THE NIGHTMARE KEEPER

THE NIGHTMARE KEEPER

VIENNA JAMES

This is a work of fiction. Names, characters, organizations, places, events, and incidents are either products of the author's imagination or are used fictitiously. Otherwise, any resemblance to actual persons, living or dead, is purely coincidental.

Published by Montlake, Seattle

www.apub.com

EU product safety contact:
Amazon Media EU S. à r.l.
38, avenue John F. Kennedy, L-1855 Luxembourg
amazonpublishing-gpsr@amazon.com

ISBN-13: 9781662536298 (paperback)
ISBN-13: 9781662536304 (digital)

Cover design by Caroline Johnson
Cover image: © LOVE_LIFE / Getty Images; © Chokniti-Studio, © vitastronomy, © Elina Leon / Shutterstock

Printed in the United States of America

For all those who were told magic wasn't real and kept believing anyway.

To Mom, who gave me my love of stories.

CHAPTER 1

Azalee

Rain drops rhythmically into the pool of fresh crimson blood.

"What happened?" I struggle under the weight of Gabriel's limp body, which I'm dragging off the rain-wet streets of a back alley in Salem and into my car.

"I . . . he . . ." Gabriel's younger brother, Logan, pales further, eyes wide, almost like *he* lost all the blood and not his broken, beaten sibling. "It should have been me, but he took my spot. Oh Gods, please, if he dies it's my fault."

"Okay, just get in," I order, slipping into the driver's seat and speeding away before Logan even shuts the door. I don't know what these two were doing in the middle of the night, in a place known for its less-than-legal activities. But if he's asking for my help, it must have been bad.

The roads are dark, the witching hour of midnight come and gone, but dawn is hours away. I glance over my shoulder to Gabriel's crumpled form seeping blood onto my interior. "Salem Med isn't too far." I offer a reassuring statement, but little of it comes out in my tone.

Gabriel looks like he's already halfway to the Gods, ready to knock on those pearly gates and request entrance to the afterlife. He's always so self-assured, head held high above everyone else. But those usually keen green eyes are masked with purple-and-black bruises.

Logan's grip on my arm is so sudden and fierce I nearly swerve off the road. "*No*, you can't take him there. Grandfather can't know about this."

My heartbeat quickens at the mention of the High Witch. "Where, then? He needs a healer."

"Can you do it?" Logan's voice cracks.

"You seriously want *my* help?" I know what his family thinks of me and those I surround myself with.

"You had the same friends, right?" One friend, but semantics aren't what this shaking kid needs right now. "That must mean Gabriel and you had some common ground. I just . . . please . . . I can't lose him."

Instead I offer, "I'll try. But without a trained healer . . ." I don't need to finish. Logan and I are both witches, but my specialty doesn't lie in the physical realm.

Logan directs me to a private entrance on the High Witch's estate nestled in the heart of the Salem town center. "Gabriel's apartment is there." A palatial, Gothic-style mansion looms over us, sprawling across a few acres. Prime property in the magical capital of the United States.

Together, we manage to get Gabriel inside and onto the expensive sofa.

As Logan clicks on a few lamps, I wipe Gabriel's sticky blood that's coating my hands onto my cloak. "Get some warm water. I need to grab something."

Logan looks like he wants to argue, but I slip back into the cold night before he can. Not caring that I'm covered with blood, I pull my hair into a ponytail, tingeing my silvery blond locks with red.

Throwing open my trunk, I nearly break the old thing. But my mind is singularly focused. Gabriel Ford is not my friend, and on most days, I might go so far as to call him my enemy. But I can't sit by and watch someone die—not even him. I don't know what I'll need, so I grab my whole potion box and carry it inside.

"Why is he on the floor?" I drop to my knees next to Gabriel's body, which is now sprawled on the ground.

"He tumbled off the couch—having a fit or something." Logan doesn't look much better. I squint, bringing his aura into my vision. Everyone has one, but not all witches can read them. The orange color is vibrating, pulsing out from the center of his body. His worry and distress for his brother causing erratic bursts.

I shake my head, pushing the colors away. I need to save my energy. "Doesn't matter," I mutter, my knees coating in the blood flowing out of Gabriel's wounds, soaking the carpet.

I swallow the lump in my throat, hands shaking as I riffle through my potions. I've done some basic healing magic, but that was for a small cut or infection. This . . . fuck, I don't know what to do. It's a sensation I don't care for. I *always* come up with a plan—risky and stupid, some might say, but at least I have one. But *lifesaving* magic, I don't know if I can do it. I work in dreams. Wielding magic to help people heal from trauma or just have a really good time. My magic is mental, this is physical.

Azalee, just do what you do best: improvise.

I grab potion vials, ripping the corks out with my teeth. Starting with the basics, I use Wipe Away to clear some of the blood and let me see the wounds. Gabriel's frustratingly handsome face is nearly unrecognizable behind the puffy skin and cuts, but the damage doesn't appear to be more than surface level.

I turn my attention to his chest. Using scissors, I cut away what's left of his torn shirt. I suck in a sharp breath, the smell of blood permeating my senses. It's . . . oh Gods . . . it's horrible. Jagged cuts mar his tanned skin, open wounds sustained from an unrelenting attack. I'm once again wondering how this happened. He's the High Witch's grandson. That offers him a plethora of respect and privilege.

But like me, there are others who aren't so keen on the Ford family. Still, a beating like this is disgusting.

"I can't . . . I'm going to be sick." Logan scrambles to his feet and runs to the bathroom. Under normal circumstances, he wouldn't leave me alone with Gabriel in this state, but his desperation is overriding his years of conditioning.

The world darkens. No—not the world, Gabriel's aura. I hadn't even realized I was attuning to it until I see it fading away.

"Don't you fucking die on me, Gabriel Ford." I need him to fight, to stay with me. So I use the magic I know to my deepest levels. Twisting my fingers, I weave an infinity pattern around his head, closing my eyes and wielding a daydream. This form of my dream wielder magic isn't as potent as a full dream, but it's enough to give him a reprieve from the pain I feel reverberating in his mind.

I breathe out slowly, aware Logan could return any second and discover what I am—or rather, confirm what his family already suspects. Magic is commonplace in our world, coming in many forms, with witches possessing varying degrees of it in their blood. Like mediums and psychics, I hold an aptitude for more skills than the average witch.

But unlike them, my magic is feared.

Fully aware what I'm risking, I use it all the same. The familiar surge of energy courses through my veins as I blend my magic and Gabriel's mind, creating a scene in his head. A pleasant tickle runs over my spine, the familiar warmth of dream magic filling me up. The high of it easing the panic gathering in my gut at the state of Gabriel's wounds.

In Gabriel's daydream, I conjure a vision of a sunny afternoon. A small lake surrounded by willow trees rustling in the warm breeze. Gabriel stands beside me, black hair glistening lighter in the rays of crystalline sun. Here, he is unbroken, the pain consuming him in the real world forgotten.

"Gabriel." My voice plays like a melody in the wind.

He turns to me, face relaxed. He half smiles, the sides of his pink lips tilting up. "Azalee." He would never say my name so softly if awake. The tinge of hatred for who I am, the magic I possess, is far away.

"Wait here. It won't be long," I tell him as I pull myself back to the blood-soaked room. He'll stay occupied in the daydream for a little while. The room feels colder and I shiver, wrapping a hand around the crystals hanging off my necklace.

The next sequence of events happens in a blur—no time to think. I barely register what I'm doing as I throw anything I can at his ripped-open chest, the wounds deep and angry. His skin is too pale. *Is there enough left in him to fight?*

"Please, don't die." My voice is softer, calling to the Fates to not take their victim tonight. But when have the Fates ever answered prayers? I spare a moment to ask the Gods to guide my hands. They might ignore me since I only invoke them when I need something.

I press my hand against his hot flesh, muttering any incantation I can remember, dipping into the deep crevasse of my brain for lessons learned in school.

I don't consciously realize it's happening until it's too late. His soul tugs on mine, the stitches of golden thread I'm weaving with my own life force. I feel him in every part of me, our tangling spirits melding together until there is no way to separate the two, not without destroying us both. If I were a trained healer, I would have recognized the magic I was creating, been able to stop myself, but I'm not. I'm just desperate and reckless, and unwilling to let Gabriel die—even if I hate him.

A heat rushes out of my fingertips, a final flood of magic into his broken body. His aura surges bright gold, mine mimicking the shade exactly. His eyes shoot open, the aquamarine color dulled by bloodshot whites. He grips my wrists, an unspoken understanding passing between us, before he passes out again. Acknowledgment of what I've done—what I've created.

A life debt.

Binding me to a man I've sworn to hate.

Life debts are rare nowadays because the witch creating one must give a piece of themselves for the connection to be forged. Over the centuries, they've all but disappeared as witches have developed safer methods of healing and protection. Because the link can be deadly if the other person is unlucky in fate. So, until Gabriel is able to return the favor and save my life, our two souls are bound together. If he or I should die before the debt is paid, we will both perish.

My hands are shaking, either from the immense magic I just expelled or the high from weaving the daydream—probably both.

"Is he . . ." Logan stumbles out of the bathroom a few minutes later, oblivious to the bond now tethering me to his brother. Life debts aren't visible to anyone other than the subjects of the magic.

I stare at Gabriel lying on the floor. His breathing has steadied, the color of his aura still blackened, but less so. I should stay. Wait for him to wake up, to talk about what I just did. But I can't. I need to get out of here before anyone notices me.

"He'll live." I stand, grabbing what's left of my potions and walking out the door. A gnawing thought scratches away at my brain: What if more than one magic was created this night?

CHAPTER 2

AZALEE

Two years later

"Seek not the Fates for answers, for they do not listen to the prayers of the earthbound. The Gods are where salvation lies. Discover their teachings in these hallowed walls."

I lean against the trunk of a tree, its orange leaves dancing in the soft setting sun as I listen to the preacher spouting his sermon on the steps of the old church across the street. His aura is almost pure white. But I've always been able to wade deeper into the colors than other aura readers—so I spy the faint lines of black running through his. He's not as pious as he'd like his flock to believe.

"Witches and humans are welcome. You are all the Gods' children." His eyes drift to me on those last words, my back stiffening.

That would be my cue to move along.

I avert my eyes, tugging my cloak tighter as I head down the main street of Salem. I believe in the Gods and Fates. I've seen their handiwork in too many things not to. But organized religion isn't my thing.

Organized anything, really.

And besides, the last time I prayed to the Gods, I got exactly what I asked for, and the consequences fucking sucked. Lesson learned. You can't trust help from otherworldly beings—if you want something done right, you have to do it yourself.

As the sun sets, Salem truly comes alive. It's the beginning of October—tourist season. The fall leaves and Halloween draw them in droves, the streets bustling with adventurous explorers.

Magic may be everywhere, but everywhere is not like Salem.

It's full of old magic—a mystery to even those with magic swirling in their blood, maybe because it all started here when our witch ancestors saved the regular folks from a plague. Where it would have once been heresy to flaunt potions and tarot readings, it's now commonplace throughout the world.

MISSING THE DEAD? LEARN HOW TO CONNECT TO THEM YOURSELF! CALL US NOW TO BOOK A TRAINING APPOINTMENT WITH OUR WORLD-CLASS MEDIUMS!

My hands curl into fists inside my cloak pockets as I enter the most populated part of downtown. Advertisements fill shop windows and notice boards. Some of them legit, others not so much.

GOT SOMETHING TO HIDE? FEAR NOT! WITH OUR 5-STEP AURA-BLOCKING SERUM, YOUR SECRETS WILL BE SAFE FROM EVEN THE STRONGEST WITCH!

That one is scrawled across the window of an apothecary. A neon witch pouring a potion into a cauldron flashes beside it. I would like to scoff at the tackiness, but I can't argue with the sales strategy. The Retreat, where I live and work, sells the same kinds of things. Albeit in a little more upscale fashion. It's an exclusive wellness day spa that markets more to high-end clientele and less to cheating partners trying to hide their infidelity.

These types of novelties are one of the main draws to a place like Salem—humans and witches flock here from all over the world. Sure, you could buy your hair-thickening tonic at your local chemist, but it just sounds so much more powerful saying you bought it in Salem.

I shrug off these types of businesses easily enough, but I falter on the cobblestones when I see a pop-up table selling tarot readings. It's only one of many. Psychics of varied strengths, offering visions of the future, fill these historic shops. Not to mention the plethora of stores selling all types of paraphernalia associated with divination.

All witches possess at least a modicum of magical abilities, but specialties like aura reading, healing, divination, and dream wielding can be rarer—certain skills more so than others.

"You look troubled." The tarot reader startles me with her high-pitched voice. "Twenty dollars for a three-card spread and we can sort out those wrinkles marring that pretty face of yours."

My frown deepens said lines. "No, thanks. I'd rather buy a bottle of Cloud9 and just let those troubles find a place to sleep for the night while I have some fun." Troubles never go away, not really. No use having a stranger tell me something I already know won't solve my problems.

"The Fates have dealt you a heavy hand, no? I can show you what path to take in the future to avoid such unpleasantries." She speaks about her connection to beyond the veil without fear. She knows that no one waits in the shadows to condemn her to the pyres for her magics.

Anger pulses in my veins, burning white-hot at the inequality among our kind.

Dream wielders aren't illegal *per se*, but we aren't exactly welcome in polite society. It's why we've congregated in secret covens around the world for centuries. Most people are scared of those who can walk among their dreams. Wary of how we might influence or poison their minds while they sleep.

Before my anger can get the best of me, I quicken my pace, leaving the witch to her business.

"Ready?" I say to Meera when I catch her as she closes her family's shop.

My best friend gives me a once-over, raising an eyebrow. "Did you run here?"

I frown, smoothing a hand over my hair. "Just getting in some quick cardio before our evening." Out of habit, I home in on her aura. The buttery yellow lined in indigo, the colors associated with dream wielders, burns bright. She's focused—good. Only a witch who is both attuned to auras and a dream wielder can see the colors that indicate dream wielder magic. While I excel at reading strangers' auras, seeing the finer details, I've always struggled to get that kind of clarity with those I'm closest to. It must be because my emotions are too tightly intertwined with them to allow me an objective reading.

Meera rolls her eyes, giving me a look only someone who has known you for over twenty years can. "You should probably save your strength."

That washes all my previous annoyance down the drain. I've got real problems.

Like stopping the Nightmare before she kills someone.

Meera sits in the passenger seat of my car, her hand lazily floating out the window, catching the wind on her fingertips. With the sun set, the cool mist of Salem seeps through the window, giving the car an unearthly chill. These back-road towns don't invest in streetlights—the moon and the stars are their guides.

I stare straight ahead, iron grip on the steering wheel as I focus on finding this girl before she does any more harm—both to herself and the reputation of all dream wielders. Fear already taints the rumors surrounding our gifts. I don't need a rogue Nightmare making it worse.

"If you don't unclench your teeth, Azalee, they'll get stuck like that."

"How do you think I get such a chiseled jawline?" But I loosen the tension from my face. I've got Pep Up in my bag. The energy-boosting spell would keep me focused, but it also makes my nerves even more jittery.

"How much farther?" Meera rolls up the window, the cold finally getting to her as she wraps her shimmering cloak around her arms, burrowing herself inside it. With her black hair and ethereal clothes popping against her brown skin, Meera looks like a shining star. My dark clothes are designed to make me blend into the night.

I glance at the GPS. "Ten minutes." We had to leave Salem to find this Nightmare—*no*, she has a name: Inez. When I heard rumblings of strange happenings a few towns over, I took it upon myself to investigate. It didn't take long to figure out she was a Nightmare, not when you know what to look for.

Meera and I shouldn't be doing this alone. The coven dictates that groups of four are required to secure a Nightmare. But they demand too much paperwork and talking about it—I'd rather just get it done on my terms.

Inez is in stage three, based on the description I got from my sources. People reported barely touching her skin and slipping into horrible visions. Visions aren't unusual among witches. But these don't tell of the future or speak to those beyond the grave. Their only intent is to cause terror.

We should have known about Inez sooner. Found her when she first started showing signs of dream wielding, but more are popping up every day. Dream wielder magic is not inherited, which means there's no way to track who will present with the powers. They simply appear to protect us when a witch experiences significant trauma. But not everyone is strong enough to fight against the darkness it also can bring . . . which is how Nightmares are born.

Mom and the rest of the coven's leadership are struggling to keep on top of the new dream wielders.

So I volunteered my services. To which I was promptly told *no*. Apparently, I am *too reckless* and have *an aversion to authority*.

Whatever. Didn't slow me a bit. I'm not going to stop trying to save those like me.

Last I heard, Inez was still coherent, but that won't last long. Soon, she'll be entirely consumed by the nightmares in her head, unable to function. That's when the nightmares become deadly to everyone involved.

I turn onto a side street of crammed houses, matching cookie-cutter structures in neat rows. Her family doesn't know we're coming. They may be fine handing her over, or they may not want to let her go.

Unfortunately, in most cases, the families are happy to let us take the infected witch. Nobody wants to live with a Nightmare.

As I get out of the car, the bundle of nerves in my stomach grows heavier. Meera pulls her long black hair into a sleek ponytail. I grab the soft leather sachet of herbs from the trunk along with the potion I made earlier. The steady thrumming of the magic soothes my anxiety without even touching the liquid. This will help contain the Nightmare for transport.

I clear my throat, the sound echoing in the quiet night as I zip my leather jacket higher. It's too cold for just the leathers, so I don my black cloak too. I hand Meera a milky white potion. "Bottoms up." I cheers her with my own before knocking it back in a single gulp. I shiver as the magic slides down my throat, the tendrils of the spell weaving into my bones and flesh. This spell will slightly alter our appearance for the next hour. Not that it's really needed. We'll make sure that once we leave this house, none of Inez's family will recall we were even here.

"Don't forget the gloves." I run my hands over the crystals in my belt and the ones around my neck before slipping on my leather gloves, ensuring I don't have any flesh showing.

If you touch skin to skin with a late-stage Nightmare, you'll be dragged in, and you don't get out of a nightmare unless they let you out. Not even the ability to wield dreams can help you, making our magic—and everyone else's—useless.

We're greeted by screams from the house. My feet slip on gravel as I reach the door before Meera, knocking loudly. There's rustling behind it, and I grip the sachet, ready to throw the contents and recite the spell. We'll ask nicely for Inez, but we aren't leaving here without her.

"Yes?" a shaking voice calls from behind the wooden door. Through the glass panels peers a gray-haired woman. According to my research, this is Rosa, Inez's mother.

"We're here to help. Will you let us in?" My words are steady. I'm the authority here. At least, that's what I need her to believe.

"We don't need help." A loud wailing sounds behind her.

"I beg to differ." Meera clucks her tongue. "We can take care of her."

A pause, then I hear locks clicking, and the door opens—scattered around the entrance are herbs and crystals meant for protection. Not every person in the world has magic flowing in their blood, but everyone has access to potions and magical objects. Most of the time, it's hard to tell who's a witch and who's not nowadays.

We don't have time to linger as moaning from the living room draws our attention.

Rosa surveys us with bloodshot eyes, dark circles making them heavy. She must see an answer to her prayers. "We've tried everything, but she keeps getting worse."

Walking cautiously around the sofa, I kneel in front of Inez, who's curled into a ball on a chair near the fire. I recognize her from the pictures—jet-black hair with high cheekbones and a button nose—but her brown skin now has a gray tinge and is covered in frantic cuts. Her eyes are sunken, hollow, gaping black holes as the nightmare eats away at her from the inside. A muddy aura surrounds her, the color lashing out in jagged offshoots. I can barely see the standard dream wielder colors—soon they will vanish into the swirling darkness.

"We'd like to take Inez with us." I straighten, stepping back as Inez thrashes a hand out, nails crusted with blood from the scratches covering her face and body. "She'll be well cared for."

Rosa glances between Meera and me, then back to her daughter. "Are you healers?" I hear the hopeful uptick in her voice.

"We run a wellness spa in Salem. Cases like this are our specialty." I pull my gloves higher, not taking my eyes off Inez.

There's a long pause as the pieces click into place, realization forming in her tired eyes. "You're dream wielders," Rosa whispers, clutching the crystal around her neck. "I knew something was wrong with Inez after the accident. I took her to a healer, but she wouldn't speak."

Meera places a hand on Rosa's arm. "Dream wielder magic is something certain witches are born with, and it might never be awakened. But after a traumatic accident, the ability will appear as a result."

"But you don't look like her. She's rotting away." Rosa's voice cracks.

One of the benefits of dream wielding is that we can't dream. We don't relive the traumas that granted us our powers time and again in our sleep. But that doesn't always protect us.

"I'm afraid sometimes," Meera continues, "the tempting darkness drags them in."

"Can you save her?"

A year ago, my patience would have worn thin, but now, the gnawing in my gut won't let me forget what I did. Nightmares aren't just dream wielders gone bad—a problem to be handled with swift hands—they're someone's child, parent . . . *friend*.

I lick my lips. "Imagine that fear you experience when you wake up from a bad dream, the cold dread seizing your body, holding you captive until your brain can rationalize that it wasn't real. For Inez, the nightmarescape has now become her reality. Her mind is no longer capable of using logic to get itself out. Because of this, her fear and despair are all that she knows. But we'll help her find the way out." Or at least that's the goal. I haven't seen it happen yet.

Rosa slumps into a chair.

"If you can give us something of Inez's, a blanket or a favorite item of clothing, we will make sure to keep it with her as a reminder of home and what she's trying to get back to."

"She's my only daughter, I can't just—" But she doesn't get to finish, as Inez leaps straight for Meera.

This is why I didn't take my eyes off Inez. I rip open the sachet, throwing it at her back, the powder coating her hair. Next, I chuck the potion, the glass bottle shattering and drenching her skin. She whirls around, eyes narrowing on me. Where there would typically be bloodshot eyes of red, hers are streaked with black.

"The day is done, the night hast come, thine eyes will close till moon meets sun." I chant the spell quickly, my words stringing together the magic, tingling over my skin and whispering in my ears.

Inez collapses to the ground, silence falling over the house. "Take her," Rosa whispers, clutching her necklace with a shaking hand. In the end, this is how it always goes. People fear nightmares, the heart-stopping unknown, and just want it to stop.

"You're doing the right thing for her." Meera hands Rosa a hard candy. "It helps with Nightmare exposure."

Rosa is so tired, she doesn't even pause to question what it is before popping it in her mouth. "What do I . . ." Her voice grows heavy as her eyes drift closed.

"Watch Inez," I say to Meera, kneeling in front of Rosa.

Grabbing a moonstone and an amethyst from my pocket, I grip one in each hand, focusing on Rosa. Magic fills me up, the warmth a soft caress as I dream wield. The sleeping tonic coating the candy is a light dose, since I only need a minute. To enter into an individual's dream, I have to go through a door. Each is unique and reflects the dreamer in some way. Rosa's is made of white and brown feathers that sway as I step between them.

Sunlight shines on Rosa as she pushes a younger Inez on a swing set, the scent of fresh-cut grass dancing through the breeze. The dream is a bit hazy due to the sleeping potion, but I don't need a complex narrative to get the job done.

"Higher, Mommy," Inez says. Rosa is younger, the stress of her daughter's condition nowhere to be seen on her features.

I approach, tapping her on the shoulder. "Hello, Rosa."

She turns and smiles.

"Inez is okay," I tell her, my voice even and strong. I weave the words into her mind, letting them become her new memories. "She was feeling much better and decided to go away for a while. She told you that she wouldn't be able to call, but that you shouldn't worry."

Rosa frowns, but then nods. "She's better?"

My chest tightens with the lies I have to make her believe. But it's better this way. We used to have families sign magical contracts that bound them from speaking about where their loved ones went, but that still caused too many questions. And while potent, there are ways to break magical contracts. The coven found it easier to just alter the memories so that families believe the person has left and is healthy once more.

Dream manipulation is wrong, I know that. I'd never use it in another circumstance. But it's not like we can have visiting hours with the Nightmares. Eventually, the coven will inform Rosa of Inez's fate—the same one all Nightmares reach one day—but for now she will believe that her daughter is living a wonderful life.

"Inez is happy and she loves you. Remember that. You never saw us this night. Inez said her goodbyes and you went to bed early. Okay?"

She nods.

Taking a last look at Rosa, I pull myself from the dreamscape.

"We good?" Meera asks when I open my eyes.

"Yeah." I swallow, my lingering guilt bitter on my tongue. I'm always the one who has to do this. It's not that Meera isn't capable, it's just that my aura-reading abilities make my dream manipulation more effective because I have a stronger connection to the emotions of a dreamer.

Meera, like many witches, can perform spells and make potions, but doesn't possess a specialized magic like mine.

Meera and I carry Inez, placing her in the back seat with the utmost care, draping a quilt from her bed over her. The potion is strong. She won't wake until we have her secured in the dungeon on The Retreat's property. An owl hoots as we pull out of the driveway.

CHAPTER 3

Gabriel

The potion tastes bitter on my tongue as I swish it around before swallowing. Clearing my throat, I slide the vial into my suit's interior pocket. If I'm going to get through this evening, Simmer is a necessity.

Despite being an inanimate object, the oversize portrait of my grandfather and late grandmother judges me as I feel the potion taking its calming effect. I will need it to keep me from jumping out the nearest window to be free of the vapid sycophants attending this political event. But as a part of Grandfather's inner circle, something I've been working for nearly my whole life, I'm required to rub elbows with the guests who attend these galas.

Hearts aren't won sitting at a desk, Gabriel. Grandfather's words echo in my mind. Winning hearts is always easier with a dash of mourning and despair. It's why he scheduled this memorial gala for the thirtieth anniversary of my grandmother's murder. She died five years before I was born, but Grandfather made sure her image, and the memory of what took her from this life, was never far from my mind.

The crystal chandeliers sparkle across the cream wallpaper as I make my way toward our table in the center of the dozens of others arranged in the ballroom of the Grand Salem Hotel. With its high ceilings, everything in this room screams money, from the marble floors to the gilded curtain rods on the shimmering gold-and-silver twenty-foot walls.

Fuck, *I* scream money with this $1,000 tux and the two others hanging in my closet at home, along with the plethora of other designer clothes. It's something I'm still getting used to after nearly a decade of attending these things. But we've got an image to maintain. Being the High Witch's protégé is not a job I take lightly. Pulling on my sleeves, I twist the gold cuff links to ensure they're secure.

"Gabriel." The mayor stops me before I reach my destination. "Nice to see you, despite the sober affair."

I shake his hand, grip firm just as I was taught. "Sir, pleasure as always."

"It's been thirty years"—he swirls the dark liquid in his crystal glass—"but to hear the High Witch speak, you'd think a dream wielder just killed her yesterday."

My hands dangle loosely at my sides, untamed energy vibrating through me despite the magic I took to quell it. "When a soulmate bond is severed so violently, like my grandparents', the pain it leaves is everlasting. That's not something you ever stop fighting to make right." The company line falls off my lips in a well-practiced cadence.

"I wanted to commend you on the recent success overseeing my new security staff's hand-to-hand combat training."

I nod, chest filling with pride. "I was happy to pass along my skills. In our line of work, we face many threats. We can't rely solely on potions or weapons to defeat an assailant."

"If you ever get tired of working for your grandfather, I've got a position on my team for a smart, skilled young man like yourself."

"Careful not to let the High Witch hear you talking like that." I offer a half smile, but it doesn't reach my eyes. "He's rather protective over his people."

The mayor keeps his politician smile in place, but his hand tightens around his glass. Movement on the stage catches our attention as they ready the podium for the High Witch's speech. "If you'll excuse me, Gabriel, I must get to my seat." He scurries away, suitably chastised.

"Colette, I don't know if I'm allowed back in the French embassy after last month's party. The security team wasn't too happy with our creative use of the fountains." My brother, Logan, grins at the daughter of a French diplomat. As is the way when he flashes his weaponized dimples, the woman's features light up with intrigue, fingers running over the lapel of his tux.

I clear my throat as I approach the table. Colette gives me a nod, whispering something into Logan's ear before dashing away.

"Please, say you swiped a Simmer bottle for me too?" Logan says, handing me a glass of expensive champagne when I sit beside him.

"It's not a party drug." I sip the drink before placing it back into the neat table setting.

"Of course it's not a fun potion. Because my big brother, Gabriel, doesn't do that kind of thing anymore." Logan rolls his eyes, finishing his glass in a single swig. "I, on the other hand, am going to take advantage of anything I can, as long as the old man's footing my bills."

Logan is a good kid. He just knows how much power our last name gives him and isn't afraid to toss that clout around.

There was a time, not too many years ago, when I would've taken any potion offered to me. Trying to drown myself in magic to forget my future and erase the past. But when I graduated from university and started working with my grandfather, everything changed. A lot of things have changed since then. I rub a hand across the slick fabric of my shirt, to the scars beneath that still burn.

When your grandfather is the High Witch, you fall in line. There's too much at stake in his world for people who don't behave. My options were limited to being conscripted into the military and sent off to a European counterpart, or I could sober up and play the dutiful pupil.

Grandfather is formidable, but he wants what's best for us and the rest of the witches.

"Did you do the rounds?" I ask, ignoring Logan's earlier dig. I still have plenty of fun. I'm just more discreet about it. You won't find me skinny-dipping in the embassy fountains.

Logan waves at the waiter. "As the old man instructed. Worked for me, though—got to collect on a few gambling debts I was owed." He chuckles. My long-healed scars sting just thinking about the last time I had to protect Logan when the debt collectors came calling for him. If he just bet money, then it'd be fine, but he was into more exotic bets. Despite the aftermath, I'd do it all again to keep my little brother safe.

"Where's your anniversary pin?" Logan nods at my lapel.

Fuck. I forgot to stick it on in my rush to get here after staying late at the office. "Grandfather didn't give me one."

"Bullshit. I saw it when he ordered me to wear one too."

"You must have taken too much Pep Up and were seeing double."

Logan shakes his head. "Dude, why can't you just admit when you're wrong? You've always been like that." The laugh in his voice tells me he's not that upset about it.

"If I'm ever wrong, I'll give it a try." I nod to Grandfather. "Speak of the devil."

Any clinking glasses or lively chatter ceases as a hushed reverence falls over the crowd, all eyes turning to follow the High Witch taking his time crossing the stage to the podium.

Mikael Ford has been High Witch for nearly forty years, and at seventy-five, he's showing no signs of slowing down. The potions he gets specially made help halt the aging process pretty efficiently. But there have been a few more vials added to the rotation recently, which has my interest piqued.

The office of High Witch is an honorable one. He represents us as a magical community. While the president and the rest of the politicians in DC rule over the country at large, anything related to magic is the High Witch's domain—laws, justice, sentencing—it's all him and the Apprentices he appoints to uphold his rules in each state, respectively.

"Welcome, friends." As Grandfather smiles at the audience, his rare golf ball–size red beryl crystal necklace, polished to perfection, shines in the spotlights. "It warms my heart to see so many prominent community members here to pay tribute to my late wife on the anniversary of her senseless death at the hands of dream wielder magic." His words echo in the vaulted room.

I shift, the chair's squeak magnified. I clamp my jaw to keep my face neutral. Grandfather doesn't falter in his speech, but for a brief second his eyes land on me while he scans the crowd. Some nights, when I walk by his bedroom, I'll hear him discussing his day with a picture of Grandmother or just talking for talking's sake.

A person in his position must keep a strong front. Sometimes the ghost of my grandmother is the only thing I believe he thinks can see him as mortal, and not the unshakable leader he shows to the world.

"As you all know, my wife was coerced by a dream wielder into attempting to assassinate me. Thanks to my quick wits and skills, I was able to thwart the attack and capture the dream wielder responsible for the plot." He pauses, fingers turning white where they grip the edge of the podium. To the audience it might seem like a surge of emotions overtaking him, but nothing the High Witch does is without planning.

"But the victory was short-lived. The trauma my beloved suffered at the hands of this abominable magic was too much. And she fell victim to the same fate. I am grateful to the Gods that I was not touched by the same disease. That is why I have worked tirelessly ever since to stop this same tragedy from happening to another . . ."

Heads around the room nod their approval.

"Eclipse is reopening tonight," I say to Logan, ignoring the speech I've already heard a dozen times over the last week in practice. "Want to hit it up with me?" I might have cleaned up my act, but we're still allowed to let off some steam.

"Gods, yes."

The High Witch finishes his speech, and dinner is finally served when he sits at our table.

"Gabriel," an Apprentice named Ulrick says. "Your grandfather tells me you're considering taking an Under Apprentice position next year."

My eyes flick to the old man, who's busy chatting, but I can tell he's listening to us.

"It's something to consider." My forced smile is tight on my already exhausted face. My future is fast approaching, like a ticking bomb about to explode in my chest.

"Well," Ulrick continues, oblivious to my inner turmoil. "If you choose to pursue that, we'd love to have you in our district. We could use bright young minds like yours."

What he means is, he would love to have the High Witch's kin on his side.

Grandfather drops into the conversation like he was always there. "Ulrick, I'm afraid Gabriel will be staying nearer to home. He'll be working closely with me on an initiative we're putting into motion."

It might be nice to finally get a chance to lead my own projects and take a step out from behind his shadow. The High Witch is not an easy man to love. He doesn't give affection freely, but I imagine it's hard when many regard you as a king. But despite all that, he is family and has always provided the best for Logan and me.

"Mikael," Armand Santos says, coming up to the table. "I commend you on your continued actions regarding the dream wielders."

My back stiffens, the tiny hairs on my neck standing on end. I force my gaze to remain on my plate.

"I'm afraid it's an escalating problem we've learned needs to be handled with an iron fist." Grandfather's face is the picture of concern. "It's why we've been working tirelessly in the office these last few months to create laws that will keep us safe from these unpredictable terrors. Magic is only beneficial when it is contained and regulated. A sentiment I believe all citizens can agree on. Right, Gabriel?"

I nod, offering the correct and only response the High Witch will accept. "Dream wielder magic is dangerous when unchecked. So rest assured the High Witch's team will work to find a solution to protect everyone."

In public, Grandfather won't risk a quarrel, but his nostrils flare with annoyance that I didn't just spout vitriol about dream wielders.

The duty of the High Witch's office is to regulate and deter the misuse and deadly force enacted with magic. That means we must protect the people—*all* the people, dream wielders included. It's no secret, even to dream wielders themselves, that their magic, unchecked, can be dangerous, but that doesn't mean every witch who possesses it is a threat. It took me way too many years to finally realize that, but since I did, it's been a point Grandfather and I have fought about on many occasions.

Everyone at the table signals their agreement, even Logan. It's a belief we've had drilled into us from the time we were born. There are a few potions on the market that supposedly aid in protecting you from intrusion into your mind. But based on my research, it doesn't do much good if you're up against a well-trained dream wielder.

My grip is so tight on my fork that it bends in half. I quickly shove it under my napkin as Logan gives me a sideways look. I take a deep breath, focusing on my watch and the black tourmaline built into the watch's face. I had this custom made in Spain when I visited last year on the High Witch's behalf. The tourmaline, combined with the runes etched inside, creates a powerful concealment charm.

"Whatever you need, Mikael, you know my company is happy to help. We want to see the streets of Salem and the country protected. We owe it to the children."

Biting my tongue, I taste blood, ignoring it as I eat my meal as if all is well.

CHAPTER 4

Azalee

Nature repeats herself as we drive the darkened roads encased with thick trees, the sameness lulling me into a memory . . .

Iniko's face is electrified as he lies on the floor at the top of the bell tower located on the edge of The Retreat's property. "Best birthday ever. From my bestest friends." He grins at me. His Black skin glistens with the effect of the spa treatment Mom gifted him earlier. He requested extra Dewy Morning to give him the desired look.

"Don't wear him out, okay?" Meera leans against the safety rail, face half lit by the full moon.

"Fear not, Meera, dear," Iniko assures her. "There is enough of me to go around."

I scoff, kneeling beside him. "I'm so glad your birthday is only once a year because you would be insufferable otherwise." I bite my lip to keep from smiling.

"You only turn sixteen once." He closes his eyes without instruction. This isn't the first dream wield I've performed on him. He's let Meera and me practice with him for years. I know he wishes he could be like us, but his magic is even rarer. He's a Seer. But just like us, he keeps his abilities hidden. Too much interest from powerful people.

I would be curious to see what a Seer could do in a dream wield. Witches with specialties have an extra boost when they dream—healers are better at healing mental wounds, mediums can dream wield into the dead for a brief span of time, master potion makers make wicked-strong sleeping draughts, witches skilled with wards can infuse crystals to help conceal dream wielders' identities, and aura readers, like myself, can manipulate emotions to make the dreamer believe almost anything and carry that into the waking world. Those each come with varying degrees of success depending on the strength of the witch's magic.

But since true Seers are so rare, we've never had a documented case to know what they could do.

"Shh, you need to sleep." I wave the sachet I made earlier in slow circles around his head. The lavender, chamomile, and sage mixed with a few drops of Simmer will help ease him into sleep.

I ignore Meera's chewing behind me as she finishes her slice of cake.

When his breathing slows, aura calmed to a soft robin's-egg blue, I know I can enter his dreams.

"I won't be long," I tell Meera. We both wanted to give him a dream as our presents, but since only one dream wielder can enter a mind at a time, we drew sticks on who could go first. I won.

Closing my eyes, I hold my hands over his body, a moonstone clutched in my left hand and an amethyst in my right. I've been dream wielding for eight years, so it's as easy as breathing. The surge of warm magic in my chest fills me, radiating outward toward Iniko. All magic comes with risks, but I could never hurt Iniko in a dream. It's a safe space to have experiences you couldn't in the waking world.

Some minds are trickier than others to access, but Iniko's is an open book when I step into the dreamscape. His door is a dusty blue with pirate-themed stickers on it.

I twist the silver handle and step inside.

Iniko waits for me in the gray concert hallway, giddily bouncing on the balls of his feet. "I hear music." His voice is lyrical like the tune blasting through the double doors behind him. "Please tell me this is what I think it is."

Reaching into my back pocket, I withdraw two VIP lanyards. "Go ahead and see."

He snatches one, tossing it over his head before yanking me with him. He pushes open the doors to reveal a packed arena, but we have the best seat in the house—center stage.

Of course we do. It's a dream of my creation, and I would give Iniko nothing less.

The stage lights flash, the colorful display reflecting in Iniko's wide eyes. All around us the stadium glows with tiny dots of white lights as people hold up lanterns.

"I almost forgot." I barely have to think it before the dream reacts to my request, matching souvenir T-shirts appearing on us.

"You're a legend. You know that, right?" Iniko pulls me into a side hug as we sway to the music of the K-pop group performing all of Iniko's favorite songs.

"I know," I yell. I wrap my hand around Iniko's wrist, a glowing bracelet appearing. "You've been telling me as much since we were four."

One day on the swing set, Iniko came up to me and told me I was special and I was going to change the world. I'd barely played with him before that. But ever since we've been inseparable.

"Must be true, then."

"Care to elaborate?" I spin him in sync to the song.

"It's my birthday, lest we get distracted and think otherwise, little witch. It's all about me." He grins cheekily, blowing air-kisses to the singers.

In dreams anything is possible. We stay for hours, the group playing three encores. Time moves differently in the dreamscape—hours are mere minutes in the waking world. We sing, voices never getting hoarse, dancing among the crowd before joining the group onstage. Seeing Iniko spinning, arms wide as the sparks of fireworks explode above us, I know this is my happiest place.

"She's making a lot of noise." Meera jolts me from my memory as she glances at the body in the back. "You sure this potion will hold?"

Shaking my head, I force the now painful memory away. "It'll hold, she's just mumbling. If she starts screaming, then we know there's a problem. I made this potion fresh this morning. It only failed last time because it was old." The car vibrates as I increase our speed. "I heard about another possible Nightmare—outskirts of Cambridge. Maybe tomorrow we can go take a look?"

Meera shakes her head, popping a jelly bean into her mouth. "Nope, sorry. I've got kitchen duty at my parents' apothecary." She picks through the bag on her lap to find the red ones. "Besides, Az, you're not responsible for every dream wielder, *and* it's not your fault if they become Nightmares."

Instead of responding, I grip the steering wheel tighter. There are thousands of dream wielders. I couldn't possibly find them all. But that doesn't mean I'm not going to try. The coven thinks The Retreat is a good enough effort to help dream wielders. It's our haven. Those who have newly gained their powers or want additional training can participate in classes under the guise of going to a wellness retreat. It's also an excellent place for the coven to meet to discuss affairs without drawing attention to ourselves. That's obviously not common knowledge, so we offer treatments to other clients to maintain the ruse.

The wind becomes wild, the trees speaking their own language in its wake as we near our destination.

"Human . . . gate . . . dark," Inez mumbles incoherently.

"I can't listen to her anymore." Meera switches on the radio, fiddling with the dial.

"The victim was found late this evening in an alley," the reporter says over the airwaves.

Meera starts to change the station, but I grab her hand. "I want to hear this."

"The victim—who has yet to be identified—was declared dead on the scene. Early healer reports are suggesting the victim might have been killed in their sleep, leading many to believe a dream—"

"I'd rather listen to the mumbling." Meera clicks the radio off.

I inhale sharply. Fire racing through my veins makes my skin itch.

"Leave it," she warns.

"I didn't say anything." My fingers turn white on the wheel. The crystal around my neck thrums against my chest, the cold metal turning warm.

"No, but I know you. It's just some random person showing up dead. Nothing we need to concern ourselves with." She pops another jelly bean in her mouth, chewing it aggressively.

I release a heavy breath, my locket cooling slightly. "But they said—"

"They didn't say anything," she cuts me off, shoving the candy into her bag. "It's all speculation. Leave it. We have other problems. Like getting our asses handed to us when we haul in another Nightmare without prior consent."

"Fine," I concede, which means I'll keep my mouth shut. Not that I'll stop thinking about it.

About fifteen minutes outside town, I turn onto the private drive leading to The Retreat. The night is clear, thank the Gods, because these roads can be a real bitch in the winter. My headlights shine through the large iron gate marking the secured entrance.

The Retreat has been my permanent home since my father's murder when I was eight. The same night my dream wielder abilities manifested. Mom didn't want to stay in our house after that, and since she founded The Retreat, it made the most sense to move in.

Mom's been a dream wielder since she was a year old, and has always had an innate ability to sense other dream wielders. She passed that trait on to me, which manifested in my aura reading, making us invaluable to the coven when searching for new members. This definitely pisses them off in my case since they aren't my biggest fans.

I place my palm on the hand reader, and the gate groans open. The property is spread across thirty acres, encompassing a lake, dozens of tiny cabins, walking trails in the woods, and a spacious main building with the spa close to the front entrance, which is the only thing non–dream wielders ever see. But I don't stop at any of those. Instead, we head toward the right of the property and the cathedral, which has been my home for the last seventeen years.

Parking the car, I steel my nerves for the incoming lecture. Inez isn't going into the former house of worship. She's headed to the dungeons below. The coven had them retrofitted decades ago to house the Nightmares.

As if on cue, my mom, Genevieve, comes out the side door. "Not again, Azalee." She was a psychic by trade—which means it's hard to sneak anything past her. She used to spend her days reading tarot cards and palms, telling people if they would ever find the rare soulmate bond so many wish for or to watch out for the number seven.

Mom's blond hair is pulled into a tight bun, a thick red velvet cloak flying behind as she reaches us. "The coven is going to have a fit." She peeks into the back seat.

"Do you have space for her?" I say as a way of an explanation.

She might not like me going rogue, but I know she'll never turn anyone away. "We have a room." She never calls them cells, even if that's what they are.

We carry Inez down the narrow, dark stairs until we reach the dungeons. No witches guard the rooms. The risk of exposure is too great. The Nightmares aren't violent for the hell of it, but if given the chance, they'll seek out another warm body. Whether for comfort or to share the terror, I'm not sure.

I unlock the door, this time with blood. I prick my finger with the pocketknife I keep on my keys. I place the blood pooling on the tip against the locking runes carved into the door. Energy spreads across the wood as I grab the handle.

The smell hits me first, dampness from being underground with an undertone of blood and sick. I fight my gag reflex as the musky scent invades my senses.

I blink, adjusting to the dark. The rooms themselves have one small window, and this is the only door in or out. A single bulb hanging in the middle of the hall casts a yellow halo below it. The Nightmares don't like the light, it aggravates them, so we'll have to be fast.

"The one on the right." Mom's voice is labored as we carry Inez's deadweight. Her muscles twitch as we enter the room, my fingers slipping with the jerking motion.

The rooms have thick iron doors, each sealed with blood magic, and a single square hole in the middle. I hate this place. Hate that they have to stay down here, even if we decorate the rooms with the comforts of home. But we haven't found a better way to protect them. The High Witch—and head of the anti–dream wielder fan club—would get rid of us all if he could. I doubt he'd see any difference between us and the Nightmares. His whole family is irredeemable, no matter how irritatingly handsome his grandson Gabriel is.

One of the first things new dream wielders are taught is about the possibility of becoming a Nightmare. We must be vigilant for the appearance of the signs in ourselves and others.

Nightmares' conditions worsen with overexposure to other people, like they're feeding off others' pain. The truth is none of us knows what to do with them. Mom has been trying for years to reverse the late-stage damage with little success. It's a hotly debated topic at coven meetings. Some want to kill the Nightmares, save them from themselves, as they put it. But I, Mom, Meera, and others among us have fought for their protection.

I'm not giving up hope that they can be saved.

We place Inez on the narrow bed in the corner of her new room. "Let's leave her be to rest," Mom says, carefully smoothing Inez's quilt over her fragile frame.

I turn to walk away, but Inez's hand grabs my wrist.

"Argh!" Spit flies from her mouth. My gloves block her from touching my skin, but the fabric is slipping away.

"Meera!" Mom yells, placing a gloved hand on Inez's forehead. She whips her head back and forth, but Mom holds her still.

Inez chokes, words getting caught in her throat. I stare into her eyes, and I can't move. She's trying to tell me something, but I can't understand her. Meera holds Inez down as I unclench her fingers. My heart beats wildly. My brain knows the danger I'm in, but a part of me is not afraid. Inez doesn't want to do this, she's just begging for help.

Mom mutters an incantation, loosening Inez's grip enough for me to yank my arm away. Her lids grow heavy, and she falls back to the bed.

"Fresh potion, huh?" Meera mutters, backing out of the room.

The click of the lock echoes in the dim hallway. I take a deep breath, rubbing my wrist, the cold ache deep inside. I always expect to find an imprint left, but whatever remains is below the surface. Dozens of cells compose the dungeon, not all full, but the one at the end draws my attention.

"Well"—Meera claps—"I'm going home." She bounds up the stairs. She hates it down here.

"Are you all right?" Mom asks. I nod, clasping a fist around my locket. "You should get some rest. The coven will want to talk to you tomorrow."

"I'm going to check on him." I look over her shoulder to the back cell, chest aching deeper than any magic can reach. Believe me, I've tried.

She sighs, smoothing out her cloak. "I don't think that's a good idea, darling."

"I won't be long."

"They aren't . . ." She pauses. "They aren't who they used to be."

We have this discussion all the time, and more often than not, it becomes a full-blown fight. I want the Nightmares to know someone is still searching for them.

One of the first lessons The Retreat teaches is the difference between bad dreams and nightmares. Everyone has bad dreams. Any run-of-the-mill dream wielder could give you one.

But if you've ever woken in a cold sweat, the paralyzing fear still controlling your body. The lingering terror chilling you to your deepest core long after you're safe from the dreamscape. That's a nightmare.

"Mom."

"Iniko needs his rest. Your energy is everywhere, and you don't want it to upset him."

I take a long look at the door that holds my friend behind it. I've come here at least once a week for the last year, and he's never responded. He's just a hunched figure on a bed—his skin ashen, bones protruding—the nightmare taking form. A nightmare tears away every part of you. Most of the time, they die within a few years.

The memory from earlier clogs my throat.

A year ago, Iniko was working during a robbery. The attacker cast a powerful hex that caused those in its path's skin to melt from their bones. Iniko's brother jumped in front to protect him—his death was painfully slow.

I remember that for days after, Iniko wouldn't speak. I saw the signs he was losing his fight, but I just never thought it could really happen to someone I knew—not someone as joyful as Iniko. If only I had, maybe I could've prevented this. Iniko was always the light in our group, the easiest to laugh and the first to smile. I thought he would bounce back, that he needed time to grieve, and then it would be okay.

I was wrong.

By the next week, whatever darkness had begun to grow inside had overtaken his body. Hollowing out the person I knew until he was nothing but a shell. The story his family told was that Iniko died from injuries sustained during the robbery. But I won't let the Gods take him without a fight.

Following Mom up the stairs, I stop short when I see Rozzel waiting in the entryway. In their late fifties, Roz shows no signs of aging, whether magic or genetics, I don't know. "What are we going to do with you, Azalee Saunders?"

"Roz," Mom starts, but the head of the coven holds up their hand, and Mom goes silent.

"You have been warned about this. Nightmares are only to be secured with the assistance of four or more witches and *never* without prior approval from the coven." Roz clicks their tongue, shaking their pale bald head. "This reckless behavior must come to an end. You are putting yourself and the coven in jeopardy."

"I'm trying to help." I run a hand over the crystals on my belt, centering my energy. "Those Nightmares, they could be any of us. We owe them for not finding them soon enough."

"We owe them nothing." Roz's words carry an echo. "You are on thin ice. Don't think just because you are a Saunders that your mother's good reputation can save you. Report to the main office in the morning. I'm sure we can find something to keep you occupied."

I offer my most scathing look as I push past them and back into the night.

CHAPTER 5

Gabriel

My teeth vibrate as the music thrums through the club. The smooth taste of whiskey, sugar, and orange peel coats my lips as I knock back my second drink. The sharp hit of magic at the end sends an electric shock across my body, leaving a pleasant tingle in its wake. Eclipse is at capacity, unsurprising given it's opening night and the locals are here as well as the tourists who swarm Salem like locusts this time of year.

Everyone wants a piece of that old magic.

Logan and I are lounging on ruby-red velvet upholstered couches in the back section. I run my pointer finger absentmindedly along the glass of my watch, eyes scanning the crowded dance floor. With my training, I'm conditioned to categorize threats and locate the quickest exit routes. Side door: lets out onto an alley with direct access to the main road. But based on my quick assessment, I doubt we'll need it.

My head snaps to the doorway as a loud group shuffles in. It's too dark and densely packed to make out specifics, but the tugging in my chest from an invisible-to-anyone-but-me rope makes me groan. The all-too-familiar sensation demands for me to acknowledge the presence of the person tethered to the other end of the golden thread.

Gods and Fates be damned. I ignore it, just like witches tune out auras. I force the thread to disappear. It only ever lasts for so long, though.

My energy is finally normalizing now that we're away from Grandfather's supporters. The obsequious fawning makes my stomach curdle.

Some might say that's what I do too. But it's not the position of High Witch I've spent my life trying to garner praise from, it's my grandfather I want to impress. Being good enough won't cut it. I have to be indispensable. There's a security in knowing I can achieve that.

"I'm good," I say as Logan passes me another cocktail. "I've got to be at the office early."

"Gabe, that's why they invented Milk Thistle Gummies."

"All the same." I don't like instant hangover cures. They lessen most of the symptoms, but I feel shaky after. I could make my own, but brewing potions from scratch takes ages and most of us just use instant. That's why ready-made magic companies are worth billions. They're especially beneficial to humans or to witches whose magic is on the thin side.

Not that I have that problem. Mine is as thick as they come.

Lacing my fingers behind my head, I lean back on the sofa and resume my surveillance. I've always enjoyed studying how people interact, the subtle stories they tell without words.

As my eyes drift across the hazy club, icy-blond hair flipping over a shoulder catches my attention as the delicate hand reaches for a smoking glass of purple liquid. The gold thread flares back to life, slithering along from me to her.

Azalee Saunders.

It's like the rest of the club disappears, my vision consumed with her and the color red. I grind my teeth, watching her tilt her head back and laugh at something the guy she's with said. Her fingers run along his chest as she whispers in his ear. We are the only ones who can see this connection between us, but she's doing a stellar job at pretending like she hasn't noticed me.

Azalee and I have a complicated history. We both grew up in Salem, and while we didn't go to school together, we had a friend in common. Iniko. So our paths crossed here and there at parties in the woods or bonfires on the beach. Whenever they did, it always seemed to end in flames.

Then, two years ago, she saved my life. I hate her for it. For what I became after. If she'd just let me die, I wouldn't be burdened with this secret, infected with the same magic she has.

I wouldn't be a dream wielder.

I curl my hand into a fist, pressing it into my chest, and the scars left from where she healed me. Having your fate tied to a woman who despises you and who you equally hate in return is fucking miserable. I wish I could keep my distance from her, but I have to keep an eye on her because if she does something stupid to get herself killed, I'm dead too.

Mutually assured destruction.

Grandfather lost a piece of himself when his soulmate bond broke after my grandmother died, but that connection isn't a deadly one. At least not physically anyway, but the longer a couple is together, the stronger the link becomes, meaning after decades, the sudden absence of it is a hole that can never be filled. That's why he always claims unshakable moral character as the reason he didn't develop dream wielder powers after Grandmother died. But from my research, dream wielding magic is something you're born with. A trauma as deep as losing your soulmate would have awoken it. So it wasn't fortitude that kept the old man from his greatest enemy—it was the Fates.

"What?" Logan asks, following my gaze.

I huff, yanking my bow tie off and undoing the top buttons of my tux shirt. "Saunders." The words spit from my mouth.

"Is she here with friends? Got a dare going on whether or not I can get a dream wielder into bed." Logan scans the club.

I shake my head, scraping a hand through my dark strands of hair. "Logan, stop that shit. If word gets back to the old man, you're going to be fucked, and not in the fun way." I've been keeping him from stepping too far off the rails since we were kids. Somehow, even then I knew that after our parents died, I had to keep us in Grandfather's good graces or else what would Logan and I do? Where would we go? He's the only family we have. So I didn't have a choice but to follow his rules if I wanted to keep Logan and me together.

He scoffs. "I didn't say I'd actually sleep with them; I just have to get them to agree."

"Find another conquest." He doesn't listen to me much now that we're older. Probably because he's seen the things I got up to in my youth and knows I don't have room to talk.

Azalee admitted she was a dream wielder when she found out what I was after my incident. But I have no evidence on the others who go to The Retreat. On the surface, it seems like a regular, albeit expensive, wellness center. My grandfather has his suspicions too. That's why he's been pushing against Genevieve and Rozzel, the owners of the place.

Dream wielding isn't illegal—not yet, anyway. But Grandfather's doing an excellent job of making them pariahs. I've worked overtime behind the scenes the last two years to make sure he didn't overstep the line.

Azalee moves from the bar, hands tangled in the guy's shirt as she pulls him onto the dance floor. I watch her hips sway to the music, luring me into a trance.

I take the drink from the waiter before Logan can. "Dude, that was mine."

The ice hits my teeth as the lemony basil mixture slides over my tongue, the sharp tang of hibiscus cresting on my taste buds before I swallow. The magic trickles into my veins as the view before me becomes drenched in starlight, the cocktail giving the world a glow. The Star Burst potion relaxes the taker. It's not very strong. It'll last for twenty minutes max. Hopefully, Azalee will be long gone by then.

But twenty minutes pass, and she's still dancing. This time with a petite guy, her back pressed against his front. As the potion fades, I see more clearly what she's doing. She's working a spell. Her fingers glide over the crystals in her belt, touching each in a practiced motion. Her other hand is on his cheek, sliding rhythmically across in an infinity symbol.

I've never dream wielded. But I sure as hell did my research once I realized what I'd become.

I'm out of my seat and moving toward her before my mind has a chance to catch up to my feet. I squeeze through the crowds, their sweaty bodies writhing as the music reaches a fever pitch.

I grab Azalee's hand, dragging her against me. "What the hell do you think you're doing?" I hiss in her ear. Her scent is too strong this close: bright honeysuckles and fresh oranges in a grassy field.

Her eyes open lazily, clearly just as *aware* of my presence as I am of hers. She likely sensed me drawing nearer, that thread between us tightening with every step into each other's orbit. She shoves against my chest, and I step back. "I'm dancing," she yells over the bass.

The guy she was dancing with tries to resume their activities, but I step between them, once again feeling the press of Azalee's flesh against my shirt. My hand grazes the pale skin of her stomach. She wears a black crop top edged with silver stars, a short leather jacket, and a high-waisted black miniskirt.

"We should talk outside," I say, attempting discretion.

She spins, hands in the air, giving me a further peek of her midsection. "No thanks."

I loop my fingers around her belt, halting her to a stop. *"Now."*

Her eyes flick to where I'm touching the skin of her navel before she looks up at me through long lashes. She draws each word out: "Make me, Ford." I don't need to read her aura to know she's not bluffing. She'd fucking love a fight tonight.

Heat rises from my lower abdomen, the challenge in her eyes infuriating. "Don't think I won't."

The music surges, and the crowd increases their frenzy. Someone bumps into Azalee, and she stumbles into me. I grab her, hand splaying across her lower back. The burn of her flushed skin presses against the entire length of me as her hands slide up my chest to catch herself. My heartbeat thrums in my neck.

Her green eyes catch the flashing lights, tongue darting across her red lips. "Fine."

I don't take any chances, holding her wrist until we're in the chilly air and away from the line waiting to get in the club. She yanks away, wrapping her jacket around her. "What do you want, *Gabriel*?" Her voice is rough.

"Do you know how dangerous it is to stand there and flaunt your magic like that?" My jaw spasms with pain as I try to hold in my anger while scanning our surroundings.

She scoffs. "I wasn't flaunting anything. No one knew what I was doing. The only reason you did is because you haven't been able to take your eyes off me all night." She wears this aggravating smile like she's caught me peeping.

"I only watched you"—I step closer—"because I knew you'd do something stupid. I don't want to be collateral damage just because you don't give a rat's ass about getting yourself in trouble."

"I was doing just fine. You're the one who dragged me out of there like a criminal." She stares me down, unblinking, waiting for me to say that's what she is. I've said just as much countless times in interviews and public forums.

I spent my whole life with my grandfather pounding into my brain that dream wielders are unnatural, dangerous witches. That because of them, I never got to meet my grandmother. Just because I suddenly found myself one of them doesn't mean that ideal evaporated. But it did mean I educated myself on them far beyond what the old man preached.

It's the fucking reason my brain can't pick a lane to stay in and surge ahead. I don't see black and white when it comes to them like I used to. And it's why I haven't been able to just let the High Witch pursue forceful aggression toward the dream wielders, even if I work against it in the shadows. If I exposed myself as a dream wielder, not only would my family hate me, but I would lose my access to the High Witch's office and the resources to make actual change from the top down.

I reach into my pocket and hand her a pack of Milk Thistle Gummies. "Sober up and get home."

She makes no move for the potion.

"It's not poison," I add.

"Sorry if I don't take your word for it. Besides, I don't want it."

I do my best to contain my frustrated growl. "Whatever. Have it your way."

She pulls out her phone. "You ruined the buzz I was getting from the daydream anyway. So, if it eases your precious little mind, I'll order a Broom to pick me up."

She turns her back on me, pretending like I don't exist. There was a time after the accident when she wanted to be my friend and offered to teach me about dream magic. But I shut her out, ignored every attempt she made at contact. I had morphed into this horrendous monster my family had been bred to hate. As unfair as it is, I blame her for that. She saved my life, sure, but I didn't ask her to do that. Maybe I was ready to see what the light at the end of the tunnel held, and she took that away.

I go back inside, but I watch her until the car comes to pick her up. Life debts are old magic. The kind that you can't settle with a box of cigars or a nice dinner by the river. So as much as it fucks me over, I keep a watch out for her. I hope one day that tug I feel toward Azalee Saunders, that cord of fate tying us together, will finally release me from its grip, and I can forget all about her.

Walking the streets of Salem well past two a.m., everything is quiet. The only sounds are the whispers in the trees and the hoots of owls deep in the woods. Magic is everywhere, palpable in the movement of all things.

But it hits differently at night. It's almost like you can feel magic seeping up from the ground, asking you to join it.

Tourists love Salem because it's the hub of magic: with the High Witch's office and it being the location where magic was set free all those centuries ago. Most people find it commercialized nowadays, but there are those among us who fear Salem. Who think that the magic here is too untamed. The first sighting of dream wielders was in Salem, but my research shows they're worldwide now.

I stop my wanderings when I come to the iron gate that leads into the Salem City Cemetery. The gravestones date back to the 1600s, the oldest still preserved in the state. You'll find Fords among them, going back to the original Salem witches.

But I'm not here to see those old witches. I'm here to see my parents.

My steps are reverent as I shove my hands into the pockets of my tux trousers. The grass squishes under my feet. I'm ruining my shoes, but I don't care.

My parents are in the back. The last section that holds the newer corpses. Most are taken, only a few spots reserved for the High Witch and his grandsons. Morbid to know your final resting place is already picked out.

I left Logan at the club. Not that it really mattered. He was well on his way to finding more than one person to go home with. Besides, he doesn't like to come here.

I stop in front of their matching graves, dropping to my knees. The mud cools my skin and stains this expensive suit. They died nineteen years ago. I was barely six years old. The healers did everything they could, but fate comes for every witch in the end. It was a car accident. They'd been traveling to a party in the next state over. Logan and I were sent to live with Grandfather after that.

I used to dream about what my life could have been if Mom and Dad were still here. They always said I could do whatever I wanted. But they're dead, and no spellwork can fix that.

At university, when I got my first glimpse of some freedom, I went off the rails. I guess I finally let out all those repressed feelings I had about their deaths. I just wanted everything to go away. It almost did. But when I woke up from the dark, I wasn't dead. I was something new.

"Hey, Ma, Pops." I grip the top of the gravestone, my fingers pressing against the cool granite. I run my nails along the carved stone.

ANNABELLE TESSLY FORD

LOVING WIFE AND MOTHER

WESTLY FORD

DEVOTED SON AND FATHER

Whole lives distilled down to a few words. I'm lucky to remember them in pieces, but Logan was too little to recall much. I've tried my best to keep their memory alive for his sake. I clear my throat to unclog the tears gathering there. The cool wind whips across my face, and it almost feels like a hand gripping my skin, trying to rip it off.

Am I the son they would've wanted? I'm certainly not the heir Grandfather dreamed of. Somehow, no matter what I do, he always finds a higher threshold for me to meet.

I bow my head, laying it against the stone's top, wishing I could see them, but they're gone, and I should be happy about that. Moved on to wherever the good people go.

Sometimes, I wonder if I'll ever see them again. Or if I am truly an abomination destined to a hellfire eternity.

CHAPTER 6

Azalee

I regret all my life choices as I stare at my bedroom ceiling. My mouth tastes like throw up—which is concerning, as I don't recall vomiting. Every cell in my body screams as I flip my arm across my face to block the sunlight while my other hand searches my nightstand for Milk Thistle Gummies. I know I stashed a pack in here for safekeeping.

"Fuck," I hiss, flopping onto my stomach when I can't find what I'm looking for. I rub my eyes to clear the haze in the room. "Where are you, you sneaky bastard?" I use my eyes this time and riffle through the drawer but still come up empty.

The room spins when I stand, and I grab the headboard to keep upright. I'll never drink again if I can just find this *damn* potion. But after searching the room, I realize there is nothing to find.

I recall using them a few nights ago, but I swear there were more. "Past Azalee is screwing me over once again, Dad," I say to the picture on my desk. It's of me and Dad from my sixth birthday. I sport a toothy grin while squeezing a pink bunny in a choke hold. The pang of grief in my chest is still there, but it's a dull ache more than a sharp stab.

I opt for a Pep Up to keep me moving until I can grab a hangover smoothie in town. After splashing water on my face, I slip on my running gear and sneakers before heading to the kitchen.

“Unbelievable,” Mom mutters to the morning news as I enter the brightly lit room. Rainbows dance across the porcelain as warm yellow light streams through the stained glass window over the kitchen sink. I used to think it was creepy that we lived in the cathedral over the dungeons, but this place has become home.

“What?” I start the kettle, grabbing a mug and preparing a cup of peppermint and willow bark tea for the headache I can’t squash. I recognize the guests on TV. “Is that Caroline?” I grab a bowl from the cupboard, pouring too-sugary cereal inside, leaning against the counter.

“Yes.” She draws the word out a little too long. Caroline was part of the coven until she went MIA a few years ago. “She’s flouncing around the country selling false propaganda on dream wielding, teaching people how to protect themselves against us. Poppycock. She knows very well a dream wielder can’t put a spell on you from across the parking lot and jump into your head. She is doing nothing but spreading fear.”

“Well,” I say with food in my mouth, milk dribbling on my chin, “apparently people disagree, because it made her a *New York Times* bestseller.”

“Roz shouldn’t have let her into the coven.” Mom sips her coffee, staring at the screen like she could burn a hole in it. “I knew from the beginning she was ambitious. I just didn’t think she’d turn against her own kind. Dream wielding is a sacred gift. And she’s going around telling people that we’re a bunch of hell-raising creatures of the night.”

I pour hot water into my tea, dropping in a round clear quartz for extra cleansing. Sometimes, I wish I could give my powers back. Magic is all around us, but some magics come with a higher price, and it sucks when you didn’t get to choose whether you wanted to pay it.

I glance at the clock. I want to get a quick run in before I have to report to Roz’s office for my *assignment*.

“This is a special news bulletin.” Intense music comes over the TV. The shot flashes to a reporter standing outside a home I recognize from town.

The reporter is stocky, with a bushy head of hair that looks to be courtesy of a thickening potion. "I'm Henry Ochoa, and this is WSM2 live from the scene of the crime, which police are estimating took place at around one a.m. A passing jogger found the body early this morning." The camera pans and shows a woman in athletic gear standing beside him. She's pink-faced, holding tight to a crystal necklace.

"Can you tell us what you saw?" The reporter shoves the microphone in the lady's face.

She shifts, lips quivering. "Um . . . well, it was dark, so I didn't really see anything at first. I actually tripped over the . . . body." Her voice cracks at the end.

"And did you know the victim?" Henry Ochoa pushes.

She shakes her head. "No, I didn't think it was a body at that point. I mean, I knew it was a body, but I didn't know it was a *dead* body. I leaned down to check for a pulse. I'm a healer in training at Salem Medical, and I tried to revive him." She stops abruptly, her eyes welling up.

"And as a healer, did you sense the cause of death?" Healers are not a rarity, but ones with empathic abilities are. They can feel the energy at the source of the injury and dive into how the death blow occurred.

"No . . . no, I'm not that good." She regains a bit of composure. "I mostly work with potions." Police exit the house, the camera panning and zooming in on them.

"Poor girl," Mom mutters. She has never loved the press. They don't tend to be too kind to dream wielders.

"Officers, can you tell us anything?" The reporter jogs to reach them. "What do the owners of this home have to say about a body being discovered in their yard?"

"This is an ongoing investigation. We have no comment at this time." They wave him off, their cloaks flapping in the breeze.

"Can you at least tell us the cause of death?"

"The victim appears to have died in his sleep," an officer concedes, adjusting a pendant around his neck.

"Of natural causes?" Henry Ochoa's face drops at the news it might be a mundane death.

The officer pauses, looking at the camera and then at the reporter, jaw clenched. "No, it looks like a dream killed him."

The spoon slips from my hand with a loud clatter. "A dream." Just like the death they were talking about on the radio last night.

Mom clicks off the TV, standing as the lines of her face deepen.

"Were they implying one of us did it?" A fist grips my heart, squeezing tighter with each beat.

She takes a deep breath. "Be careful today."

"Mom?" Two deaths with blame being pinned on dream wielders is *not* a coincidence.

She runs a hand over my arm and squeezes my hand. "We're an easy scapegoat. They'll investigate and find that a dream wielder had nothing to do with it."

"What about a Nightmare?" Nightmares leave no visible injuries on the outside of the body, but brain examination would indicate the person died in their dreams. We have healers in the coven who have conducted medical examinations in secret to help us better understand. Not much mainstream research has gone into the taboo subject—most people don't even know about Nightmares.

"If there is a loose Nightmare out there . . ." I could skip out on Roz and go find it, make the case that this is more important than whatever they had planned.

"I'll look into it." Her voice is firm—conversation over.

"I'm going on a quick run. I'll see you later."

"Be careful, Azalee. You know how people get when there's a murder."

Despite the cool air nipping at my face, I take a longer path for my run than usual. The unfortunate side effect of this detour means I have to pass by the High Witch's house. Drawn by the magnetic force of that ever-present golden rope, my eyes slide to a window on the top floor.

Gabriel Ford stares down at me as he runs a hand through his raven-black hair. Piercing aquamarine eyes accent his straight nose and strong jaw. I can still feel where the dark stubble grazed my cheek last night.

Stupid, handsome bastard.

Last night, when he was trying to *help* me, all he did was stop my good deed. The guy I was dancing with recently lost his dog. He's been sick over the whole thing. I was working a daydream. It was a lovely walk on the beach with his dearly departed canine.

Then fucking Gabriel had to step in where he was very much not wanted.

I've despised him ever since we first met at Iniko's fifth birthday party, when he couldn't stop parroting off his grandfather's hateful rhetoric about dream wielders. I only extended my help after he became a dream wielder because it's the same thing I'd do for any of them.

Still, apparently it's true what they say about no good deed going unpunished, because now he owes me a life debt. Which means he keeps showing up in my business uninvited. I've thought about flinging myself in front of a moving vehicle near him just so he could save my life and get the debt cleared.

I drag my eyes away and pick up my pace. A few blocks down the road, I slow when I reach the house I was unintentionally—*or purposely*—running to. The news crew hasn't left, but they look to be wrapping up. Stationed near the gate to the house are officers in neatly pressed cloaks.

I stand a little too long, catching the reporter's attention. "You're not a medium by chance?" His eyes gleam, hand already inching toward his microphone.

"What? No, I was just looking." How macabre. *Don't mind the woman leering at the house where they recently found a dead body.*

His face drops as he turns back to the WSM2 news van. "Too bad. That would be a great angle. Get the news straight from the victim about the dream wielder who killed them."

"You don't know it's a dream wielder," I say before thinking better of it. I bite my tongue, but the words are already free.

His attention returns to my direction, studying me. "The officer said he was killed in his dreams. Doesn't leave much room for interpretation."

Shut up, Azalee. Leave it alone. "Dream wielders can't kill people." *Or just keep talking, that works too.*

"And how would you know?" He steps closer, expression too curious.

"I have to finish my run." I turn around, breaking into a sprint.

CHAPTER 7

Gabriel

"Gabriel." Grandfather slaps hard on my back as I walk into the office.

I cough, covering my mouth with my fist to keep the coffee I was swallowing inside. "Yes?" I manage a rough response through the burning in my lungs.

"We're going to the police station. Car's arriving now." Grandfather's valet places a cloak on the High Witch's shoulders before handing him a gold-tipped cane. He doesn't need it to walk, but the old man enjoys the looks it gets with the large alexandrite on top.

"Police station?" I stay a step behind as the black town car pulls along the curb. The High Witch's office is located in town hall. The red bricks, charcoal roof, and white shutters make the place timeless. In the spring and summer, fragrant flowers line the walks, but as autumn descends, orange and yellow leaves cover the paths.

A few tourists stand outside, taking pictures in front of the iconic bronze statue of the founding witches of Salem. When they spot us, they whisper and point. Grandfather offers them a hearty wave and dazzling smile as the driver opens the car doors. The High Witch's security gets into an SUV that will follow behind us.

Logan and I had personal details when we were younger, but as a way to demonstrate to the citizens the High Witch was taking finances seriously, he dismissed our protection officers when we turned eighteen. Instead, he sent Logan and me to the best combat classes.

Grandfather probably expects me to jump in front of a hex for him if I have to.

It's not until we're settled into the plush leather seats, the car driving away, that he responds. "Terrible thing." He shakes his head, watching out the tinted bulletproof glass as the shops pass by. It's early, but the pop-up stalls are already selling magical wares to eager visitors. "There was a murder yesterday and another this morning. I've called for the Captain to arrange a briefing for us. I want answers. I've dedicated my life to protecting Salem, and I will not let it be terrorized. I've also recast the wards around the manor." Grandfather has always excelled at protection magic. It's one of the traits that got him elected. Citizens loved the idea of a High Witch who could guard them from evil magic.

Neither Logan or I inherited that specialty, but instead took after our mother, who was a master potion maker. Now that I'm a dream wielder, my sleeping tonics and calming draughts are more powerful than ever before.

I heard about the murders on the news this morning. And who they're blaming for them. Dream wielders. It's been a hot-button topic for centuries, but with Grandfather's vendetta against them, he makes sure it's forever at the forefront of citizens' minds. Non-witches have embraced magic because it could help them and could be regulated with laws and policies, but dream wielders are another matter. A delicate hand is required when establishing ways to make sure their magic doesn't become deadly, and a delicate hand is not something the High Witch is known for.

I keep my face in a practiced neutral state. "The Apprentices will want a statement." I make a note on my phone to call them later.

"They'll get one, don't worry, my boy." *My boy.* The term of endearment meant for a grandson. But on the old man's tongue, it's as sharp as a blade, a show of ownership over all those born with the Ford name.

Reaching into his jacket, he withdraws a black vial. The opaque exterior hides the liquid inside. He shoots it back as fast as Logan was hitting the elixirs at the club last night.

I choose my words carefully. "Is there anything I should be aware of?" I give a slight nod to the bottle.

His expression is unreadable. "The healers found some reasons for concern."

My heartbeat quickens. Grandfather and I have never been close in the traditional sense. But he and Logan are the only family I have. We have each other's backs. "What does that mean exactly?"

He gazes at the vial as he twirls it in his fingers. "I thought I'd have decades before I was reunited with my beloved wife, but the Fates might have other plans."

Swallowing does nothing for my dry mouth. "You're dying?" I always assumed he would outlive us all.

"My dear Ella was the light of my life." His tone becomes wistful as he loses himself in a memory. "Our soulmate bond was among the strongest witches had ever seen."

I'm not sure how true that is, but I don't interrupt. Over the years, the moments of softness that come from talking about my grandmother have lessened.

"As the years without her increase, I find it harder to manage the pain of that missing chunk of my soul without some assistance." He looks up at me, eyes glossy. It's not the show he puts on for his followers, but genuine grief. "If only you'd got to meet her, just once. You'd understand—her light shone so bright it lit up the whole town."

"You've kept her alive for us, Grandfather. I know what a gift she was." Her pictures line our walls, making sure neither Logan or I could ever forget her.

Slipping the bottle back into his pocket, he regains his full stature. "However, the Gods will have to put up a fight if they want to take me before I'm ready."

Not really an answer about the dying part, but exactly what I'd expect from him. I have never known a world without the old man, even if I've sometimes dreamed about what that might be like—to have a chance to choose my own path. Still, when faced with the real possibility, I'm far more conflicted than I thought I'd be.

Grandfather takes calls the rest of the drive and I catch up on emails, both pretending like nothing happened. The Salem Police Department is a bustle of activity. A few reporters wait outside for a chance to speak to anyone willing.

"Handle them," the old man says as he exits the car.

I take the lead with the press. "The High Witch will release an official statement on the recent events later today. If you have any follow-up questions, please contact our offices. Thank you." I nod to the reporters as they shout questions I have no intention of answering.

The High Witch and Captain of the police are already deep in conversation when I catch up. "Disturbing trend, Captain." Grandfather clicks his cane against the cement for emphasis.

"We're putting our best people on this." Captain Mendoza is a stout man with wide shoulders and a buzz cut.

"I should think that would be obvious. This is the peak season for visitors. We wouldn't want any issues with the public thinking the High Witch can't keep them safe."

Mendoza leads us into an interrogation room with stark white walls and a corkboard on the left with information the police have on the two victims.

The heat is stifling, and I loosen my tie to ease my breathing. "Do you think they're connected?" I ask, examining the evidence, my leather-soled shoes slipping on the polished floor. Pictures and stats cover the papers, but there are only a dozen. I've never run an investigation, but this seems a little sparse.

I don't miss the beat in which Mendoza looks to the High Witch for approval before answering. "We're still assessing, but we do believe it is the same killer."

"How so?" I clasp my hands behind my back.

"Early healer reports from our medical examiners indicate the victims were killed in a dream. Residue of magic left from dream wielding was found in the brains, similar to other cases we've had in the past where the murderer was found to be a dream wielder."

My heart stops as the blood in my veins turns to ice. I tighten my grip on my watch, hoping to hide the shaking. I've read conflicting research papers, but some suggest that only a Nightmare can kill, while others say any dream wielder is capable of such acts. I'm guessing the Salem police aren't exactly discerning when it comes to assigning blame or differentiating between dream wielders and Nightmares. "You're confident a dream wielder did this?" Straight and to the point, just like I was taught.

Grandfather has taken the seat at the head of the table. "Of course. It was only a matter of time before we started seeing this happen. It's as I've been saying for decades: Leaving them to grow would put us all in danger."

It's like he's giving a speech to sway a crowd and not myself and the Captain.

"Residue of dream magic doesn't definitively confirm the victim was killed *in* a dream. That residue is left in the dreamers' brain after any experience with dream magic," I say, careful with my words. It's not strange that I would be familiar with the effects of dream wielders, given Grandfather's crusade. But too much familiarity could raise suspicions. "Was there any other evidence to prove a dream wielder was there at the time of death?"

I turn back to study the faces of the deceased—a woman in her late forties, found in an alley near the edge of town. The second man was discovered this morning in the front yard of a house that didn't belong to him. They've already cleared the owner of suspicion. Other than the apparent dream death, the victims don't appear to have any connection to one another.

"It's likely the killings took place elsewhere and the unsub dumped the bodies after. We've only just got initial reports on the vic from this morning. But the woman wasn't from Salem. Best guess is she was in town for the holiday. No witness at the scene, but the evidence found by the healers leads to that being the only likely conclusion."

"What if it was a Nightmare?" I know I've said too much when Mendoza's eyes narrow. Instinct makes me reach for my watch, but I stop myself from fidgeting and looking suspicious.

"Nightmares aren't common knowledge. Average Joes don't know the difference between them and dream wielders." He leaves off the question, *So how do you know?*

I stand at my full height. "I'm not common. I'm a Ford."

Mendoza backs down ever so slightly. "It's impossible to tell which one was responsible. They leave the same traces."

"That's because there is no difference." Grandfather leans forward, pointing a bony finger at Mendoza. "I want this crazed psychopath found. You understand? I don't care if you have to knock on every door of a suspected dream wielder. We owe it to the people of Salem."

The final desperate acts of a dying man. Grandfather is always in control, and if he feels like this sickness is something out of his hands, he will try to gain back dominance where he can. Suddenly, it makes sense why he's been pushing even harder against dream wielders as of late.

Mendoza's face pinches. "I wish it were that easy, sir. But since most dream wielders don't tend to advertise their powers, we only have speculation to go on."

The High Witch nods like he expected this response. "Then I trust you'll be giving your full support to my proposed bill Gabriel and I will be finalizing shortly."

Even though High Witch is a position granted for life, he still needs to keep voters on his side to pass any bills he wants to implement into permanent laws. Every citizen is allowed to vote, no matter their magical status. It was decided early on that to keep things peaceful, witches and non-witches needed to have an equal say.

Senses tingling, my eyes narrow. "What bill?" He keeps hinting at the new project I'm supposedly spearheading with him, but the details are coming too sparsely for my taste.

"I've recently had it written up, but I plan on introducing it to the public soon, with your help." He picks at invisible lint on his cloak. "If it passes, we won't have any trouble knowing who the dream wielders are. And hopefully, in a few years, they will no longer be an issue."

Heart raging against my chest, I bite my tongue. I don't trust myself to speak. Discovering dream wielder magic isn't simple. There are very few potions that will detect it, all of which require herbs that are illegal to grow because of their dangerous nature. I need to know what this new bill entails, but when confronting Grandfather, it has to be a strategic strike. Perhaps now that he's facing the end of his mortal coil, I can persuade him to see that a legacy dripping with hate is not the imprint he should leave on Salem.

Mendoza's face gives nothing away. "I'm sure we can arrange a letter of support."

"Excellent." Grandfather stands. "In the meantime, I have a place you can start your search."

CHAPTER 8

Azalee

Orange leaves dust the surface of the calm lake, the clouded sky coloring the liquid a murky gray. When I tap my finger against the glass of the sliding door, the sound reverberates through me. My reflection in the glass looks even more defeated than I feel. It's the beginning of the month, which means we're booked up at The Retreat with the returning non–dream wielding guests desperate for their aura cleanses and antiaging spell treatments. I've had my hands full all morning filling requests from them.

"Azalee?" Sam says behind me.

I take a last look outside before turning. "Ready?"

Sam is in his late fifties with deep-tan skin from years of working outside. He's a farmer by trade and the newest addition to the dream wielder coven. He gained his powers five weeks ago, after he and his partner were swimming in the ocean. A current swept in and took his husband under—Sam nearly drowned too, trying to save him.

He twists his wedding ring. "I don't think I can do this."

I put an arm around his shoulders and lead him through a silent hallway before entering a treatment room. "You can, Sam. I can help you through it. Dream wielding will allow me to create a safe space for you to process the trauma and fear left by it."

Tears fill his eyes. "Will I see him? Noshi?"

I could show him his deceased loved one, but it's not advised. Dream wielding can make things feel so real it's hard to separate it from reality. If you allow it, you could get lost in the dream world—it's another way to get pulled into a nightmare by losing your grip on reality. My heart aches, the deepest kind of fissure you can't ever repair. I know exactly how Sam feels, because I, and many other dream wielders, can relate. While we can offer comfort to others by sharing a final moment with a loved one or revisiting a memory, we ourselves can never risk immersing into that euphoria.

"This is about healing your mind. Noshi is with the Gods now. But you're still here, and we want to help you move forward."

Sam looks disappointed but nods.

"Please, lie down, and we'll get started." When I saw Roz this morning, I thought they were going to give me some shit job like cleaning the chicken coop, but instead they told me to assist with Sam. It's not that dream wielding and helping someone through a trauma isn't tiring—all that sadness is overwhelming if you don't cleanse right—but it's *so* rewarding.

The treatment room smells like lavender and chamomile from the potion I have bubbling away on the warming plate. This concoction was created by dream wielders centuries ago to help aid in the dreaming process and promote calm energies. Sam lies on the table, tension muddling his aura. I click on the soothing sounds of rain.

Sitting on a stool at the end with his head, I place crystals around him. My moonstone will center me as I dream with him. You can dream wield without any of this, but they make it easier. "All right, Sam, slow breaths in and out. If you need to stop, all you have to do is ask. Okay?"

He nods, closing his eyes. I do the same and focus on channeling myself into his mind. Finding the way into a dream wielder's mind is simpler than most, and his door appears to me after a few seconds. It's a wooden gate made with iron nails and found pieces of metal. I flip the latch, and I'm in his dreamscape.

"Sam?" I've brought us to a beach. Not like the one where he experienced his trauma—that was a Nantucket shore with Atlantic tides. We're at a tropical beach adorned with palm trees and clear blue water.

Sam holds his arms around his stomach, gazing at the sea, jaw popping with tension.

"You're safe." I make the breeze sway the palms and kiss his cheeks. Sam has no control over this dream. I'm in charge. He's too fresh in his pain for it to be safe to let him take the lead. "Let's move a little closer. The water is warm, I promise."

I take his hand and lead him to the water's edge with baby steps. A familiar tug in my stomach makes me look toward the tree line. We're alone, but in the real world, someone is coming.

Gabriel.

Why is he here?

Sam is unaware of my sensation and keeps glaring at the waves.

I feel a phantom vibrating in my pocket—my phone ringing. I ignore it, focusing on Sam and his therapy. The sensation stops, but it starts again a moment later. "Sam," I say softly. "I need to pull us from the dream. But you can stay asleep while I take care of something. All right?"

His nod barely registers, but I take it as consent and pull myself from the dream. He stays sleeping on the table while I step into the hallway.

It's a number I don't recognize, but they've called twice, so I had better just see what's up. "Hello?"

"Where are you?" the rough voice says.

"Who is this?" Although I'm pretty confident of the answer.

"Gabriel."

I hang up. Maybe that's why I sensed the tug. The Fates giving me a caller ID.

The phone rings again. "What do you want?"

Gabriel's voice is muffled, as if he's holding his hand over the phone to conceal his words. "Where are you?"

I step into the reception area and watch the raindrops trail down the glass as I peek into the driveway. "Why should I tell you?"

"The High Witch has official business at The Retreat." He's so quiet I have to squeeze my eyes closed to focus on the words. "I suggest you find a charmed place to hide anything you wouldn't want found."

That stops my fidgeting. "What's going on?" My eyes spring open, scanning the landscape for any clues of danger.

"You have five minutes." The phone clicks off.

I call Mom before I even take another breath. "The High Witch is coming," I say. "Or his lackeys. Either way, we need to make sure there's nothing to see."

"Here?"

"Yes. We've got five minutes." My heart pounds in my chest, rattling my rib cage.

"Stay there. We're on our way."

It's not like we keep signs up advertising DREAM WIELDERS THIS WAY. But certain crystals or books might tip them off. Mom will need to double-check that the wards protecting the dungeons are secure. I don't want to imagine what would happen if they found the Nightmares.

The new dream wielders on-site have come for a two-week retreat to train and learn their powers in private. It has all the pretenses of any regular retreat, but it could spell trouble if they're looked at too closely. Sometimes, in the beginning, when you're still learning to control your powers, it can be easier to give it away.

I hate waiting here like a sitting duck, but Mom will handle alerting the rest of The Retreat. I check to make sure Sam is still asleep and lock the door back to the treatment rooms as a precaution. The coven has plans for these things. It's not the first time we've come under fire, and with the way the wind is changing, I have a sinking feeling it won't be the last.

The gauzy white button-down and khaki linen pants we wear as part of The Retreat uniform stick to my skin, the rain soaking my clothes as I head out the glass doors when I see the black SUV and police cruisers pulling into the rounded gravel driveway.

Taking a calming breath, I run my hand over the crystals around my neck to ground my energies. "To what do we owe the pleasure?" I say to Gabriel as he gets out of the SUV. "I didn't see you on the appointment list."

Gabriel is wearing dark aviators and a pristine gray suit. His black hair is perfectly styled by a hair potion, unbothered by the misty rain. "We're here on business from the High Witch."

Despite my insides quivering, I don't show it. "Oh? Does he need a crystal massage or energy alignment?"

Gabriel glares at me briefly without responding. The Captain of the police gets out of the cruiser. "Miss, I'm Captain Mendoza. We need to speak to the owners of the spa. Can you call them?" I've never met him, but I've researched who to avoid.

"No need." Roz and Mom approach on a golf cart we use to get around. Roz is wearing a hard expression I thought was reserved for me. "Is there a problem, Captain?" Roz holds their ground, looking every bit as intimidating as the High Witch.

"I'm sure you've heard about the recent murders on the news," the Captain says.

Mom looks completely at ease, face the picture of an angel. "Tragic, lives cut so violently short. But what does that have to do with us?"

We all know what it has to do with us. But we'll play this little game of pretend.

Gabriel scoots closer, and I force myself not to look at him. "Stay quiet," he whispers so only I can hear. My jaw pops from holding in my snide retort.

Mendoza looks over the spa building. "The High Witch wants to assure our citizens that actions are being taken to find the culprits of these terrible crimes. And given that the victims died in their sleep, we're investigating all suspected dream wielders."

I can almost hear the trees shake in anger as a gust of wind passes through.

Roz folds their arms. "You can search this place all you want, Captain. You won't find any murderers here."

Muttering rushes through the gathered officers. "All right, we will." Mendoza orders his people to search the grounds and outer buildings. Roz will already have coven members waiting to keep an eye on them.

"What can we assist you with, Captain?" Mom says, ever the diplomat—a quality I sure as hell didn't inherit.

"I suppose you thought that little warning would clear the debt?" I hiss to Gabriel, keeping my eyes forward and moving my lips as little as possible.

He sighs. "I was hoping. But"—he motions between us, that golden rope taunting us—"no such luck." His hand grazes mine, and I yank it away like I've been shocked.

"So, you didn't just want to help your *kind*." I trail out the last word.

His eyebrow twitches. "You are not—" He stops himself short when the Captain looks at me. "Captain?"

His eyes travel over us, clearly aware we weren't paying attention. "We need her to come with us inside."

My confidence falters as I try to recall if I left anything sitting around. "We do offer a day pass to the pool if that's your question." I swallow my anxiety with deflection.

Mom and Roz give me a warning shake of their heads.

"Miss, if you'll please. We need to test you and the others."

"Test me?" My voice shakes.

"For what?" Roz's eyes narrow.

"The High Witch has authorized us to test for dream magic."

I stiffen, glancing at Gabriel. "What?" That testing is only possible on the dead—you have to slice open their skulls to get a look at it.

Gabriel looks equally surprised. "The potion that reveals that requires use of nightlock powder. That was outlawed in the 1800s. The only place you can find that now is in a single preserve in the North Pole where they have seed storage of all known species."

Nightlock is a highly dangerous plant that was eradicated because it had similar effects to Nightmares. It would torment the mind before eventually killing the person after they slipped into a coma. I wonder for a second if that's what killed those two people, but a healer would've been able to detect that. Also, the effects of nightlock are swift and then very slow. The person experiences symptoms within hours and then slips into a coma—the coma can last up to a week or, in some cases, as long as a month.

I'm surprised to see Mendoza's uncomfortable look at Gabriel's question. I forget some people might actually be scared of the High Witch's grandson. *Can't relate.* Hatred, sure, that I can get on board with.

"I don't know the details, sir. I just know the High Witch ordered it."

I shouldn't be surprised the High Witch gets to bend the laws to benefit him.

"So, if you'll come inside," Mendoza orders. The officers head toward the door, Mom and Roz following.

"So, now the High Witch is just going to round us up and *kill us*?" I hiss, eyes wide. Even if I thought I could make it, I can't just run away. Mom and the other dream wielders need me.

"He's not going to kill you," Gabriel says, slipping off his watch. "Put this on."

I frown, brows pinching together. "What? No. I don't want a bribe in the form of an overpriced watch."

Gabriel grabs my arm, sparks flying over my skin. "It's got a powerful concealing charm that cost me a fucking fortune." I struggle against his touch, but he doesn't let go until he's strapped on the watch. "They won't be able to get anything from you with this."

"What about the others?" Gabriel's watch is warm on my wrist from where it sat against his skin.

"I can't do anything about them."

"My crystals will be good enough. We have them for a reason. You should know by now we are more than capable of taking care of ourselves." I start to take the watch off, but he covers my wrist with his large palm.

"Azalee, just do it, okay?"

He doesn't care what happens to me. He just doesn't want me to die before he clears the life debt.

"Miss Saunders," the Captain calls from the door. "If you will, please. We can wrap this up and be on our way."

Yeah, with the dream wielders being hauled back to the station, ready for the gallows for crimes we didn't commit.

"Why are you wasting time with us when the real killer is out there?" I say to Gabriel.

He straightens his cuffs. "We're checking all options."

"Oh, fuck off, Gabriel. You know we didn't do this."

He doesn't answer as he holds the door open. Maybe he does think we're capable of murder.

Mom and Roz stand near the desk, watching as Mendoza opens a case and removes a vial with shimmering purple-black liquid. I remember studying potions in school, but the chapters on the real bad ones were scant. I guess they didn't want us getting any ideas. I do recall one we learned about that emitted bright-orange smoke and had to be kept in a bottle lined with gold. That was one of the most deadly potions a witch ever created. It was taught as part of the warning against using magic for crimes due to the strict punishments associated with them.

I wasn't lying when I told Gabriel our crystals should do a good enough job concealing us. But they're usually just used to tone down our auras. Only other dream wielders can see our buttery-yellow and indigo aura, but sometimes, you can't even trust the people who share your gift.

Gabriel being a great example. Still, I grip his watch, pushing it farther up my arm to hide it under my sleeve should the officers notice it's his. But this will only protect *me*.

What I need is a distraction.

I study the room, deciding how to get that vial away from the Captain as he sits it on the desk and withdraws a few more items to perform the test. I hear the dogs bark from behind the building, and I have my answer. Stepping away from Gabriel, I head toward Mom and Roz but take a little detour to the back door.

Roz is the proud owner of two oversize white huskies. They like to control a room, so they aren't usually allowed in the spa. But today their dominating nature is just what I need.

Gripping the handle behind me, I pop the door open just enough for them to get Roz's scent.

"All right, Mrs. Saunders, why don't we start with—" Captain Mendoza doesn't finish as the two hounds come bounding through the open door. The dogs don't even pause as they leap toward the police. I'm not sure if Roz trained them this way, but I'll take the assist.

"Frost, Ace," Roz yells at the huskies, reaching for them as they knock over a potion that begins to emit waves of heat across the room.

In the chaos of trying to wrangle the dogs and stop the spreading potion, I make my move. Dipping low, I reach forward and grab the vial off the table. I close my hand to conceal it, taking quick, backward steps as fireworks start from Wild Flames we bought to use on Halloween.

Hiding the potion behind my back, I press myself against the wall, pretending to be terrified I might catch on fire, while I search the wall for a gold medallion. My finger runs along the smooth plaster until my nail clips on the cool metal. Still out of sight, I press the sequence of symbols I was taught years ago but never had to use.

The round metal pops open, and I slide the vial into the open space, snapping it closed as it disappears down the hidden chute. This system of pipes was installed decades ago to communicate in secret. The pipe leads to another hidden opening in the back part of the spa by the swimming pool.

It takes five more minutes, but we manage to get the dogs back outside and the potions under control.

"Sorry about that, Captain," Roz says, not really sounding sorry at all. "The hounds don't much like strangers. Makes them jumpy."

Mendoza's jaw is tight. "Then we'll make this quick." He reaches toward the table, pausing where the missing potion should be. "Where the hell is it?" he shouts at his men before turning on us.

Gabriel quickly meets my gaze before I look away.

"We were helping fix the mess," Mom says.

I hold out my hands. "Feel free to check us if you like."

He does just that and searches every drawer and cupboard in the entryway but comes up empty.

"Well," Roz says, "you don't have any more potion, and based on the radio chirping at your hip, you've found nothing of interest on my property. So why don't you and your men leave us to run our business."

The Captain looks like he wants to argue, but Gabriel steps in. "They're right, Mendoza. We have nothing to charge these people with. We can tell the High Witch we did our search."

Mendoza concedes, brow furrowed. "Fine. But just be aware, should we find new evidence, we'll be back."

I give Gabriel a middle-finger salute as he heads back to his car. Only after he's out of sight do I realize I'm still wearing his watch.

CHAPTER 9

Gabriel

When will I be free of this damn life debt? Surely, what I've done so far qualifies as saving her life. Fine, she wasn't in mortal peril at that exact moment, but if circumstances played out the way Grandfather seems to want, that could easily be the case. But apparently, the Fates have other ideas.

I should have taken the Milk Thistle Gummies instead of trying to prove something by acting like I didn't need them. I've had a nasty headache all morning, interfering with my ability to think rationally and analyze possible outcomes. Which, given the energies flowing through the city today, I can't afford to slip.

When I return to the office, I check my watch to see how much longer I have to be here. Only my watch isn't there. *Shit.* I forgot to get it back from Azalee. Pain grips my gut. It feels like I'm walking through the office naked with the words *dream wielder* tattooed on my forehead. I shove my sweaty palms into my pockets to dry them.

"Are you all right, sir?" Grandfather's receptionist asks.

My brows pinch. "I'm feeling a little under the weather. Could be coming down with something," I lie, tongue heavy. "I'm going to go home for the rest of the day. Will you tell the High Witch?"

I don't wait for her response before heading toward my SUV. Not having the watch doesn't mean they'll be able to tell I'm a dream wielder just by looking at me. Even now that they have a nightlock potion that can detect dream magic, I still doubt they'd be able to deduce that I'm afflicted with that power.

From my research in Grandfather's library, potions used for detecting dream wielders would only be useful if the subject in question had recently dream wielded. Which I've never done. I might not be able to rid myself of this curse, but that doesn't mean I'm going to actively participate in it.

When I get home, I pause briefly in the entranceway as I always do, staring up at the oversize oil painting of my late grandmother.

"Never forget who took her from us, my boy." Grandfather holds four-year-old me in his arms. "Dream wielders killed her, and we will not let that crime against us go unpunished. It's your duty to keep the world safe from dangerous magic. Never forget."

He has repeated the same speech every time we've walked these halls. *Never forget. Never forget.* I used to see the High Witch in my sleep. A judge in a courtroom, slamming a gavel as he chanted the words.

But I haven't experienced any dreams since the night Azalee saved me. I'd been spiraling for years, but was finally getting back to a stable state. It's like Logan saw that as his opportunity to take my place as the reckless brother. The memories of that night come in bits and pieces . . .

"You sure you want to do this?" the club owner, Geoff, asks me. He looks behind me like the High Witch is waiting to pop out and arrest him. All that's there is Logan—he's the reason I'm even here to begin with.

"Didn't realize we had a choice." I'm getting really fucking tired of people second-guessing my every move. Like I don't have the option of making my own choices. Just another fucking cog in the magic machine that is the High Witch's life. Logan and I are nothing but chess pieces, sympathy cards he'd play to gain favor.

Logan shifts nervously beside me. I shouldn't have let him tag along, but he would've just followed anyway, so I thought that I might as well keep him in sight. It was supposed to be his fight. He's been gambling for years, each bet greater than the one before. He usually gets himself out with little more than a lighter wallet for his troubles. But this time, the player he lost to is out for blood. I've always protected Logan and I'm not going to stop now. So I'm taking his place. I'll take the punches so he doesn't have to.

"I just don't want the blowback on me if this goes south." Geoff's cigar hangs from his mouth, whiffs of smoke circling the small office. This facade looks like the entrance to a storage facility, sad and forgotten in a back alley on the Salem outskirts. I've reconned the area enough to know the ins and outs.

My jaw aches as I grind my molars. "Am I on the roster or not? Because I can find another place that'll let me fight," I growl. A viper ready to pounce. I'd insisted to the guy Logan lost to that I pick the venue. I wanted the upper hand where I could.

Geoff's eyes narrow. "Can you?" His tone scratches at my last nerve. I want to call the High Witch on him just to fuck him over.

I yank out another hundred and throw it on the counter. "Good enough?"

He smiles, yellowed teeth on full display. "Welcome to the fighting rings. Wait in the back until you're called." He points toward the fighters' waiting area.

Logan and I head back as I shake my arms to loosen the tension building in them. I've mastered all the fighting styles they've thrown at me over the years in training, so I'm confident I can end this quickly.

The authorities have shut down plenty of these clubs over the years, but like cockroaches, they always find a way to survive. All it took was cross-checking a few names in the High Witch's computers and I found one.

The strong scent of mildew and metallic blood fills the air. I sling my bag over my shoulder and find an empty locker to shove it in. I didn't think this through other than I have a fire burning inside me, and if I don't find a way to release it soon, I am going to explode.

"I can do it, Gabriel. You don't need to take this beating for me," Logan says.

"Yes, I do. Just promise you won't make a bet that stupid again."

"I promise." A lie and we both know it. He goes to join the audience, leaving me to focus.

I sit on a bench, listening to the sounds of fists hitting flesh, and the cheers and boos of the crowd, until my name is called.

"The only rules," Geoff says as he walks me to the ring. "There are no rules. Mercy is only offered if your opponent feels like granting it. Same goes for you. We don't suggest you kill the other guy, but if you get killed—ain't our problem."

I clench and unclench my fists, offering only a nod that I've heard him.

"If you need a doctor, do it on your own time. Good luck," he adds before dropping me off at the swinging doors that lead out to the crowd and ring. I can just make them out through the dingy plastic window.

I get my ass kicked. But in my defense, it was never a fair fight. I was here a week ago, studying how they conducted the matches. One-on-one, that's what it always was. Until I walk into the ring and see five guys against me.

I guess everyone wants a piece of the High Witch's grandson.

I initially hold my own, taking out the first guy with a single punch. I get cocky. I let myself think I can best the onslaught. But I don't have the stamina of five guys.

I don't recall much after the first five minutes. Just the constant bombardment of fists. The blur of the audience's jeering faces. And the pain.

So much pain.

It's like every single inch of my skin is having the flesh ripped off. I get in a few punches, but as the attack continues, I can't fight anymore.

I wouldn't say I give up. But I'm no longer in my body, I'm floating somewhere beyond.

If Logan is still there, I don't know. At least he didn't get hurt.

As the world turns black, my vision narrows to tiny pinpoints. Everything is ice. The noise goes away, not that I can hear much over the pounding blood in my ears. I am so cold. I can't feel my arms. The pain is subsiding, and even in my rattled mind, I know that isn't a good thing.

Then the movement stops, and I vaguely realize I'm outside. Rain dropping on my face feels like acid. It'll all be over soon. Nothing will matter in a few more minutes.

Then she is there. Her blond hair glows like a halo in the streetlight.

"Help . . ." That's Logan.

". . . Gabriel?" she says, voice so far away I think I'm dreaming.

I don't speak. I can't. But I reach out my broken and bloody hands toward her, and she grasps them, curling her fingers into mine. I close my eyes and let her take me away.

I don't remember much of the next several days. She healed me, used magic and potions, and a bit of herself. She saved me and connected us for who knows how long.

Logan said the Fates must have made her appear that night, but she told me she'd been seeking out a dream wielder nearby. Coincidence was to blame for my misfortune.

CHAPTER 10

Azalee

Typically, the moment I walk into the apothecary, Meera's mom, Tali, will thrust a steaming mug of a mystery concoction into my hands. She is well known for finding the perfect drink mixture for what ails you. This usually means there's a line all day, but when I arrive shortly before closing to pick Meera up for the coven meeting, the closed sign is already up.

"Oh, thank Gods," Meera says when she opens the door, apron soaked in a purple liquid. "Please tell me your baking skills have suddenly improved since you almost burned your house down in high school?"

"They have not."

Meera yelps, running behind the register and slipping into the tiny kitchen they added a few years back to expand their offerings. I follow her through the swinging doors. It looks like a potion exploded. Flour covers the floor, while three kettles overflow on the stove.

"Where are your parents?" I rub my temples.

Meera's worked here for years, but she's never been in charge of the kitchen. She wipes her forehead to get the flyaway pieces out of her eyes. When she brings her hand away, flour streaks her skin. "They . . . left—a few days ago to see my brother in Florida."

"A few days ago? Have you been running the place yourself this whole time?" She didn't say a word to me.

"It was fine the first day, but then we ran out of baked goods, and Dad is the one who makes them so . . ." Smoke floats out of the oven as she removes what I think are supposed to be muffins, but they look like pools of melted goop.

"Meera . . ." I trail off. I don't know how much help I can be in a kitchen. "Can you call them? Ask them for the recipes."

"I have the recipes. That's not the problem." She throws the destroyed pan on the counter, collapsing onto a stool.

"At least it's not as busy as normal." I try to find the bright side, but that's usually Meera's department.

"That's because the usuals realized I'm in charge and stopped coming. I don't have my mother's talent for remedies."

I rest a hand on her shoulder. "You should close for a few days." She looks up at me, eyes wide. "Just until your parents get back. If you burn the place down, I don't think they'll be too happy."

"They didn't even close when we had that huge hurricane when we were kids."

I examine the room. "It kinda looks like a hurricane already hit it." She puts her head in her hands, shoulders slumping. "Meera, what's up? You seem off."

She yanks off her apron, throwing it on the counter. "Az, I . . ."

My phone beeps: a text from Mom asking where we are. "Can we talk about this on the way? Roz will flay me alive if we miss the meeting."

"No need, I'm just fucking exhausted is the gist of it." She closes the shop and gets into my car. "So, I heard you got in trouble."

I aggressively put the car into drive. "Yeah, I had to pay the piper this morning. But that was the least shitty part of my day." Meera knows all about that unfortunate night with Gabriel two years ago. I had to tell someone when I realized I was bonded to a fucking Ford. She and Iniko are the only ones I ever told what happened.

Meera's eyes widen. "Oh Gods. Spill."

❧

I shift in my seat, rolling my neck to release the tension with little success. A headache has slowly overtaken my brain as the day creeps on. Meera and Mom sit on either side of me in the underground room with the curved concrete ceiling. It used to be a bomb shelter or for food storage—either way, long before my time. Now we use it for *serious* coven meetings.

Meera's head droops, and I elbow her to wake her up. "What, huh?" Her head snaps up, and I press my lips together to hide my smile. If I have to sit through this, so does she.

Roz cuts us a glare but doesn't miss a beat. "I know this is alarming for most of you, but I assure you this renewed interest in dream wielders will die down as it always does." They've been explaining the day's events to those lucky enough to miss out on the police.

"Really?" a witch named Beoak says. He's one of the new dream wielders—only about six months into his powers. "Because two murders in two days seems like something that isn't just going to *go away*."

"They raided The Retreat," another adds. More voices join in with concerns, a fever pitch overtaking the cramped space.

Roz raises a hand to silence them. "The police found nothing and went on their way with very little trouble." I don't miss their eyes sliding over me.

They asked me after the police left what I did with the vial of potion. I told them I didn't do anything with it. The Captain must have lost it. Roz didn't believe me. But I wasn't going to tell them where I'd stashed it because they'd make me give it to them, and I already have plans for it.

"Everyone needs to remain calm," Mom adds. Dad was always level-headed, while Mom kept hers in the clouds. When he died, she took on his persona. Someone in the house had to keep chaos from reigning. "Losing our heads and acting rash isn't going to do any good. That's exactly what they're hoping to accomplish by ruffling our feathers."

That only moderately satiates the group, but at least they're quiet, so Roz can wrap this up and I can be on my merry way. "It's no secret that throughout our history there have been bad apples among the dream wielders. Those who use their power for ill intent." Roz speaks so painfully slowly I have to force my eyes wide to stay open. "But the good the majority of us do is not enough to tip the scales in the eyes of the High Witch and many of the public. As a coven we must take care of ourselves . . ."

After a few more instructions outlining what we should do to keep vigilant, the meeting lets out.

I grab Meera's hand, steering her toward the door. "I have something to show you," I whisper.

"Azalee," Mom calls before I can escape.

"Yes, Mother dearest?" I don my most innocent smile.

"You wouldn't be going anywhere that would get you in trouble, would you?" Her brows dip into a familiar frown.

"Ye of little faith," I scoff. "Meera and I are going to Big Witch Pizza." I kiss her cheek, leaving before Roz can lecture me.

"So, what are we doing that will get us in trouble?" Meera asks when we're in the cool night, walking back to my house. The rain has cleared, the sky glittering with stars, but moisture still clings to the air.

My lips twist into a sly grin. "Just a little arson."

"Pardon?" Meera says in a French accent.

I slip the vial of potion from my pocket. "This is what they wanted to use earlier. It has nightlock powder in it."

Meera stiffens. "Should you be keeping that on you? That's dangerous shit to be messing with."

"As long as it doesn't leak, it's fine." I shrug, wrapping my hand around the cold glass. We slip into the greenhouse. I snuck in earlier and set up my ingredients. Many people use this space, but with the rain, no one's been in today. Most of what I needed was here, so I figured it was the quickest place to perform the spell.

"Anyway, I'm guessing they have a stash of nightlock growing somewhere. I want to use a finding spell to locate it."

"And then set it on fire?" Meera frowns.

She's generally up for any wild plan I can concoct, but she's looking less than enthused. "I read fire is the best way to destroy it. If we dig it up, there's a chance we could ingest it or have it touch our skin."

"Az, this is the High Witch's doing. We could get in major trouble if we fuck with his garden."

I roll my eyes, grabbing herbs and powders, twisting off lids, and tossing the ingredients into my copper bowl. "And we're majorly fucked if they use the potion on us to test for dream magic residue. Then any anonymity we wanted is long gone."

I lay out the map of Salem on the wooden table. "Look, I get it if you don't want to come with me. Head to Big Witch, and I'll meet you there when I'm done. Just save me some pizza."

Meera is my best wingwoman, but I won't make her go if she's uncomfortable with this. I'm more than capable of doing it on my own.

"Az, just leave this alone. This is bigger than going rogue to help some Nightmares. This is the High Witch we're talking about." Meera's face pinches as she plucks at the ends of her curls.

"Go get some pizza, Meera. I won't be long."

Meera looks like she's going to say something else but leaves without a word.

I know she's right. Other than my entanglement with Gabriel, I've done a pretty good job of staying out of the High Witch's orbit.

But I can't sit back and let us all be at risk. Sure, the dream wielders can conceal themselves, but Nightmares can't. We're their last line of defense. If we fall, the police will round them up. They might hesitate at killing dream wielders, but I don't think the same constraints will be afforded to Nightmares. Iniko is trapped in his nightmares, and I didn't protect him before, so I sure as hell will not let him be made a sacrifice to a political agenda of bigotry.

After I mix the potion, I pour it over the map, the gelatinous mass sliding down the lines of streets. It twists and turns, leaving a black trail to follow in its wake, until it stops on a section of land near the river, the potion glowing brighter as it finds the garden's location. There isn't much out there, but that's probably the point.

Slipping on my cloak, I glide into the night.

CHAPTER 11

Azalee

Following the trail burned into the map, it takes about twenty minutes to reach the plot of land the spell indicated the nightlock came from. As I suspected, the field is full of security cameras surrounding the fencing. Even though I don't spot any guards walking around, there are plenty of other ways to ward a place.

I park far enough away that the cameras won't spot me and open my trunk. I like to keep a wide variety of potions, herbs, crystals, and anything else that might come in handy when seeking out dream wielders or Nightmares. Tonight, I added some accelerants and a box of matches. I don't want to burn the whole forest down, so I'll sprinkle some fire-control powder on the plant beforehand to keep it contained.

The first problem, however, is hiding myself from the cameras. I run my fingers over the glass of Gabriel's watch. He said it had a powerful concealment charm. Let's hope it works on whatever the High Witch has set up here. But I'm not leaving my safety entirely up to a Ford.

If I had Essence of Night, I could mask the grounds in darkness, but that would also block my view. But that's a moot point because I never owned any of it to start with. I riffle through my wooden box of potions. I've got lots of calming draughts, a few energy boosters, and dozens of odds and ends.

My finger skims on a sparkling heart-shaped bottle. This was a gift from Iniko—Twinkle Twinkle. It makes the person who ingests the potion sparkle and glow for about half an hour. Two years ago, he drunkenly purchased three overpriced bottles from an apothecary on the way home from a party as an early birthday present for me. After quickly consuming two, we executed a series of questionable dares, documenting them on my phone. The next morning, when we went to erase the evidence of our stupidity, we were nearly impossible to recognize in the pictures because we were shining so bright the cameras couldn't pick up our features.

Which is precisely what I need tonight.

I place the bottle to my lips and take the sweet liquid down in one swallow. It takes a few minutes to get to full potency, but then I'm sparkling like a disco ball. I sigh with relief, glad the expiration date was more a suggestion than a firm stopping point.

I wave my hand in front of me, and a trail of light like a shooting star follows in its wake. My heart twists as my throat grows thick thinking about Iniko. The heavy pit in my stomach that never really goes away rears its ugly head. I miss my friend and the way things were. Sometimes, I look in the mirror and don't recognize the face looking back. It's like I lost myself along with him.

Squaring my shoulders, I walk to the fence, using my cutters to open a small section in the rear. As I step over the perimeter, my watch grows warm, my arm going numb before pinching with pins and needles. Guess the concealment spell's doing its job.

Thanks, Gabriel. I smile, knowing how furious this would make him.

I make it quick, in case there are more hidden wards. The nightlock is easy to find. It has pitch-black leaves and shimmering violet flowers that bloom in darkness—it might be deadly, but it's stunning. The flowers close in on themselves as I approach with my light.

I pull out my phone to get a photo of the illegal grove, but thanks to the warding magic, my pictures keep coming out blurry.

I sprinkle the fire-control powder on the dozen or so plants before squeezing out the accelerant from the bottle. Taking a deep breath, I strike the match and toss it into the heap.

I only wait a minute to make sure the nightlock is ablaze before I run back to my car, tires flinging up dirt and rocks as I speed away.

Despite the headache banging in my skull, I don't want to call off dinner with Meera. I take the long way back to the center of Salem, waiting until the potion has worn off and I'm no longer sparkling.

I squeeze the white-and-black moonstone in my pocket, hoping it will push my headache away.

"The JJ . . . for Gabriel," the announcement for a pickup order greets me when I walk into Salem's finest pizza place.

Warmth spreads across my chest at the name JJ—not Gabriel.

"I didn't think anyone else ordered that pizza," I say as he takes the pie from the employee.

He studies the cardboard box. "Mushrooms, spinach, pineapple, anchovies, and chorizo might turn a few people off, but not me."

"Me either. Of course, I grew up eating it, so I never had a choice to not like it. I'm sure they'd take it off the menu if it wasn't . . ." The rest clogs in my throat.

"Your dad's creation," Gabriel finishes for me.

I blink in surprise. Dad cofounded Big Witch. This was his signature pie. "Yeah, it was."

"He had good taste. I'm sure we would have gotten along great." He flashes me a cocky half-up grin and the slight reprieve of my dislike for him is gone.

"Well, enjoy." I step past him, but he blocks my way. "What?" I glare.

The restaurant is busy, so he drops his voice. "My watch."

"What about it?" I raise my eyebrows in innocence.

"Give it back." His low tone rumbles through me. A stupid, inconvenient fire erupting under my skin as I imagine that voice saying different—not suitable for public—things to me.

"I don't have it." *I do.* It's on my arm. But after my arson, I'm not about to part with something that offers this much protection. Also his pissed face is sweet, sweet music to my soul.

"That watch is invaluable."

"That's not what the guy at the pawn shop said." I smile devilishly.

"Azalee." His growl is barely contained.

I don't speak right away, letting him stew for a few precious seconds. Then, like the philanthropist that I am, I put him out of his misery. "Chill. It's at my house. You'll get it back. Just not today," I add before walking away to find Meera.

"I'm going to do it," Meera says when I sit opposite her.

Gabriel hesitates, glaring at me across the restaurant before leaving.

She stares down at the menu she memorized years ago. "I'm going to get the Big Witch, and I'm going to finish it this time." The Big Witch is a pizza the size of a table, thin crust and piled with almost every topping imaginable.

She places her menu down, cracking her knuckles, her spirits higher. She didn't ask me if my arson was successful. I guess she wants to have plausible deniability.

I study her buttery-yellow and indigo aura. The appearance keeps fluctuating to a muddy color. If she were a stranger, the hidden meanings would be easier to spot with my skills, but my emotions keep getting in the way of an impartial reading. I try harder to decipher it, but I wince as a sharp pain jolts down my spine. I've had trouble focusing on auras before when I'm stressed out—and today surely qualifies as stressful. I back off, hoping her words will give me answers, but words hardly ever do.

"Meera, how are you doing?"

"Fine. Why?" She waves to get the waitress's attention.

"Well, you seemed upset earlier."

She offers a dazzling smile. "I'm fine, Az. I got it all sorted. The shop will stay closed until my parents are back. Shouldn't be long. It feels so trivial after what happened at The Retreat," she whispers the last part. But I doubt it's a secret—I'm sure all of Salem is gossiping about it.

"Are your parents having fun?" I close my menu, not hungry enough to care what I get.

"Hmm?" She's still attempting to flag the waitress.

"In Florida? Are they enjoying the sunshine?"

She relaxes back into her chair. "Oh yeah . . . they love the heat. I think the waitress is avoiding us."

"I might have another *case* we can investigate after dinner," I say casually.

I've made a hobby the past year of scanning the police radios and newspapers for accidents, trying to find anyone who might have the potential to become a dream wielder. Or I do something a *little* less aboveboard and use the login of a healer in the coven to check hospital records for anyone showing up with symptoms that might have potential. It's wrong because I sort of stole the password, but I'm using it for good, so it cancels out the wrong.

"Az, don't you think you should take a night off from crusading?"

I frown, shaking my head before she even finishes. "No. There's too much to be done." *Too many people to save.*

Reaching across the table, Meera places her hand over mine. I didn't realize I was freezing until I feel her warmth. "Jumping from one risky move to the next is setting you up to be in the crosshairs of some *very* powerful people." Her usually cheerful face is sober. "Go, go, go is your default—I get that. But you work at a spa, for Gods' sake, maybe add in some time for relaxing and recharging so you don't burn out."

"That's what a steady supply of Pep Up is for." I shrug, offering a nonchalant grin. Stopping makes things real. If I don't stop, nothing has time to catch me. "So, want to go tonight?"

She rubs her lips together, knowing she's not winning this argument. "I can't. I'm going to meet up with Grant."

"Henderson?" He's a healer over at Salem Medical. I know he and Meera have gone out a few times.

"Yeah, we're going to have a coffee or something, I don't know." She waves at the waitress, who finally heads our way.

"Maybe tomorrow?"

"Yeah, maybe."

When I got home after dinner, I intended to read, but I drift off to sleep before I even start the first page.

The buzzing of my phone on the nightstand wakes me hours later. I grope for it, nearly knocking it off the table, catching it last minute. "Hello?" My words are rough with sleep.

"Azalee." The voice cracks on the other side and my eyes fly open, the moon shining through the open curtains.

"Meera, what's wrong?" My breath catches in my throat. When you've been friends with someone as long as we have, you know when there is trouble.

"I . . . I don't know what happened." She's crying. Meera never cries. "I did everything right . . . I didn't even think this could happen." I can barely make out the words through the wailing.

"You need to start over. What happened? Are you hurt?" I'm wide awake now, already pulling on my clothes as blood pounds in my ears.

"I need your help." Her voice sounds far away.

"Where are you?"

"I'm at Grant's house. I was dream wielding and . . . and oh Gods, Azalee, I'm going to hang for this."

I stop my frantic rush of getting dressed. The beating of my heart comes to a sudden stop. "What happened?"

"I killed him. I killed Grant."

CHAPTER 12

Azalee

At those three words, all the color drains from the world.

I killed Grant.

"Text me the address, and I'll be right there," I tell Meera as I stumble down the stairs. My cloak gets stuck in the car door as I slam it shut against the gusting wind. I hardly notice the strain against my neck as I speed off, the tail of it flapping in the jet stream.

Meera couldn't have killed anyone. There must be a mistake. I wrangle my chaotic thoughts into a containable beast while I drive. I will not lose a friend—*not again.*

It feels like an eternity before I reach Grant's house. Meera flings open the door, her tearstained cheeks highlighting red, puffy eyes. "Az, I don't know what happened." She throws her arms around me, and I hug her tight before walking us inside and pushing the door shut with my foot. The only light is from a lamp in the living room. The minimal furniture makes the room already feel abandoned.

"I didn't do anything different." She hiccups through her explanation. "I asked his permission. I didn't just jump into his dream."

"Wait." I stiffen. "He died while you were dream wielding?"

She nods, eyes threatening to bubble over with fresh tears. Out of habit, I home in on her aura. I get only the barest glimpse of a deep yellow-brown before scalding fire erupts in the base of my skull. I cut off my connection to the magic, her aura disappears, the burning in my brain simmering.

"Dream wielding can't cause death," I say, voice unsteady, bile burning my throat. Supposed dream wielder deaths have been reported over the years, but first the two deaths from yesterday and now this—it can't be a coincidence so many are cropping up at once. "I need you to start from the beginning."

"When we met at the café, he was fine. He didn't look sick or dying. He was just Grant. Then we came here, and I—*shit, shit, shit.* This isn't how it was supposed to go." Tears cascade down her cheeks.

"It's going to be okay. I promise." I wrap my arm around her shoulders. "So, you were dream wielding when he died? How did you know?" *What did it feel like?* I'm not sure Meera could handle that question.

She doesn't look at me, her head resting on my cheek. "Um . . . it was normal to start. We were surfing in Oahu and then—" She shudders and I hug her tighter. She starts again, voice barely a whisper. "Gods, I don't know. It's all kinda fuzzy. It was like lightning flashes, but everywhere—slicing through my body, digging into my brain until I surrendered to it. Then nothing. It was just black. When I opened my eyes again, he was dead." Voice cracking, she collapses, sobs convulsing her frame.

"It's okay, just let it out." I run my hand over her hair in a rhythmic motion.

The Retreat has the largest collection of books on dream wielders, and a few tomes recall the experience of dream wielding during a natural death. That doesn't sound like any of the accounts I've read. They stated that the dream went dark and stopped, returning the dream wielder back without harm. A few case studies where the dream wielder—only conducted by those who are mediums as well—have accessed the mind of the dreamer just prior to a natural death. They stay only long enough for the person to pass on so they can offer a final send-off. It's actually rather peaceful sounding—as far as death goes. Then the dream wielder exits the dream as usual.

But this, this was violent. I can see it in Meera's haunted expression.

"Can you take me to him?" I ask after she's calmed slightly. I don't want to see a dead body, but I have an idea. Meera hesitates, eyes wide, but finally leads me to a bedroom in the rear of the house. The glow of the moon through the windows lights our path.

Grant lies on the bed. He looks like he could be sleeping. I almost want to ask if she checked for a pulse. But I know Meera, and she is thorough. Taking a deep breath, I clench my hands into fists as I step closer.

Meera grips the white doorframe like it's the only thing holding her up.

I press my fingers to his neck to check for a sign of life. As expected, nothing beats. I note several crystals by his bed. I remove a howlite and moonstones from near his pillow meant to help in peaceful sleep.

I keep my fingers on his neck longer than necessary, hoping, *wishing* a pulse would start again, but nothing happens. I pull my hand away, wiping it on my pants. He's still slightly warm, which is even more disconcerting. This isn't the first body I've seen, but it doesn't make the chills down my spine any less bracing.

"Meera." My voice cracks through the silence like shattering glass. "I'm going to dream wield."

"What?" she croaks.

"I've read about dream wielders who can see into the minds of the dead if they arrive soon enough. If I can, I'll ask him what happened." Placing my bag on the floor, I pull out my crystals to help guide my meditation.

This type of magic is typically only possible for a highly intuitive medium.

Perhaps the Fates will be on my side for once.

Sitting on the bed, I'm careful not to touch the body. Chills run over my skin as I pretend this is any other dream wield, ignoring the intrusive thoughts reminding me death is catching. And in October, in Salem, death isn't a visitor you want anywhere near your door.

My hand catches on something, smooth and cold, next to Grant's arm. "Do you know what this is?" I hold up the clear bottle.

"He's been having trouble sleeping, that's why he wanted me to dream wield in the first place. To see if it would help."

That explains the overabundance of crystals sitting on his bedside table. "Did you bring it?"

She shakes her head. "No, he already had it."

I pop open the lid and take a sniff. There isn't anything left except a little at the bottom. I'm not an expert, but in school, we all learn about poisonous potions and how to smell them. As far as my skills go, it's a standard sleeping tonic. I put the bottle on the table and settle in.

I hold a rose quartz in one hand and an amethyst in the other. I place a clear quartz on his forehead, carefully avoiding touching his skin with my hand. Closing my eyes, I focus on bringing his spirit and mind to me.

I shake my head, squeezing my eyes tighter. The headache I still have is making it hard to relax—also, the dead body isn't helping. After a few deep breaths and internal chants, I calm down.

Before me is a handleless door, black as night. Walking with intent, I push, but it doesn't move. Some people's doors are trickier than others, requiring me to seek a hidden mechanism to open them. But Grant's is a fortress with no way in that I can determine. Whatever is behind this door will stay hidden from me. I open my eyes and shake my head.

She bursts into tears. "I'm going to hang. They're going to hang me."

"No, they aren't." I pull out my phone.

"Are you calling the police? Azalee, I can't be hung. Oh Gods, my parents." Her face twists in horror.

The phone rings as I lead her into the living room and put her on the sofa. "Mom?" I tell her what happened, and she says she's on her way. I hang up and sit beside Meera, whose face is slack as she stares, unseeing. "It's going to be okay. My mom will know what to do."

At least, I hope she will. I can't burn something down to get us out of this one.

Meera and I wait for minutes that stretch as long as hours. When I hear Mom's car in the driveway, I'm at the door before she makes it up the walk.

Meera flinches at every sound. It's disconcerting to see my ordinarily vibrant friend so shaken.

"Where's the boy?" Mom gets right to business. If anyone knows about things that can go wrong during dream wielding, it's her. She could dream wield before she could walk. Granted, in all my lessons, I never once heard about a dream killing someone—a Nightmare, sure, but *never* a healthy dream wielder. Of course, there's a first time for everything. I push that thought deep inside.

"Meera, stay here, okay?" Ever since I wandered Grant's mind, I can't shake the chill creating goose bumps on my skin. That's why I hate interacting with the dead. It's like they're always trying to drag you with them.

If Meera heard me, she doesn't act like it. She just continues staring out the window. I imagine that in the daylight, the house is lovely and welcoming, but even the plants scattered around in pots feel like they're dying.

I stop short of the bedroom, shoving my hands in my pockets to prevent them from shaking. "Do you think this has anything to do with the other murders?"

"Let's focus on the problem at hand." She weaves a strand of loose hair back into her bun.

Mom asks me what happened, and I answer to the best of my knowledge. "A dream wielder wouldn't be able to do this, but . . . do you think Meera is maybe . . ." I can't finish the sentence. The pit in my stomach widens. Even if I haven't seen the darkness creeping into her aura, maybe I missed something—*again*. I should have known Iniko was on a dangerous path, his descent was evident, and I will never forgive myself for not intervening. For assuming he would bounce back. If I've fucked up again and lose another friend . . .

"Meera is exhibiting no signs of becoming a Nightmare," Mom reassures me, the picture of calm as she kneels near Grant. After several minutes of examining the body, she speaks. "We need to call the police and report the death."

I balk. "What? No. You said she wasn't a Nightmare. This can't be her fault. What if they arrest Meera?"

Mom leads me from the room, closing the door. "They will not arrest Meera. There's no evidence to support that she killed him. They will likely question her, and based on current events, I suggest she not mention anything regarding dream wielding. She can say they were sleeping together, and she awoke to find him dead. She should mention the sleeping draught, since it was his own. There's one more thing," Mom adds.

"I'm guessing I won't like it?"

"We can't be here when the police arrive."

I shake my head. "No, no way am I just leaving her to the wolves." She might not be a Nightmare now, but the stress and pressure the police will put on her could tip the scales in that direction. Hopelessness is just enough of an open door for darkness to slither in and get a foothold.

"I know you don't like it, but if we're here too, there will be even more questions. The Captain already has it out for us—let's not give him another reason to seek out The Retreat."

"You seriously can't expect me to be okay with leaving Meera to handle this alone."

Mom places her hands on my shoulders. "I know you're not okay with it, but trust me, Meera *can* handle it. She's stronger than she lets you believe."

I take several shaky breaths before following Mom.

She sits next to Meera and explains what she needs to do. "My dear, everything will be okay." Her words are slow and comforting.

"Come to our house when it's all done. We'll have a spot for you in the guest room."

Meera stares at me, eyes bloodshot against her tearstained cheeks. "Az?"

I put on my bravest face. "Fuck 'em. You didn't do anything wrong. I'll see you in no time." My confidence has always been my easiest quality to fake.

The world feels like it's stopped, with every movement of my lungs in and out requiring more effort than usual. I curl my hand into a fist, squeezing tight before opening it slowly and grabbing Meera's abandoned phone on the table, placing it in her hand.

She looks like a zombie, eyes unfocused as we leave.

"Night, Mom," I tell her as she heads upstairs when we get home. I make a show of needing a cup of tea to soothe my nerves. But tea isn't strong enough to do that—even the best brew.

My mind is going a million miles an hour, and I need to talk to someone. Even if it's a fucking terrible idea.

Sneaking into the dungeons, I tiptoe past the other Nightmares' cells and let myself into Iniko's room. Nothing moves when I prop open the door, so I push it enough to let me step in through a sliver.

I've never had a problem here, but I'm afraid if the Nightmares wanted to consume me, there'd be nothing I could do. A nightmare while you sleep can be paralyzing, unnerving for the rest of the day, but a nightmare in the waking world . . . that leaves an imprint.

"Iniko?" I whisper. But I don't know if he can hear me. We used to sit for hours and talk about our dreams, about boys we liked, and how maybe one day we'd leave Salem and see the world. But neither of us will probably ever get out of this place.

I tried my best to make the room as comfortable as possible, even though the healers insisted he couldn't tell. I hung up a picture of the three of us from a few summers back. I brought in his favorite blankets and pillows, anything to remind him what he was fighting to get back to.

Sitting on the stool near him, I rest my head against the wall. Like always, he doesn't look at me. His brown eyes stare, unseeing, at the wall as he sits with rounded shoulders. I close my eyes, relishing the darkness.

"I don't know what to do, Iniko. Meera messed up, or maybe she didn't. Either way, we're all in trouble." A tear falls down my face. Maybe I'm more tired than I thought—I never cry. "And what do I do about the High Witch? I'm sure he'll use these events to make people fear us. To him, we are all Nightmares, but even Nightmares aren't to be feared."

My eyes flutter open at the sound of movement. Iniko sits with his head on his knees, back against the wall. "Will you talk to me, please?" I lean toward him. "Please break out of this. I need you." I want to shake him, my hand hovering over his bed.

Then Iniko reaches out, grabbing my hand and dragging me into his nightmare.

CHAPTER 13

GABRIEL

It's only been two years since I last closed my eyes and could escape into a dream. I wonder how long it will take to forget that sensation. I don't care most of the time. But it does feel like something is missing.

I wake to pounding at my door. Fumbling for my phone, I squint at the bright screen. It's barely two a.m. I grab my robe as the knocking persists and head down the stairs from my loft bedroom. My modest apartment is within the High Witch's estate, but I get some privacy at least.

Opening the door, Captain Mendoza strolls in without an invite. "Sorry to wake you, Mr. Ford, but it's urgent business. We've had another death."

I scrub a hand across my face, still groggy with the dregs of the sleeping potion I took only a few hours ago. "All right," I say, unsure why he needs to wake me at this hour. Unless . . . "It wasn't someone I know, was it?" Thoughts of Grandfather lying in a casket invade my brain, making my chest tighten in a conflicted kind of way.

Mendoza realizes his misstep, shaking his head. "No, no, nothing like that. But the High Witch's office told us to call if we caught another case, and when I did, they said to bring you to the scene this time."

The old man's clock is still ticking. "Right." Going to see a dead body in the dead of night is just the kind of horror I like to avoid.

"Time is pressing. My guys are there securing the suspect and the victim, but we need to get a medium on scene ASAP."

"Suspect? You're detaining someone?"

"It's the person who phoned in the death. But we can discuss further on the drive." He glances at my robe and bare feet. "I'll wait outside while you change. My SUV's out front." He leaves without giving me much choice in the matter.

Stripping off my robe, I head naked to the bathroom. I splash cold water on my face to wake up before grabbing Pep Up from the medicine cabinet and knocking it back, followed by a glass of water from the tap. It's the best I can manage in the interim.

Looking into the mirror, I note dark circles under my eyes and a paleness to my skin that wasn't there earlier. Is this how it felt for Grandfather when he had to see my parents' bodies in the middle of the night? I don't know the victim, but somebody did. My stomach churns, threatening to send the potion I desperately needed back out the way it came. I clamp my jaw tight, using techniques I learned in combat training: three breaths, and it settles.

I quickly throw on some jeans and a black tee, grabbing my cloak as I head out the door. It's more casual than the High Witch would approve of, but I'm not wearing a suit and tie if I have to be dragged from my bed.

"We have to make a quick stop on the way," Mendoza says as we pull onto the deserted road.

"Who's the victim this time?" I stare out the passenger window, watching the rain mist and drizzle in the streetlights. We aren't about to encounter an active threat, but I maintain situational awareness should the tides turn.

"Grant Henderson, twenty-seven."

"And he died in his sleep?" I hedge by not saying *dreams*. But there's no reason I'd be here if it were an ordinary death. Not that any death is ordinary, not for those they leave behind.

"Got the call from a woman who was there with him. She said they were sleeping together, and he went to bed and didn't wake up." He huffs. "Name's Meera Kumar. Reports from undercovers say she hangs out with those other dream wielders—so I suppose you can connect the dots."

Meera probably *is* a dream wielder. She and Azalee are so close it would surprise me if she weren't. But my first thoughts aren't for what kind of trouble Meera might be in. My mind immediately goes to Azalee and if she knows.

I reach for my watch out of habit, and the empty skin screams her name.

"Where are we going?" I ask, pushing Azalee to a space in the back of my mind. I'd love for her to vacate altogether, but that isn't happening as long as this bond connects us.

"We've gotta pick up a medium."

The medium is none other than Carmen Juanita. She's known nationwide for being one of the very best.

"Glad you were in town, Carmen," the Captain says after she settles in the back seat.

"Always happy to assist." She's a petite woman with auburn curls and a Spanish accent.

"We've got a bit of a trend on our hands, and we're hoping you can shed some light on it for us."

She raises her hand to silence him, gold rings catching in the dim lights. "No more. I like to go in fresh."

We drive silently to the house, and I'm glad the Pep Up is kicking in because otherwise, I'd be drooling on the window. We stop in a nice neighborhood with historical houses and manicured lawns. Inside, they've set up an interrogation center at the kitchen table. Meera is hunched over in a chair, head in her hands as she answers questions. Her tone suggests they've been repeating them for a bit.

"Captain." One of the officers nods at us. "The body is this way."

Meera glances up at that, her eyes meeting mine. My heart twists ever so slightly, and the instinct to offer her some reassurance surges, but I keep my mouth shut. I'm here to observe and report back to the High Witch. I don't think my interference is wanted. Still, this is the first dream death where someone else has been present to report it. It breaks the pattern.

Based on that, I doubt Meera is responsible for the other deaths, but we'll have to confirm her alibi. Which means none of them could be connected. But three people dying from three random dream wielders is odd nonetheless. They've been around for centuries and now they just decide to rise up in a killing spree? It doesn't feel right.

When I see Grandfather, I should bring it up. He wants me to participate, I'm going to.

I follow behind Mendoza and Carmen. This should be pretty straightforward. Mediums can speak to the spirit of the departed and get a straight answer on who killed them, if they're willing to talk. They had no luck with the last two spirits, but maybe that's why they brought in the heavy hitter.

If Carmen gets Grant to identify Meera as the killer, we should be out of here before breakfast, and I might get a few more hours of sleep. The thought should be a grateful one. But I imagine the devastation on Azalee's face if they arrest her friend, and it sours the mood.

The bedroom is in the back, with a few officers standing guard. The body can't have been here more than a few hours, but the skin is ashen, and I cover my nose to protect it from the smell of death that lingers in this place.

Carmen sits on the bed, placing three candles on the bedside table. She lights them while muttering an incantation. She closes her eyes once the candles are lit, and the room goes silent. If we were in a different world, maybe no one would put their faith in the words of a person who says they can speak to the dead, but here, it's as good as a confession from the criminal.

My heart pounds in my ears as the time stretches by in unending seconds. It's like I feel the presence of a dozen dearly departed souls pressing against me. All of them trying to get a word with Carmen.

The medium opens her eyes and shakes her head. Grant's spirit, wherever he is, didn't want to talk.

I look over at the Captain, his lips pressed into a thin line. "Well?" I ask.

"It's not cut and dry that she's innocent just because we couldn't get a spirit confession, but we don't have anything to hold her on." He looks at his officer. "She give you anything in the questioning?"

"No, sir. Just what we reported."

Mendoza stares at the body. "Get the coroner in here. I want a full report by this afternoon." He pushes past me without a word and heads to Meera. "Looks like you're free to go for the moment. But," he adds, "don't go skipping town. We'll have some follow-up questions."

Meera looks like a zombie, but she nods, teary-eyed.

"What about me?" I ask Mendoza.

He's staring at his phone, brow dipping into an angry V. "It's your lucky night. We got another murder."

CHAPTER 14

Azalee

Unlike dreams, I remember nightmares.

It's a feeling you can never quite shake, no matter how hard you try. The way your heart pounds like your chest is too small to contain it—panicked that you'll forget what it feels like to beat normally. Unending fear creeps through your blood—nothing is real, or maybe it's too real. Nightmares become your new reality, and you know you'll never find the way back into the light.

Iniko's nightmare is all these things and more. I can't wake up. It only ends when the Nightmare wants it to, and Nightmares never get enough.

My skin is on fire, bubbling from invisible flames. I try to rip it off, but my hands won't move—none of me will. I'm in the middle of an empty field, surrounded by shadows that plunge on forever. The sky is crying, not rain, but tears, the droplets wet and salty.

At first, I thought the field was grass, but the closer I examine it, the more I wish I hadn't because grass doesn't move that way. It could be all manner of creepy-crawly things my mind could conjure. Dreams are a pain in the ass like that. Not thinking about something is nearly impossible. I've trained for years to overcome the trait, but in the nightmarescape—it's hopeless. The *not* grass sways against my bare feet, and even through the fire, I feel its stringy tendrils wiggling up my legs.

Self-preservation takes over. All I have to do is wake up, and everything will be fine. But even if I could pinch myself, it wouldn't do any good.

Raw terror rips through me into a shriek. I wail, my throat burning like the rest of me, until there is no sound left. And then I cry. The fire on my skin will never stop.

Nothing will ever be okay again.

Out of the darkness stumbles a figure coated in fog. Its twisted fingers extend as the fog envelops me too. Another torturer come to enact its pain, the unending imagination of nightmares. Then the thing is in front of me, and it has a face. Not just any face: Iniko's.

His features distort in pain, ripped in the wrong direction, extending too far to be real. His ordinarily brown eyes are red with flames, but through them, I glimpse the sadness, the hollowness. I notice his teeth have rotted away when he lets out a screech even more painful than mine.

And in that moment—as his scream echoes around us, consuming the world—I'm not on fire anymore because I know this isn't my nightmare: It's his. This isn't a scream of anger, of hate meant to frighten; it's a cry of pain. This sorrow, the never-ceasing darkness, isn't mine to bear. That terror is worse than the first. The knowledge that there's nothing I can do but sit and watch him wither away.

I want to speak, but words don't work here. No salvation from the kind lies we tell each other. Iniko screams, and I feel it in my entire being, ripping away pieces of my soul with every breath.

Then it stops. We aren't in the field anymore, but a bar. Iniko isn't with me. I'm alone except for two people sitting in a booth. They're talking, but I can't understand it. I don't know the one guy, but the other is the High Witch.

What is Iniko's nightmare trying to show me now? The High Witch certainly does count as a nightmare.

The High Witch places his hand on the man's hollow cheek, and bit by bit, where their skin touches, the man turns to ash. His whole body fades away into a gray cloud of cinders. Another man appears, and the process repeats itself. This happens over and over again until I've lost count of how many witches have died at the High Witch's hand.

Then Iniko is at my side. He opens his mouth and screams. I drop to my knees. My cries join Iniko's, pain rippling through my body.

The world collapses around us in one fell swoop, and I'm lying on the floor in his cell once more. It's silent, but I still hear the screams in my soul.

I steady myself the best I can, squeezing my shaking hands into fists. Nightmares don't leave you as quickly as dreams. I glance to the bed where Iniko lies, his back to me. The nightmare must have meant something. He's never tried to grab me before. He must have a reason.

But what was it?

"I promise we'll find a way out of the nightmares, Iniko. I won't leave you in the dark." It feels like a lie as I shut the door. Stopping at the bottom of the stairs, I open the kit we keep down here for emergencies. I grab a hard lemon candy, popping it in my mouth. A few seconds later the calming magic tingles across my taste buds. The simple spell takes the edge off the terror left from the nightmare.

I'll consult the many books on dream theory upstairs, but that'll have to wait until tomorrow. I have a feeling if I still dreamed, they'd be dominated by the bone-chilling screams and vacant eyes of my lost friend.

After a fitful sleep, I'm the last one to breakfast the following day. I know it's impossible, but I swear I woke to Iniko's screams. I tossed and turned all night, worried about Meera. She was meant to stay in the spare room, but she was asleep in my bed when I got upstairs. A promising sign that they let her leave. But I know better than to think this is close to over.

I grab a mug, hoping a cup of coffee will be enough boost to get me through the morning. Meera and Mom have their eyes glued to the TV. "Anything noteworthy?" I ask, pouring a bowl of cereal.

"Someone's been arrested," Meera answers. Her mushy cereal sits untouched.

"For Grant's death?" My stomach clenches as I slide into a chair.

Mom answers, "No, there was another death last night. A woman. They've arrested a dream wielder as the murderer."

The cereal I'm attempting to swallow scratches all the way down. I push it away. "Another one? What the fuck? That's really bad for us." I give Meera a hopeful nudge with my elbow. "But at least you have a solid alibi for that one and I was with you when the others happened, so they can't blame you for all of them. With someone in custody they might investigate if that person killed Grant too. That's something."

She doesn't respond.

Mom moves her teacup around, but doesn't drink. "The dream wielder isn't anyone the coven is familiar with. It happened on the outskirts of Salem."

That doesn't make it any better.

I spin my wheels, trying to find a solution. "Maybe there's a serial killer. Grant's death was obviously an outlier. He probably had an undiagnosed illness, so we'll exclude that from the events. But anyone is capable of murder—even dream wielders. Maybe it's not a dream wielder murder, but just a murder committed *by* a dream wielder. How did they die?" Not that it would matter to the authorities and ever-growing concern among the public whether the dream wielder used a poison to actually do the killing. The second they're identified as a dream wielder, that's all anyone will focus on.

Meera flinches beside me, and I bite my lip. This topic might be a bit too fresh for her. But she answers the question. "The woman died in her dreams—like Grant. The dream wielder pled guilty to killing her in a dream."

"No." I stand, pushing my chair back. I trip over the leg as I distance myself from the TV. "It's not possible. We can't cause enough terror to send someone to the grave. Something isn't right."

The same reporter as yesterday is on TV. "A bottle of sleeping tonic was found on the male victim we reported on earlier, but after testing, it's been ruled out as the cause of death."

Meera stills in her chair, fingers turning white from her iron grip on the table's edge, the other in a tight fist around a purple amethyst. My shoulders slump. I'd really hoped that tonic would prove Meera wasn't responsible.

Meera collapses her head on the table. "What am I going to do?" she asks, voice muffled through her arm.

My voice rises steadily. "Maybe they missed a clue."

Mom runs a hand over Meera's hair, meeting my eyes. "I don't know what happened with Grant. I don't think you're responsible for his death. But we don't have another explanation to provide to the police at the moment."

"Then I'm going to find one." I leave without another word.

CHAPTER 15

Gabriel

It's nearly six a.m., and I've seen two crime scenes already. The last one was outside in the drizzling rain, the body covered in a black plastic sheet, but an arm hung out the side. If I had nightmares still, that would haunt them. I push a hand through my soaked hair. Perfect, it'll just add to my already disheveled appearance.

At least I look better than the guy in handcuffs.

"Why don't we use the nightlock powder potion?" I say as they drag the suspect to the interrogation room in the police station. It's warmer in here, making our rain-drenched clothes smell like wet dogs.

"We would." Captain Mendoza hands me a cup of steaming liquid. "But the only potion we had disappeared yesterday at The Retreat. It takes a while to brew a new batch, and even if it didn't, we're out of nightlock. My officers are investigating a fire last night that destroyed a crop. Another fucking thing to add to my plate."

Fire? Gods, Azalee, can't you take a breather for, like, five fucking minutes.

A thud echoes from the cramped room as the suspect stumbles into the metal table. He looks like shit with his hollow cheeks and red-streaked eyes. If you'd told me he was dead, I'd believe you. It's like there's no spirit left in his body.

"Two different people were at these murders." I take a sip of bitter coffee from the Styrofoam cup. "So, what, now we've got dream wielders of every shape and size committing murders at random? It doesn't add up."

Mendoza stands at the door to the interrogation room. "Well, that's what we're gonna find out. Why don't you go to the other room and observe through the two-way mirror."

Pungent disinfectant and cedar permeate the halls as I open the door to the adjacent room. When I step inside, the High Witch greets me.

"What are you wearing, Gabriel?" Grandfather, as always, is dressed impeccably in a bespoke suit.

"Sorry." I shake out the tails of my wet cloak. "It's already been a long day. Didn't realize I'd be starting my morning so early." I down the last dregs of coffee and toss the cup in the trash. The room is dark so as not to give away we're here. Not that I think it would matter. I doubt the guy on the other side of the glass even knows where he is.

The Captain takes a seat at the table across from the suspect. "Would you like a glass of water?" He pushes the cup toward the man, who makes no move for it. The other officer in the room clicks to start a recording.

"Can you tell us your name?"

The man gazes at the recording device. "Jeremiah," he says after several minutes. His words are low and slow. He must be on some serious shit. Flying high as a fucking broom. Maybe that's why he did it.

"Jeremiah, you were found with a dead body. Can you tell us how that happened?" Mendoza's voice is even and efficient. He wants to get this done as much as we do.

Once again, he takes too long to answer. "I killed them." The words have no emotion. It's like he's reading a list of facts off a flash card.

Grandfather shuffles next to me, cane hitting the floor.

"And how did you kill them?"

One blink. Then two. "In a dream. Sweet, deadly dream."

I can hear Grandfather's breath catch as he leans forward. It's like he's been waiting for this moment his whole life. I swallow, the acidic burn of the coffee making it difficult.

"Care to elaborate?"

His eyes roll around as the rambling starts. "I'm a dream wielder. I dream, dream—don't dream. They dream. I dream for them. So many colors, too many. Sweet dreams killing you quickly. I dreamed their death."

"Why did you do it?"

This time, I swear he looks straight through the mirror at me. "Because. Because. You can't hide in your dreams."

A beat from Mendoza. "Because *why*?" he pushes.

"It's who I am. I had to. Had to." He scratches at his face, eyes drooping. "It's the only way to make it stop. Stop. Stop."

Grandfather shakes his head. "I told you, Gabriel. These dream wielders are a scourge on the magical ecosystem. This is the first step to stopping their spread. We've got a confession. Mark my words; there will be more where that came from when I finish my bill. They'll have nowhere to hide as I burn the house down."

A chill runs down my spine at the same time my blood boils. Conflicting feelings of fear and hatred. He would condemn me with the same fate if he found out what I was. Not even being his grandson would save me.

"Then," he continues, "I can leave this earth knowing when your grandmother and I reunite, I can offer her justice for what was done to her."

Focusing on the other room so I don't have to meet his eyes, I poke the glass. I need to get him to realize that dream wielders must be assessed as individuals, and treated accordingly should they break the law. "Look at him. He's rambling like he's mixed potions he shouldn't. That is not the face of a mastermind. He's clearly disturbed."

"Exactly."

"No." My voice wobbles, and I double down on my willpower. "You got justice for Grandmother by capturing the man who used her. And while I understand the desire to regulate magic so it doesn't happen again, we need to make sure logic is guiding our actions, not emotions."

Grandfather cuts me down to size with a glare. "I will not be questioned on the motivations behind my actions. My record as High Witch speaks for itself in the good I have done for this country."

Licking my lips, I stay the course. "I didn't mean to offend you. I just wonder if perhaps this isn't a dream wielder problem." Turning his attention toward another issue might alleviate some of his aggression toward them. "Maybe there's a bad dealer out there selling illegal potions that's making these witches unstable. We need a healer to take blood work and test him and Meera."

Grandfather frowns. "Meera, is it? Are you on a first-name basis with these criminals?"

I close my eyes and take a breath before answering. "I was there at the scene this morning. That's it. Have you located a Seer who can give us some insight?"

The old man's jaw tightens. "Since Theodore died last year, we've yet to procure a new Seer."

True Seers are rare. Most governments recruit them extremely young and guard them as tightly as any crown jewels. I sense the irritation radiating off the High Witch that he hasn't been able to get a new one.

"I'm going to ask the Captain to make sure they check his blood."

"Check all you want, Gabriel. But I've warned about this for decades. My prophecies are now coming to pass."

"Grandfather, what if we offer a creative solution to this problem? Like training in schools. A way to make sure the dream wielders are learning safely." These are the programs I've been introducing to Apprentices that lean the opposite way of the High Witch on dream wielder issues. If I can gain enough pushback against him from others in power, we can create a dialogue for change that might actually help rather than sow prejudice.

He looks like I threw a boil hex at him. "Don't be absurd. I will not make their deadly magic mainstream in our schools. But since you're my grandson, I suppose you can have a preview of my plans." He takes out a scroll from his cloak, yes, a literal scroll like it's the 1600s, and hands it to me.

I read over it quickly to absorb the major points. My chest constricts the more I read, pain shooting across my ribs. "You're . . ." I try to speak, but my voice won't go further. I clear my throat. "You're going to force them to register themselves?" I hope he chalks up the shaking in my tone to the lack of sleep.

"Indeed *we* are. Too long they've been allowed to hide in the shadows. This way, we'll know who holds these powers and can apply restrictions to their magics and movements."

"Don't you think that's stepping over a line?" If I know the High Witch, this bill is only the first step in a much stricter plan to control dream wielders.

He takes the scroll back from me, rolling it up with care. "You've had your disagreements with me in the past, but in the end, you've always come around to my side. But if you don't want in on this legislation, I'm sure the historians can use you at the library. It might do you some good to learn the history you seem to have forgotten."

This isn't right. But I don't say it. Because while he thinks I was swayed to his side in the past, he doesn't know the small changes I've made to tame his rhetoric. If he relocates me to the library, I lose the access I have from within his inner circle to continue to do that.

I also know if I push too hard against him, he might be suspicious of my motivation, which could lead him to finding out what I really am.

After the interrogation, I head home to change into something more work appropriate before I have to continue with the rest of my day. I want a hot shower and a decent cup of coffee first, though. But it doesn't look like I will get either because when I walk to my door, Azalee is lounging on the steps. Her long legs are kicked out in front of her as she leans back on her elbows. Sleep deprivation makes my usually controlled brain slip and take in the curves of her body with hungry desperation.

Snap out of it, Gabriel.

I stop short, assessing the surroundings for any staff that might be there. But this is my private entrance, and it's quiet as usual. There are security cameras, but I made some adjustments to their positions to keep my privacy. "What are you doing here?" I keep walking toward the door, sliding the key in, but not opening it.

She stands, body brushing against mine in the fluid motion I witnessed on the dance floor. "I wanted to give this back before you arrested me for theft." She holds out my watch.

A weight lifts off my shoulders when I take it, sliding it onto my wrist. It feels like I can breathe easier with this protection back where it belongs. "Thanks. You can go." I push the door open, expecting her to leave, but she doesn't. I hold in my groan, glancing over my shoulder. "Was there something else?"

Rudeness is my default to keep her at arm's length. Any association with her might lead to my undoing, even if the only people present are the two of us. I'm not about to start a bad habit of being nice to her. I have a feeling it would be a slippery slope to a whole lot more.

She stares at the sky before making eye contact. "Look, I didn't plan on coming here—I was just walking and sort of ended up in front of your house."

My mom used to say it was the way spirits guided us to where we were needed. I can't imagine Azalee and I together will be anything good. Even if the way her teeth tug on her bottom lip pulls at something in my lower belly, my fingers begging to touch her skin.

I clear my throat, shoving the door open with my hand. "You have to be fast."

"Trust me, I will." She slides under my arm and struts into the living room like she owns the place.

I stand across the room, leaning against a chair tucked into a large wooden desk behind the sofa. "So . . ." I say, face pinched, waiting for her to jump in.

She does a slow spin, taking in every part of the room with keen eyes. She lands on a spot of carpet next to the sofa. "How did you get the bloodstain out?" There'd been blood everywhere that night she found me. When I told her later not all the blood was mine, I thought she'd see me as a monster, but it just made her eyes sadder.

That's how she looked at me the next few weeks when she kept trying to get me to join her coven. To embrace my new powers. Until I told her to leave me alone, but in a much less civilized way. Then she just looked at me like she's doing right now. Disdain and annoyance. Maybe a little bit of lust as I slip off my cloak and hook it on the back of the chair.

"We didn't—had to rip out the old carpet and replace it." I fold my arms across my chest. I notice her eyes snag on the underside of my bicep and the tattoo peeking out. I flex a little to give her a show. "The High Witch caught me taking out the soiled carpet rolls. Had to convince him I was doing some redecorating."

"Redecorating with the same carpet?" She raises an eyebrow.

"We're a very boring family. All white bread and milk for us."

She laughs, its warmth surprising me. "Oh, Gabriel, we both know you're anything but boring. A dick, sure—but boring, I don't think so. The rumor mills about you could power this whole town."

When that smile twists up her lips, I feel the tug in my gut again. The steady burning string that won't let me forget we're connected. That's why I'm itching to step closer. To push her against the wall and show her just how unboring I can be.

Not fucking happening, Gabriel.

I won't let some ancient magic trick me into doing something very stupid with her. "Did you come here to talk about bloody floors and nights I'd rather forget, or did you come for something else?" I get back on track. Grandfather will be bitching and moaning if I'm not back soon.

"Did you hear about Grant Henderson's death?" She leans against the kitchen island.

That question surprises me. "Yeah, I was there. Meera didn't tell you?"

Frowning, she shakes her head. "It was a bit of a night—as you can guess. I'm sure she just forgot. You are pretty unmemorable."

I don't take her bait. I'm not in the mood for a fight.

When she realizes I'm too tired to play with her, she continues, "I'm assuming you also know about the dream wielder arrested for murder this morning?" She's playing confident, but I hear a slight tremor in her voice.

I nod but stay quiet. She came here to see me. I want to know why. If it was just for some verbal sparring, I'm afraid I'm not ring-worthy just yet.

"He didn't do it," she says.

My brows scrunch together. "Do you know the guy?"

She shakes her head. "Nope, never met him." Looking away from me, she grabs an apple out of a bowl and twists the stem.

"Then how can you be sure?" I scratch the back of my head, my hair sticking up when I pull away. My eyes drift to the bathroom and the hot shower.

She frowns, opening her mouth, closing it, then shrugs. "Fine, I don't *know* he didn't do it, but if he did, it wasn't from dream wielding."

"That's not what he says."

Her eyes widen in shock. "Where did you hear that?"

She thought she could use the High Witch's grandson to get the dirt. "Azalee, this is an ongoing investigation, and I've already said too much." I push off the desk and head toward the door to let her out.

"Come on, Gabriel. You have to give me something."

I pause, hand on the door handle. "I'm sorry, did I forget the part where we're friends and I share things with you?"

She barks out a laugh. "We are not friends." Fire erupts in those green eyes, yanking at the thread between us.

I stride toward her with the winds of fate. "Exactly. So why would I tell you anything? Especially something that could get me in trouble?"

She rises on her toes to reach my level, but my height keeps her looking up. "Because despite your denial, we're the same, you and me."

The same. She doesn't need to say more. If shit goes down for the dream wielders, I'm going to get hit in the cross fire.

I bite my cheek, breathing heavily as we square off in a stare-down. Flecks of gold dance in her irises from this close. Her pink lips twitch, and my hand struggles to stay at my side and not reach up and touch them. "I sat in while the police updated my grandfather on the situation," I tell her as I head into the kitchen and start the espresso machine to put some distance between us. I can't shower yet, so might as well get some caffeine pumping in my veins.

"And?" she presses when I pause to pour in the beans.

"The guy admitted to it. He said he killed her while he was dream wielding." My hands shake as I click the start button. "Didn't even say it was an accident. Said he did it because he could." Shame coats my face as I turn back to her, hating that something like that could live inside me. "I can admit something wasn't right with that witch, but I can't prove that he didn't kill that woman in a dream."

"Then he can't be a dream wielder. He must be something else. A psychic maybe or a Nightmare . . ." Azalee pales, looking like she might vomit.

"I thought Nightmares couldn't function. This guy was talking just fine." The screeching of the machine fights to be heard over us.

"You're right, a full-blown Nightmare wouldn't be up and talking." She looks physically pained to say I'm right. "But in the very early stages, they look like us—so it is possible."

I grab two mugs and place them on the counter between us.

"Did they have a medium? What did the victim's spirit say?" she asks.

I pour the dark liquid. "They didn't need a medium. The guy admitted his guilt freely. They're already prepping for his execution."

Hanging, fire, drowning. These are the punishments for using witchcraft for dark intent—old-school justice.

I push the cup toward her, and she accepts. "Doesn't that seem weird to you?" she asks, heading to the fridge to help herself to milk. "He'd willingly admit to killing this woman? And say he did it with magic, full well knowing the punishment is always more severe for that?"

She's not wrong. My guard was already up about these cases, and she's just reaffirming the inconsistencies.

"They don't even have to give you a trial," she continues before I can respond. "If they want a show or to stir up hatred for the convicted, they'll have a mockery of a trial. A farce to show they're giving justice, but once the High Witch decides you're guilty—that's it. It's how they keep magical crimes down."

I take a few sips of my bitter espresso. "Look, I was there for his confession. He wasn't right in the head; I'll give you that. But he confessed. The High Witch won't just let that go."

She bites her thumbnail, pacing in front of me. "What if his confession was planned? Maybe this murder isn't about him per se, but about creating fear for the dream wielders?"

"You think the High Witch is behind this?" I push myself off the counter, avoiding her gaze by looking out the window. I know Grandfather wants his legacy securely in place now that he believes his days are numbered, but murdering innocent people to do it? I don't think he'd go that far. Despite his flaws he has always wanted the people of Salem to feel safe. Creating this mass panic would do the opposite of that.

"I didn't say that, but the fact you'd jump to that conclusion speaks for itself." I can hear her tapping her foot.

"I just jumped on the ship you were already captaining. He may not like dream wielders," I say, and she snorts. "Fine, he hates dream wielders, but he'd never stoop to having someone killed to make a point."

She meets me by the window. "Even if it meant he could get his law passed requiring dream wielders to register themselves?"

There she goes, surprising me again. "How did you hear about that? I only just learned about it today."

She smiles. "The coven has its resources."

I tap my index finger slowly against the glass as rain falls. "I don't have an answer for you," I say quietly. I don't even have them for myself. "But maybe we can get some." I meet her gaze, holding it for a few beats too many before walking back to my desk.

"I'm listening," she says to my back. If I didn't know better, I'd say she sounds a little breathless from our staring contest. I know my heart is racing too much for my liking.

I rustle through the drawers, pulling out a card. "Do you want to see a medium with me?"

"No, but I'll take that card and visit her myself." Azalee makes a grab for the card, but I hold it in the air. "Don't be a dick, Gabriel. Which I understand is very difficult for you."

"She won't see you without me." If there is evidence to be found, we need to do it methodically and by the book. That's the only way to assure it sticks to the real culprit. Knowing Azalee, her impulsiveness will fuck this up and get us both in trouble if I leave her to her own devices.

"I can be very persuasive." She jumps to reach the card, but I grab her waist to keep her down, my fingers dipping into the soft curves.

"So can I." I bare my teeth in a grin.

Her tongue flicks across her lips. "Just give me her name before you embarrass yourself by pretending you're a human with real emotions."

That cuts deeper than I should let it, but my sleep deprivation has my nerves raw.

"I'll just find my own medium." She crosses her arms.

"Yours isn't as good as mine." I rest my hands on the V of my hips, and her eyes rack across my body in a quick flick. "Azalee, we can both get what we want here."

"Doubtful. I don't think you could ever give me what I want." She bats her eyelashes, lips twisting into a smile. "But I'll see your medium and be the judge of that."

We agree to meet this evening after work, and I'm hoping I haven't made a grave misstep in trusting her.

CHAPTER 16

Azalee

The high ceilings of the chapel reflect light in from the dazzling stained glass as I step into the dark wooded room. It doesn't get used for religious purposes anymore—primarily for indoor yoga classes and nighttime dream wielding sessions. A memory rises to the surface as the musty smell of old herbs fills my nostrils . . .

"All right, class," Mom says, walking around us as we lie on the floor staring up at her. Frankincense burns at the altar. "Today's lesson is an advanced form of dream wielding. Astral projection. It might not be commonly used and takes great patience and concentration, but it comes in handy should you need to contact someone who is otherwise unreachable through normal means of communication."

I shift on my yoga mat, patience already wearing thin and we haven't even started. This isn't the first time Mom has tried to teach me astral projecting. But when I wasn't instantly great at it, I gave up. But this is Meera's first time and she dragged me along.

"Align your crystals, focusing on areas that feel most off balance." She waits for us to finish before continuing. "Now, close your eyes and connect with the dreamscape. Unlike typical dream wields, you don't have a subject to dream into. In the astral plane, the entirety of the

dreamscape is accessible to you. It might feel overwhelming to have all of it at your fingertips—call on your magic to keep you present. Release your physical form."

My jaw aches with tension as I squeeze my eyes shut. The only thing I see is the back of my eyelids.

After several minutes, I stand in frustration.

"Where are you going?" Meera hisses as I hastily roll up my mat.

"Iniko is at the ice caves today. I think I'll join him."

Mom calls to me as I head toward the door. "Magic takes time, Azalee. You must practice."

"I will." I leave before she can detect the lie.

I flip on the lights to get an idea of the state of the space that's sat undisturbed for the last several months. We don't use it much in the summer, and Roz instructed me to clean it since the weather is turning cold.

"Meera, what are you doing here?" I say in surprise when I spot her on one of the yoga mats, staring at the sky. The air swirls with dust as I sit on the floor with her.

She turns her head to stare at the altar. "Do you remember when we were kids and snuck in here with Iniko to make a love potion?" She runs her fingers along the stained glass pictures of fallen angels that line the bottom of the altar we've left for aesthetics—or maybe just in case some vengeful Gods didn't like us using this holy space to get sweaty.

"Iniko was convinced his crush just needed a little push, and he'd fall madly in love with him after that." I smile at the memory swimming up from the depths of long-forgotten good times.

"Too bad he got the wrong ingredients and made a wart-growing spell instead." She chuckles, still looking at the glass.

My laugh echoes through the room. "Poor Iniko. He still wanted him after that, so I guess it was true love." We fall into a long silence.

"I'm sorry, Az," Meera says, finally meeting my eyes.

"For what? You didn't do anything wrong." I run a hand over her dark hair, pulling her into a hug. "It's going to be okay."

"Promise you'll forgive me?" She stares up at me, dark eyes brimming with tears.

"There's nothing to forgive." I don't want to push, but I need to know. "Why didn't you tell me Gabriel was at Grant's house?"

Her brow furrows. "I guess I forgot—there was so much happening. It felt like I was stuck behind glass in a fish tank."

"Did you get any answers from the cops?" I didn't get a chance to ask her this morning before I went off half cocked on my little adventure to Gabriel's house. *Which I guess paid off?* I don't know. He's so fucking hard to read. For all I know, tonight's plan might be a trap. But for Meera and the rest of us, I have to try.

Meera shakes her head. "No. Just the old *don't leave town, little missy.* Misogynistic bullshit. Or maybe that's just what they say to murder suspects."

"You're not a murderer."

"I guess we'll see." She lies back on the mat and closes her eyes.

"Do you remember anything else from last night? Now that you've had some time to process."

She doesn't open her eyes. "I've been trying, but you know how dreams are. It felt like it happened in a blink of an eye. One minute he was smiling on the surfboard, the next I was waking to his vacant stare."

"We could get a clarity potion. It might help."

She shakes her head. "Clarity won't make the Fates change their course."

It's later than I would have liked when I finally make it downtown to the medium. But I don't care because I got to help a few dream wielders prep to take their first solo dream trips. Seeing them achieve this step is a rush of pure joy. It's like watching them leave a cocoon and flap their wings.

Gabriel can wait an extra twenty minutes. It'll be good to knock down his ego several pegs.

He pushes his foot off the brick wall he was leaning against when I stop in front of the shop. His hair is wet from the slow drizzle of rain pouring all day. His aquamarine eyes are leaning more blue against his five-o'clock shadow.

Fuck, he looks terrific. He did this morning too. I enjoy the rough-around-the-edges vibe he's sporting today. The suits are nice and all, but he looked like an ad for law school. This Gabriel looks like he could show me a good time.

I try not to squirm when his eyes run over me, a hot flush creeping up my neck. "You sure you're still up for this?" he asks, brushing a hand through his hair.

"Did *you* want to back out? Afraid the High Witch might find out?"

He flinches, and I feel a stab in my chest. Sure, it was a joke—a little mean-spirited, but that's our usual temperature. Instead of delving into those pesky things like feelings, I reach for the door handle, but he places a warm hand over mine. His body presses close to keep us under the small awning. I'm trapped in his scent of clove and rain. My head has already been foggy enough for the last two days without him making it worse.

"Contacting the dead is not an endeavor to undertake lightly." The warning in his voice makes me still. We both know what it's like to be touched by death. "You don't want to be messing around if you aren't ready to hear the answers they might give."

The hair on my neck stands on end as if the ghosts have already heard us talking about them. If he knew me better, he'd know how desperate I must be if I'm seeking the help of a medium.

I press my trembling hand into his solid chest, the expensive sweater soft against my skin. "I need the truth. Something is off—and

I'm going to figure out what it is." I push in front of him, opening the door.

Bell chimes greet us as we enter, and the pungent smell of patchouli tickles my nose. The medium's shop doesn't offer any frilly nonsense. Similar shops like this also sell other items and services, but not here. It's strictly her place to perform séances.

The compact space is accented with a table and a few chairs on one side and an overstuffed love seat and a window bench on the other. Gabriel made an appointment for us, but unsurprisingly, when it comes to interacting with a medium, we aren't late for it, we're right on time.

A melody of wind chimes signals her appearance from a door in the back. A round lapis lazuli crystal wrapped with silver thread hangs around the medium's neck. This cobalt stone flecked with pyrite helps with challenging psychic powers and communication with spirits. I'm not sure if this is what makes her the best medium in Salem or not, but according to Gabriel, she is.

Or should I say, the best medium in Salem who doesn't work with the police or the High Witch. She won't worry about a paycheck if the spirits give her an answer the High Witch might not like.

"I am Opal. Please, take a seat." She's in her mid-sixties with salt-and-pepper hair twisted into a bun. She walks with a slight limp over to her chair.

Velvet fabric in deep eggplant adorned with embroidered gold stars and constellations covers the small table we sit around. There are no tarot cards or crystal balls. The only adornment is a golden rutilated quartz point about a foot high. It's a light yellow with strands of gold running through it. She may not have a lot of adornments, but the few she does have are pretty fucking powerful. Less is more, I guess.

"Do you have someone specific you've come to see?" Her voice is heavy, like it's coated in caramel.

I glance at Gabriel. It might be a bit weird if we say we want to talk to the lady who was murdered last night.

"You needn't tell me who you wish to commune with. Just keep them in your mind's eyes to focus them to you. But remember, we are not the controllers of the dead. Only those who wish to speak will come forward."

Spirits are temperamental beings; they don't always show up when called. I focus on the woman from the news this morning. I've never met her, but maybe my desire for the truth will win out.

Opal burns blackthorn for protection against harmful spirits that might try to find their way in. The familiar tickle in my spine starts. I've done a very good job of not visiting mediums until now. But if it helps dream wielders, I'll do it. Gabriel, sensing my uneasiness, takes my hand under the table, squeezing it. I begin to jerk away but realize I want a hand to hold. Not because I enjoy the feel of his skin against mine—*I don't*—but it calms my racing heart.

Opal closes her eyes, and nothing happens. No lights flicker, no sudden chill. We just sit quietly in our chairs and watch her. My eyes slide to Gabriel, who gives me a reassuring nod as if telling me this is what's supposed to happen. I want to punch his smug face. Instead, I untangle our fingers and put my hands in my lap.

"I see a person," Opal says after a few minutes. I perk up. "It's a man." My heart sinks again. It's not the woman from this morning, but maybe it's Grant. That'd be a good start too. At least we can get solid evidence Meera is innocent.

"He's showing me a yellow balloon. He keeps trying to hand it to me." This is the thing with mediums: What they see isn't always straightforward. They're given images by the spirit, and it's up to us to interpret their meaning. "He's showing me a number eight." She reaches up and grabs her head. "I'm sensing lots of pain. So much blood. He died from trauma to the head."

My brows furrow as I piece together the riddle. A bloody head wound? Grant didn't have any visible damage to the head. "He's petting a pink bunny."

Suddenly, the room is crashing in on me. I can't breathe as the pressure gathers on top of my chest. This isn't Grant she's seeing.

It's my dad.

CHAPTER 17

Azalee

My dream wielder ability manifested the day my dad was murdered. It was over seventeen years ago, but I remember it as clearly as yesterday. My mom was out of town, so Dad took me to the carnival. It was the best day of my life.

Then it became the worst.

It was late on a new moon night. The darkness was so consuming, but the warm breeze of summer kissed the air. I'd been asleep in my room when the noise jolted me from my last ever dream—*the shattering of glass, smashing of wood.* The police later told us it was most likely a home invasion gone wrong. They probably didn't expect us to be awake or for my father to try to stop them. He did, though, and I ran downstairs at the sound of fist punching flesh, of cracking bone.

I always wondered what would've happened if I'd stayed upstairs. If I hadn't seen my father get struck in the head with a marble bookend. Would I have become a dream wielder? Maybe the trauma wouldn't have been as bad. When I saw my father's body hit the ground and the two guys ran out the front door, I bolted after them, slipping in the pool of blood spreading across our floor.

I don't know what I thought I could accomplish. But I knew I had to catch them for what they'd done. I didn't even stop to check my father's body. I could see his aura, and I knew he was gone.

I raced after the men, nowhere near fast enough to catch them, but I ran until I couldn't breathe, until my lungs were lead in my chest. Then I fell to the ground and curled into a ball, hot tears sticking to my cold face. I must have fallen asleep and someone found me and brought me home. The days after are a blur. It took me a week to realize I wasn't dreaming anymore.

"Azalee?" Gabriel's voice sounds very far away.

"What is he saying?" I ask Opal, ignoring Gabriel.

"He's warning you to be careful. That the path you are headed down will lead to danger."

"Should I stop?" The words scratch my dry throat.

Her eyes gaze unfocused past us. Then she shakes her head. "Even dangerous things must be done, but use caution, for everyone is not as they seem." Her eyes flick to mine, a knowing that wasn't there when I first met her. "I'm sorry. He's gone. He was very weak. His connection to this world was only held by a string."

Tears prickle my eyes, but I wipe them away. I will *not* cry in front of Gabriel Ford. "Can you try to reach someone else, please? A woman." I change the subject, but Gabriel wants answers.

"Who was that?" His voice is sharp.

Swallowing, my throat burns like I'm drinking sand. "My dad." I look back to Opal, not in the mood for more questions. "There was a woman who died this morning, supposedly killed by a dream wielder." Opal's brows arch slightly, but she doesn't comment. "Can you reach her?"

"I can try, but as I said, spirits aren't always cooperative." She places her hands flat on the table, eyes moving rapidly under her lids. After a few minutes, she opens them. "I'm sorry, I can't find her."

"What about Grant Henderson? He died last night. Can you try him?"

Gabriel shifts, jaw clenching as he presses his lips together. This is clearly not going as he planned. *Fuck it,* who cares if we have to tell Opal what we're up to.

She hesitates, reading something between the two of us, but closes her eyes and tries again—nothing happens. "There is only blackness where these spirits are concerned."

"Is that normal?" Gabriel asks. "To not see any trace of someone?"

Opal contemplates, trailing a hand over her necklace. "Yes and no. It's common not to find a spirit when searching them out. They may have already moved on or simply don't wish to be found. But these two . . . no, there is something strange about the complete darkness around them. It's as if they are being hidden from me. Their spirits are contained, so we can't speak. Perhaps that in itself should be answer enough for you." She gets up from the table. "I'm afraid I have nothing more to enlighten you."

We don't linger in the medium's shop. She's told us everything she can and we're sent on our way—Gabriel $200 lighter. The night is cool. I pull my cloak tighter around me. Silence seeps in, the pounding of rain on the cement the only melody.

Gabriel breaks the silence. "I thought we weren't going to tell her who we were looking for?"

I kick a rock into a puddle in the gutter. "I had to improvise. We weren't getting anywhere, and I didn't want this painful twenty minutes we had to spend in each other's company to all be for nothing."

"Cute." His voice is flat. "What if she tells the police what we were looking into? Or the High Witch?" Each word echoes in my head, the painful realization we didn't learn anything useful.

"Then it's your fault," I answer with too much force. "You're the one who picked her." I don't fully trust Gabriel, but he seems willing to help me, so I add, "I just need to clear Meera's name. And stop the avalanche hurtling down the mountain before it buries all the dream wielders in its wake."

"You don't think a dream wielder could have done any of these murders?" Gabriel hedges, not taking his eyes off me.

"No." I don't hesitate. "Dream wielders can't do that." I push a wet strand of blond hair behind my ear.

He sighs, features softening. "Look, I know she's your friend, but maybe something happened in the dream. Not that she did it on purpose, but that's what accidents are."

"How would you know the first thing about dream wielding?" We're pretty much alone, the rain driving people inside. "You go around acting like you aren't one. So don't pretend you know how dream wielding works."

His growl is guttural as his hands scrape through his hair. "Don't stand there all high and mighty pretending you know shit about my situation. You haven't lived with my grandfather your whole life. You don't understand what would happen if he discovered what I am. He wouldn't just kick me out of his house; he would destroy me. I would have nothing left."

"So fuck all the dream wielders then, right? As long as Gabriel Ford gets to feel safe." I didn't realize I was screaming until the words rip from my throat. Good thing no one is around to hear our street brawl.

He steps closer, his darkened eyes burn into mine. "Do you remember the curriculum they started at schools that taught kids about the dangers of dream wielder magic and how to guard themselves against the invasions of their mind?"

I frown. Kids learn about all types of magic, but surprisingly there isn't an emphasis on dream wielders over the other types. "No. That wasn't a thing."

"Yeah, because I stopped it from happening." He smiles the least friendly smile imaginable. One of those *gotcha* grins.

My brow furrows deeper, confusion pulsing through me. "What?"

"Last year the High Witch wanted to roll the program out to schools, but I was able to drum up enough opposition from the administrators and school boards to stop it before it ever got off the ground. Not everyone needs to be a bull in a china shop to get things done. Sometimes a slower, less in-your-face approach is required."

I close my eyes, shaking my head to try to rattle out an answer to a very uncomfortable question. I have spent years hating this man, and rightfully so. He's said plenty of terrible and inflammatory things against dream wielders. Was that an act? Or is this the act? Is he trying to trick me into thinking he's the hero so I let my guard down? And so what if he's done one good thing? He's been an asshole to me and my kind.

"Were you looking for a thank-you?" I say an automated sarcastic response because I'm too stunned by his supposed good deed to think of anything better.

His laugh is harsh. "I apologize that not all of us can sit on our pedestals and preach how righteous we are. Some of us are stuck in the lion's den, hoping to get by without anyone eating us." He walks away, leaving me standing in the street.

The buzzing of my phone breaks the rain's staccato. I stare at him sulking away a moment longer before grabbing it from my pocket. I'm not preaching from my high horse. I just want him to be honest. But even I know I'm not being honest with myself. Maybe I'm jealous because I wish I could hide away sometimes. It's Mom calling, and I pick up, pressing myself close to the building under the awnings.

"You need to get home right now." No hello or greeting.

"What's going on?"

"Meera's been arrested."

CHAPTER 18

Azalee

I don't remember the drive home. The rain pounding against the windshield matched with the blood pumping in my veins. One single thought echoed in my mind—*I couldn't save Meera either.*

"Where is she?" I run into the living room, cloak dripping water on the hardwood.

Mom and Roz sit at the dining table, staring off at nothing.

"Mom?" I haven't dropped my keys into the dish by the door. I'm ready to bolt the second they tell me what happened. Meera needs my help—I have to do something.

Clearing her throat, Mom says, "She's at the jailhouse." Her blond hair hangs loosely over her shoulders. Every day it has more strands of gray.

I run my hands over my face as I pace, not caring I'm making a puddle. "How could they do this? They don't have any proof."

"Sit down, Azalee," Roz says. "Your nervous rushing won't make the Gods hear us louder."

"Sorry my worry about my friend's fate is bothering you." Phantom fingers dig into my chest, clawing at my heart.

Mom's eyes slowly come back to focus. "The police were acting on orders from the High Witch. Meera is a suspected dream wielder, and with the other murders . . . well, it wasn't hard to get the warrant."

I continue my laps around the kitchen, ignoring Roz's *tsk*s. Too much energy is cascading through my body. I need to get out the throbbing under my skin that feels like a million fire ants. "All right, so what's the plan? I'm assuming we're going to get her. Pay her bail or whatever."

Roz shakes their head, long fingers gripping their cup. I spy the remnants of tea. *What warnings did the leaves reveal?* "I've talked to our lawyer, and he's reviewing the case now. In the morning, he'll have more answers."

I slam my hands down on the table—neither flinches. "You're going to let her stay there all night?"

Mom places a hand on mine. "We don't have a choice." The words are an anchor tethered to my feet as I'm thrown overboard.

My eyes dart between them, hoping I'll see a glimmer of assurance in their stares, but I receive none. "She didn't do this," I whisper. I could tell them what the medium told me, but I already got bitched out for my *extracurricular activities*, so I don't need more reprimanding. Plus, they would throw a fit if they knew I was with a Ford.

I still believe *deep* in my bones that the High Witch is connected to this somehow. But if you're going to take a shot at him, you can't miss. *See, Gabriel, I'm not always a bull in a china shop.*

"Meera is not a murderer; I know this," Mom replies. Saying Meera's *not* a murderer and saying she's innocent are two very different things.

I lean against the chair, directing my question to Roz. "We're all in this coven together. And it's supposed to be a safe place, right?"

Roz's cool blue eyes run over me before they nod.

I swallow, knowing I might not like the answer I'm about to get. "Do you honestly believe the dream wielders are responsible for these deaths? Do you think Meera is?"

"We are all well aware that dream wielders can be dangerous when they use their powers to do wrong. The High Witch's wife is an example of that we will never be allowed to forget. However, killing in a dream has, until now, been impossible for a healthy dream wielder to do." They run their finger over the teacup's rim, gazing at the leaves. "Still, magic is always changing, growing, adapting into something new. I can't speak of the other dream wielders, but I do not believe Meera would knowingly hurt someone."

My heart lifts a little but deflates again with their following words. "*However*, we have coven members researching to see if perhaps our magic is evolving. There is no indication yet that that is the case, but we will do our due diligence to be sure. When we have all the findings, we can act accordingly."

Roz thinks Meera did it.

Not that she's guilty of first-degree murder, she didn't plan this, but Roz thinks Meera is responsible nonetheless.

"I need to consult my books." Roz leaves without a goodbye.

Mom stands too, pulling me into a hug. "Get some rest, Azalee. We'll fix it in the morning." With a kiss on my forehead, she leaves me.

I go to my room but have little hope that sleep will come easily. I want to visit Iniko, but it aggravates Nightmares to have someone with such despair in their heart nearby. See my trip there yesterday as proof.

I change without noticing what I'm doing, not even bothering to turn on a light or pick up the piles of things that litter the floor. I slip under the covers and stare at the ceiling without seeing. What is Meera looking at right now? I hope she knows I'll do anything to get her out.

I grip a moonstone in my hand, willing myself to sleep. I could use a sleeping tonic, but I haven't replenished my stock, and I'm not trekking out in the rain to go to the shop. There is so much I should be doing instead of sleeping—finding out the truth behind Grant's death, saving Iniko, stopping the High Witch's agenda. *It's all too much.* I keep saying I want to do these things, that it's my job, but I haven't done any of it. Fuck, I usually make it worse.

Maybe I'm no good to anyone.

I close my eyes and repeat a chant, willing my body to sleep. A stabbing builds in the base of my skull, but I ignore it and slowly drift off to sleep.

But it's not empty blackness that greets me.

The pounding of my head turns into the slapping of feet against packed, damp earth. Fallen branches and rocks cut into the balls of my feet, making them slick with blood. My hair whips against my face as I look behind me, getting caught in my mouth and eyes. My heart is on the outside of my skin, a bloody mess dripping with each pouring beat.

Thud. Thud. Thud.

I stop short, tripping and landing on all fours. I'm surrounded by a never-ending jungle. Torch lights flicker in the depths of the thick trees, revealing a woman peeking out at me—with each blink, she gets closer.

"Well, hello there." She's right beside me now, sharp teeth glistening in the firelight. "I haven't seen you before."

I try to speak or move, but my body is hardened stone. The oppressive heat is suffocating me.

She tilts her head, the trees swaying with her movement as if they're a single entity. A smile erupts across her features, distorting the beautiful face into a twisted nightmare. "We're going to have so much fun."

The beeping of my alarm shakes me from my slumber. I click it off, then toss the phone to the ground. Pain rips through my body when I sit. I hang my head between my knees, taking slow and even breaths. What happened while I was asleep last night shouldn't have happened. *Full stop.* Dream wielders don't dream. A slithering sensation creeps along my spine. That wasn't a dream.

It was a nightmare.

With shaking hands, I peel off my clothes, each layer scratching like grains of sand. The very touch of them makes my skin crawl. I throw them in the trash, standing naked in my room, failing to calm my racing heart.

I trip to the bathroom, stubbing my toe on the door. The pain should send shock waves up my leg, but I barely feel it. I turn the shower on full blast. The hotter, the better. I need to burn it all away. Using an energy-cleansing salt scrub, I rub until my skin's bright red, then I rub a little harder. If I can scrape hard enough, maybe I can make the memories disappear too.

I had a nightmare.

This is the first sign of trouble—the early stages of becoming a Nightmare. The hopelessness I've felt, the headaches, all early warning signs I've chalked up to stress. But I'm not past the point of no return. Besides, it wasn't *that* scary. It could've been a bad dream. It's like Roz said: Magic can change. Maybe dream wielders are adapting to have their own dreams.

Yup, that sounds reasonable. I'm fine. I'm not becoming a Nightmare.

By the time I'm out of the shower and headed downstairs, I've nearly forgotten the dream. Or I've almost convinced myself to ignore it. Mom is already waiting in the kitchen.

"The lawyer said he'd meet us at the jail in thirty minutes. Roz will stay here to monitor The Retreat, but you and I can go. Eat up." She places a bowl of oatmeal on the table for me.

I may have willed myself to push the dream to the back of my mind, but I can't do the same with Meera. I eat the oatmeal only because Mom won't stop staring at me, but I have to choke down every bite.

"She'll be all right, Azalee. We'll figure this out." Mom kisses the top of my head.

I nod, blinking back tears. I can't speak without telling her about the nightmare, and she's got enough to worry about.

Silence fills the car ride, peppered with Mom's reassurances that the lawyer is one of the best and that he'll make sure Meera gets a fair deal.

Not that Meera will be released or that Meera will be proven innocent. A fair deal. *Why does the bad choice have to sound like the best option they can give?* I'm not settling with getting Meera a fair deal—I will prove she's innocent. No way four murders, all supposedly committed by dream wielders, happen within days of each other and aren't connected. I just have to figure out how.

It appears fate is on my side because I see my number one suspect when we arrive at the jail. "Honorable High Witch Ford," Mom greets the High Witch when we enter the building.

"Genevieve." The High Witch doesn't try to hide his disdain. "Here to see your *associate*?"

Fuck, what a dick. I bite so hard on my tongue to stay quiet I taste blood.

My mother, ever graceful, smiles politely. "I would not abandon anyone in their time of need."

"Even a murderer?" His eyes bore into us.

Mom doesn't flinch, which is more than I can say for myself. Pure rage boils my insides as I stare into the bigoted face of the High Witch, refusing to let him think he's winning.

"Innocence or guilt is not for us to decide. That is the job of a jury," Mom says.

Should the evidence prove Meera did this with magic, she won't be allowed to plead her case to anyone but the High Witch, and any plea she makes to him will go unheard.

"If you'll excuse us, my lawyer is waiting." Mom steps past the High Witch, head held high. I can't say I'm as dignified, and that's when I spot Gabriel standing in the back corner. I sensed he was here the moment we arrived, the gold rope flaring to life as if I needed a reminder I'm chained to him. He looks like he wants to say something to me, but I don't give him a chance as I follow Mom.

We're led into a holding room where they have Meera, and I run to her. "Meera, I'm so sorry." She bursts into tears that spill onto my shoulder. "I should have been there. I shouldn't have let them take you." I feel the darkness rolling inside me.

This is your doing, the voice whispers to me.

"You couldn't have done anything to stop them." Fluorescent lights cast an eerie tint to her brown skin, highlighting her puffy eyes.

"If we could all take a seat." The lawyer points to the chairs around the table. He's ancient, with wisps of hair and wire-rimmed glasses covering his wrinkled white skin. "Now, let's look at the evidence so far . . ."

When we exit the holding room thirty minutes later, I feel worse than when we started. The lawyer presented a case to get Meera off, but it didn't sound easy. He also seemed to be leaning toward the idea of having her admit the murder was unintentional. Because apparently, he is fine settling with a charge of manslaughter with life in prison. Mom assured me we wouldn't do that unless we had to. I don't even want to hear it as an option.

Dream wielders are swimming with weights tied to our ankles, and eventually, the fatigue will be too much, and we'll have to surrender to the undercurrent.

CHAPTER 19

Gabriel

"Well, Senator, that's amazing to hear. Your dedication to the people of your state is admirable," I say, pacing the halls of the police station while I speak on the phone to a senator out of New York. Grandfather has me following up with critical political allies to ensure he'll have their support when he announces his bills.

Which I did do, but I've also made some phone calls to his criticizers. This senator in particular is great at keeping our conversations close to the vest. "I know that none of us want a witch hunt on our hands, and if you and your allies can present your case against this bill to the public, I'm confident we can resolve things in a way that treats all our citizens fairly."

As I start my circle again, my eyes drift to the interrogation room Azalee went into a while ago. I felt her before I saw her, my head turning just in time to watch her walk through the station doors. I didn't know Meera had been arrested until we got here this morning. Grandfather has always had a keen eye on the state of the police in Salem, but since the string of deaths, it's all-consuming. He came here to get the latest information to add to the statement he'll release about the new bill.

I frown, realizing the senator said something I didn't catch, but it seems like we're wrapping up. "Thank you again. We'll be in touch."

Grandfather is in Mendoza's office, discussing the latest case information. I take a second to breathe and turn off the Ford persona. Sitting on one of the plastic chairs that line the hallway, I rest my elbows on my knees and scroll through my phone. I have several unanswered texts from Logan. Guilt eats away at me knowing I've pushed him to the sidelines the last week.

Truthfully, I've put a wall between us since I became a dream wielder, afraid that even the smallest slip in my demeanor would expose what I've become. I've made the excuse that I'm too busy with work when he's wanted to hang out. If I keep this up, revealing what I am won't lose me my brother because I'll already have done that on my own.

I text Logan to meet up tonight to play some basketball. His immediate enthusiastic reply makes me smile.

After the medium last night, I was fired up and needed an outlet. I went to Eclipse again, which was a terrible mistake. Trying to distract myself from the emotions Azalee can dig up in me, I thought finding someone to take home might be just the thing.

It wasn't.

The woman was pretty, and she was certainly interested, but I couldn't get Azalee out of my fucking brain. This stupid string connecting us feels like a hangman's noose. I ended up closing my tab early. It was probably for the best after the long day I had.

The door to the interrogation room opens, and Azalee walks out with her mother and the lawyer. I stand as they pass me. "I need to speak to you," I whisper low enough for only Azalee to hear. Tension tightens her jaw, clearly not wanting to talk to me, but that razor-sharp mind knows I might be useful.

"Mom, I need to use the restroom. I'll meet you at the car," Azalee says, waiting until her mom's left before turning to me. "You have two minutes. This better be worth my time."

"My grandfather is pushing to have the dream wielders hung." I get right to the point. I can't say I was surprised when he told me this on the way here. The High Witch loves a grand display of power.

I can tell it shakes her by the slight dip in her facade, but she keeps up the show. "Well, thanks for the heads-up." She starts to leave, but I grab her arm. Like it always does when we touch, sparks cascade across my skin. I might find her insufferable, but I'd be a fucking liar if I said she isn't the most beautiful woman I've ever seen. I've had more fantasies than I'll ever admit about the curves of her hips and the long lines of her legs.

Clearing my throat, I continue, "The evidence they have regarding dream magic residue is circumstantial. It's not ironclad proof a dream wielder caused all these murders—other than one man's erratic confession—but that's the angle the High Witch will push. I may be . . . I've never done *it*." I glance at Captain Mendoza's office door, but they're deep in conversation and don't notice me and Azalee. "But I want you to show me." The insecurity in my voice that I assumed would make her laugh doesn't.

Her eyebrows dip as she sucks in her bottom lip. "Show you what?" It's her turn to glance around. "How to *dream wield*?" she mouths the last part.

I ghosted her before, so I wouldn't be surprised if she told me to fuck off. "I don't know what the limits are in the dreamscape. But I want to test how far you can go—since you're *so sure* killing isn't possible." Something is off, I know it, but I don't know enough about the functionality of dream wielding to say with certainty that it can't cause death. Reading books only gets you so far, sometimes you need practical experience.

She steps closer to whisper, "You want me to try to kill you?"

"I'm sure it's something you've daydreamed about a time or two," I say. She shrugs. "I just need you to show me how it works."

Her tongue flicks across her teeth. "I don't think so, Gabriel."

"I want justice for those victims. Which means I need to know who the suspects could be." We're barely a breath apart now. She smells like chamomile and lavender. "According to you, it can't be done, so I shouldn't be in danger, right?" I need the truth, whether those answers are ones Azalee or I want or not.

"What if I'm wrong—which I'm not—but hypothetically if I am. You could die."

A diplomatic response forms with ease, but I give her a piece of truth instead. "I should have died two years ago, so this is all just borrowed time anyway."

Those deep-emerald eyes study me. "So you know about the life debt loophole then?" She smiles, annoyed.

I mimic her fake grin. "Oh, you mean the rule that says if the person who saved you kills you, they don't die. Yeah, I know that one."

"You should really be more scared of me then." She flips her long blond locks over her shoulder. "It's only a matter of time before I get so fucking fed up with this rope latching us together that I off you just to free myself." I might not be able to read auras, but I know she's lying. She's not a killer.

Grandfather's and Mendoza's chairs are moving; time is running out. "So, will you show me?"

Her eyes roam over me and I'm guessing she's reading my aura. "Fine," she finally says.

I'm frustrated by the warmth that brings to my chest. That this person who is the captain of the I Hate Gabriel Fan Club doesn't shy away from me because I'm a dream wielder. She embraces that part, might have even been my friend if I'd been willing to try. Others would hate me for this magic, but she never would.

"But I can't take you to my house," she adds.

"And I can't take you to mine."

She bites her lip. "There's an old bell tower at the back of The Retreat. Meet me there at midnight."

"It's a date." I put my hand out for her to shake, but she rolls her eyes, walking away.

I bounce back and forth on my feet, fists smacking the punching bag. Sweat stings as it drips into my eyes, and it feels like nothing else exists. This overheated room with the sour smell of sweat and my skin hitting the bag is all that matters.

Tension melts away with every strike rattling up my arm. I needed this after the last two days. I had a long lunch meeting with Grandfather and a newly appointed Apprentice. It went well, but I could hardly focus, thinking about the night I'm submitting myself to in a few hours.

I stop the bag from swaying, wiping my forehead with the back of my hand. I'm sore as fuck. I took a few weeks off, and I'm feeling it. My muscles are screaming from the exertion, but I'm relishing the pain. I never want to be in the situation I found myself in two years ago. I was a good fighter then; I'm a great one now. I can't let that slip.

I spot Logan coming in the door and raise my gloved hand to call him over. He waves, shifting his heavy backpack on his shoulders, then points to the locker room, mouthing, *One sec.*

I almost miss the look on his face, the one that always spells mischief. I rip my gloves off, following him in quick strides. I might not be able to read auras and garner someone's true intentions, but I know Logan better than I know myself.

"Hey," I say, coming up behind him as he's attempting to shove his oversize backpack into a too-small locker.

He jumps, startling before replacing his grimace with a smile. "You head to the court. I just need to change."

I nod to the half-zipped bag. "What's got that so full?"

He doesn't meet my gaze. "You know me, ever the dutiful student."

I snort. "Sure." I lunge for the bag, snatching it before he can.

"Gabriel, fuck off, that's mine!" He tries to grab it, but I spin around.

"Please tell me there isn't fireworks or some other fucking trick that you're too old for." Logan has always been a little too enthusiastic about the Halloween season, resulting in numerous trips to the healers. I unzip it to find . . . textbooks and notes. "This looks like schoolwork."

"That's what I said." His arms are folded over his chest, cheeks flushing red.

There are two vials, the liquid inside a deep green with specks of red. "What class is this for?" I don't recognize the potions, which is saying something since I memorized my fair share.

Logan shrugs, looking so much like that little kid I entertained to distract from our parents' caskets and the mourners ogling us like zoo animals. "I'm taking a few advanced potion classes."

I frown. "I didn't know you had space in your schedule. You barely make it to your other classes. I never thought you were interested in pursuing potions as a career." Logan used to tell me everything, but I guess he learned from me how to keep secrets.

"Well, I actually like these ones, so it's easier to drag my ass there." He takes the bag back, depositing it into the locker with more care this time. "It's just for fun. I like to experiment with potions."

I place a hand on his shoulder, at the dip in his voice. "Switch your major to potions and become a creator. You'd be amazing at it." His name is always plastered across the tabloids as the playboy heir to the High Witch. It might be nice to surprise the vultures who think he's only useful for the next salacious story with his nerdy side.

His sad smile makes me ache. "You know the old man would never let me do that."

I release a heavy sigh. "I know."

"Will you keep it between us?" Deep frown lines crease between his eyes.

I study him for a moment before nodding. "Your secrets are always safe with me." So why can't I offer him the same?

The usual cheeky grin returns. I used to think he just didn't care, but maybe we are both wearing masks. "Did you still want to play?"

"Of course, you need another good ass kicking tonight." I rub my knuckles into his head.

I let myself forget about murders and dream wielders for the evening. Logan is an excellent distraction, as always. But as midnight hits, the witching hour calls, and I have a date to keep.

CHAPTER 20

Azalee

I stare across Salem, the cool breeze biting against my skin, reminding me this is real. I tried to bury myself in work today so I wouldn't sit around thinking about if I fucked up with Meera. A mind left to reflect can be a dangerous thing—intrusive thoughts have a way of worming deep and festering.

When we were kids, Meera, Iniko, and I would sneak up to the bell tower to eat junk food and tell each other all our secrets. Even though Iniko wasn't a dream wielder, like Meera and me, that didn't stop him from constantly asking what we learned after our lessons. He wished he could be a dream wielder too. At the time, none of us truly understood the price the tragedy required to gain these powers could exact.

There was no way to tell if Iniko was born with the dream wielder magic lying dormant inside. The only way to know was if a trauma happened and the power manifested. At first, we used to help him think of ways he could try to awaken it. My trauma was the result of a murder, so we couldn't replicate that. Meera's manifested after being stuck in a well for three days when a game of hide-and-seek went wrong. Iniko tried the well thing but only made it two hours before he just climbed out.

As I got older, I realized I didn't want him to have our powers. The risk wasn't worth it. I'd been right too, because when it finally happened, it was too much for his mind to cope with. After all that, he still didn't get to be a dream wielder.

I wish he had gone to university with Gabriel—played lacrosse or rugby or whatever fancy sport Gabriel no doubt excelled at. But when Iniko's family needed him, he traded all that so he could stay and help in the shop. A single change by the Fates made a life alter course.

Stairs creaking behind me startle me out of my trance. Gabriel's dark head appears moments later at the top of the stairs. "Were you hoping I'd fall to my death on the way up?" His cloak hangs open, revealing a gray Henley and jeans.

"The Fates work in mysterious ways." I lean against the safety rail, my back to the world.

He climbs up the final steps into the cramped outer observation ring. His commanding presence makes us mere inches apart. A swallow gets caught in my throat when his hand glides along my hip as he situates himself. His strong jaw is still etched in that teasing five-o'clock shadow. I grind my fist into my leg to keep my back from arching into him. That stupid tug from our connected gold thread makes me crave the closeness.

His long fingers run slowly over the bell, tracing the engravings. "How are you holding up?" I can't tell if the question is genuine or if he's making conversation.

I don't bother answering. Instead, I point to the sleeping bag I placed on the floor near us. "If you want to lie down, we can get this over with. I'm sure you have small animals to sacrifice for your hexes or whatever."

"Azalee, listen—"

I turn quickly, bumping into him, his strong arms entwining around me to keep me from falling. *Fucking heart, stop racing.* I should have taken a calming draught, but they can mess with my control in dream wielding, and I need to be sharp.

The tower is secluded, which is important, but I don't like feeling the heat of his body warming up my cold one. I could trace every freckle covering his nose and cheeks; it makes him feel human. Two years ago, I was all in on discovering every part of the marble statue that is Gabriel Ford, but not anymore. As pleasurable as that experience might be for a night, there aren't enough Milk Thistle Gummies to cure that hangover.

"I want you to be right," he says. I could almost think these close quarters weren't affecting him like me, but I notice how his eyes snag on my lips before darting back up. "I don't want dream wielders to be responsible for the murders." For a guy who pushed his ability so far away you'd need a spaceship to get there, this surprises me. I didn't think he cared what happened to us. Guess this is my second surprise of the day.

"Do you think they're guilty?" The moonlight is weak tonight, giving the stars their chance to shine. I find my fingers drifting to his arm, just to give my skin the briefest taste of him to satisfy the itch.

He takes in a deep breath, adjusting his belt. "Honestly, I don't know enough about them to say. But from what I know of Meera, she's not a murderer. I'm aware she's a well-trained dream wielder. If it's possible, I think she would know how to prevent it from happening."

I wish I saw these glimpses of him more often. The Gabriel who isn't trapped in his grandfather's shadow. Iniko always said he was there if you caught him in the right light. "So let me show you dream wielders aren't responsible. Then we can tell the High Witch he can fuck off and stop the crusade against us."

Ignoring me, he lies on the sleeping bag and closes his eyes. But I hear that *bull in a china shop* comment echoing in my head.

"What are you going to see?" His lip twitches slightly, but his eyes remain closed. I kneel beside him, aware of every inch of my body and his pressed against each other.

"Depends." I grab the clear quartz crystal and place it on his forehead; he cringes a little at the cold stone. "I can lead the dream, showing you what I want you to see. That's typically what we do with first-timers because their traumas are so fresh, but since yours was years ago, it shouldn't be an issue."

I only have a small lantern because while no one usually comes out this far, I didn't want to draw attention to us. Before I shut it off,

I watch the vein in his neck pulse as his heart rate ticks up each time I touch him. For a man who prefers to keep his emotions tucked away, his body is sure giving me a flashing neon sign of how he feels.

I could tease him about it, but I choose the high road for once in my life. "Or," I continue, "you can lead the dream, and I observe—or we can do a combo of both. Some people's minds aren't as creative and require more from the dream wielder. But when two dream wielders share a dream, both have more input."

I grip my pink rose quartz in one hand and the purple amethyst in the other. I have my moonstone around my neck tonight, close to my heart. "Okay." I swear I hear his teeth grinding as he tightens his jaw. Not the energy I love going into a dream. "Take deep, even breaths and try to fall asleep." I use a voice I wouldn't have with Gabriel in any other circumstance, but a successful dream requires trust.

His throat bobs. "I can't fall asleep on command. At home, I'd knock back a sleeping draught."

I smile, though he can't see it. Being in this position is a vulnerable one. I can't overlook that he's willing to do it. He's giving himself to me ultimately trusting I won't hurt him. A tiny shard of my icy heart breaks off and melts away. I didn't know he had that much faith in me.

"A sleeping tonic makes things fuzzy in the dream." I take a sachet of herbs from my bag. It contains thyme, lavender, anise, and red jasper. I wave the bag around his body in slow clockwise circles. "This will help induce sleep. We use it often with new dream wielders." I place the bag near his head, the calming scents filling the air.

"Focus on my voice," I begin.

I slowly talk him into a deep meditative state. Entering into a chaotic mind is fun for no one. I repeat the lines until I see his breath slow. I'm still having trouble focusing on auras too long, but I get enough of a peek to see it's relaxed.

He's asleep. It only takes about six minutes, pretty quick actually. He looks peaceful. I resist the urge to run a hand over his softened face. In sleep, we see a person's true colors—their auras cannot conceal themselves.

Gabriel's aura is typically a dark green edging on black with hints of the yellow and indigo of a dream wielder. But it's lightened to a forest green. He's far more caring and nurturing than I would've guessed from his waking persona. Pushing my magic further, I read deeper into the colors—faint lines of deep purple, almost black, cut through the other colors. He's extremely worried. I wince as a phantom knife of fire cuts into my brain, forcing me to shut down my aura investigation.

I can enter into a dream anytime now, but I hesitate. *What if I'm wrong?* What if dream wielding has been the cause of these deaths? My mind flashes to my nightmare-like experience last night. If something is wrong with me, this could be dangerous for both of us.

But if I can convince him that dream wielding is safe, he might be able to bend his grandfather's ear—having someone so close to the High Witch to persuade him might be our only chance to make headway. Gabriel, for all his faults, wants the truth. He wouldn't condemn someone just for being a dream wielder, not without evidence to back it up. Perhaps him not revealing himself just yet might actually be useful. Also, I don't want to kill Gabriel. He's not my friend, but he's not a monster like the High Witch.

I close my eyes, entering into his dream world.

Everyone's dreams are different. Some are almost carbon copies of our world, so much so that you might not even be able to tell you're dreaming if you didn't know what you were looking for. Others only dream in black and white. But the dream I'm letting Gabriel create is big, as in capital *B*.

Sleek silver metal walls surround me as I step through Gabriel's round door into his dreamscape. It takes me a minute to acclimate to the dream I'm letting him facilitate. It looks like a spaceship, based on the copious screens lining the hallway that provide details of planets, ship speed, and relative location of the vehicle. I don't know a lot about space observation, but apparently, Gabriel does.

I don't see him immediately, but since this is his dream, he's here somewhere. I decided not to influence his dream to start with. I was curious to see what he could come up with.

I make no sound as I walk. The hallway lets out into a giant observation room with a whole wall of windows. I spot Gabriel standing near it, gazing into the vastness of space.

It's breathtaking. The entirety of the universe is laid out before us, with dazzling stars and planets for as far as the eye can see. Every inch of the sky is more awe-inspiring than the last in bold Technicolor.

Gabriel wears a sleek white officer's uniform, with a hat tucked under his arm. He looks like he should be part of the navy in that outfit. I'll be honest: I never thought I was into a man in uniform, but this is doing it for me.

It's then I realize we aren't the only people in the observatory. Some are monitoring reports, wearing similar uniforms to Gabriel, but others wear intricate masquerade gowns and tuxedos, complete with masks and feathered headdresses. A common theme in dreams is the blending of multiple ideas and situations.

I observe Gabriel for a minute as he takes a cocktail from a passing server. He sips it slowly and gazes into the universe he's created. He may not even realize this is a dream. Some people don't. Especially new dream wielders, who are used to dreaming. He hasn't dreamed for two years; I'm guessing he might have some idea.

"Pretty impressive," I say, coming beside him.

He looks slightly dazed before recognition clicks in. "This is a dream."

"It is. You created it. And it's pretty good."

He cracks a smile. "Did it kill you to compliment me?"

"Well, it is just a dream, which means I didn't *actually* compliment you in real life. So I'll let it pass."

Gabriel turns around and looks at the rest of the room. "When I was little, I wanted to be a spaceman. Used to dream about a place like this. You know . . . before."

"I wanted to be a ballerina." I guess if we're in the sharing mode, I can offer a little something. "I remember the first few times my mother dream wielded with me after I gained my powers. I used to pretend I was performing *The Nutcracker* in front of a huge audience."

I hadn't created that experience in some time. The longer you let your dreams drift away, the more you forget about them.

Gabriel's eyes run down the length of me, taking their sweet-ass time before coming back to my face. "I think you'd make a fantastic ballerina." As soon as the words leave his mouth, my clothes slowly melt into a swirl of fabric on my bare skin. The caress feels like his hands are creating a masterpiece, turning the textile into a light-pink leotard and tulle skirt. The outfit is complete with pastel ballet shoes.

I wish I didn't want to smile right now. My cheeks ache as I attempt to hold in the encouragement I should give him. "Thanks. I was feeling underdressed."

"Apparently"—he nods toward the dance floor—"there's a masquerade ball going on. I wanted you to fit in. I'm considerate like that."

"As am I." I use a little bit of my magic to influence the dream, adding space-themed masks to Gabriel's and my faces.

"So, what do we do now?" Gabriel asks.

"We can do whatever you want. It's your dream." That might sound like a simple statement, but in the dreamscape, the possibilities are endless—overwhelming to lots of newbie dream wielders. But Gabriel likes to take charge. I'm sure he can figure something out.

The other dream figures begin to dance as a piano melody trickles out of the speakers on the wall. Shooting stars cascade across the sky in time to the music. "Seems like everyone's dancing," Gabriel says.

"That must mean you want to dance. You're controlling the dream."

"I am?" Delight flares in his features.

I nod.

"I didn't know I could do that. I thought it would be harder." For a guy who I assumed everything came easy to, the shock in his voice isn't what I expected.

"Well, it's much easier to control your dream when I'm here with you. It takes a little more practice to dream wield into someone else's dream. But you could do it." I know I said I gave up on him, but the truth is, I'll never give up on any dream wielder.

Gabriel places his hand out. "Will you dance with me?"

I hesitate, studying his open palm. "You wanted me to kill you . . . Do you think that's going to do it?"

I expect a smart-ass response, but that's not what I get. "Honestly, with you in that outfit, it may kill me not to dance with you."

Fuck me. That was a good line. How am I supposed to say no to that?

Throwing caution to the wind, I accept his hand, and he whisks me to the dance floor among the other phantoms. I call them that because they aren't quite corporeal. I expected as much. In the early stages, it can be hard to concentrate your magic on a whole scene. The more you practice and build the magic muscle, the more realistic the dreams appear.

"One slight outfit alteration," I say. I click my heels together, and my pointe shoes turn into pink wedge boots. "Perfect."

Gabriel's half smile makes my chest do unnatural things as he places a hand on my waist. "Try to keep up," he whispers in my ear, sending chills down my spine.

My lips brush his cheek when I turn my head. "Oh, Gabriel, trust me, there's nothing you can do I can't keep speed with." I let those words linger as the music starts.

We perform an intricate dance that all the rest of his creations know as well. I'm typically not into letting someone else lead, but since I'm being so charitable with Gabriel tonight, I'll let it slide. As we glide, the gold thread of fate weaves around us, glowing brighter as it tightens, drawing us closer.

"I wouldn't have pegged you for a good dancer," I say as we sashay in a large circle. The room flashes in and out of the space station, turning into a grand ballroom and back again—another signal of an untrained dream wielder.

"The High Witch loves a gala, and some of those include dancing. Logan and I had to learn from a young age." Our bodies press together as he lifts me in the air and spins. I grip his shoulders, trying and failing to ignore the strong muscles that flex under me. With a wiggle of my nose, his uniform could disappear, and I'd have free range to explore every inch of his physique, should he be willing. I could put those muscles to work in all kinds of ways.

Chill. This is Gabriel we're talking about—a no-fly zone.

Not wanting the mention of the High Witch to dampen the rather lovely atmosphere, I change the subject. "You should've danced with me at Eclipse the other night."

He slides me down the front of him as we complete the spin. His warm hands glide up my arms before resetting to the standard dance posture. "Would you have let me?"

I bite my lip. "Probably not. Don't want you ruining my street cred. I can't be seen fraternizing with the enemy."

His hand trails along my waist, the thin fabric of the leotard making me feel every part of him. "Am I your enemy?"

The universe dances across his eyes, making my throat dry. I clear it before speaking. I do not need Gabriel thinking his presence is doing anything to my body. "I didn't want you to be. But you made that choice for both of us. I was just following your lead."

The record scratches, and the music stops. The cosmos vanishes from his eyes. "Should we do what we came here for?" A stiffness has returned to his speech.

But I'm not done yet. If I only get one chance in Gabriel's dream, I'm taking my sweet time.

I roll my eyes. "You're such a buzzkill. Enjoy the dream for more than a second. What have you always wanted to do but couldn't?"

His fingers dig into my waist, his chest rising and falling as I press against him. Swallowing hard, he looks out to the vastness beyond the window before dragging his firelit eyes back to me. "Swim in the stars."

Guiding him to the window, I press my pointer finger into the glass. From the pressure point, the glass begins to crack into beautiful constellations until it breaks into a million pieces and bursts into the universe, turning into stars.

Three steps appear, and I ascend them until I'm even with the cosmos. "One star bath made to order." I spread my arms to the side like I'm about to take flight. Closing my eyes, I imagine a swirling star dancing around me as my clothes melt away, exposing my skin.

I hear Gabriel suck in a breath as he takes in what I'm guessing is a *fucking* great view of my ass. I peek over my shoulder with a wink before diving into the stars.

The water is the perfect temperature. I can't tell where my body ends and the cosmos begins. "You going to stand there all day, or are you going to join me?" I float on my back, creating clouds over myself so I don't overwhelm poor Gabriel.

Looking at him upside down, I twirl my fingers through the stars as I study him.

Unlike me, he doesn't use dream magic to remove his uniform. He shrugs off each piece one by one, keeping eye contact with me the whole time. *Dick.* He knows exactly what he's doing.

When he pulls off his shirt, I notice a tattoo on the underside of his arm. It's of the constellation Aquarius intertwined with a dandelion flower.

Any interpretation I'm about to do on that symbolism is stopped in its tracks as I follow the lines of his muscles to his abs and the deep-cut V of his lower abdomen. My mouth is full of cotton balls, and the muscles in my jaw are working overtime as I struggle to keep my face neutral.

Like me, he slips off his pants and creates a cloud to block out the family jewels. His face is unreadable when he looks at me as he dives into the water, leaving no splash in his wake.

The water glitters and shimmers as I watch his form glide underneath it. Poking his head up, he swims toward me. "I can breathe underwater." His eyes are wide with wonder, the surprise in his voice endearing.

"It is a dream. Anything is possible." With a single thought, I turn the deep-navy water into a dark purple sparkling with pink stars and galaxies all around us, going on for infinity.

"It's beautiful," he says, eyes on mine. I hope he doesn't notice how my heart beats into the water, pulsing toward him as it ticks faster. "It doesn't feel like this could ever harm someone. It's pure *magic.*"

The way he says that is exactly how I always feel when I dream wield. That all other magic feels unremarkable in comparison.

"Should we—" I start, but he grabs my hand and pulls me under the water before I can get us back on track for this outing.

We swim through underwater caverns and coral made of planets and comets. We're both naked, but the stars shimmer around us, obstructing a clear view. I'm not sure which one of us is doing that or if our subconscious is smarter than we are.

Time moves differently in the dreamscape. It feels like hours lost in the cosmos, but only minutes have passed in the real world. Since I'm in charge of this dream wield, it's just me who has the real sense of time.

And as much as I'm enjoying this little side trip—it can't last. Eventually, I will have to wake him up, and before I do, I need to do what we came here for.

Time to push the dreamscape to its limits.

CHAPTER 21

Gabriel

When I woke up this morning, I didn't think I'd end the day swimming in the stars. The unending vastness of space glides past us as I kick my feet faster, arms barely feeling the strain of the hours spent in this beautiful, ethereal water. When I used to dream about space, this is exactly what I imagined.

Of course it is, because this is my dream.

I'm the one who's creating all this, or most of it. I know Azalee is lending a bit of magic. I was terrified to dream wield. I thought I'd find myself lost in the chaos of my mind. But it feels so natural. I don't have to think about it; it's like breathing. It is the heart of what magic is: pure creation. No one could be scared of dream wielding if they experience this themselves.

As that sentiment sinks in, I know it's not true. Even if I could think of a way to explain this to Grandfather, he'd never understand. His anger and distrust of dream wielders have festered for too many decades.

"Gabriel," Azalee says beside me, taking my hand to stop my swimming. "It's time."

"Time?" I float on my back, counting the stars. It's like being in a sensory deprivation tank.

Azalee doesn't respond. The sky turns bloodred, lightning shooting across the once-pleasant vastness.

Oh, right, it's time to show me the limits of the dreamscape. I didn't forget, but I started thinking perhaps this was all a dream wielder could do. But we have a few murders to solve, and this thing I thought might be beautiful could be as deadly as a poisonous flower hiding behind a colorful facade.

Lightning continues to strike, hitting the water's surface and making the liquid evaporate in its wake. Losing my ability to float, I slam into the hard surface of a planet—razor-sharp rocks and broken glass slice into my skin on impact. Luckily, I'm back in my regular clothes or I'd have cuts in very uncomfortable places.

"Fuck." I roll onto my side, skin stinging as I rise on my elbow. "Couldn't have given a guy a little warning?"

"Sorry, but that won't work for this little activity." Azalee stands above me unharmed. I frown when I notice she's back in her regular clothes too. I'm going to mourn the glimpse I got during our swim. But those images are permanently burned into my memory.

For a moment, it almost felt like we were . . . I don't know, friends? Clearly, this is a dream.

Azalee continues, "I'm going to have to search your mind to find what scares you."

"You'll see my thoughts?" My body feels too heavy after the weightlessness of space. It's getting harder to breathe.

"I can see whatever I want. Unless you think you're strong enough to stop me." There's a challenge in her voice. I almost rise to the bait, but the words dry up in my throat.

I cough to spit them out, but can't make my voice work.

"Cat got your tongue?" She smiles wickedly.

I gasp as I try to speak.

She shakes her head. "No, that's not what scares you." She looks up like the threatening sky is giving her an answer. "Beetles.

Creepy-crawly pinching beetles." As she says the last words, I feel a slither in my throat.

I cough harder this time, my stomach contracting with each movement. Something hard hits my teeth, and I spit furiously, expelling two red-and-black beetles.

"Fucking hell." My voice is rough.

Her brows dip. "I want you to remember." Her voice is quieter. "This was your idea."

And then she's gone and I'm alone on a rocky planet with a storm for the ages brewing above me.

I steady myself, spitting one more time to get the taste of bug out of my mouth, wiping away the residue with the backs of my hands. Then I drop them to my sides, keeping them loose, ready to squeeze into fists at a moment's notice. Always stay on guard for a fight; that way, no one can surprise you. But somehow, I doubt I'll be able to punch my way out of whatever Azalee has planned.

The ground shakes as the planet spins until it disappears, and I'm shrouded in darkness—the kind where you can't even see your hand an inch from your face. I used to be scared of the dark when I was little, but I got over that ages ago. As the dark remains, the silence deafening, I realize it's not dark I'm scared of but the sensation that I'm completely and utterly alone.

No one knows where I am. No one will find me.

"Azalee," I call out, hoping she'll respond.

I feel slithering up my neck, and I scratch at my skin, grabbing the beetle and tossing it into the abyss.

I will not sit and be preyed on. I make my way through the dark, walking and hoping that I don't run straight off the side of a cliff or into a pit full of alligators. As I go, I notice the ground underneath changes into hard cement. I catch whiffs of damp earth and the subtle sweetness of windswept trees.

Why am I here?

Did I go for a walk?

It's a dream.

Lightning cracks through the sky again, and I see a house ahead of me. The one I lived in with my parents before they died. I stop in my tracks. I don't want to go farther, and not just because I see blood dripping from the windows, soiling the flowers in the window boxes.

This is mad. They didn't die in that house. None of this is real.

Or is it? It feels like the real world. The cuts on my arms sting, and the sweat dripping into my mouth is salty. All five senses are telling me I'm experiencing this.

They're dangerous, the way they can take your mind and manipulate it. I recall the words Grandfather drilled into Logan and me, telling us the story of his assassination attempt again and again, until it became the stuff of legends. My heart beats in my throat; the wind lashing around me feels like it might rip it out. Lightning intensifies as the rain thunders down.

Scurrying behind me draws my attention. I listen to tiny nails clawing against the cement. Rats. I know it's rats. Because I hate them, she knows I hate them. I should be furious at Azalee, but I'm actually fucking impressed. As terrifying as this is and as high as my blood pressure must be, I don't think these illusions could kill me.

Still, I don't want to stand here, so I keep trudging along. Gravestones pop up as I push onward, impeding my way in the middle of the road. They have my parents' names, Logan's, and Grandfather's. Every person I've ever known is dead.

I'm alone.

And then I see my gravestone. I drop to my knees, bones cracking. I run my fingers over the text.

Here lies Gabriel Ford

And although it doesn't say it, I know why I'm dead. Because I'm a dream wielder. If Grandfather finds out, I'll be dead to him. Logan too. Dream wielders are the reason my family lost so much. Everyone I care about will paint me with that same brush.

Murderer.

The scurrying gets louder and heavier. I turn to look, and I'm smacked in the face by a solid right hook. My head hits the back of the gravestone before it disappears. I fall for several minutes before landing in the middle of a gladiator-fighting arena. The stadium crowd roars. I cover my ears as the sound pounds against my brain.

"Get up." It's the voice of many, echoing around me.

I blink, squinting against the hot sun's rays. About a dozen guys circle me. They're fucking huge, well over seven feet and as wide as trucks. Each wears a different animal carcass over his head. The smell of fresh blood stings my nostrils.

The one closest to me wears a lion's head, his ripped muscles glistening with the sweat and blood of the last person he killed. "You have to fight."

I can't fight, can't move my arms at all. They feel like they weigh three thousand pounds.

"Fight." It's the chanting of the crowd now.

I want to fight. But the more I try to move, the less I can. I can't breathe. Whatever's holding me down is squishing my lungs. I'm going to drown in my own sweat and blood.

The kicking starts, cracking into my bones and flesh. The fists are next, blow after blow, my skin on fire as the burn rips into my insides.

Then I see her. Azalee. She's perched on the edge of the ring, face pinched as she watches the beating.

I'm dreaming. *I am dreaming.*

This is my dream, and I take charge.

Closing my eyes, I imagine a sunlit day by the beach. The rocky shoreline extends as far as I can see.

The roaring crowd goes silent, the rhythmic crashing of the waves replacing it. Tension oozes from my body as I relax into the soft folds of the warm sand.

My chest sings as I release a breath, no pain following.

"Well done." Azalee's voice makes me open my eyes.

"You didn't kill me."

She stands above me, sun backlighting her so she looks like the angel who saved me all those years ago. "I told you I couldn't."

I close my eyes, relishing the fresh air. "What a fucking weird night."

CHAPTER 22

Azalee

I'm not in the habit of creating scary dreams for people. But there are times in therapy sessions when you have to bring people face-to-face with the trauma they've experienced to heal. All in all, I did a pretty badass job creating a series of scary events to get Gabriel's heart thumping. Of course, there are a few other ways I would have preferred to make him sweat after our swim.

It didn't take a lot of digging to know what scenarios to conjure to scare him. Newbie dream wielders aren't good at hiding things; their minds are open books. I asked for things that frightened him, and his subconscious provided. Everything was terrible but not terrifying.

I felt the call, though—the scratching at the back of my mind to keep going, to peek a little more into the darkness. I drowned out the temptation with the thoughts of Meera and Iniko, of all the dream wielders out there who will suffer if I don't stop this witch hunt.

When it was evident I'd given him enough to placate his curiosity about what a dream wielder could and couldn't accomplish, I let him take back control of the dream. He moves us to sit on the edge of a cliff overlooking the ocean as the sun sets.

"It was a good attempt," he says. "The whole blood in the windows was a particularly creepy addition."

I laugh. "I saw it in a horror movie once."

His face glows with pinks and oranges. Ever since our swim, I can't stop imagining what it would be like to kiss him, which is super problematic when operating in a dream. You need to control your thoughts and feelings so you don't show your cards.

"My heart rate was high, but not enough to kill me." Gabriel leans back on his hands. He's so beautiful it hurts. Inside the dreamscape, we let the pretenses of who we are—of what society demands of us—drop away. But it won't last. Dreams never do.

Since we are still in a dream, I take my sweet time to enjoy the view while I can. "I told you dream wielding couldn't kill people. While I was manipulating the dream, creating the narrative, your mind knew when to stop it from going too far."

That's a tiny white lie. *I* knew when to stop it. How to quiet the call of the darkness, the things waiting on the other side of the door, ready to pounce if only I let them in. But the lie is more about myself than dream wielding specifically. Because I normally don't feel the darkness. I picture the visions I had the other night, pain spreading across my ribs.

Azalee, don't. There are too many other lives at stake to worry about myself.

"Do people ever . . ." He hesitates, biting his bottom lip. "If you can create anything in a dream, can you create people who have died?" His eyes are steady when he looks at me despite the uncertainty in his voice.

I shake my head, even as I say, "Yes. I can create a shadow of them. A figment as real as the people dancing in your space station." My heart aches as the light leaves his eyes because I know what he wanted to hear. It's the same thing I wish were true too. That dreams could bring back the dead. "But those wouldn't be your parents, Gabriel. Just like any version of my dad I conjure won't be the one I knew."

He nods, staring out at the ocean instead of looking at me. But he doesn't need to for me to feel his anguish. His dreamscape seeps the feeling into the rocks and grass beneath us, turning it cold.

I take his hand, the warmth welcoming. "I'm sorry. I wish I could give you another answer."

Still avoiding my gaze, he looks at our joined hands. "You get it more than anyone else would, I guess. Did you ever try it? Creating your dad?"

"Yeah, one of the first times my mom let me control a dream wield. I knew I shouldn't because it can really fuck with your head, but I did it anyway."

He laughs and the warmth returns to the dream. "Of course you did."

I push his hand away, casting him a withering glare, but there is no malice behind it this time. "*Anyway.* It looked just like him, but it was wrong, like a wax figure in a museum. But if my mom hadn't been there to force the dream to restructure, I might have made myself believe it was him." That's the danger of a dream—even when you tell yourself it's not real, inside it can be hard to believe it isn't.

We sit in silence, both contemplating another lifetime that might have been. Before he clears his throat and says, "So, I guess it's possible the dream wielders are innocent. Maybe you weren't wrong in thinking someone else is responsible." Gabriel's hand finds my cheek, turning my head toward him. I don't pull away. "I only ever wanted the truth. This was the next step in finding it."

I lean my face into his hand because *fuck it*—I want to. I want to forget about my failures in the real world for just a moment. I let the dreamscape do what it does best and distract my conscious mind. "Gabriel . . ." Everything is more intense in dreams. The urgency of my desire dances like musical notes on my skin. That can be the only reason I lean into Gabriel farther, my lips lingering inches from his. Our warm breath mingling, the smell of chocolate and mint dancing in the air.

His eyes drop to my lips as he licks his own. "I have a terrible idea."

"I'm sure you're used to those," I say without thinking.

He shakes his head, those lips calling to me as he gives that devastating half smile. Did I always think he was this sexy? Surely not. It's the dream. But right now all I want is to feel him, *taste him.*

"Azalee . . ." But he doesn't finish the sentence before my lips crash into his, forgetting every line I ever drew between us. I want him, and I can tell when someone wants me. He tangles his hands in my hair as mine run up his chest and neck, my fingers grazing his skin, burning at the touch. For one minute I want only this to exist.

I moan into his mouth as he drags me into his lap, pressing me into him until there's no way to tell where one starts and the other begins. The hard muscles I spied earlier flex under my hands as I tear at his shirt. His skin is ablaze, the heat radiating against my palms as I explore the lines of his well-earned physique. Not to be outdone, Gabriel's fingers slip under my T-shirt, sliding along my hips and dip of my waist. Our breaths are ragged as we kiss furiously, knowing it's a first and should be a last.

The world slips away, and we're floating on a pink cloud. My head is full of nothing but his lips, the hint of mint and chocolate on my tongue, his hands removing any thoughts I might try to conjure. I want all of him. I need it. The fire burning inside me will burst if I don't get it.

Gabriel and me. Me and Gabriel dreaming.

A dream.

This is a dream.

The heaviness he vanished with his touch settles back into my bones. I pull away first. When he wakes up, the world will still be crashing around us. Dreams can only keep you safe for so long.

Azalee, there are more important things at stake.

Taking the wise path is a pain in the ass, but I do it anyway. "You need to speak to the High Witch." I remove myself from him, straightening my shirt. I press a fist into my lips, trying to forget what he felt like. Somehow, I don't think that sensation will ever truly leave me.

His brows dip in confusion at my sudden change in subject. "I'll ask him about the murders. Push to see if there is other evidence that was overlooked." His breath comes out rough, laboring to bring himself back to the present. "But until I gather more rock-hard evidence, I need to be in stealth mode. I'm not going to blow things up just for the hell of it and make it even harder to find answers through the wreckage. If he thinks something is up, he'll double his wards, and they're already a bitch to break."

I shake my head, forcing myself not to look at his lips. "No, I mean you need to tell him you're a dream wielder. You can't keep hiding it. If you tell him, maybe he'll let up on the rest of us, and realize we aren't the enemy. You're in a unique position to get him to listen. You're his blood." I get slow and steady wins the race, blah, blah, whatever. That might work fine if people weren't dying and our kind weren't being hunted like monsters.

The dream changes, and we are back at the space station. I stumble at the sudden transformation, caught off guard.

"You overestimate my grandfather's love for me. He won't stop because I'm a dream wielder. He'd make sure I never saw my brother again, for starters."

Despite all the times I've fucked up, my mom would love me no matter what. Is it fair I push Gabriel into surrendering the only family he has left? Even though half of his family is a tyrant?

Gabriel continues, "Hell, he'd probably use me as an example. Lock me up for testing, for all I know."

I blink, losing my other train of thought. "Does he do that?"

"What?" The dream is flickering in and out as he loses concentration.

"Testing—has he got dream wielders locked away somewhere?"

His eyes narrow. "No." The temperature drops, thunder roaring in the distance. The station disappears, and we're in an orange desert.

"No? You know this for sure?" I press my cool hand against my flushed face, brushing hair from my eyes before the wind blows it right back.

"I've never seen any dream wielder prisoners."

"Doesn't mean there aren't any." A bolt of lightning shoots across the black sky. "So you're content to stay hidden away, living a lie? Knowing maybe your grandfather is experimenting on innocent dream wielders." My blood boils as the wind thrashes against my bones.

He runs his hands over his mouth, bringing them to rest on his hip bones as he looks up at the sky. "It's not as simple as you're trying to convince me it is." His eyes find mine again, lines creasing his forehead. "Some of us only have a lie. It's the only thing allowing us to keep our thin grasp on our lives."

I frown, shoulders sagging. "I don't get it—*you.* You said you stopped the High Witch's bullshit before, but now you won't."

The lines on his forehead deepen, his eyes hardening into a glare. "You don't have to *get it* because it's not your life. I'm sorry I can't be this perfect, stand-up guy you want me to be. I'm trying the best I can to get through life. I don't know any other way."

I fold my arms, bracing myself against the harsh gusts. "You're content to let others suffer so you don't have to?" I'm kinda being a bitch, but I need to make him wake up and see things my way.

"Don't you dare twist my words. I said I wanted to find the truth." A flash of lightning hurls across the sky, followed by a clap of thunder rattling my teeth. "That bill the High Witch proposed is extreme, and the likelihood of it passing is pretty slim. So, let him stay busy working on something that is dead in the water while we continue to gather evidence. Dream wielders are fine for the moment—there are no secret prisons we're aware of. They aren't being rounded up and executed."

"Except for the ones that are." My voice rages louder than the approaching storm. The dream is magnifying my voice to unearthly levels. "The ones being accused of murder."

He throws his hands in the air as sheets of freezing rain bounce off my skin. "What do you want from me, Azalee?" he asks, his voice suddenly quiet. "I am doing this the best way I know how to get an outcome that is going to stick. The High Witch is the law, so we need an equally strong one to oppose him."

I press my lips together. "I want you to grow the fuck up and stand up to your hate-mongering grandfather."

We wake up on the bell tower, the anger still flowing through my veins brought back through a dream.

CHAPTER 23

Gabriel

My feet pound against the treadmill, legs cramping, but I push forward. I take a swig of my water infused with Energy Boost. I don't slow my pace as I stare at the wall with laser focus. It's been a few days since I dreamed with Azalee, but the experience is burned in my fucking brain. Sleep hasn't come easy now that my brain remembers that dreaming used to be a thing. It's decided to toss and turn until I pass out from exhaustion or too much sleeping tonic.

Which is why I've been up late every day arranging my investigation wall like a man possessed. When I got home from work, I jumped on the treadmill to focus my thoughts into a useful vision. Over the last few days, I've collected as much information as I could about the murder victims and the suspects. I've arranged them on my wall to give me a visual in hopes of finding the missing link that will crack the cases wide open.

Three of the murders are people with tiny footprints as far as the social landscape is concerned. They were all unassuming, with scant backgrounds and social circles. The second victim still hasn't been identified. They make perfect targets in the eyes of someone who wants to get away with these crimes. The only oddity is that the culprits left the bodies in places they would easily be found. From a profiling perspective, I'm guessing that says something about the killer. I just don't know what it is yet.

I know what Azalee would say. *Someone is trying to draw attention to these deaths and blame them on dream wielders.* I'm not saying she's wrong, but we also have no proof she's right.

A vision of Azalee naked in the stars flashes into my mind. The way the cosmos danced off her pale skin, her icy-blond hair filled with the colors of the universe.

Cut that shit out, Ford. We don't need Azalee distracting us when she's not even here.

I turn up the treadmill faster and regroup. My headphones blare to drown out any external stimuli that might get in the way of my investigation.

The other death, Grant's, doesn't fit the profile. He had lots of friends and was a well-known healer, and his killer, Meera, was at the scene. Hell, she called the cops. That's an outlier, which could mean it's not related to the other three, but I've kept it on my board because it's still connected to the dream wielders, which means it's important.

The killing spree took three victims, possibly four, in two short days, but we've had nothing the last few. Tonight is the annual Salem October Festival, and I have an instinct that might mean our luck is over. My talents don't lie in hearing spirits or messages from the other side, but I know when to trust my gut.

I reach for my water bottle to take another drink, but it's empty. Troubling, since I barely noticed the energy potion doing anything. I should get ready for the festival, but I keep running.

Some might argue I'm running from something, but I'm racing to it. If I keep going, the answer will reveal itself. *Nothing stays hidden forever.* Azalee told me that when I refused to acknowledge I was a dream wielder. I prayed she was wrong, I guess we'll see.

When I gathered the case reports from the police, I was hoping they'd discovered evidence with a finding spell or an autopsy, but sadly, they seem as lost as I am when it comes to possible suspects. Some elements of these crimes feel highly calculated, and others are totally sloppy. The one suspect they have confessed to the last murder, but nothing is tying him to the others. Meera has alibis for the other two—so while she hasn't been totally ruled out, there also isn't anything to charge her with.

I jump when someone touches my arm. "Gods, you scared the shit out of me." I rip my headphones from my ears, staring at my brother. "What are you doing here?"

"What am I doing here? What are *you* doing here? We're supposed to be leaving for the festival."

I glance down at my watch. "Fuck." Grandfather told us to be ready at six forty-five, and I'm not close to presentable.

Flipping off the treadmill, I jog to the shower, undressing and stepping into the hot stream. "Go, tell the old man I'll meet you there."

"Nope, can't do that." Logan whistles. "Apparently, he needs a united front. I'm here to round you up."

I swear, scrubbing soap into my hair and rinsing it quickly. My fatigued muscles quiver with their disapproval, but I ignore them.

"Dude," Logan says when I get out of the bathroom. He sits at my kitchen counter, adding a few sprigs of eucalyptus and a ground powder to the potion I made on the stovetop. I don't bother to ask what he's doing. Logan is wicked skilled at potions. "What's up with the murder board?"

"It's not a murder board." I sprinkle Quick Dry on my hair. My scalp tingles. I don't love the texture it leaves, but I'm rushing. Plus, it's not like anyone's going to be touching it.

"Are those not murdered people?" He runs a hand across his dark scruff. Grandfather hates when we aren't clean shaven. The old me would have made Logan shave before we left so as not to incur the old man's wrath, but today I'm siding with the subtle rebellion.

"Yes, those are victims of a crime I'm attempting to solve. So, some might call it a murder board if they wanted to be insensitive to the dearly departed." I take the stairs to my bedroom two at a time. I draw my suit from the closet. Most people aren't wearing suits to a festival, but the High Witch plans to make a speech, and when we stand behind him, this is the armor he prefers.

"Did you solve it?" Logan yells, then adds a few beats later, "You don't think dream wielders can kill people? How the hell would you know? Have you been doing some moonlighting that I need to know about?"

I freeze in the middle of buttoning my shirt. I hadn't expected anyone to come in and scrutinize my board and I'm suddenly wondering if I put any information on it that might give me away. "I . . . read it in a book. The evidence from previous crimes can't definitively say dream wielders can kill people."

"Seriously? They're all monsters. Aren't they?"

"You think so?" I say, meeting him back in the living room.

He frowns. "Isn't that what the old man preaches? You always told me we needed to listen to him. That he was our family, and he wouldn't steer us wrong."

Pain radiates across my ribs, and I rub hard to make it stop. I haven't told Logan what I know about Grandfather's ailing health. But if the end is near, I should sooner rather than later. "I did say that." Logan hates dream wielders because I encouraged him to listen to the High Witch. He doesn't make public statements on the matter like I have being in the High Witch's office, but he's never spoken against it either. I wanted to keep Logan from making waves with the old man and getting himself in trouble. It was easier if we just acquiesced. But now I wonder if I did Logan more harm than good. "I'm just covering all of the bases."

"I wouldn't let Grandfather see that part when you make your presentation."

"I'm not presenting anything, at least not until I have some leads. Ready?"

He glances at the potion bubbling away on the stove. "Don't leave that on past midnight. It'll burn and fuck up the magic."

"I know." It's a high-dose sleep tonic—a pain in the ass to brew even with my specialty in potions, which is why you usually get them from healers. But I don't want to explain to Grandfather's healers why I need it.

Sitting in the back of the SUV with Logan and Grandfather, I let my mind drift to the kiss with Azalee. It absolutely should not have happened. But I didn't know how badly I wanted it until I had it. Now it's like I can feel her touch all over me—her tongue in my mouth. Fuck me because I need to do it again.

That evening ended like all conversations with Azalee and me: in a fight. She wants something from me I'm never going to be able to give her. If it were just sex, we'd be fine. But we're too intertwined in bullshit to leave emotions out of it. Like that life debt, for example. I wonder if that's making these emotions stronger.

"Gabriel, were you listening?" Grandfather says.

"Sorry. Work stuff." I'm usually a better multitasker. Logan's brows are dipped into a deep V and I'm worried I missed something important. "What did you say?"

Grandfather huffs, hating to repeat himself. "I was telling you boys that I plan to introduce my new bill to the public tonight."

I stiffen as my body senses danger ahead.

"To register dream wielders . . ." Logan drops off, unsure. This must be the first time he's hearing about this since he doesn't work in the office. He's allowed to be blissfully unaware of the politics. "Sounds . . . uh . . . aggressive."

"I wasn't under the impression we were ready to formally introduce that yet." I choose my words carefully, not letting any emotions in. "I know a few senators have requested meetings with you to discuss the details first."

"They can talk all they want, but this is clearly a magical issue. Which means it belongs in our purview. It's my duty to inform the citizens of legislation I'm bringing to a vote."

I grind my molars, jaw aching with a sudden pop.

Logan glances between us uneasily. "Do you think that's a good idea?" He comes to my aid. Gods, I don't think he understands how much that means to me. Because I'm afraid I might lose it if I opened my mouth right now. "The festival is supposed to be a tourist thing. It's fun. Do we want to bring politics into it?"

"Son, politics are everywhere. And we have a captive audience. You do not want to let that opportunity go to waste. The murders have put citizens on edge. They want reassurance from their High Witch."

After momentarily collecting myself, I push back again. "People want answers, sure, but this bill is no small motion. It's bound to have a polarizing effect. Many might think it problematic that we're trying to make dream wielders second-class citizens."

He levels me with a piercing stare. My hand closes around my watch. "Monsters seek shelter from storms just like anything else. If non–dream wielder citizens speak out against this bill, it will reveal to us who would assist them should the situation arise. That information would be prudent to have."

I switch tactics. "Grandfather, I haven't had enough time to study the bill. The office will be inundated with emails and calls after this and I want to make sure we have all our ducks in a row, lest we look unprepared." Maybe if he thinks he'll look like a fool I can delay him a little longer. I do believe what I told Azalee—that getting this bill passed would be a fucking miracle—but just the idea of it is a dangerous enough situation. Perhaps her concerns weren't totally unwarranted.

"When you are the High Witch, you can make such decisions. But as of now, that position is mine alone. And as you are aware, time is not on our side." He pats his jacket pocket where he keeps his vial from the healers. As if I need a reminder of the mortality knocking at his door.

Logan frowns, glancing between us, but stays quiet just as we were taught.

I recognize the tone for what he's not saying: *end of discussion.*

Azalee said I might get my grandfather to listen, but I don't think I can. And once I tell him I'm a dream wielder, there's no going back. Not only will I lose my valuable access to the High Witch's resources, but I will be cut out of this family and Logan will be left to fend off the wolves of this world alone. I couldn't survive losing my whole family, even if that does make me a coward.

"You'll be on stage in ten minutes," the festival director tells us when we arrive. "High Witch, if we could get a few photos beforehand?"

"Of course." Grandfather and the director leave while Logan and I are left in the waiting area behind the outdoor stage.

My stomach gurgles, unsettled as I watch the gathering crowd. "I'm taking a quick walk," I tell Logan. I ignore the twinge in my chest when I see his frown. We always did the festival together, but I need a second alone to center myself before I have to play the dutiful Ford in front of an audience. Can I really fucking stand there and say nothing while the old man announces this heinous legislation? I *know* that my strategic approach can pay dividends if done correctly, but that also means I can't rock the boat so far that we capsize before I get the evidence I need.

I take the outer loop of the booths set up to sell goods and food. This is a substantial economic boost for local businesses. It's also just a hell of a good time. I usually look forward to it, but it's been a weird month.

Up ahead is a large crowd, and I take a shortcut around a building to avoid them. On the side of the back wall is written:

DEATH TO THE UNNATURAL DW.

Dream wielders.

Bile burns my throat. How many people have seen this? The paint is a bright red, dripping down like a bloodstain.

Thinking fast, I sprint into the booths and find one selling cleaning potions. I buy the most powerful, then get hot water from a tea booth. Throwing the potion onto the letters, I watch them bubble away until they're unreadable. Then I toss the water to rinse it.

I can clean all the walls I want, but that won't stop the incoming tide.

As I walk back, I reach for my watch, my stomach dropping as I realize it's gone.

CHAPTER 24

Azalee

The day flew by, occupied by the task Roz assigned me to clean the greenhouse. Water sloshes in my bucket as I scrub the windows, the sun finding its way back into the space. It's nearly time to get ready for the festival, and my aching back will be glad for the break.

After my dream with Gabriel, I've welcomed the hard labor distractions. I'll admit I was a little worried after dream wielding into Gabriel's mind what my sleep might bring. But the last few nights have been restless but no dreams as it should be. The nightmare must have been a one-off—a hallucination caused by a fever. That's a far more logical answer than me having a nightmare on my own. But even as I rationalize my way out of spiraling, my churning gut isn't buying it. Sure, I proved to Gabriel that dream wielders aren't dangerous, but the big takeaway: I got myself in more trouble by giving in to my desires.

I *never* would've kissed Gabriel in the waking world. The dream corrupted my judgment. And even after I proved to him dream wielders are safe, he still won't talk to the High Witch. He's too fucking worried about his well-being to care about the rest of us. Sure, I need him to stay alive for my own sake, but if that means our kind suffers to save us, I can't do that. And while I hate to admit it—and never would out loud—it seems like he has been doing *some* good for the rest of us. Albeit while hiding in the shadows.

After finishing at the greenhouse, I drop by Mom's office. I stop before going inside to give a little love to the plants growing on the windowsill in the hallway, remembering when we planted them . . .

"Just a few drops, Azalee," Mom says over my shoulder. "Remember that potions are best used with a light hand."

I grip the thin glass jar with my tiny fingers. I give the potion a swirl, just so I can see the pink-and-purple mixture shimmer in the light one last time. Licking my lips, I use the dropper to place three drops in each pot of dirt. One breath passes before I ask, "How much longer?" I look up at Mom.

"Patience. Watch and wait. Just as we had to take time to brew the growth potion, it's going to take time for the seeds to absorb it."

Fidgeting the whole time, I wait with Mom for thirty minutes until the little sprouts burst to life out of the moist dirt.

That was one of many lessons she taught me about magic. Even before I was a dream wielder, she imparted her years of experience onto me. I learned how to brew potions from scratch, grow herbs and flowers, memorize incantations, purify crystals and recharge them. My education was vast—even if I didn't always practice as much as I should.

"I was thinking of seeing Meera before the festival. Did you want to go with me?" I ask when I walk through her open door. Her office has a large stained glass window of a garden and a rising sun sitting behind her ancient mahogany desk. But she's stretched out on the floor with tarot cards and runes spread in front of her.

She answers without glancing up. "The lawyer said it was best we keep a little distance from her."

"Seriously?" I grab a lollipop from the stash in her desk. "Meera is all alone in the viper's nest, and his advice is just to let her think we've abandoned her." I pop the red sucker in my mouth. I've barely eaten all day, so I need the sugar boost to keep going.

"Meera knows why we need to do this." Pieces of her hair fall into her face as she scrunches her nose, shuffling the cards before dealing them again in a Celtic cross.

"I'll make the visit quick." I reach down and grab a card that's found its way under the desk. *The Fool.* I roll my eyes, handing the card to her.

She places it at the bottom of her spread before finally looking at me. "Azalee, you have always been a free spirit, and I love that about you." She keeps going when she sees me opening my mouth, "In fact, I encouraged it. But I need you to remember that all that the coven does is for the good of the whole. Please don't put that in jeopardy." She taps her finger on The Fool card as if to make her point.

She's got me there. I nod. "Okay," I say, even though it feels like chewing glass. "Maybe we should stay away from the festival too. With everything going on, I can't imagine the public is going to be welcoming to suspected dream wielders." I've read plenty of news articles and posts online the last few days with interviews from Salem residents about their growing fear with a possible serial killer or killers running around. The longer the culprit remains at large, the worse it's going to get.

I hate the idea of not attending the festival—it's one of the best parties of the year. But it's never been the same without Iniko, and now, without Meera, it might be best to call it on the festive occasion. All I'm going to feel the whole time is guilty that I get to walk free while two people I love are trapped in cages.

"The High Witch is supposed to give a speech beforehand. Whatever he's going to say, we need to hear it firsthand."

My mouth is dry, the lollipop sticking to my tongue. "I know what he's going to say. It's about the fucking witch hunt of a bill he's trying to ram into law." Despite Gabriel's confidence that the bill won't pass, I'm not so naive. The High Witch had plenty of supporters to help facilitate shoving his law on dream wielders before these murders started. Now it'll probably be a landslide.

"What is coming will happen, but that doesn't mean we have to stop the fight against it." She gets off the floor, wiping the dust off her cloak.

We walk back to the house to get ready, but as we approach the front, I spot a police car and an officer beside it. He straightens when he sees us. "Good evening."

Neither of us says anything. My jaw clicks as I grind my teeth.

He continues when we don't speak, "May I come in and have a word?"

"It's a nice night, why don't we talk right here?" Mom is so graceful. Gods, I wish I had a bit of that. I wanted to tell him to get the fuck off our property.

"All right." He nods, clearly uneasy, as he shifts back and forth. "Miss Saunders, one of the properties of the High Witch was the subject of arson last week."

My heart skips a beat, but I remain steady as Mom's gaze darts to me. "How terrible," I say, my voice not showing the slightest bit of remorse.

"A high-value, very rare plant was destroyed. You wouldn't happen to know anything about that, would you?" The officer is only a few years younger than me—no doubt trying to earn his cred by coming after the big bad dream wielders.

I rub my lips together, shrugging. "Why would I know anything?"

"Earlier that day, a potion containing the rare herb was *misplaced* on your property."

"Nightlock," Mom chimes in. "That plant is illegal to cultivate, as I'm sure the High Witch knows."

"So," I add, "if someone *had* burned his crop, the High Witch should be grateful to them. Otherwise, you'd have to arrest him for illegal witchcraft."

"The High Witch is not under investigation—the arsonist is." His eyes narrow on me. "Where were you six nights ago?"

"She was with me," Mom steps in.

"And then out to dinner with a friend," I add.

"We'll need to get a witness statement from them."

I tilt my head and try to read his aura, but I can't get a fix on it. All I get for my troubles is the start of a migraine. "If you had any evidence that I was responsible, I'd already be in handcuffs. So"—I turn away from him, taking Mom's arm and moving to go inside—"if you get some evidence, you know where to find me."

We're both silent until we hear the car driving away. "Azalee, please tell me you didn't burn the High Witch's property."

I play with a bundle of blackthorn on the entryway table. "I can't tell you that."

"Azalee Saunders, what the hell were you thinking?" Mom so rarely gets angry I jump at the outburst. "You put us all at risk."

"We were already at risk." My voice rises to meet hers. "If the High Witch was allowed to keep growing nightlock and using it to make potions, it was only a matter of time before we were all fucked."

Mom's face is pinched. "You can't keep making these rash choices. We have the coven for a reason. If you want to protect dream wielders, be more active in meetings."

"Whenever I try Roz always shuts me down." My face flushes with anger. I'm so fed up with waiting for the coven to come to a consensus when I can just do it myself.

"Probably because your solution to a problem is to light it on fire." Mom shakes her head before glancing at the clock. "We will discuss this later. Go get ready for the festival."

I don't feel like going, but I get dressed. I squeeze a few Aurora drops in my eyes, the potion turning my green irises a deep purple. That's about as festive as I'm feeling tonight.

As the sun sets Salem comes alive with the spirit of magic, which is extra thick for the tourists. The festival is more crowded than in years past. No doubt when word that the High Witch was making a speech got around, people wanted to be a part of history. Dark-purple fabric covers the podium on the main stage while cascading lights hang from it, giving an unearthly glow. Ready for the High Witch's arrival and the doomsday talk I'm sure will accompany it. My stomach twists as I wait for the axe to drop on all our necks.

Mom and I are thrust farther to the front as the attendees increase. Other members from the coven are here too, Roz among them. I clutch my locket, hoping the charmed crystals within will calm the panic inside me—but it needs a cleansing refresh because it doesn't seem to be working. There are too many people slowly draining my energy—my limbs become heavy, while the pounding in my head increases.

The faces of those around us are far less jovial than at past festivals. And the number of protective crystals hung around necks and sewn into clothes and headgear just further pushes the ongoing narrative that the people of Salem are truly worried.

The High Witch arrives looking pompous as ever in a full suit and cloak with the High Witch sash he wears for special events and ceremonies. His oversize, rare red-beryl necklace looks like it's made of blood in this low light. I'm going to hurl.

"I am here today to ease the worry of our citizens. Not only here, but around the country," the High Witch begins, cameras pointed at him from every angle broadcasting worldwide. Gabriel is at his side, dressed in a black suit, looking like he's attending a funeral. At least he has the decency to look ill at all this. His brother, Logan, stands on the other side of the High Witch—a united front. But after my talks with Gabriel recently, I know there is more of a crack in that facade than is visible to the naked eye.

"I want you all to know I am doing everything in my power to protect this city from the dangers that have become ever prevalent." The High Witch lets each sentence hang before starting the next one.

At this rate, we'll be here all night. "In light of recent events, we have decided that for the safety of all our citizens, we shall vote on a bill that would require the registration of all current and future dream wielders."

I thought a roar of approval might follow, but instead, a low buzz begins, people glancing around. Questioning eyes look for someone to step forward, to be the voice of reason. Apparently, dream wielders aren't the total outcasts the High Witch wishes us to be. *Do something, do something,* I beg Gabriel in my mind, hoping the tether between us gives him the message. The life debt might as well make itself useful for once. Despite my disagreement with it, I know what he feels is at stake if he speaks out. Still, a little dramatic speech opposing his grandfather in front of a crowd would be very helpful right about now.

But Gabriel's silence is the loudest I've ever heard.

"You can't do this. It's unethical." Mom steps forward from her place beside me. I don't know if she planned this all along, but I knew she could never stay silent. She talks about me being the reckless one, but I had to get it from somewhere. I, however, started my fire in the middle of the night—alone in a field—and she's putting her neck right up to the lion's mouth. Sweat gathers on my palms despite the cool weather. My ever-increasing heart rate sending my body into fight mode.

The High Witch's head turns lazily in our direction. "If you have a complaint, feel free to file it with my office. This is not the time for an open forum."

The crowd around us has stepped back, clearing a path as Mom approaches the stage. "Of course it's the time. There is no other time than now because it will be too late. Stop this witch hunt for dream wielders—they're not responsible for these heinous murders. Dream wielders cannot kill in dreams." Mom looks to the crowd for others to stand with her, but even the other coven members stay quiet.

Throwing myself into danger has never bothered me—hell, I welcome it most of the time, but that's risking *my* life. Mom sacrificing her safety isn't a situation I'm used to. Since Dad's death, she's always been the cautious one. I could rely on that knowing she wasn't at risk. I can't lose the only family I have left.

I sort of understand Gabriel's hesitation now. *Fuck, I hate agreeing with him.*

I look up at Gabriel, but he refuses to meet my gaze. I step forward, but Mom shakes her head in the tiniest movement. I pause, brows pinching together, before fading back into the crowd. My stomach knots and clenches with protest at the inaction, angry I'm going against my nature and sitting still. If this is our point of no return, our line drawn in the sand, I want to be on those front lines.

"Dream wielders are dangerous." The High Witch's jaw twitches.

"No, they aren't. At least no more dangerous than anyone else could be given the chance." Mom's voice is soft, begging for him to understand.

A vein in the High Witch's neck pulses. "And how would you know this?"

Gabriel stares straight ahead, his right hand clasped tight over his left wrist.

I don't know how many of the crowd suspect we're dream wielders. But we've never done anything to threaten or harm anyone in this community. What happens if Mom admits she's a dream wielder? Do those once friends suddenly turn their backs on her? Would they rally with us?

Mom looks to be pondering the same thing as she glances at me. I nod, giving her my blessing. I hate that it has to be her and not me making this admission, but I'd fall on the sword for her and she'd do the same for me. Sometimes, bold action is required to get things done. Just like I had to do what I thought was best for the whole, so does she. Come what may.

"I know dream wielders aren't dangerous because I am a dream wielder." She doesn't turn to face the High Witch but instead addresses the people. My insides twist, heart rattling against my rib cage. No going back now. There's an old saying in Salem: *The trees hear every word, so take heed when speaking, for their roots go deep*. Basically, you better be fucking sure of everything you say out loud because it's out there forever.

Mumbles ripple through the crowd, many saying they knew all along. "Then you can be the first to sign your name on the registry." The High Witch smiles like a lion catching up to its prey. "A signal of good faith, if you say dream wielders, like yourself, are not dangerous."

She faces the High Witch now. "I will not sign a registry that makes it easier for you to persecute us." Mom doesn't budge. For all her agreeing with Roz, it sure sounds like she's practiced this speech before. Maybe she always knew a day like this would come. "We should be free to express who we are, but if we wish to remain hidden, that is also our choice."

"As I said, this bill will go to a vote. As always, the people will decide." He dons a charming smile as he scans the crowd. "But for now, no more talk of bills and laws. This is a time to celebrate our great city. Let the festivities begin." He gives a quick wave before exiting the podium, Gabriel on his tail.

CHAPTER 25

Gabriel

"Well, that unexpected revelation will work nicely in our favor," Grandfather says with smug satisfaction as we exit the stage. The rumbling of the crowd grows as they spread out into the festival. "We haven't even passed the bill yet, and we've already smoked out our first dream wielder. The rest will fall in line."

"That admission felt like the last-ditch effort of a desperate person to stop an unlawful crusade. I don't see the rest being so willing to reveal themselves." I shove my hands into my pockets, clenching them into fists. My nerves are in heightened-awareness mode now that I'm without my watch. I asked the organizers to bring it to me immediately if it's found. But the tides of fate don't appear on my side as of late.

I saw the way Azalee looked at me. She wanted me to fight for them. But if I wasn't going to say it to Grandfather in private, there's no way in hell I would admit my powers in front of a crowd. Plus, now that the bill is out there for public commentary, I need my access at the office more than ever if I'm going to get the pendulum to sway toward axing this bill.

"We have them right where we want them." Grandfather turns so his valet can put his cloak on him. "Desperate people act irrationally. Which will only further prove our assessment of them."

Logan isn't looking at us when he speaks, too busy eyeing the festival's dazzling lights. "Didn't seem like the crowd had the reaction you were looking for." Always a sly one, Logan speaks the comments in a nonchalant sigh, but the tension around his mouth is a dead giveaway to me that he's uncomfortable with this situation too. Maybe not to the extreme that I am, but clearly he's questioning our grandfather's rhetoric and sudden aggression.

I don't think I'm ready to tell him about my magic, but if I can keep moving him toward acceptance that dream wielders are not the enemy Grandfather describes, perhaps he won't think I'm the monster under the bed when I do finally tell him.

"Change comes in waves, boys, and I've started a tsunami. The witches will fall in line."

"Or drown," I mutter.

The High Witch either doesn't hear or chooses to ignore me. "Gabriel, Logan, if I need you, I'll have my secretary call you. But for now, you're free to enjoy the festival. Do remember you are ambassadors of my position, so act accordingly," Grandfather says before walking off with the head of the festival to garner more favors, no doubt.

A cool wind whips through, and Logan pops his collar to block it. "I'm meeting with some friends for festival games, want to come?"

My scalp itches from the quick-dry potion. "I'm not feeling it this time."

"Oh, okay." Logan's voice is stiff. "It's just tradition that I destroy you at ring toss, so I thought you'd like the opportunity to redeem your sorry ass, but whatever."

He's right. I used to practice all year, but somehow he always beat me. As the older brother, I was both proud and irritated. "I just . . ." I stare into the crowded festival. There's someone else I'd like to find first. "Let me handle something and then I'll come find you. Cool?"

Logan shrugs. "You know where I'll be."

I know seeking Azalee out is a fool's errand. But since I haven't stopped thinking about her the last few days, I'm not sure I'll be able to stay away. It isn't too hard for me to find her; I just follow the tug in my gut.

When she senses me behind her, her shoulders tense, and I swear I can see her head move from the eye roll. "Hers is on me," I say to the vendor of the funnel cake stand, where she's next in line. I place a fifty on the counter between them.

Azalee finally graces me with her beautiful face, only to throw daggers at me with her eyes. "He's not paying for mine." She takes my bill and shoves it into my jacket pocket before pulling out her own money.

I drop my voice. "Seriously, Azalee? It's just a funnel cake." It's not just a funnel cake. I'm hoping it's an olive branch and an apology of sorts.

"I don't take bribes." She grabs her fried dessert covered in powdered sugar and berries. "Goodbye, Gabriel."

I follow her as she weaves into the throng of people dressed in eclectic holiday attire. Everyone joyfully celebrates the season. But I don't miss the scattering of patrons whose eyes linger on Azalee. It's not a secret who her mother is or that she works at The Retreat, and after the speech, tensions are even higher.

"I understand why you're upset with me." I try to give this conversation an amicable start.

Ignoring me, she takes a bite of funnel cake, the red juice coating her bottom lip, before she flicks her tongue across it. My body roars with heat, my brain fritzing for a second when all I can think about is pulling her into a back corner and kissing her again, just to see if the real-life thing feels as good as the dream.

"Azalee, the High Witch—"

"I don't want to hear it. Just leave me be and go congregate with the witches you wish you were." She sends me a deadly glare.

I groan. I knew this was a bad idea. "I'm still trying to figure out what's going on." I have to stay closer to her so we aren't overheard. Because even in this group of partiers, we're both people who draw attention. "But I can't act without information."

She spins on her heels, nearly shoving her dessert in my chest. "You have information. I provided it to you on a fucking silver platter. In fact, it was the exact info *you* requested. And then you've done shit with it since. Just let us take care of ourselves. It's what we're used to."

Azalee walks away, leaving me in the center of the booths. I contain myself as the crowd does its best impression of not gawking at me while clearly watching the whole thing.

"Is that the High Witch's grandson?" Chatter like this spills into the crowds as I duck my head to become invisible.

Other conversations consist of rehashing Grandfather's announcement and Mrs. Saunders's admission to being a dream wielder. Some agree with the High Witch and want Mrs. Saunders arrested. While many still think it's a bit extreme to require them to register. Everyone knows that's a slippery slope. If we start doing that with dream wielders, what group could be next?

I think back to the graffiti and how Grandfather's ability to sway a crowd could've gone either way, and he picked the path that would lead to more unrest. I know he believes he's protecting the witches, but this is not the way to do it. It's a lot easier to rationalize this topic in my head than when I'm faced with the man who raised me as his own after my parents died. I do love him. In a different way than most people probably love their grandfathers, but he made sure Logan and I had a home and were given the best start in life we could. Am I okay with him dying knowing he hates me? Is there really no other way to come to a compromise?

But even as I say it, I know it's not true. The High Witch has spent too long villainizing the dream wielders to suddenly change course now.

I head toward the games, taking the back way. I always wondered if one day I'd feel like I'd outgrown the festival. I guess that day is today. But before I reach them, I hear shouting from the far side near the barn. There's a loud bang and I take off running in that direction, where the tug in my gut tells me my life debt is kicking in.

CHAPTER 26

Azalee

I wanted to go home after the speech, but Mom says she won't back down now. I got a funnel cake to soothe my nerves, but Gabriel ruined that experience. When I find Mom again, Roz is with her.

"What were you thinking, Genevieve?" Roz hisses. "I would expect such antics from your daughter, but I thought you had more sense."

It's nice not to be on the receiving end of Roz's wrath, but I don't appreciate it coming for my own blood.

I open my mouth to tell them to back the hell off, but Mom speaks first. "I know this is not as we planned, Roz. But I had no choice. Someone has to show the people that this dream wielder crusade is ill-founded. The community of Salem has known me for decades. They know I am not a threat. Perhaps having a friendly face to think of when dream wielders are whispered about will give us some sympathy."

Roz shakes their head. "Or it'll give them a face to plaster on the propaganda posters. You have no idea what Fates you have put in motion."

"And neither do you." I can't keep quiet. Even though I hate that Mom put herself in the hex crosshairs, I'm standing by her side when it's against Roz. "The way of the Fates is never known by mortals. We just act and hope they blow us a favorable wind."

"I'm going home," Roz says. "You two fools can stay here if you like. But don't say I didn't warn you."

As if the Fates are listening, the wind kicks up as they stomp away. I shiver, pulling my cloak tighter.

"Mom . . ."

"I have made my choice, Azalee. I will not let the High Witch believe he's won."

I can't help a small smile. "You know, you and I aren't so different."

She squeezes my hand. "Why do you think I scold you so much? I know just how much trouble you could get into."

People are buzzing about the High Witch's new registry, but since most of the crowd aren't dream wielders, they quickly get over their initial shock. This proposed law won't affect them. They won't have to put their name on a list to be checked on and documented for the rest of their lives.

I hold my head high as we walk among the booths. The lively music contrasts with my uneasy mood. Normally, I wouldn't mind attention from a crowd. I'd strut and flitter to the best of my ability. But tonight's attention is not the kind I fancy.

My fingers dance over my crystals. "I hate to agree with Roz, but I don't think we're safe here," I whisper as we walk past the Ferris wheel, screams of delight echoing. A thought to seek out Gabriel tries to take hold, and I bat it away. I do not need his protection. More like he'd only provide a nice distraction in the sheets.

Mom doesn't shrink away from the crowds gawking. "Have faith in your fellow witches. They will see there's nothing to fear, and that idea will spread. If we cower, then the High Witch wins."

"Technically, he doesn't want us to hide either. He wants us all to be known by our name, birth date, and address."

She gives me a small smile. "Showing we are strong by not hiding and putting our names on a registry for all to see are two very different things. He wants to segregate us; we want the option to move about of our own accord."

While I don't disagree hiding would be a victory for him, us getting our asses hexed will probably be okay with him too. I hate that he wins either way. As if summoned by the Fates, a large cup of hot chocolate flies past our heads and slams into the wall. We jump back, but a splatter of chocolate hits us anyway, dripping down my arm and cheek.

"What the hell?" I wipe my face, turning to see the deranged guy who's going to get my shoe in his ass.

A man in his mid-thirties stands with a few other guys, forming a half circle. "What'cha gunna do about it, dream wielder?"

My jaw tightens as my blood boils. The High Witch's fear of dream wielders and blanket discrimination have given freedom to others to follow in his footsteps. "We don't need any trouble." Mom raises her hands as a sign of peace. She may not be up for a fight, but I have energy I need to dispel.

"You're an abomination, unnatural piece of filth. No one should have the power to create nightmares," the man spits.

"Okay, first of all"—I step in because I can't listen to this idiot anymore—"dream wielders don't make nightmares. So, if you are going to insult us, why don't you get your facts straight." I level him with my most vicious stare.

His hand bunches into a fist. "Watch your tone. I won't be spoken to like that."

"Then you should walk away." I cross my arms. I will not let some man intimidate me.

The guy next to him grabs a small leather pouch from his pocket.

Mom grabs my arm. "We don't want to start any fights. This is a place for fun."

The dude with the bag smiles a crooked grin. "This is gonna be fun for us."

Mom whispers from the side of her mouth, "Run." She barely gets the words out before the hex bag hits her in the chest, the contents flying out in a burst of light. She shoves me to the side to keep the magic off me. The bag falls to the ground, the powder clinging to her. She tries to dust it off, but it coats her hands. She grabs her chest, eyes rolling back in her head as she collapses to the ground.

"Mom!" My throat constricts as I scream, running to her.

"Don't touch her!" Gabriel yells, racing toward us. "Hex bags are illegal." He turns to the men, voice full of the authority of the High Witch's grandson.

I hover my shaking hands over Mom, knowing I shouldn't touch her and spread the hex. I feel so helpless just watching the magic seep into her skin.

"You need to call 911." I think Gabriel is talking to me, but the world closes in, my vision tunneling.

I turn to face the attackers. I take heavy steps forward, blood pounding in my ears. Gabriel tries to stop me, but I swat him away. "You want to fear us? Then fear us." I run at the man who threw the bag. My hands slam hard against the sides of his face, my nails tearing into his skin as I call upon the seeds of darkness sprouting inside me.

What I show him brings him to his knees.

A dark cave. Thousands of bat wings flapping against each other, beating high above us. The droplets could be rain, but that would be too tolerable. Bat feces cascades from the creatures with beady red eyes and sharp claws. He thrashes against the ropes holding him, his body sinking into the waste matter, weighted down by the corpses tied to his ankles.

Guano should be the least of his worries. Residing inside the years of excrement are carnivorous worms, feeding on any living creatures unlucky enough to get caught in their home. They pick and peck at his skin, wiggling inside until they feast on every part of him. His screams are futile as his open mouth only gives them more landscape to eat.

It could be hours or seconds before two strong hands pull me off my victim. He's writhing in agony but manages to get up and stagger away from me. "You crazy bitch." His friends have already run for the hills.

"What did you do?" Gabriel's eyes are wide, cloak hanging half off his body as I struggle from his grip.

"Mom." I run back to her, ignoring him. Sirens buzz through the air as I fall to the ground. I lean down, still not able to touch her, but the ebbing of her aura tells me she's okay, weak but alive.

He crouches beside me, voice low. "Azalee, what did you do to that guy?"

I keep my eyes focused on Mom as the pain splits my head in two. "I only gave him what he deserved."

"Which was?"

A nightmare.

CHAPTER 27

Gabriel

"Azalee, what did you do?" I try to keep my voice low, but the festival crowd is gathering around us. The chatter grows louder with each passing second. I stare at the side of Azalee's face, her eyes glued to her mother, hands hovering midair, shaking with the strength it's taking not to touch her. Pushing Azalee about what the fuck just happened isn't going to get me anywhere right now. But it's something we're going to have to circle back to.

The wailing of the ambulance drags me from my analysis.

"The ambulance is here," I tell Azalee, standing and offering her my hands. "You need to step away so they can treat her. They know how to reverse hexes." She doesn't even look at me. She's lost in a fog, in a dream . . . in a *nightmare*. I put my hand on her shoulder to pull her up, but she wrenches away from me.

"Don't." The single word sends a shiver down my spine. It's almost like I hear it echoing in my mind, rattling around until it eats away at my resolve. I look at her eyes to see if they're bloodshot, but her hair is blocking my view.

Before I can persuade her to move again, the EMTs push through the crowd. "Step back," the healer commands as they arrive with a stretcher. They're dressed in protective gear so they don't get affected by the hex still seeping into Mrs. Saunders. "Did anyone touch her?" He looks at Azalee, then at me.

"No." I shake my head.

"Miss, please step back," the healer tells Azalee in a gentler tone this time. He places a hand on her shoulder like I did, but she doesn't throw him off. When she finally looks up from her mother, who is a putrid shade of green, Azalee's wide eyes aren't bloodshot, just filled with tears. My body sags with relief at the sight of clear pupils. But the joy is quickly replaced with an ache. I've never seen her look so afraid and helpless. Azalee's headstrong determination is a pain in the ass most days, but I realize I miss it now.

"Can I come with you?" Azalee asks when she finally lets them put her mom on a stretcher.

"Of course. But hurry."

Azalee doesn't give me a second look as she runs off to the ambulance. It speeds away, and I glance around the mass formed in a few minutes. Spectators with phones out to document the scene, the second one Mrs. Saunders was involved in today: cause and effect.

But most of these prying eyes missed the crucial part where Mrs. Saunders was attacked unprovoked with a hex. I'm glad, however, that they missed Azalee's rage revenge attack. The man wasn't asleep, so it wasn't a dream she made and she didn't do the correct sequence for a daydream. So what did she do?

Based on the man's fear-stricken, pale face as he bolted away, I'd say it was a nightmare. I've done my research, and physically, Azalee isn't showing any early signs of transforming into a Nightmare—but it's the inside mutation that's harder to track. If that man were still here, I'd beat him to a pulp and let the police arrest me.

"Mr. Ford, what happened?" someone in the crowd yells.

"Did the dream wielders attack someone?"

"What is the High Witch's position on this?"

Fucking hell. I scratch the back of my neck. Realizing my cloak is all askew, I fix it quickly, putting on the persona the High Witch's team must have.

"The High Witch has no comment at this time," I say to no one in particular. A bunch of phones are raised, and I'm sure this will be all over socials in minutes, if it isn't already the biggest story. Just one more thing for people to fear when tensions are already high enough.

I scan the crowd, hoping to spot one of the men involved in the attack. But they're smarter than they seem because they've disappeared.

"What's going on?" Grandfather parts the crowd like a God descending the heavens.

The phones turn to capture him, giving me a second to collect myself.

Taking a rattling breath, I shake out my hands before answering. "There was an attack on *Mrs. Saunders*." I emphasize her name to avoid saying what I'm really thinking. This was an attack on a dream wielder, and Grandfather is responsible for this increased frenzy that led to the hexing. "The men ran off in that direction." I point to the left.

The High Witch nods to his security detail. "Find them." Grandfather raises his hand to calm the crowd. "We will recover the *supposed* men responsible. I understand the concerns of our citizens regarding dream wielders. And I promise you, all actions we take moving forward to protect them and ourselves will be for the greater good."

Them. Us. The High Witch is gifted with words. He knows precisely the inclination those specific phrases have. They are different from us. They are other. The High Witch didn't need to elaborate; he's been making his point for decades.

"Gabriel, you were here? Tell me what happened." Grandfather puts his hand on my shoulder, leading me away.

"I didn't arrive until they were throwing the hex bag. But I got enough context to know it was an attack on a dream wielder."

Grandfather continues to walk us through the festival as if nothing has happened. Waving and nodding to the partiers like it's all fucking fine and dandy. Like a woman isn't being taken to the hospital right now drenched in an illegal hex.

"Gabriel, we know that people are scared. Dream wielder magic is frightening. Of course, I don't agree with these actions, but I do understand their fear. And we cannot belittle it."

"It wasn't fear, it was hate." But what Azalee left in that man was fear.

Grandfather stops to study me. "Are we going to have a problem?"

I know what he means. Grandfather pretends he likes people who have critical thinking skills. But he only likes it if it benefits him. "I'll ensure the festival situation is contained, and we have no more escalation."

The old man smiles. "That's what I love about you, my boy. Always able to jump into the fray and solve a problem. You like getting your hands dirty. You've never been afraid of a little action."

For the first time, that doesn't feel like a compliment.

Grandfather leaves and I do a sweep of the festival, looking for the men. I didn't get a great look at them in the dark, but it was enough. If only I'd grabbed a piece of clothing or something so I could do a finding spell.

When I saw that attack, for a minute, I thought the bag had hit Azalee, and my heart lodged in my throat. And that's the moment I realized I actually care what happens to her, beyond the fact that her death would be my undoing because of the life debt. I wanted to save her. I know she'd laugh if I told her that, so I'll keep that tidbit to myself.

I've been trying to figure out these murders alone, but I don't think I can. And the longer we wait, the more likely another attack will happen, and the next one could end in death. I need to make sure that there is no more collateral damage from my family's actions.

CHAPTER 28

AZALEE

The ride to the hospital is a blur. The healers in the ambulance act quickly to remove what they can of the hex bag from her skin. She's taken away when we get to Salem Medical, and I'm left to wait in the cold hallway. But I barely notice through my numbing body. I stare at the white tiles, unmoving, lost in my memories . . .

I squeeze my eyes tight, forcing them to stay closed as I finish counting. "Nine, ten." I open them, leaping up and weaving my way through the dreamscape of my mother's mind. This is only my second time dream wielding, but I'm determined to show Mom I'm a natural like her.

"Remember, Azalee," Mom's voice whispers in the sunflowers that are growing twenty feet high, intertwining to create a maze. "You're controlling the dream. I can't hide from you. You just have to know how to command it."

Using my dream magic to light the way, I follow a glowing pink path. I tiptoe under a mammoth mushroom before gliding down a slide made from the limb of a willow tree. I'm deposited near a river made of chocolate.

I close my eyes and focus on finding Mom. I am a dream wielder. I control the dreams. The whole of the dreamscape is my domain. I use my senses to feel for her, stretching my magic muscle. It's tiring, but the more I do it, the stronger I feel.

When I open my eyes, I'm standing in the hollowed trunk of a tree. I push open the door and step out into the meadow. Mom sits on a picnic blanket surrounded by empty plates.

"Fantastic job, Azalee," she says with a proud grin as I join her. "Now, let's try making lunch. Food is one of the trickiest parts to achieve, but when you can get it right, it's magic."

My phone buzzes and I blink, hardly able to read the name. I didn't realize I was crying. "Hello?"

"How is she?" Roz's voice cuts through the haze.

I swallow the lump closing my airway. "I don't know." The words are scratchy, and I cough to clear them. "The healers are working on her now."

"Gods, I should have insisted you both leave with me. I knew something like this would happen." The sharp tone is present, but I hear the worry underneath. Years ago, Mom and Roz had a brief fling. It didn't last, and I didn't ask questions because I was too young to care about my mom's love life. But while they aren't a couple, that affection still stands.

I don't answer Roz because I don't have anything to say.

"We're having a coven meeting tonight. Witching hour. I need you to be here."

That ignites a fire back in my veins. "I'm a little busy."

"Visiting hours have long since ended. When they heal Genevieve, they'll send you home." Roz is back to a commanding mood. "This meeting isn't optional. There are lives at stake. I thought your little crusade to save us all would make you more interested in the coven's business."

"Sorry, Roz, a nurse is calling me." I hang up the phone, staring into the empty hallway.

Fuck Roz and the coven meeting. It doesn't do us any good. Iniko is a Nightmare. Meera is rotting in jail for a crime she didn't commit, and Mom is hexed, lying in a hospital bed. Nothing we do is enough—*nothing I do.*

Pain shoots through my skull, and I press my hands onto either side of my head to snuff it out. But it's useless. When I open my eyes, a shadow in my peripheral vision startles me, but nothing is there when I turn to look.

Sometime later, a healer tells me they successfully removed the magic from Mom's body and that she'll be okay. She needs a few days to recover at the hospital to monitor her progress. The hex wasn't too strong—not surprising, seeing the idiots who made it. I ask if I can see her, but with hexes, they require the patient to be in isolation for twelve hours to make sure there is no residue left that could harm another.

So, even though I hate it, I leave Mom to be watched over by the expert staff.

Driving through The Retreat property, I'm careful to avoid others, lest I be dragged into the coven meeting. Our house, which is usually so inviting, is dark, no life shining through the stained glass windows.

I don't bother to click the lights on as I stumble inside the dark house, dropping my bag near the door. I don't give a shit what Roz wants. The last thing I feel like doing is sitting in a bomb shelter, reliving tonight's events with a bunch of panicked dream wielders. While I feel like I could pass out, my mind is too wired to sleep. Everyone I would generally turn to is in jail or the hospital. I only have one person left here to talk to.

I need to see Iniko. I know it's a completely terrible idea given my current energies, but I have to risk it. I need *someone.*

After the storm yesterday, the winding stairs to the dungeons are muskier than usual. I grabbed an extra black tourmaline protection crystal before coming down here. Going into Iniko's nightmare might have triggered the nightmare in me, a residual effect. I could use an extra boost of protection.

Despite the dangers and the repercussions it might have, I'm curious to see into his mind again. It was nice to be with him, to show him that I'm still here too. And he did give me that weird vision of the High Witch; maybe it means something.

I flip on the overhead light. It blinks a few times like it might have other ideas, but it finally stays on. I walk with purpose toward Iniko's door, opening it slowly. He's sitting in the same spot as always, darkened face looking toward the tiny window high above.

I sit on the stool near his bed, resting my head in my palms. Before I know it, tears cascade down my cheeks. "I don't know what to do, Ink. I've tried so fucking hard to protect us, but no matter what I do, it ends in tragedy." I wipe away the wetness, glancing up at Iniko pondering me. "Iniko . . ." I breathe.

He shifts, leaning closer. I resist the urge to back away—he won't hurt me. We stare at each other for a beat. I search those brown eyes for any sign of the friend I knew. "Ink, can you—" The words are ripped from my throat as he clamps a cold hand around my wrist and pulls me once again into his nightmare.

Thick tree roots cover the dark hallway's floor, making me trip, the skin of my knees tearing as I hit the ground. Blood drips down my legs when I manage to stand again. Winding branches crawl up the walls like spindly fingers, making the smell of dank earth cling to the air. I hug myself tight as I walk, the sounds of screams coming from behind the walls—or in the walls. There are no windows or doors. I shiver as my blood runs ice cold. What little I can see of my skin in the dim light is a shade of unnatural blue.

There is no ceiling, instead it's a sky full of rolling dark clouds—thunder and lightning rattling through them. My bare feet are cut and bleeding, stinging with each step. I can't stop; I'll never leave this place if I do. I'll become one of the howling lost souls in the walls. The heavens open, freezing rain descending upon me.

A flock of birds sweeps overhead, cries cutting through the storm. My dress clings to my legs as the water soaks through. My beating heart and pounding feet are the percussion that keeps me going. Eventually, the hallway releases into a large circular room. In the center sits Iniko, his chin pressed into his chest, unmoving. In front of him is a table with four objects arranged in perfect symmetry. I move closer to get a better look.

As I approach the table, the rain stops just around us like I've stepped under an umbrella. The first item on the table is an open amber glass bottle with orange smoke. In the middle is a bloodied rabbit's foot—the gray rabbit it belonged to lies dead beneath the table. I pull my bare feet back to keep from touching it. A tarnished gold trophy with the words SPECIAL RECOGNITION is toppled over on its side. The last piece is a small handgun frozen in an ice block.

I open my mouth to speak, but no sound comes out. I claw at my throat, my hands coming away covered in blood and skin. I'm choking on all that I want to say. My words are my weapons, but in the nightmarescape, they've been stripped away.

Stepping around the table, I shake Iniko, trying to wake him. He falls off the chair with a loud thud but still doesn't move. Slowly, a pool of blood begins to seep around his body. I kneel, searching for the source of the injury, but there doesn't appear to be one.

My white dress soaks the blood into its skirt, creating a pattern that looks like the world's continents. My fingers shake violently as I attempt to wipe it away, only coating it more. The pool beneath me grows wider the more I fight against it.

Another clap of thunder rattles the room. The phantom sounds of my unheard screams ringing with it.

I get up, tripping back and catching myself hard on the table as I examine the room for an exit. There are no doors other than the one I came from. No windows either, just a patterned wallpaper in dark browns and reds. A chanting begins around me, inside me. Dark drums beat against the inside of my head. I crash my hands furiously against my ears, willing the sound to end, for everything to stop, but nothing works.

I slam my palms on the table, and it shatters as if it were made of glass and not solid wood. Small cuts appear over my already blood-soaked hands. The amber bottle spills on the floor, the room filling with orange smoke—the only color in this hollow place.

There's a clawing at my ankle, and I look down to see Iniko reaching for me, trying to get up, his legs twisted at awkward angles. He opens his mouth, and an awful death rattle escapes. I shake my head, forcing words that won't come. Tears burn as they travel down my cheeks, acid on my skin.

Heavy footsteps sound in the hallway as I lift Iniko. He's so much heavier than I remember, yet he is skin and bone—I can see the outline of every one of them. A hooded figure steps out from the dark hallway. They're the source of the chanting, yet they have many voices.

Iniko digs his fingers into my skin, drawing blood.

My white dress is crimson.

A flash of lightning cuts through the room. "Azalee." I hear the voice calling me from the sky.

Iniko digs deeper into my skin. The chanting of the hooded figure grows louder. Iniko's bloodstained fingers grab my face, forcing me to look at him. *"Find them."* The words sound ripped from a forgotten story, not quite clear.

Then a hard tug yanks me from the nightmarescape and back to the dungeon.

CHAPTER 29

Gabriel

I struggle to keep hold of Azalee, who's thrashing in my arms. My eyes don't shift from Iniko as he shrinks back in pain, clutching his head, which is covered in a dark-green liquid I used to subdue him. Until five seconds ago, I thought he was dead. Any joy I might have felt at seeing that wasn't true was overpowered by the realization at what he has become. Hands gripped under Azalee's arms, I drag her out of the room, slamming the door shut with my foot. The scraping metal echoes in the silent hall.

"Azalee, are you okay? I heard you screaming from upstairs." I grip both sides of her face, eyes wild as I examine every inch of her.

She shoves me away, hitting the stone wall and sliding to the floor. She scoots her knees to her chest, covering her face with her hands. Visibly shaking, I hesitate before reaching for her. Azalee and I have never been friends, and under normal circumstances, she wouldn't want me anywhere near here. But whatever she just experienced is anything but normal.

"Azalee." Crouching, I remove her hands from her face. "It's okay, you're okay. That wasn't real. It was a nightmare."

Squeezing her eyes tighter, she takes a deep breath before blinking them open. "Iniko," she manages.

"He'll be fine." I choke back the unexpected tears clogging my throat. "I always carry Wilt Away with me just in case." It contains attackers for a short period. I've kept it on me since the night in the fighting ring. I wasn't sure if it would work on a . . . Gods, calling my friend a Nightmare feels so wrong. Still, I don't think the potion should have worked on one. Which means Iniko let Azalee go.

Tears fall silently as she presses her back into the wall and staggers to standing. She wipes her eyes with the back of her hand, staring at her skin like she expected to see something different. "What are you doing here?" Her voice is stronger.

"I went to the hospital, but they said you went home. I was following up after the incident." Better to let her think I'm here on official business. Not that I was actually worried about her. "When I arrived, your door was wide open, and I heard screaming."

"I don't need the High Witch's help. So, kindly, fuck off, would you?" She pushes past me, heading up the stairs.

The moist air dries with every step I take after her. "Azalee."

She doesn't turn around.

When I get to the kitchen, she's ripping open the freezer and grabbing a pint of lavender Earl Grey ice cream. Slumping into a chair, she eats straight from the container. "You can go home."

I linger near the door, arms folded across my chest. She's okay now, and part of me wants to leave. Tension radiates between us, my molars suffering as I grind them. But the ghostly expression on her face makes me forget our past grievances. Before I can change my mind, I sit in the chair opposite her.

"Do you want to talk about it?" I rest my elbows on my knees, hands clasped together as I lean forward.

"What *it* would you be referring to? That my best friend is in jail? That my mom is in the hospital because she was attacked for being a dream wielder? That you sat idly by and let the High Witch condemn us all?" She shoves the spoon back into the ice cream, the other end breaking through the side of the container.

"Actually." I shift in my seat, rubbing the empty space where my watch should be. "I was referring to the nightmare you just had and that Iniko has apparently been alive this whole time, but I guess if you want to talk about any of those things—"

She cuts me off. "I don't want to talk about any of it. Especially not with you." She shovels a large spoonful into her mouth. "Just because we shared one dream doesn't mean we're friends."

And a kiss. But I guess we aren't mentioning that. Fine by me. I'd rather forget it. She pushes her hair back, and I notice the blood.

"You're hurt." I stand, coming to her side and reaching for her to examine the source of the blood.

She frowns, hands gingerly touching the area. "I . . . I must have done it down there."

"Where's your first aid kit?"

"I'll be fine." The brush-off is her automatic response.

"Azalee, just let me help you."

"When did you suddenly grow a savior complex?"

I clamp my jaw, the dull ache all too common the last few weeks. "I'm not trying to save you—trust me. I'm trained in basic first aid."

"Good for you."

She's egging me on, thinking it'll distract me. But I'm not that easily deterred. "The kit?"

She sighs. "Kitchen. Top cupboard on the right behind the cereal."

I rummage through the cupboards until I find it. It was not where she said, but I'm guessing that was part of her little game. "Take off your jacket so I can get a clear look," I say, kneeling beside her chair.

Unzipping the leather jacket, she winces, trying to hide it with a stony expression. She undoes the sheer blue shirt she's wearing underneath it too. "Thought you'd need good access," she says while making full eye contact. Daring me to look down because all she has on is a black lace bra.

With my eyes, I trace a smattering of moles along her left ribs. They could almost be the constellation of Aquarius—like my tattoo. I watch the way her chest rises and falls as her breathing quickens, a slight flush radiating across it the longer I gaze upon her.

"Thanks," I manage. Licking my lips, I focus on opening the kit and searching for gauze and disinfecting potion. Finally looking up once I've calmed my erratic heart, I skim my fingers over her warm skin to move her hair. She sucks in a breath but doesn't say anything.

There are several scratches where I'm surmising she dug in her nails during the nightmare. "This is going to sting," I say as I dip the gauze in the light-blue potion and place it on the bloody cuts.

She hisses. "There should be numbing potion."

"I have to clean it first." I place my other hand on her shoulder, the touch of her bare skin against mine sending tingles down my arms all the way to my lower abdomen. This close, I can smell lavender on her breath. She turns her head, lips so close I have to press my feet into the ground to keep myself steady. Just a kiss. One, two, thirty, that's all I'm asking for. Just enough to quench this thirst.

"Gabriel?" she prompts, and I realize I've stopped moving.

I clear my throat, removing my hands from her body and grabbing the numbing potion. "It's not too bad. Should be gone in a few days." I apply one more potion before covering it with a bandage. I leave her to get dressed and wash my hands at the sink.

When I'm done, I retake my seat. She's fully clothed again, but I'm never going to get rid of the sight of her. The dip and curve of her breasts, a place I've tried very hard not to imagine. I decide a subject change is needed. "I talked to the nurse at the hospital; she said your mom will make a full recovery. That's great news."

"I know she will." She bites her lip, a war clearly raging inside her on whether she wants to keep talking to me. "I'm more worried about it happening again. Fear makes people angry, and then they do violent things to make themselves feel better. This is only the beginning." She puts her ice cream on the table.

"You're right."

She frowns at me.

"Don't get used to me saying that."

Concealing a smile, she lays her head against the back of the chair, closing her eyes.

My eyes drift to the wooden door that leads to the basement. "Why did his parents let everyone think he was dead?"

She doesn't open her eyes. "What were they supposed to do? It's not like they could explain what really happened or where he was. It was easier to just let you and the rest of the world think he died. The people that really matter to him knew his fate."

I clench my jaw, ignoring the implied dig. Sure, Iniko and I weren't as close as he and Azalee, but he was still my good friend. "It's nice to know one person I thought I lost is still here. Even if he's . . ."

"Find them," she whispers.

"Sorry, what?" I frown.

She shakes her head, eyes opening. "It's something Iniko said in the nightmare. *Find them.*" She clicks on the fireplace, watching the flames dance.

"Nightmares are nonsensical. It probably didn't mean anything."

"Iniko's a Seer." She glances at me for the first time.

My brow furrows as I process her comment. "I don't know what him being a psychic has to do with nightmares."

"No." She stands and paces. "He's a true Seer. He's been Seeing into the future since we were kids."

"What?" My stomach turns. "I've known Iniko for years; he never mentioned being a Seer."

"It's not a talent he went around telling anyone who would listen."

"We were friends, I thought he might have . . ." I trail off, scratching the back of my neck. The shock of knowing someone you thought you were close to had lied to you for years. My arms tingle with numbness as I search for any clues I missed that he was a Seer. Is this how Logan would feel if he learned I'm a dream wielder?

"Guess you weren't that good of friends." Her venom slices deep.

"True Seers are rare." Her poison is in her words. She knows it too. I won't let her see she's got me. "They usually get high-position jobs with the government."

"Iniko didn't want any of that. He wanted to live a simple life—if you're his friend, you should know that. He knew if people got wind of what he could do, they'd want to use him for their own gain." She sits again.

I take a deep breath, looking past Azalee into the kitchen. "He looked . . ."

"Skinny?" she supplies. "Nightmares don't eat very well. That's one of the reasons they wither away so quickly."

"Sad." My eyes meet hers, holding the gaze longer than I mean to.

Clearing her throat, she warms her hands with the fire. Strands of hair have fallen across her face, and my fingers itch to push them away—to feel her skin against mine. "As much as I've tried to make that room homey, it's still a cage."

"I'm sure you're doing the best you can." The comforting words slip out without a thought.

I expect her to fire back a biting retort, but she doesn't. "If you want to see him, you can. I don't know if he really understands what I say to him, but maybe your presence might make him happy."

"But you can't relate?" I offer the dig for her.

She keeps her head down, hiding the smile, before sadness creeps back in and she looks at me. "I may not get it, but he did call you a friend. So I'm sorry you thought he was dead. As much as I hate seeing him like this, at least I knew that maybe he had a chance to come back to us. You just added him to the list of people you lost."

"Thank you." I really mean it. "We both don't need to add anyone else to that list."

She bites her lip, obviously thinking of her dad and what could have happened to her mom. "What if he can See even though he's stuck in a nightmare?" She changes the subject.

"You think he was trying to tell you something?" I shift in the chair, knees knocking into hers.

"Yes. He's been a Nightmare for a year, and it wasn't until a few days ago he pulled me into one with him." Her voice gets louder as she gains confidence. "Maybe he Saw a vision he's trying to warn me about."

It's my turn to stand. Shoving my hands into the pockets of my cloak, I turn toward the dungeons, looking back to that horrible place as if I were there again. "That's one possibility, but it's also possible his condition is deteriorating and he's lashing out." I usually don't pull punches when talking to Azalee because she's always up for a verbal brawl, but when it comes to Iniko, I need to tread with more grace.

"I'm right. I just have to find a better way to communicate with him."

When I turn to look at her, she's already standing beside me. "You can't have a real conversation. They no longer see reality. The worst parts of the mind have taken hold, locking them inside their nightmares."

"How do you know so much about Nightmares?" Her eyes narrow.

I massage my upper arm, shoulders tense. "I wanted to learn more about what happened to me."

A sudden anger sweeps over her face, but under it there is a hurt. "I offered to help you."

"My grandfather tracks my every move. My presence here would've just put you all at risk." True, but not the reason I didn't accept her offer. I just wanted to pretend it didn't exist. That I was the person I'd always been, not the outcast I'd become if my family discovered my new powers.

"I *really* don't want to talk about the High Witch." She pinches the bridge of her nose.

Before we can fuel this argument further, there's a knock at the door.

Her eyes dart to the front and then to me. "You need to go."

"Who is that?" I ask.

She frowns, face disgusted. "I'm sorry, are we friends? Did you think we were sharing and caring tonight?"

"Azalee, seriously?"

"Gabriel, one heroic save from a Nightmare doesn't make us good. It didn't clear the life debt." The knocking increases. "Do you think whoever is at that door wouldn't ask a million questions about why the two of us are together?" she asks.

She's got me there. Whether it's her people or mine, I don't want to explain my presence.

"I don't think we're done with this conversation," I say.

She shakes her head, eyes turning sad. "Just a second," she calls to the door before saying to me, "There's only one thing I have left to ask you, Gabriel. What's the real reason you didn't finally just stand up for us when your grandfather made his speech?" All the fire is gone from her voice. "And don't give me the slow-and-steady bullshit again. Because fine, I sort of get that. Perhaps my wrecking ball approach might not always work. But that moment at the festival was a point of no return. I'm sure even you can see that."

I take a slow breath, shoulders rising and falling. I could lie to her. But to figure out what's happening, we will need to work together. So I offer an olive branch I would have burned rather than given only a few weeks ago.

When I finally speak, my words are rough whispers. "I know who the world expects me to be. I'm the grandson of the High Witch. I should be righteous and strong, knowledgeable and assertive. I know who *you* want me to be—honest and fair, the defender of the dream wielders—like you." My eyes meet hers. "I'm not sure if I can ever be enough of any of those things. But I do believe that my plan to fight from within will work, but your *enthusiastic* approach might not be a bad way either—we just need to find a way to balance what we both bring to the table."

I almost stop there, but add one final truth. "Truthfully, I was also scared. Scared of what my grandfather might do to me. That he would cut me off from the only family I have. That my brother wouldn't ever look at me the same."

"You're not the only one who's scared."

She keeps her lips pressed together as I step toward her. "Azalee, when I saw those men attack you, I realized my desire to do this by the book can't overshadow the real and immediate danger all dream wielders face." I put a hand out between us, waiting for her to shake. "I've always followed the High Witch's lead, but it's time I follow the path I know is right. Fate will find me either way."

She studies my hand, tracing the lines up my arm over my shoulder until she lands on my face. "I don't trust you. Not really. You need to earn it. But." She takes my hand. "You might make a useful ally."

"Such a compliment. I don't know how I'll recover from the flattery."

She lets out a sharp laugh. "I'm sure your ego will inflate again soon enough."

The knocking resumes. "Azalee Saunders, open this door."

"Fuck," she mutters.

"Roz?" I guess.

"Forever the consequences of my actions coming to bite me in the ass." She turns away, heading toward the front. "You let yourself in; I'm sure you can find a discreet way out the back."

I slip into the night and onto a new, unknown path. Waiting for the Fates to judge the consequences of the actions I've performed tonight. Whether they are in my favor is still up in the air.

CHAPTER 30

AZALEE

The wind slashes at my face, threatening to peel the skin off. I crouch to make myself as small as possible, huddling on the jungle floor. Then the screams start. The high-pitched panic in them consumes me until I'm nothing but screams and blood.

All at once, it's silent, except for a giggle. "Welcome back, darling."

Prying my eyes open I see the woman with the pointed teeth, her sparkling dress shining in the firelight as she spins a large wooden roulette wheel. It's night in the jungle, the moonlight cutting through the palm leaves overhead.

"No . . . no . . . no . . ." another helpless cry echoes behind me, but before I can get a proper look at the person, my head is snapped back. The crack that follows is so loud I wonder for a moment if my neck is broken. But the searing pain in my arms and legs as I attempt to stand tells me I am still whole.

"I wondered where you got off to." The woman twirls a knife between her fingers. "Never fret, though, we got all the time in the world."

I press my eyes shut. "This isn't real."

A tongue clicks. "'Course it's real, what a terrible thing to say. You'll upset our other guest." Her eyes drift over my shoulder, smiling so large I think it might tear open her face.

I close my eyes. *Wake up, wake up, wake up*, I repeat the phrase again and again in my head until the words lose all meaning.

I wake, clutching my chest, fingers digging into the fabric around it, trying to rip my heart from my body. My hair is slick against my face and neck. I push it off to get fresh air while I lie there, staring at the ceiling. Waking from a nightmare and having your heart beating a million miles an hour is totally normal, but I'm not sure my heart is beating at all.

Because dream wielders don't have nightmares.

A nightmare.

The same one I had before.

I close my eyes, taking deep, calming breaths.

To wash away the negative energies, I think of everything I have to be grateful for, of things that make me happy. Happiness is the opposite of fear.

Mom: She is the light of my world. She always knows the right things to say—and now she's in a hospital bed. I hear the screaming again.

No. Okay, something else.

Meera: My best friend, always my partner in crime—and she's rotting in jail.

Fuck. This isn't working. Scrambling out of bed, I head to the shower. The only way I will set my mind straight is through action. When Roz came by last night to bitch me out, they made it very clear that I was to remain at The Retreat, keeping a low profile, unless I went to visit Mom.

Roz was pissed I missed the coven meeting, but I don't care. I can't add more worried witches to my plate. I already have enough people I'm failing. And I'm sure as hell not just going to sit here and hide while the High Witch gets to keep up his crusade.

The scalding shower doesn't stop the pounding headache. So, while I grab the first clothes I find, I take a double shot of pain potion, grinding some piper nigrum fruit and adding it to it for a boost to banish the nightmare and gain inner strength.

The moment my feet touch the bottom step, there's a knock at the front door. "I swear to the Gods if this is Roz again," I mumble.

When I open it, Gabriel is waiting on the front steps. "Morning." White steam puffs from his mouth in the cold. He's sporting a dark scruff. "Mind letting me in? It's freezing," he adds when I don't move.

"Were you just standing there all night waiting for me to wake up?"

His brow furrows. "Of course not. Just the last two hours," he adds. His cheeks are flushed pink, and his eyes are softer—toned down from the usual glare he offers me.

"Fine." I turn, leaving him there and heading toward the kitchen. After his confession last night, I hate to admit it, but my feelings for him have shifted. Instead of giving me more reasons why his plan was better than mine, he admitted his failures and that my approach might not have been totally shit. It was actually kind of nice to have him listen to my ideas and not write me off straightaway like the coven always does. We're more alike than I cared to see before—each of us carries a weight on our shoulders that's been dragging us down.

His hair is a mess, bits and pieces sticking up all over the place like he's been running his hands through it. "I told my grandfather I'd be out of the office today, following up on leads from last night's attack. So I thought you might like company to go to the hospital with you."

I pour myself a cup of coffee, raising the cup to my lips. I pause before grabbing another cup and pouring him some too. "I don't need a babysitter," I say, handing him the drink.

"You certainly don't, but I thought you might like a friend."

I take a slow sip, pondering him. "I didn't realize we were friends."

"A generous term." He leans against the counter, fingers wrapped loosely around the mug. "The world is full of too many people wanting to be enemies. Partners in crime?"

Shaking my head, I swallow more coffee, my throat raw from the screams. "Crime and Gabriel Ford don't exactly pair well. How about mutually interested parties who are working together out of necessity?"

"Kind of a mouthful." I don't miss the way his eyes flick to my lips.

I twist them into a teasing smile. Even if I'm softening to him, I still need to mess with him a bit—have to keep up appearances so he doesn't start thinking I actually agree with him on all fronts.

I drop my mug in the sink. "Let's go. My car's out back."

"My SUV is newer and gets better gas mileage."

"I'll alert the media." I go for my keys, but Gabriel swipes them before I can.

"I'm also a better driver. So we'll go with mine."

I'm trying to maintain some cool so we might accomplish something, but he's testing my limits. "How do you know you're a better driver?"

His long legs already have him out the door several paces ahead of me. "Just an educated guess." He opens his car with a beep.

"You have control issues." I stand by his arguably nicer SUV, not getting in.

"We can have this discussion all day if you'd like. But I thought you wanted to see your mom?"

I narrow my eyes. "Fine. It'll save me gas money." I shrug, getting into the luxe interior. He didn't win this argument. I just conceded because I do need to check on Mom. Gabriel will soon find out I always get what I want, one way or another.

I won't admit this, but I am glad I don't have to drive. My mind is racing, and the road is the last thing I want to focus on. When we arrive at Salem Medical, there's a small group of press waiting outside.

"I'll go around back and tell the guards I'm here on official High Witch business," Gabriel says. "You can use the front entrance. But might I advise you don't speak to the reporters."

"Gee, thanks for that stellar advice." I get out of the car, leaning back in before I shut the door. "You don't really need to come in. I'm fine alone." I hope he doesn't notice the crack in my voice.

"I'll meet you inside."

I ignore the camera crews, ducking my head as I slip through the sliding doors. A security officer keeps the vultures outside.

"I think it's best if you wait in the hall," I tell Gabriel when we meet at the elevators. "The less people that see us together, the better." I'm not nearly as well known as Gabriel, but better safe than sorry.

"I can't argue with that."

Butterflies zoom in my stomach as we fly upward. "Glad you're learning." When the door dings open, I head toward Mom's room, not waiting to see what Gabriel does with himself.

I open the door slowly, peering into the sterile room. Mom is lying in the bed, eyes closed, the soft-blue blanket pulled up to her neck. I place a vase of flowers I bought downstairs on the table near the bed. Beeping machines fill the otherwise quiet space.

Not wanting to wake her, I stand perfectly still, arms wrapped around my stomach as I hold in the sob tearing at my throat. It's disconcerting to see her so helpless and pale. At least she can rest in a dreamless sleep. Whatever wounds the attack left aren't on her skin. But hex trauma can manifest in all kinds of ways. I can't lose her—not after everything.

She's okay, I remind myself. The healers did their job, and she'll make a full recovery.

Time marches on, each tick of the clock a beat against my skull. The hours are slipping away and I'm nowhere closer to getting answers. But I'm not waking her when I know she needs her rest, and I'm not going anywhere until I speak to her first—just to verify for myself she's okay. To dispel some of my restless energy, I shift from foot to foot, my shoes squeaking on the linoleum.

Mom mumbles, head turning toward me as her eyes blink open. "Azalee." Her voice is soft, but strong.

"Hey." I paint on a bright smile, taking her outstretched fingers. "How are you feeling?"

She squeezes my hand. "I'm fine, Azalee. Please, put that worry away."

I sit on the bed beside her. "Mom, I was so scared you'd . . ." I glance at our clasped hands, not wanting her to see me cry.

"I'll be out of here in no time. I'm made of far stronger stuff than that—as are you." Her finger lifts my chin. "While I'm away, I need you to take my place in the coven should Roz need you to assist. People look up to you."

"Highly doubt that."

"They do. The young dream wielders need someone like them to emulate. It's why Roz and I expect so much from you." She kisses my hand. "Stay close to the coven. Gallivanting off into the night isn't wise in present circumstances."

"Mom, I can't just sit around and twiddle my thumbs."

Tension lines her forehead. "Azalee, slowing down, taking the time to read the full situation before acting, is important."

"It's not fair that I get to slow down." An ache too deep to reach swallows my insides. "That I can take a breather when Iniko doesn't get that. Every second I waste is another monstrous moment Iniko is trapped in that nightmare. What right do I have to a reprieve when he doesn't get the same?"

I'm saved from having to hear her answer when a healer walks in. I quickly wipe at my eyes in case a stray tear decided to escape.

"This must be your daughter?" the round-faced man asks, smiling brightly.

"The one and only. Azalee, this is Hartley. Do you remember him?" I squint, trying to place his face, but I come up blank. "He attended a retreat many years ago."

"You're a dream wielder?" A weight lifts off my shoulders. I thought Mom was a sheep among wolves here.

He nods. "Your mother is in good hands. I promise no harm will come to her."

"Thank you." The words are barely audible.

"But I need to take her for a few tests." He unhooks Mom from the machines.

I kiss her before heading for the door. "I'll come see you later."

"Azalee," she adds. "Don't do anything rash. The universe is in a delicate balancing act at the moment. A single ripple could cause a tidal wave."

I nod but slip out before she can tell I'm lying.

I didn't expect to still see Gabriel in the drab waiting room, but here he is, sleeping on a faded flower-printed chair. I kick him in the foot. "You waited?"

He blinks, stretching his arms above his head. "Of course, I'm your ride." His features are softer, eyes still heavy with sleep.

"I could have found a way home." *But I'm glad you stayed.* Why can't I say those words out loud? He's been relatively helpful the last week, and despite not being able to tell his grandfather that he's a dream wielder, he helped in the way he thought was best. He also wants to find out the truth about these murders, which is priority one right now.

Still, giving him even a little of my gratitude feels like I'm losing a bet I don't remember agreeing to.

"Did you want me to leave?" He stares at me with those blue-green eyes, trying to extract more from me than I'm willing to give at the moment.

I avoid the question and the twisting in my gut from his gaze. "Well, since you're still here, want to find some bodies with me?" I say, walking over and clicking the down button.

He meets me at the elevator, whispering, "What kind of bodies?" He steps close as the doors slide open, and a woman exits.

"Dead ones."

I move inside, poking the button for the lowest floor. I haven't figured out where the morgue is, but lower seems the smartest.

"Azalee, what bodies?" he says, stepping in after me.

"The ones supposedly killed by dream wielders. I want to see if I can dream wield into their minds." The silver door slides closed, locking us in with the crackling elevator music and smell of tea tree oil.

I'm looking straight ahead, but I can see him studying me in our reflection. "You can't dream wield into a body that's been dead as long as these victims. There's no soul left to dream."

I shrug. "I want to see them anyway. There might be clues." I've tried the metaphysical; now, let's try the physical.

"Clues the police didn't see, but you can?" The elevator slows to a stop.

"The police saw what the High Witch wanted them to see." The door opens on the ground floor, and I step out, not waiting to see if he follows. I go to a map of the hospital and look for the morgue, but it's not listed.

"You aren't going to find it on the visitors' map," Gabriel says behind me.

I spin around, crossing my arms. "Okay, how do we find it?"

He dips his chin low, running a hand over his neck, before sighing and lifting his head. "My grandfather and I toured the building a few years ago, when they added the new wing. I know where the morgue is." His eyes flick back up to me.

"By all means then"—I sweep my hands in front of me—"lead the way." People filter by, not paying us much attention.

He steps closer, voice low. "They aren't going to just let us into the morgue."

"Then we won't ask permission. Partners in crime, remember?"

He stares at me a moment longer, but when he realizes I won't be changing my mind, he starts toward the back of the hospital. We have to wait several minutes for a healer's aid to scan her badge to open the restricted section.

"Excuse me," I call, stopping her before she slips away. "I was wondering where the cafeteria is?" I put on a forlorn grimace. Gabriel is waiting to cover the lock with a sticker to stop it from engaging.

Annoyance edges her expression, but her voice is kind. "It's on the third floor, just follow the signs."

She starts to head inside, but Gabriel hasn't been able to block the lock.

"And the elevators are where?" I frown, my voice heavy with sadness—some real, some for show.

She sighs, stepping back from the door and walking me around the corner. From my peripheral I see Gabriel grab the door before it can shut. The healer shows me the elevator and I thank her profusely, squeezing as much time from this interaction as I can to buy Gabriel precious seconds.

As the healer disappears around the corner, Gabriel appears. "Shall we?" He smiles. We wait until the area is clear and slip unnoticed into the unlocked door.

I follow Gabriel quickly as we weave through the maze of white halls and stairwells, each looking the same as the last until we reach the bottom floor and see a door marked MORGUE. Just as I'm about to grab the handle, a voice behind us calls out. "What are you two doing down here?" We turn to see a guy in a lab coat and scrubs.

I start to formulate my lie, but Gabriel speaks first. "Finally. Are you the one who was supposed to meet us?" he says impatiently, pulling his cloak tighter to conceal his jeans and T-shirt underneath, showing off the large crest of the High Witch on his chest. I try to keep the bewilderment off my face.

"Excuse me? Meet you for what?" The man frowns, confused. His eyes dart to the High Witch's crest.

Gabriel lets out a haughty sigh. "We were supposed to examine the bodies from the dream wielder murders. My grandfather, the *High Witch*, wanted me to take a look." For a guy who didn't want to play by my rules—he's sure good at it.

The man's eyes narrow but widen as recognition spreads across his face. "I'm terribly sorry, Mr. Ford. I didn't know we had anything planned. Um, let me just . . ." He fumbles with his badge and a wrapped sandwich, scanning his card across the keypad. The door opens, and Gabriel signals for me to go in first.

The room isn't bitterly cold like I was expecting, but there is a chill the hallway didn't have. The gray-tiled floor squeaks under our shoes as we head to the giant silver doors on the wall opposite the one we entered.

"May I ask why the High Witch wants you to examine the bodies again? We gave him a thorough report." The man's badge reads HEALER WALES.

"We do not question the High Witch's orders," Gabriel says, unbothered as Healer Wales pulls the four bodies of the victims out from their metal tubes. The air in the room drops several degrees cooler as I stare at the bodies.

I suppress a shudder as I glance at Gabriel, mouthing, *Distract him.* Because I can't dream wield with Healer Wales watching.

"Healer Wales, can you come show me your reports, please." Gabriel places a hand on his shoulder, leading him to the opposite side of the room, where a desk sits, and turning their backs to me.

I waste no time grabbing my crystals and getting started. I don't bother with Grant since nothing happened last time. Instead, I begin with the man from the first murder. I close my eyes, gripping my crystals tight until they cut into my skin. I squeeze harder, trying with all my might to connect to something—even if it's just a glimpse—but nothing happens.

I give up, moving on to the next two. I don't have time to linger. Once again, I summon all my powers, but the result is just a growing headache. Gabriel was correct; there is no mind left to see in. Gabriel glances over, and I shake my head.

"Well," he says to Healer Wales. "I think we got everything we needed here. We'll see ourselves out."

"Did you already see the patient in the coma?" Healer Wales asks as we head for the door.

I pause. "What patient in a coma?"

"The fifth victim. She was brought in yesterday evening. The police got there before the dream wielder could finish the job. Lucky too, or she'd be down here like the rest." He looks at the bodies, shaking his head. "The dream wielder got away, though."

I glance at Gabriel. I hadn't heard of any other attacks, and based on his face, I'd say neither had he. "Take us to her."

We follow Healer Wales in silence to the tenth floor. "All brain functions register as normal, but she won't wake up," he informs us as we enter her room.

The woman lies motionless on the bed. Beeping machines and birds chirping right outside are the only sounds. Her hands rest gently at her sides, chest rising and falling with even breaths.

"Where's her family?" I step closer to the bed.

Healer Wales looks over her chart. "She's a Jane Doe."

"You've been most helpful, Healer Wales. I will make sure my grandfather knows this." Gabriel shakes his hand. "But you look like a busy man, and we can take it from here."

He shows his first sign of uneasiness at the dismissal, but Gabriel keeps his charming smile plastered on. "Yes, all right, thank you. If you need anything . . ." he finally concedes.

"We'll be sure to call on you," Gabriel assures him. Healer Wales lingers a moment longer before leaving.

"Did you know about this?" I pull crystals from my pocket again.

"No, my grandfather didn't mention anything about a failed attack."

"Probably didn't want to admit his failure." I'm expecting a sharp comeback, but there is none. Maybe he's starting to believe me.

I've never had the opportunity to dream wield into a mind in a coma, but I know it can be done. The problem is people in comas aren't helpful. They don't know you've dreamed in because they have no point of reference to know you entered their mind. Still, this is the first break we've gotten, and I'm taking advantage of it.

I sit on the bed. "Keep an eye on the door. I don't want any unexpected visitors coming in and thinking I'm trying to finish her off." Gabriel nods, closing the curtains around the bed, leaving us in privacy.

I grip my crystal and close my eyes, feeling the immediate pull into her dreams.

CHAPTER 31

Azalee

Fog conjugates around me, twisting in swirls of grays, blacks, and whites. It tastes like orange Creamsicles. Fog can be a result of medication and drugs or can be a symbol of the dreamer's confusion. I'm on a city street filled with odd-shaped, colorful buildings: some with oversize roofs that reach upward forever, others with doors too small for anyone over two feet tall to use.

I study an upside-down bakery, serving things on platters made of sunflowers, when a rustling in an alley a few buildings over draws my attention. I head in that direction, hoping for a run-in with the dreamer. Jane Doe has to be nearby.

Molasses coats the sidewalk, making each sticky step take five times longer. My muscles burn with the added exertion. I need to move faster. I don't know how long we have before a healer decides to check in on her in the real world. I crouch, focusing on building power in my legs, before I push off. Flying through the air, I land gently in the alley.

The fog lightens as I come upon Jane Doe standing alone. Her hair is a bright sunshine yellow, while lines of red tears streak her dark skin. Arms folded, she keeps glancing down the alley.

When she spots me, her shoulders tense, hands forming fists. "Are you it?" she asks. Her voice stays for only a moment, floating away on a sandstorm breeze that cuts like glass against my exposed skin. At my will, a jacket forms around me, covering any bare skin to protect against the wind.

"Who are you waiting for?" I ask quietly, but my voice booms. Interesting, despite it being her dream, she feels like she has no voice.

"Are you the dream wielder?" Once again the voice stays for only a second, words clipped and fleeting.

"Is that who you're waiting for?" I step forward, avoiding the frogs on the ground—another symbol. Something is being overlooked, hiding in plain sight. I walk gingerly on the lily pads; the water beneath only looks like an inch or two, but dreams seldom act how they appear.

She looks around, face contorting in confusion, her bright yellow dulling. "I was told to wait here." The frogs begin a chorus of croaking.

"Who told you to wait?"

"They paid me." A bush springs from the water, dollars growing off it. "A lot of money." There's an explosion as gold coins tumble out of cracks in the brick walls on either side of us.

"What did they want you to do?"

She blinks rapidly. A figure appears behind her in the shadows, cloak and hood hiding them.

"Do you know who that is?"

She doesn't look at us, just stares at the brick wall. The gold coins dry up and blow away. "They told me all I had to do was dream." The money bush bursts into bright purple flames.

All she had to do was dream . . .

"Did they pay you to let someone dream wield in your mind?" I lick my lips to steady my breathing as pieces click into place.

"It hurt." A rattle of thunder shakes the buildings. They sway side to side like palm trees in the island breeze. The frog croaks drowned out momentarily by the cracking of lightning. "I wanted it to stop. I asked for it to stop." More red tears flow from her eyes, slipping down her neck and lining her throat.

"Who did you ask to stop?" I talk faster as the world falls apart around us. "What did they look like?" I need a description—anything to go on. If this was a failed attempt, they might try again, and I need to find this dream wielder before they kill someone else.

Jane Doe turns to me, eyes crying black tears now. "I want to wake up." The last word flies through the air, dancing around me. "Up . . . up . . . up."

I've never tried to wake someone from a coma. Typically, I can pull myself out and wake the sleeping person, but I don't know if that will work now. I take her hand. "Then wake up."

Another rattle of thunder shakes the buildings. The frog chorus grows louder. The person in the shadows steps closer. "Don't let them take me. Don't let them show me those things." Jane Doe falls onto me, clinging to my shirt, ripping at my skin.

"Who are you?" I shout to the figure. "Reveal yourself." I'm a dream wielder; I should be able to manipulate what's happening. It's almost as if she is still stuck in someone else's dream . . . or nightmare.

The figure stops, turning toward me—nothing but an endless black sits behind their hood. Either she can't or won't remember the face of the person who did this to her.

Jane Doe's weight is too much for me as she pulls me to the ground, ice-cold water splashing my face. Rattling thunder and croaking frogs consume us.

I feel a jerk behind me as I'm pulled back into the real world.

Gabriel shoves my crystals into his pocket and drags me into a closet. "Shh." He presses against me as he shuts the door softly. The only light is from the sliver around the doorframe. I'm breathing heavily, chest heaving. Gabriel places his hand over my mouth to silence my breaths.

"Morning, honey," we hear a nurse saying on the other side of the door, going through the motions of checking her patient. "It's a lovely day outside. You should wake up and see it."

I try to stop my oncoming panic left from being ripped out of the dream so suddenly. When you're torn from the dreamscape, your mind can't tell what's real. I reach up and run my hands over Gabriel's chest.

The solid muscles under my fingers ground me back in the real world. I breathe deeply, inhaling his minty aroma.

It's not working.

Breathe, Azalee. You're awake. You're awake.

My mind spirals. I hear the screaming again. Not Jane Doe's—mine.

Fuck it.

I rip Gabriel's hand off my mouth, snaking my arms around his neck and slamming my lips into his. He stiffens against my body. My pounding heart no doubt beating against his chest. But as I keep kissing him, he returns it. His fingers dig into the small of my back, pulling up my shirt. Each place where they touch leaves a burning-hot scar I'll never get rid of.

I flick my tongue against his lips, and he opens his mouth in return, twisting his tongue against mine.

Real. This is real.

The crack unleashing screams into my brain seals up as the dreamscape evaporates, and I'm firmly back in the real world. And securely pinned against the closet wall with Gabriel's full weight on me.

"I'll see you later, dear," the nurse says, opening and closing the door behind her.

Gabriel and I stay smashed together a moment longer. I go to pull away now that the coast is clear. But he kisses me one last time, long and deep, biting my lip as he falls away.

He opens the door and steps out. My chest is still pounding, but for a totally different reason. "We should . . ." His lips are pink, and I notice a few scratches on his neck.

Whoops.

"Yes, we should." I run a hand over my hair, collecting myself before stepping out of the closet and back into the hallway.

That was a terrible decision. Which I really want to fucking make again.

"Well?" he asks when we're alone in the elevator.

"Hmm?" I bite my lip.

His eyes glow with desire as he looks at the movement. "Jane Doe?" His rough voice scrapes on every nerve in my body.

I could push that emergency stop button and let us finish what we started. The fire in my veins would really, *really* like that.

Nope. Stop.

"Oh, right . . . uh . . ." I take my time moving my crystals from my pocket and back into my bag. "Someone paid her to show up and have them dream wield in her mind. She couldn't or wouldn't remember who the dream wielder was or who paid her." *This is good. Let's focus on what we came here to do.*

"She was set up." He says the words slowly—processing them with each syllable. He looks happy for the distraction as well.

"She's a Jane Doe. They probably figured they'd go for a target who needed money and wouldn't be missed. They wouldn't have to worry about friends or family asking questions." We head out to his car, which is parked in the back and away from prying eyes. The fresh air is a nice reprieve after our closet session. "There was someone there in a dark hood. I couldn't make out their features."

Gabriel leans against the car, staring at me. The sunshine makes his freckles pop, the highlights of lighter brown in his hair breaking through. "So we still don't know anything."

"Not nothing; we know all these people were most likely paid before they were killed. That means there's a money trail."

"You don't know they were all paid," Gabriel counters.

"It's a safe bet all but Meera were. She was probably targeted because the High Witch hates my family and since Mom and I were safe at The Retreat, she was the easiest person close to us to target. Anyway, this money theory makes more sense than a bunch of random dream wielders killing people. Gods, if only I could get into Iniko's mind. Talk to him for a minute without the nightmares." He might be able to show me where the next attack will be. I could stop another person from dying or ending up in jail for a crime they didn't commit.

"Have you tried researching to see if Nightmares can be communicated with?"

I give him a deadpan stare. "My friend has been a Nightmare for a year, but no, I didn't even think of trying to find a way to talk to him." I hit my palm against my forehead. "Gosh, Gabriel, what did I ever do without you?" I get into the passenger seat. It's delayed, but he gets in a minute later.

"I just meant, have you extended all your options."

"I looked through every book The Retreat has. I couldn't find anything." I lean my chair back, staring out the front window, orange leaves dancing off the trees.

"But maybe you didn't look through *every* book."

I turn my head, raising an eyebrow.

"My grandfather's private library has books on everything. Where do you think I did my study on dream wielders and Nightmares?"

"And you think he has books we don't?"

He puts the key into the ignition but doesn't start it. "He's the High Witch; his books have been passed down for centuries. I'm sure he's bound to have books you don't."

I grab my seat belt and click it into place. "Then what are we waiting for?"

"There are hundreds of books. It would take days, if not months, to search them all."

"Does he have a librarian?" I ask cautiously, knowing what I'm about to suggest might evaporate the trust we've been cultivating.

Gabriel frowns. "He has a historian who looks after books and documents in the High Witch's collection, but even if I was willing to risk exposure to ask her, I doubt Pricilla would tell us how to connect with a Nightmare."

I bite my lip, pondering not saying what I'm thinking, but hesitation isn't really my style. "She *might* tell us, if we ask her in a dream."

The word *dream* hangs heavy in the air. The car grows hotter the longer we sit in here without starting it.

Hands tightening on the wheel, Gabriel doesn't meet my eyes. "You want to use your magic to influence her into telling you what she knows. Like that dream wielder that tried to use my grandmother to assassinate my grandfather." The hate I'm used to hearing in his voice when he talks about dream wielders is back in full force.

As much as I didn't want to work with Gabriel before, I know I need him now. Using a softness I don't typically offer him, I place a hand on his arm. "No, not like that. That dream wielder—they were wrong, they did a terrible thing to your grandmother. Even I can admit that not all dream wielders are good people."

His eyes finally drift to mine. A mixture of terror and sadness.

"I will only enter her dream to ask a few questions. No harm will come to her. I swear. And if anyone could get it done with as little risk as possible, it's me. I can control emotional responses in dreams—as you've experienced." I don't mention that I've done dream manipulation like this many times before. That nugget of info won't make him any happier. "Or, if you like, maybe you could do it?" I gauge his reaction. And just as I suspect, he shakes his head vehemently.

"No. I don't want—I don't know how." He rakes a hand through his hair. "If you promise she won't be harmed, you can try."

"I promise."

And while it's true, I hear the echo of the nightmare's scream in the back of my mind.

CHAPTER 32

Gabriel

"Give her this." Azalee withdraws a vial from her bag. "It's a sleeping tonic. It's not very strong, but it will be enough to get her to sleep for about thirty minutes. More than enough time for me to get in and out."

I stare at the purple liquid, not taking it from her open palm. All the words my grandfather poured into me over the decades sound off in my head.

"It's not poison."

"I know," I say without hesitation. And it's true. Despite everything we've said to each other over the years, I do trust Azalee now. Hell, she's the only person I can truly be totally myself with and know that she won't back away from it. It's rather freeing not to hide behind a mask.

Taking the vial, I pour the liquid into the cup of tea we bought on the way. Pricilla always raves about this specific brew from a shop in town. "Stay in the car and I'll wave you in when she's asleep."

The historian's office is located in a museum downtown. While she works for the High Witch, the rest of the staff isn't on his payroll. Still, we'll need to make sure Azalee isn't seen.

I head inside, walking past the many displays of artifacts from Salem's past, until I reach Pricilla's office.

"Mr. Ford," Pricilla says when I step inside. She is in her early eighties and has been at this job longer than grandfather has held his. Her brown skin is wrinkled, gray hair neatly trimmed in a pixie cut. "I wasn't expecting a visit from the High Witch's team."

The large office feels cramped with all the shelves and boxes stored in every corner. It smells of ink and old paper with a hint of clove and licorice.

"Nothing official, I was just in the neighborhood and wanted to drop by and offer thanks from the High Witch on your continued dedication to preserving his position's history." I place the tea down in front of her.

"Always charming, you Fords." She opens the lid and smells the pungent tea. "But I never turn down a good cuppa."

I wait for her to taste it, but she doesn't. "Is it the right one?" I press.

"Smells like it."

"Mind making sure?" I offer my most charming smile. "I don't want to leave without knowing I got the job done."

She shakes her head with a chuckle. "You are your grandfather's kin." She takes a sip, and I watch her smile in delight. "That's the one. It always reminds me of . . ." Her eyes flutter and close, head resting back on the chair as she falls asleep.

"Pricilla?" I ask. When she doesn't respond. I wave to Azalee from the window to come inside.

A few minutes later, Azalee is in Pricilla's dream. I don't take my eyes off them. I've never been awake with Azalee when she dream wields, but this close I can feel the magic tugging on our golden thread. I have to remind myself Azalee isn't going to harm Pricilla, but the more minutes that tick by, the harder it is to resist the instinct to stop her.

"I got it," she says, opening her eyes after five minutes.

"She told you a spell?"

Azalee bites her lip. "No, but she told me which book in the High Witch's collection might have the answer. So, let's go."

"What about her?" Pricilla sleeps peacefully in her chair.

"She'll wake shortly. All she'll remember is that you brought the tea, then you left and she fell asleep."

"So you did influence her then?" I grind my teeth.

"Only a little." Azalee frowns. If I didn't know her, I'd think it was guilt. "Enough to cover our tracks."

I know it had to be done. But that doesn't mean it sits any easier in my gut.

I pull around the back of the High Witch's house and tell Azalee to wait in the car while I check if the coast is clear. I'm guessing, like me, her brain is still a little rattled from that kiss; otherwise, she might think this is a trap. I wouldn't have blamed her if it had been a few weeks ago. Turning her and the other dream wielders over is what Grandfather would have expected from me. But I couldn't, especially not now that we are inching toward the truth of these murders.

After doing a quick sweep, I motion for her to come in. "The High Witch is in Boston for the day, and my brother should be in class." *Should* being the key word. "We'll have a few hours." She follows me down a long hallway until we reach a carved wooden door.

The expansive wood-paneled room is the High Witch's private collection. It's two stories with a spiral staircase on the left, a fireplace in the back set between two floor-to-ceiling windows, and, of course, books.

"Oh my Gods." Azalee sucks in a breath beside me. "Not even the Salem Public Library has this large a collection. I didn't realize this fortress was hiding books."

I glance over at her. "I'm sure it's hiding a lot more than books."

"Like a money trail?"

I press my lips into a thin line. I know she thinks Grandfather might be involved in these murders. That he's the puppet master who created a play to lead the masses to vote his way, and she might be right. The old man will do whatever it takes to get his way. I just never thought it'd be serial murders. But I started this endeavor to find the truth, and I'll see it through to wherever it leads me.

"Pricilla said the book was *Call of the Darkness*." Azalee continues, not waiting for my response. "But she didn't say *where* it was. This could take hours. If another attack is imminent, we need to hurry."

"If you were someone who hated dream wielding, would you keep those books front and center?"

She nods. "Right, to the back. Does he have a protection circle around them? You know, in case those evil dream wielder powers try to leach out." She smirks.

When we reach the far end, I open a glass cabinet with runes etched into the glass.

"Oh my Gods, he does." Her face twists in disgust.

"He *really* doesn't like dream wielders." Over the last two years, I've separated myself from the idea. I wasn't one of them. It wasn't *me* he despised. But over the last few days, as I've immersed myself in that world, separating the two is getting harder.

"Gabriel, if your grandfather can't love you for who you are—"

"I thought we were looking for answers, not bringing up family drama." The venom I'm used to spouting at her comes firing out, if a little tamer than before.

Taking the hint, she backs off.

Running a finger along the spines, I spot the book we're looking for. It could pass for leather, but a heaviness stirs inside me when I pull it out. "This is it."

"It's made of human skin, FYI," she says. That must be the reason she didn't yank it out of my hand right away. "Put it on the table."

I set it on the massive wood desk and flick on the light, casting a yellow glow over the pages. A storm is settling over Salem, dark clouds turning day into night. Salem's weather is magic; it seems to adapt to the moods.

We both lean over the tome, Azalee using her pointer finger to flip it open. "Pricilla was a little fuzzy on details thanks to the sleeping tonic. So she couldn't give me an exact page."

The first few chapters contain things I would've preferred not to know. Like detailing how to make a Nightmare from scratch, as in starting with the trauma and manipulating them into becoming a Nightmare. We jump over that chapter quickly.

Rain drops on the window as Azalee grabs my arm when we reach a page in the middle. "Gabriel." Her hair tickles my cheeks as she leans closer. "This is it."

The passage is a spell, handwritten in the margins. The book says that to reach a Nightmare, you must use more than one dream wielder. The combined strength will increase the power of dreams over nightmares. It won't last long, and depending on the strength and will of the Nightmare, it might not be successful at all.

"You think it will work? It's just scribbles in the margins." I look over at her, my lips grazing her cheek. My stomach clenches, my mouth going dry.

She straightens, pressing her hand to the pages, but must remember the questionable binding because she pulls away, wiping her hand on the back of a chair. This isn't the kind of book you want to get up close and personal with. "Everything starts as someone's scribble. I've never tried to use more than one dream wielder for anything—let alone to dream wield into a Nightmare. So I don't know if it'll work, but I'm willing to try."

I run my fingers over the text. "If this goes wrong, the Nightmare might fight back. You could be trapped. There's a reason people don't willingly seek out Nightmares."

"Iniko will fight the darkness. I know he will." She clasps her hands in front of her, skin turning white from the iron grip.

"Then I guess we better find the ingredients." I take her hand, a hum vibrating between us. Whatever we keep unlocking when we kiss is growing stronger. A siren call I don't know how much longer

I can ignore. I release her grasp, scanning the list. "Some of these are extremely rare, but I may be able to find them in my grandfather's stores." I glance at the clock. It's later than I thought. "Shit, he'll be home soon. You need to go."

"You check here, and I'll raid The Retreat—pun absolutely not intended." She glances at the large clock in the corner. "Can you meet me at my place at midnight?"

"It's a date." I test the waters with a smile.

"No, it's not."

Azalee opens the door the second I arrive. "Got everything?" she asks, letting me inside and heading straight toward the dungeon.

"I almost thought we would have to do without the *Spilanthes acmella*." Grandfather had wanted to chat about the festival and his trip to Boston over a long, drawn-out dinner with Logan and me when he got home. But when he took a call from New Zealand, I was able to find what I needed—with Logan's help. He pestered me for why I needed such odd ingredients, but I managed to convince him it was for a project the High Witch wanted me to conduct that I wasn't allowed to discuss.

I'll have to answer Logan's questions later, but I'm clear for now.

"But I found a tin in my grandfather's desk. It's nearly gone, but it'll be enough." If he notices it's missing, he'll think Logan took it. He has a habit of doing that. I'm carrying my ingredients in a wooden box, while Azalee's are in a mirrored one. Mirrors have always been windows to the soul.

We reach the door, and she draws a knife to prick her finger, but I grab her hand just as the blade touches her skin. "We don't have to do this. We can find another way."

"That might be true, but we don't have time. If doing this gets us a few steps ahead, then I'm willing to risk it."

"As long as you're sure."

"I am. Gabriel . . ." She pauses. "Thanks for trusting me on this and not shooting down my idea. It's not exactly something I'm used to."

"Don't get me wrong, I hate when you have good ideas." I smile. She doesn't hide her laugh from me this time. "But while you and I might go about things in different ways, our end goal is the same. So I'm willing to listen to whatever absurd plan you concoct, if you're willing to hear out my more stable ideas too."

She rolls her eyes like always, but that cute grin doesn't falter. "I guess that's fair."

We decide it's best to make the potion outside Iniko's room, so we're ready to go as soon as she opens the door. Iniko can't be the one to pull Azalee into his nightmare; she has to initiate the dream.

Azalee's delicate hands tremble as she lays a blanket on the ground, carefully smoothing it until it's wrinkle-free. I'm mesmerized, unable to take my eyes off her as I strike a match to cleanse the space.

Taking turns, we each remove one ingredient at a time, placing our intentions into them before arranging them in a circle around a central bowl. The blackthorn is in its own copper bowl beside it, smoke drifting upward in soft tendrils.

We alternate pouring the ingredients, carefully referencing the picture of the spell on my phone to make sure the order is correct. With each drop added to the potion, I feel the energy changing. After I place the last herb in the bowl, Azalee submerges the necklace we'll use around Iniko's neck and its twin she'll wear. A hematite stone at its center for grounding, its metallic sheen shines as the brew swirls around it.

Azalee takes my hands, linking us around the bowl as we chant the spell three times, followed by a minute of silence. Pressing my eyes closed, I sink all my energy into the brew. There's a flash of warmth across my skin and a humming in my ears, a weight pressing heavily against my limbs. Then it's gone.

I open my eyes, blinking at Azalee, before dropping her hands. Withdrawing the crystal necklaces, she blots them dry on the soft gray cloth. I take a deep breath; the hum of the magic audible around us is an excellent sign.

"It's now or never." She puts the necklace on and grips the other tightly.

"I've never been in charge of a dream wield before. What if I screw this up?" This fear has been eating away at me all day.

"You won't be dream wielding; you're just my boost of energy. Focus on channeling your power to me."

Iniko doesn't stir as we enter the room. She needs to get the necklace over his head without him touching her. Opening the chain as wide as she can, she leans over, tossing the necklace. It gets caught on his ear, but it startles him enough he pulls it down the rest of the way.

She motions for me to get closer. "It's okay," she says calmly to Iniko. "We're going to try something new today, all right? This is going to let us speak."

I take her hand, an amethyst pressed between our palms and rose quartz in my other. The hematite stone hanging from her neck, the twin to the one now slung around Iniko's, should be the connecting force between them. Normally, there is a thin string between dream wielders and dreamer; the hematite turns that string into a thick rope.

As she takes Iniko's hand, I hope to the Gods it holds.

CHAPTER 33

Azalee

I reach out, fingers shaking as I take Iniko's hand. The world jerks away, and his mind sucks me in.

I can't let the nightmares discover me before I get a foothold in his dreamscape. I find a crevasse hidden in the depths of despair—the last dregs of a dream shadowed in a nightmare. I'm not seeing with my eyes; my vision is too fuzzy. I use my other senses to guide me.

Bitter cold stings my exposed skin—I tug harder on my connection with Gabriel's energy, letting him warm me. Slowly, my skin doesn't feel like someone is stabbing it with little knives. Sun radiates from me, pushing outward as I light the way into Iniko's mind.

Gabriel isn't here with me physically, but I feel his presence nonetheless. That life debt rope is suddenly no longer the bane of my existence.

"Iniko," I call through the darkness. It may be receding, but its force barrels against me, trying to consume me. I don't let my hopes get too high that I might get to talk to my friend again. Here, with my mind intact, I get the sense the nightmarescape is far more extensive than we ever imagined.

Gritting my teeth, I force the final bits of darkness away, pain slicing through my skull. I've performed difficult dream wields before, but nothing like this. Gabriel's steady energy thumping in my veins is what keeps me going.

"Iniko?" Only one shadow remains, a cloud of it huddled in the corner. We're in Iniko's childhood bedroom. Energy spent from keeping the darkness at bay, I don't have any left to create a dreamscape. This is what Iniko's mind has chosen.

Home.

I step toward the huddled mass of billowing darkness, a shape moving underneath. I reach my hand inside the cold smoke, goose bumps appearing over my arms. The resistance is strong as my fingers search for something solid. My hand grasps firmly on a shoulder; swallowing the lingering fear, I tug the person toward me. In that moment, Gabriel's strength exerts itself once again, helping me drag Iniko from the dark. Gabriel can't see what's happening, but he must feel my needs and act accordingly—clever piece of magic.

"Iniko," I say again softly. "It's me, Azalee."

He blinks a few times like he's blinded by the lightness of this room. He studies me, hand grazing over my hair, then my face before his eyes drop to my shirt. "I can't believe you haven't burned that ugly thing yet."

I burst into tears. I've worked so hard this last year to put on a brave face. To not let the sadness and despair win. But it was always there, digging deeper and deeper, eroding who I was. "I missed you." I throw my arms around his neck, pulling him into a bone-crushing hug. My heart thrums in my throat as I cherish the rise and fall of his breaths against me.

"I missed you too, my special, special Azalee." His voice is missing something; part of him is still lost in the nightmare. "I always knew you would get me out. How did you do it?"

I swallow. "It's only a temporary dream. I used Gabriel to help me dream wield. It was the only way I could be strong enough."

He nods, looking around the room.

"Iniko, are you . . . how do you feel?" I'm not sure what to ask or if I should. I'm afraid it might pull him back under, but it feels wrong not to.

"Right now, I feel light, and sometimes all you can live for is the right now. I don't know how much time we have, and I have a lot to tell you." A bench of black stone appears in the room. Iniko pulls us to sit, his hands still clasped in mine.

"You need to be careful. Things are happening. Plans put into motion." His bloodshot yellowed eyes burn into mine.

I flinch back. "What do you know?"

He looks at his palms, running his hands over his bare arms and then mine. "The nightmares confused me at first. I didn't think I was Seeing anything more than a new terror, but then I realized it was something else, something beyond myself." A wisp of darkness twists itself like a cat around his feet. I tense my muscles to keep from visibly trembling.

"There are so many of us, hidden deep underground, but it's nothing like here. It's a true prison. The smell of decay and sadness is nauseating."

I fail to conceal my shudder. "Who's in this prison?"

He looks up, his dark eyes sad but alert for the first time in a year. "Nightmares. He's keeping them to experiment on. To change the course of fate."

"The High Witch?" I need to move this story along. As much as I want to sit and talk to Iniko, I don't know how much time I'll get. The nightmare is like a wild cat on the prowl just outside these walls, searching for its way in.

He nods, scratching his head. "He's using them to bring about terror—hidden—he's hiding them away. The dream wielders are not safe." He suddenly grabs my hand, clawing into my skin. "The spirits are wrapped in darkness, chained to the earth by dirt and stone. They cannot be free to rise to the next world or to stay and tell their truths.

You must release them. For locked spirits can only bring about pain and suffering."

"Whose spirits, the Nightmares'?" A framed picture of a baseball player falls off the wall with a thud. A low rumbling like right before an earthquake sounds.

Iniko ignores it. "No, the victims'. He locks them away to keep the truth hidden from those who could See it." The medium said the spirits were wrapped in darkness, but a binding spell strong enough to hold spirits from moving on? That would have to be fucking powerful and require immense magical abilities.

"What else, Iniko? Can you tell me if there will be another attack?"

He rests his head in his palms as the world becomes dark. I sense the nightmare beginning to regain control. The ground shifts, and we're in a densely wooded forest. "Is this where the attack will happen? Where are we?" My words come out fast because I feel the nightmare bearing down, skulking at the back of my mind.

"Salem Woods, tomorrow night. What was missed will be completed."

"The attack on Jane Doe? Are they going to try again with her? Or someone else?" I have too many questions and the time for answers is running out.

"Watch." Images of the path fall into my mind. He's using the little energy he has left to show me how to get there.

Iniko shakes, and I curl him into my arms, letting him leach my warmth. "I know this is hard, Ink, but I need you to fight it. Please, just a little longer."

He nods against my chest.

There's another question I need him to answer. "Can you See anything about Meera's future? About the night Grant died. Something I can use to help her." I told him what happened to Meera when I visited a few days ago. I hope he was listening.

He grits his teeth, straightening up. "I can try, but it's fuzzy."

"It's okay, tell me what you See." The world darkens again, and this time, we're outside Grant's house. Connected events are more accessible for him to See.

Iniko steps away from me, walking toward the house. The world is slightly blurred, like when I was in Jane Doe's mind. "It's not fuzzy because I'm weak. It's because there is a charm concealing it—a very powerful one."

"Meera was charmed? Something to make her not know what happened?" That's why when I asked her, she wasn't able to give me details.

Iniko nods. "Perhaps."

"Maybe that's what they do? They enchant the dream wielder and then bring in one of the High Witch's hidden Nightmares to finish the job." *Yes*, that would make sense. I knew it was impossible for a dream wielder to kill someone.

Iniko turns back to me, tendrils of darkness swirling around him. "I cannot see that far. Azalee, I've given you all I can. It's up to you, it always has been." He runs a hand through the dark clouds surrounding him. "I can't keep them away any longer."

"I'm sorry, Ink." Hot tears slip down my cheeks. "I'm sorry I have to leave you here. I haven't given up trying to find a way to free you."

Iniko reaches out to me, but he's too far away now, and I'm stuck to the ground. "I know you come to see me. I don't always know what you're saying, but I feel you there. I feel your guilt."

"I will get you back."

Iniko smiles sadly. The darkness has consumed all but his face. His mouth opens to speak, but all that comes out is a scream.

CHAPTER 34

Gabriel

I yank Azalee from the nightmarescape and clutch her tightly to my chest. My clipped breathing makes me lightheaded. I keep my eyes pressed shut to stop the room from spinning. Azalee pants in my arms, face flushed and wet with tears.

"Take it slowly," I whisper, running a hand through her sweat-drenched hair. "In and out. Good, yes, just like that." As I continue to help bring her and myself back from the dream's grip, I move us into the hallway.

Azalee's breath slows to a normal rhythm. She finally opens her eyes, gazing up at me with her head resting against my chest. "Thank you." It's the softest I've ever heard her.

"Did it work?" I still hold her in my arms. When she was here before, it was a fiery lust that sizzled across my body. But now I offer her comfort and safety, which she absorbs like a sponge.

"My mind's still like scrambled eggs, but I think I got some answers." She pulls away, heading toward the door, tripping on uneasy feet. I'm two steps behind, ready to catch her. "But let's not discuss them down here."

The ghostly expression on her face makes me wonder how this experience left Iniko. Getting dragged from the darkness for a brief moment makes it harder to go back in.

Azalee beelines for the kitchen, placing a saucepot on the stove and filling it with cream. "Mom always said a good cup of hot chocolate could push away nightmares." She stirs absentmindedly as I lean against the counter beside her. She's looking better already, but I still want to keep my eyes on her. Or maybe there's another reason for that.

"I was nine when my mom first told me about the existence of the Nightmares and how they came to be," she continues, oblivious to my longing gaze. "After, I used to sneak down and leave mugs of cocoa for them. I did it every night for a month until Mom caught me." She smiles at the memory. "She wasn't mad. I remember her leading me up the stairs to make another batch for the next night."

She pours rich chocolate nibs into the pot, watching them melt into the milk, turning it a light brown. "And then one day, I stopped. I realized whatever magic my mom told me was in this cocoa wasn't real."

"I was six when I realized magic wasn't the answer for everything." I hand her a sprig of chocolate mint from the plant growing on the window. "Growing up like we do, with magic in our veins, you think anything is possible. But then my parents died. I read every book in that library, looking for a way to bring them back. But as we all finally learn, death comes for everyone eventually. A fate we cannot escape no matter how powerful we are." Grief squeezes my lungs. A pain I thought long since buried over comes back in a giant wave.

"A devastating truth we both had to understand far too young." Azalee grabs mugs from the cupboard, pouring the steaming liquid into them. "Magic feels like the answer for everything. But it's not—unfortunately." She puts a heaping handful of marshmallows on top.

"Do you remember when you came to my sixth birthday party?" I ask.

She frowns, adding more marshmallows to her cup. "I try to forget most of my interactions with you." Bringing her hot cocoa to her lips, she sips it to hide her smile.

"Highly doubtful you forgot this one." I wrap my hand around the warm mug to take away the chill left from the dungeons.

"Why's that?"

I level her with a smolder. "Because you kissed me."

She barks out a laugh. "No, I didn't."

"Yes, you did. We had just eaten cake and ice cream, and I was sitting alone in the ball pit because my grandfather had scolded me about getting my new shoes covered in frosting." The memory drags me right back into those feelings. It's the first time I recall knowing where my place in the High Witch's world was. "I was crying, and you came over and kissed me."

Her lips twist up. "Oh, that's right. You tasted like strawberries, and it was so wet."

"Hey, it was my first kiss. I've improved." I delight in watching her eyes flick to my lips. "But it did make me feel better. You, me, and Iniko didn't leave that ball pit for hours. That was the first time you came to my rescue. Guess I shouldn't have been surprised when you did it again years later." I couldn't conceptualize it at the time, but it meant a lot to have someone show loyalty to me like that.

"I guess you weren't always so bad. Even if you were still trying to boss me around."

"*Trying* being the key word. You were a stubborn pain in the ass even at six."

She tosses a marshmallow at my face. "Didn't stop you from following me like a lost puppy."

"If we'd been born to different circumstances, maybe we could have been friends."

"Let's not go that far." That biting tone is there, but her lively eyes tell me there is no heat behind them. "You'd have needed a miracle for that."

"When our forefathers saved everyone from the plague, the Puritans thought magic was a miracle." I stare at the bobbing marshmallows.

"I don't think I believe in miracles." She moves toward the living room, but I stop her.

"I do."

She tilts her head, raising an eyebrow. "Name one."

"You didn't poison this hot chocolate to kill me."

She cracks a genuine smile, and it shatters my resolve.

Placing my mug down, I step closer until our bodies are pressed together. "I've got another miracle."

"Oh?" Her voice is hoarse.

Slowly, I start at her ear, tracing the line of her jaw, and watching her shiver under my white-hot gaze. "Us." I tilt her chin up, my lips hovering above her. I want to taste the minty chocolate on her tongue.

"What about us?" I watch her resistance melting like the marshmallows in our abandoned cups.

I lick my lips, her pupils dilating in response. "You know, sworn enemies to lovers."

Without dropping my gaze, she slides her hand along my abdomen, pulling my shirt up so her fingers graze my well-earned muscles. "We aren't lovers."

My lips twitch. "I'm sure we can arrange that."

The gold flecks in her green eyes shimmer with a pulse of magic through our bond. Using her nails, she teases a swirling pattern across the sensitive skin of my hips. Tilting her head, she raises an eyebrow, a dare flashing in her features.

Do it, I say with my stare.

"Fuck it. I've had worse ideas." She pulls my head down, lips exploding into mine. I reach around, lifting her into my arms and placing her on the counter so I can slide in between her legs.

My large palm splays over her upper thigh, the heat radiating between us sizzling just under the surface. "Happy to assist in your destructive nature for a night," I say, and she nips at my throat in response.

A roaring fills my ears, and I slide my tongue into her mouth to keep her from getting the last word. She doesn't seem to mind. The kiss is rough and fast, the years of fighting manifesting in a frenzied need for each of us to keep the upper hand. She scoots closer, wrapping her legs around me as I dig my fingers into her hips, searching for the satisfaction we both crave.

Azalee is usually hard angles and stony glares, but right now, she's soft against me. All the pieces of us slide into place. That string linking us together that I've wanted to cut away so often now burns bright, a flaring white light pulling us ever closer.

It's the best fucking thing I've ever seen.

She scratches my skin, pinpricks of pain receding as waves of pleasure replace them. *More.*

"Bedroom?" I pant against her ear, kissing along her neck. I can feel her heart thrumming against my lips.

"Where's your sense of adventure, Gabriel?" She shoves hard against my chest, and I stumble into the table, barely catching myself from falling. "There's a perfectly good dining table underneath you." A mischievous grin graces her perfect lips, and I'm happy to go wherever she leads me.

Striding forward, she pushes me down on the table, flipping a leg over and straddling me. I run my hands up her waist, taking her shirt with me and pulling it over her head. My breath hitches as I take in the stunning view. My thumb traces over her newly exposed body, goose bumps covering her skin in my wake. I grip the back of her neck. "Azalee . . ."

Her nails scrape across my scalp, playing with my hair. "Is this the part where you tell me it's a bad idea?" She offers the barest of kisses, biting my bottom lip. "That this is my chance to back out?"

"Both things are valid." I say this even as I'm unclasping her bra, the thin lace strap dangling precariously on her shoulder. I run my fingers under it, each painful millisecond dragging on as I wait for the final yes I need to keep this going.

Her eyes soften, and she sucks in her swollen pink lips.

Gods, I hope she's not going to back out. She should. I should. But we've been skating around this moment too long.

Leaning into me, she guides my hand to slip the bra the rest of the way off, allowing me free range of her body. "I'll be the best bad idea you've ever had," she says.

Fuck. "I don't doubt that."

With complete disregard for my clothes, she rips open my shirt, the buttons ricocheting across the kitchen. The wicked grin is too much, and I wrap my arms around her back so we're skin to skin, and I'm lost in blissful oblivion.

"Try to keep up, Ford."

I do just that and a whole hell of a lot more as I find the spots that make her moan again and again.

I start a fire in the hearth, the crackling our background music before I rejoin her on the floor. After the table, we made good use of the couch and floor. Pillows and blankets create our makeshift bed. "How was Iniko?" I say when I've settled back in, her naked body hidden away under the quilt. It's probably time we revisit the reason I came here tonight.

"Okay—terrible. He was him, but not." She stares toward the door to the dungeons. "He was stronger than I thought he would be. But pieces of him had been hacked away, lost in the darkness. It's not something he will be able to fight forever. Eventually there will be nothing left."

"We'll save him." I kiss the top of her head. "What did he show you?"

She rests her head on my chest, hands running over my tattoo. "Dream wielders didn't kill those people. A Nightmare, or more than one, did. The High Witch is keeping several locked away. Iniko couldn't pinpoint where, but it was dark and cold—probably a dungeon or cellar."

I twirl my fingers through her hair, trying to keep my voice steady as I say, "He was sure it was the High Witch then?" I still had hope that my grandfather wasn't responsible.

"I'm sorry. I hate the High Witch, but that didn't mean I wanted you to have a shitty grandfather." She kisses my chest in a surprisingly sweet gesture. "He's also keeping the spirits they kill bound to this earth so no mediums can connect and get the truth."

"And you saw my grandfather with the Nightmares?" I need 100 percent proof before I can hope to win the public's favor against him.

"I didn't see him in the vision, but Iniko said it was him." When I don't respond, she props up on an elbow to look me in the eye. "I know you wanted to believe that your grandfather wasn't capable of this level of sadisticness."

"I never thought my grandfather was perfect—far from it. But I didn't see him going this far. Framing dream wielders and killing innocent people." I sit up, pressing the heels of my hands into my eyes.

"Desperation makes people do crazy things. His bill is up for a vote, and he doesn't want to lose."

"It's more than that," I admit, knowing I need to share everything with her or this isn't going to work. "He's dying—of what and how long he has, I don't know." I answer the questions I know she's going to ask.

"Fuck." She lets out a heavy breath. "That's why he's so up our asses all of a sudden."

I nod.

"Do you want to talk about it?" she asks slowly.

"No." I'm only now fully coming to terms with his true deeds. I can't afford to mix in sympathetic feelings for my dying grandfather when I need to focus on him as the dangerous High Witch.

She nods. "When you do, you know where to find me."

"Did you ask Iniko about the attack?" I change the subject.

Her back is bare as she sits with her arms wrapped around her knees. I run my fingers along the curves as she speaks. "Yeah, he showed me the location of the next attack. It'll be tomorrow night"—she glances at the grandfather clock—"scratch that, tonight at Salem Woods."

"You think we can stop them? Maybe catch whoever is behind it?"

She looks over her shoulder to me. "Yes, and yes. I won't let another person die or have another dream wielder take the blame. You don't have to do this with me, Gabriel." She plays with the stone around her neck that she didn't remove after the spell. "But I'd have better luck if you were with me."

"Was it hard to get those words out of your mouth?" I press a kiss onto her shoulder.

"Like swallowing glass." She smiles, grabbing my chin and lifting my lips to hers.

I kiss her deeply, and she sighs in pleasure. I don't think I've ever seen her relaxed—she's always racing a million miles an hour to the next bad decision. But as I cup her cheek, my thumb softly tracing over her skin, I don't need to be an aura reader to feel the shift in her energies.

She smiles ever so slightly against my lips, and without breaking our kiss, I pull her back to lie on me. My body thrums with the need to keep her close. Her heart beats in sync with mine as I slide my hand over the curves of her body I'm not done exploring, but all too soon she pushes away.

"It's late. You should get home." She stands, taking the blanket with her and leaving me naked on the floor.

"You're kicking me out?" I try not to sound hurt, but there's a sting in my chest. It's been too long since I shared a bed with someone. That desire aches deeper than I realized now that I was this close.

"Imagine the scandal if someone showed up and found us like this together." She motions to my body. "Best not risk it."

Her words make sense, but I can tell she's lying. Putting on that bravado she uses as her weapon of choice.

I don't call her on it, though. "Okay. I'll see you tonight at Salem Woods?"

She nods. "I'll text you the details."

The bitter cold greets me as I walk out to my car. That tug toward her I always chalked up to the life debt is stronger than ever, and I'm pretty sure it has nothing to do with her saving my life and more to do with what she's done to my heart.

CHAPTER 35

Azalee

I'm strapped to a spinning board, knives stabbed into the wood between my legs and by my ear.

"I'm sorry," a frail woman wrapped in a shawl whispers from a chair in the audience composed only of her. We're in a circus tent, but a hint of the view outside shows I'm in the dark jungle once more.

I try to speak, but with every attempt, metallic blood fills my mouth.

"She's coming." Fear paralyzes the woman's features.

A staccato of music, off-key and thunderous, scratches at my brain. Then the wheel starts spinning as the scene blurs with my tears.

I don't jolt up like they do in the movies after startling awake from a dream. My eyes fly open, but the rest of me is paralyzed.

Sleep paralysis: the next stage of becoming a Nightmare. I attempt slow, deep breaths, reminding myself repeatedly of who I am. It wasn't real. Nightmares aren't real. Dreams are nothing more than a fabrication of the mind. They don't control me.

But nightmares are real. And sometimes dreams are all we have.

This is why I didn't want Gabriel to spend the night. After having him touch me in a way I'm not sure I've ever felt with any of the lovers I've taken to bed, I wanted to curl up in his arms and sleep. But I knew, especially after my encounter with Iniko, that the nightmares were lurking inside my mind, waiting for their chance to sneak in. I couldn't risk him seeing me like this.

After a few minutes that feel like hours, my body returns to me. This time, I jump out of bed, tripping and knocking a plate of crystals to the ground. I sink to the floor, wanting nothing more than to close my eyes, but I'm scared of what I'll see.

Instead, I slowly pick the crystals up one by one and force my racing pulse to slow itself to a normal rhythm. I lean my head against the bed, exhausted from the simple task.

I need to get out of here.

I'm dressed and on my way to the jail, not bothering with breakfast. The knots in my stomach occupy all the space usually reserved for food. I sit in the station for an hour before they let me see Meera—she looks better than I do. I don't know if that's saying more about her or me.

"How are you holding up?" I ask through the glass between us.

"I don't know." She plays with a hole in the faux wood tabletop.

"I might have a lead that will help you," I whisper into the phone.

"Really? What is it?" Her wide eyes are alert for the first time in days.

"I don't want to say anything just yet. But can you tell me again what happened that night with Grant?" I have to be careful with my words. I have no doubt this conversation is being monitored.

Her gaze drops. "I don't want to talk about it, Az. That's all I ever talk about now."

I lean forward. "Please, Meera? It could really help."

She frowns but nods. "It's a blur. I remember going to Grant's house, and we had a few drinks. Then I asked him if I could dream wield, and he agreed. The dream wielding was going fine, but then it went dark and when I woke up, he was dead."

"And you *do* remember dream wielding?" I push.

"Yeah. Why?"

Adrenaline rushes through my veins. "Was there anyone else there?"

"No, just us." Her eyes narrow.

"Do you recall anything weird happening? Did the drinks taste funny?" I'm searching for some clue about the fuzziness Iniko described around Meera.

"What are you getting at, Azalee?"

"I'm trying to figure out why you and the other dream wielders are here." I want to fill her in on what Iniko showed me, but it's too risky. "Listen, I'm close to finding answers. It'll all be over soon."

Meera places her hand on the glass, and I put mine on the other side. Her fingers curl, trying to reach me. "I don't want you getting hurt too."

"I won't. I'll be fine."

"I'm serious. You placing yourself in the middle of all this to protect me will only get you in trouble too." She looks around the room at the guard near the door.

"Of course I'm going to protect you—you're my best friend. I won't let someone frame you for murder." I stand. "I have to go, okay? But I'll check back in soon." She tries again to convince me, but I'm in too deep now.

Cool mist fills the air, clinging to my skin and hair and absorbing into my clothes—the shadow of a rainstorm on its way. Iniko wasn't clear on *when* the attack is supposed to take place. So I got here as the sun was setting. It didn't take long to find the clearing. The vision he gave walked me through the path leading to it.

I sent Gabriel my location, but he hasn't texted back. It's nearly midnight, and I'm starting to wonder if he will show up at all. Maybe he regrets last night. We both would be wise to, but I don't. Still, it doesn't mean it'll happen again.

I roll my spherical black onyx around in my hand. This is the most powerful one I own. My mother gifted it to me after my father died. I glance up at the sound of twigs cracking, my body tensing.

"Sorry." Gabriel raises his hands as his face becomes bathed in moonlight.

"I wasn't sure you'd show." I slide the crystal into my cloak pocket, my body aching from lack of movement.

He scans the surroundings. "Did I miss the party?"

"Hasn't started yet." I tug him into the shadows with me. The full moon is on our side tonight, lighting up the darkness to hopefully reveal the bad guys and get us some fucking answers.

"You sure this is the right . . ." He trails off when a figure moves in the darkness, moonlight guiding them to this spot. Instinctively, we move as one, hiding ourselves deeper behind the tree. Sounds travel differently in the forest.

A flashlight illuminates their path as they enter the moonlit clearing. It's a woman around our age with thick braids and a flowing pink dress and gray cardigan. She stops in the middle of the clearing and stares at the space she came from. A few minutes pass and my anxious feet are itching to move, but then another person exits into the clearing.

It's a teen boy with a reddish-brown pixie cut. "Are you Amina?" His voice is high-pitched, edged with suspicion.

"Polaris Haan, we can begin," is all the woman says.

Gabriel's warm breath tickles my ear. "Now?"

I shake my head, snapping a picture with my phone—not that this is proof of anything yet. We need to wait for the Nightmares to show up. Or the High Witch himself—that would be even better. Gabriel's body shifts beside me, and I lean into him without thinking, reacting to his warmth. His hand glides along my upper thigh and over my hip, coming to rest there with a reassuring squeeze.

"Shall we?" Amina's voice is soft, singsongy, like a lullaby. She must be under an enchantment to make her malleable. Just like Iniko thought.

Polaris doesn't speak but lies down on the cold earth. If he's anything like the Jane Doe at the hospital, he's just doing what he was paid to do. I squint through the trees, waiting for the Nightmare to enter the scene and play their part.

I've never seen Amina before, but she's moving through the motions of preparing to dream wield like a pro. Gabriel and I watch silently as Polaris slowly drifts off to sleep, aided by a draught Amina gave him. As Polaris's breaths slow, Amina rises from the ground and stands perfectly still.

Dried leaves rustle to our left, making Gabriel's body tense. A breeze tickles my face, a hissing warning in my ears to get away. Pulling my cloak up to my chin, I ignore the whispering.

Four cloaked figures withdraw from the shadows, walking unhurriedly toward Amina and Polaris. I wonder if all the attacks happen in the privacy of the forest, and then the bodies are moved to whatever location the High Witch wants them found. I snap another photo.

One of the mystery figures is shorter and has a slim build. They're to the left of a towering, broad-shouldered person with a shortened gait. They're having trouble staying upright without the other to steady them—probably the Nightmare. The other two burly strangers hold a metal stick with a cuff at the end clamped around the Nightmare's wrist. Their height is similar to Gabriel's, just more bulky.

Their robes are deep purple, almost black, and each has the symbol of twisting knots on their chest I don't recognize. Gabriel's grip tightens on my wrist.

None of them speaks, but the more petite figure lowers the hood of the Nightmare. His skin is waxy and pale, his blue veins trying to leap from under his sunken features. Shoulders slumped forward, his hair hangs limply over them, a tangled mess of brown. His mouth is open like it's attempting to speak or scream. This Nightmare is nearing his end—whatever is terrorizing him is about to win the battle.

Nausea rolls through me with visions of the place where the High Witch might be keeping the other Nightmares. I have to save them. They don't deserve this.

The Nightmare steps toward Polaris as Amina retreats, expressionless.

"Now," I whisper to Gabriel.

Nightmares will attack or run off if given the chance, but this guy is a late-stage Nightmare—which means his death won't be far off. When they get to this point, their fight is nearly extinguished. I doubt he's even aware he's been moved from his dungeon. He won't be much of a problem. Which means we can focus on the escorts.

As Gabriel and I appear from behind the tree, the two guarding the Nightmare drop their hold on him and move toward us. Gabriel and I don't talk as we head for different guys. I duck, pushing the Nightmare out of the way, not needing him to get hurt or interfere in the fight. I hear grunting behind me, and my gut twists at the sound of flesh hitting flesh.

I withdraw a pouch from my pocket and throw it at my attacker. A burst of pink powder flies into his face. Rose-Colored Glasses. This charm is supposed to make the person see everything in a happier light. The escort staggers back, trying to wipe the powder from his face. He looks like he put on too much blush.

I grab a heavy stick from the ground, weighing it in my hand. They teach all kinds of exercises and self-defense at The Retreat. I dabbled in hand-to-hand combat. *Let's see if I still have the moves.* I circle to the left, the escort looking at me perplexed, but his hands are still in a fighting stance. The charm confuses his motivations.

Out of the corner of my eye, I see the smaller escort pulling a bag out of their pocket. I only have time to say the words "Watch out!" before the forest is plunged into total darkness.

CHAPTER 36

Gabriel

Essence of Night.

It's complex and tedious to brew, requiring a blood moon and a steady hand to stir it continuously for hours. Some dupes work as a party trick or for a quick getaway, but to create *true* darkness takes real talent. Even the sound is gone. My heart hammers as my lungs heave against the effort of my fight with a surprisingly well-matched opponent. I take the opportunity to stand still. Straining fruitlessly to see anything in the magical darkness. I call Azalee's name, but the night swallows everything inside its perimeters.

There's no telling how long the Essence of Night will last or how far it extends. It can vary depending on the strength of the caster. I move at a snail's pace, shuffling my feet so I don't trip and waving a hand to keep from colliding with a tree.

It's incredible how much more infinite the world seems in the dark. My foot connects with something, and I fall hard, but it's not the ground I land on; it's a body. I scramble off the person, hitting into something that wobbles. I feel an unmoving foot under my hand. The dream wielder and the person on the dirt must be Polaris if neither has changed positions during our scuffle.

I stay on the ground, closing my eyes and gripping the crystals around my neck for protection, muttering any spell I can think of to bring the light back. But without the ingredients to cast, most words are as useless as prayers to uncaring Gods. When I open my eyes, the darkness begins to recede. I don't know if I should thank my magic or those aforementioned Gods.

"Gabriel." Azalee's voice carries on the moonlight toward me.

"Azalee." Relief floods me, my body growing weak with the sudden release of panic. We both look around the clearing. The hooded figures and Nightmare are gone. "Are you okay?"

"Yeah." She nods, reaching into her bag. "Here." She hands me a small glass jar filled with a yellow opaque liquid. "Wave this under Polaris's nose, that should wake him up. I'll get Amina."

Azalee opens a bottle with what looks like water. "What you need is a little clarity." Tilting Amina's head back, Azalee puts one drop in each of Amina's eyes.

Amina blinks rapidly, eyes locking with Azalee as she stumbles back. "What . . . Where am I?"

"It's okay, Amina. You're going to be okay."

Crouching, I wave the jar under Polaris's nose. His slim body shivers as his eyes flutter open. "Here." I offer a hand to help him stand.

Azalee steps forward as Amina's eyes glaze over, once more entranced. "Shit. Whatever they used is strong. We need to get her to Roz. They'll have a stronger potion."

I sling Polaris's arm over my shoulder to help him walk. "What about Polaris?" If he only took a sleeping draught, there wouldn't be any lasting effects. "After this wears off, Polaris might be able to get us some answers."

"Let's take them both back."

We drive separately, Amina with Azalee and Polaris with me. Azalee leads the way to the far back of The Retreat property, where a small cabin sits on the edge of the woods near the lake. Guiding Amina around is simple since she walks and stays where we put her. While Polaris is a little more coherent, the grogginess will last a bit. I fling him over my shoulder for ease of transport. When I saw this kid walk into the clearing, all I could think of was Logan. Polaris can't be more than fifteen.

Where's his family?

Azalee bangs on the door. "Roz, wake up! We need help!"

There's a swear and rustling on the other side before it swings open to reveal Roz in a bathrobe and slippers. Their eyes skim over us, quickly assessing. "What did you do now?"

"She's been enchanted," Azalee says, indicating her head to Amina. "I tried a clarity potion, but she reverted almost immediately."

Polaris twitches in my arms, and I adjust my grip to keep the kid from smacking the ground.

"Oh, and he took a sleeping tonic," Azalee adds. "We used Rise and Shine. He should be fine."

"Come in." Roz heads to the small kitchen in the ample open space.

I drop Polaris in a chair, and he makes a soft mumbling sound but doesn't wake. I roll my shoulders, pain cutting through the left one. I took a strong punch to the back when I was tussling. But I did him more harm than he did to me.

"Amina, would you like to sit down?" Azalee asks.

"Amina, sit," Roz says with more authority. Amina complies. Roz runs a hand over Amina without touching her.

My eyes survey the tidy space, categorizing the nearest back exit and other potential threats. After the fight, my adrenaline is still hanging tight to my nerves, ready for the next attack.

"Roz was a healer once," Azalee whispers, dragging me from my analysis. "A fucking good one. They could make a lot of money working in the private sector, but they've always had a soft spot for my mom."

"Hmm," Roz mutters, searching a bag they retrieved from a safe.

"What did they use?" I ask, keeping my hands balled into fists in front of me.

"She has been both enchanted and dociled. A mix of calming draughts, I'd guess. She must be a stubborn one." Roz pulls out a bundle of herbs, placing them in a mortar and pestle. "And a Do as I Will spell, I think."

"Really?" My jaw spasms with my clenching. "That's illegal." A Do as I Will spell is a highly advanced combination of potions and spellwork that allows you full access to control a person—a spell you might only find in the High Witch's library.

"Quite right, Mr. Ford. They were banned well over two centuries ago." Roz puts a crystal goblet on the table and pours the herbs into the bottom. Then they pull two glass bottles from the kit. One is a brown amber, which they pour into the cup, and then a jade-colored liquid is next. Stirring the contents with a silver spoon, they mutter a spell under their breath.

They hand the goblet to an unmoving Amina when they're done. "Drink." Amina finishes the whole thing in one long sip before returning the goblet to Roz.

"How long will this—" Azalee starts, but Roz holds a hand up. Amina's eyes begin to roll back, her hands gripping the chair. She goes completely rigid, then relaxes, and her eyes focus on Roz.

"Welcome back." Roz closes their case.

"What?" Amina glances around at the room. "Where am I? What happened?"

"That's what we wanted to ask you." I step forward, dropping my hands to my sides.

"I'll see to the other patient." Roz heads to Polaris, who has fallen back asleep.

Amina wraps her arms around herself. Azalee takes a seat next to her. "Do you remember what happened?"

I lean against the counter so that I can keep an eye on Polaris as well as the door. We got away, but if I learned anything in my training, you never underestimate an opponent.

Amina closes her eyes, pressing a thumb into her forehead. "Last thing I remember was going to a café on Main, and then, nothing. It's all blank. Where am I?" When she opens her eyes, she's more alert.

"You're safe. You're at The Retreat." Azalee puts a hand on her, but she pushes her away.

"You drugged me and brought me here?" She attempts to stand but wobbles and collapses.

"We found you in the woods. Someone enchanted you." I study her face for any signs of concealment.

"They wanted you to pretend to dream wield. They were going to frame you for murder," Azalee adds. I don't know if that was helpful information to calm her, but at least she's paying attention.

"Dream wield?" Her eyes are wide. "I don't know how to do that. I don't want to know how." Her eyes dart to the door.

"Do you remember anything from when you were taken?" I press.

Amina closes her eyes, trying to remember.

"Maybe she needs more clarity," Roz suggests.

Azalee reaches into her bag, pulling out the clear potion. "This will help bring clarity to your thoughts. One drop in each eye."

She stares at it. "Maybe I don't want to remember."

Azalee opens Amina's hand and places the bottle in it. "I know you're scared, but you may be able to help us save a lot of people. And yourself, should the authorities try to tie you to any other murders. Please."

Amina turns the bottle over before leaning back and putting the drops in. "There was a man in a hooded cloak. I thought he might be here for the festival. I ignored him and kept walking; it was super foggy, the kind that pops up out of nowhere. I was taking my usual route, but I don't . . . somehow, I got lost." Her hands shake as she squeezes them together. "Then there were two hooded people. One of them pulled something out of their bag, and everything went dark. The next thing I remember, I was waking up here."

My alarm bells start ringing. "Were you walking home from the festival when this happened?"

Amina nods.

Azalee and I exchange a look. The festival was three days ago. Where was she held that whole time?

"Jane Doe," Azalee whispers to me. Amina was probably the one meant to take the blame for that attack.

"She needs to rest." Roz guides Amina to lie down on the bed. "That one"—they point to Polaris—"is awake now."

Roz grabs Azalee's arm. "Does your mother know what you are up to?"

She doesn't meet their eyes. "This is going to help all of us."

"You can't keep me here," Polaris says. "I have rights."

Azalee looks at me with a *you take this one* smile.

"We just wanted to make sure you were okay. Maybe call your family?" I reassure him, using the voice I reserved for a younger Logan.

"And to see what you remember," Azalee adds, unable to stop herself from being in control.

He leans back, pinching the bridge of his nose. "That is the last time I answer an ad from the PennySaver."

"What ad?" Azalee and I say at the same time.

"I don't know. A stupid ad asking for help with a school project. When I answered it, the chick said I wouldn't have to do much but lie there and sleep. The money was wicked good—too good—which should have been my first tip-off."

"Do you still have the ad?" I ask, hope flaring in my chest.

"Nah, I threw it away after I called them. The number should be on my phone, though." He reaches into his pocket and pulls out an old flip phone. "Here."

I copy the number. "Do you have family we can call?" I repeat my earlier question.

He shakes his head. "There's no one—it's just me. I was going to Chicago, but my funds were running low. Thought I'd try for a bit more cash before I left."

"Did they pay you yet?"

Azalee is looking for a money trail. The real evidence we'd need to catch my grandfather.

"Half. The other half was to be delivered after the experiment was complete. It was cash," he adds.

"Do you remember what they sounded like, or did you see anyone when you picked up your payment?" Azalee is asking all the right questions, but there aren't any answers to be given.

He shrugs. "It sounded like a girl, nothing distinct about the voice, just a girl saying she'd give me a bunch of money to sleep for a few hours." I must look skeptical because he clarifies. "I know it sounds shady, but desperate times. And no, I didn't see anyone other than her." He points to Amina.

I debate telling him he just escaped death, but what good would it do? I can tell he's done answering ads for a while.

"You're welcome to stay here as long as you like. We've got extra cabins," Azalee says.

"Am I welcome to go too?"

"I'd advise leaving town right away if you do. The people who paid you probably won't want loose ends." I don't know if that's true, but better safe than sorry. "Thank you for talking to us." I get up and head toward the door.

"Amina . . ." Azalee trails off when she reaches Roz.

"I'll offer her a place, as I would any dream wielder." Roz looks like they might stop there, but continues, "Azalee, whatever it is you're digging yourself into, you need to cut it out."

Azalee's cheeks suck in like she's trying to quell her annoyance. "You heard what they said. This scheme to entrap dream wielders isn't going to stop unless we stop it."

Roz pulls at their earlobe. "You stubborn girl. You keep acting as if this situation is all on you to solve. It's not. And if you continue to proceed that way, it's going to spell trouble for all our kind."

"So, what then?" Azalee's voice is low so the others don't hear, but the intensity is fierce. "I'm supposed to just sit around and wait for the coven to get their shit together? Even if by some miracle we did come to a consensus, we never take any real action. The time for idly waiting to see how the tide turns has long since passed us by."

"Roz, I promise that Azalee and I are being careful with our investigation." I offer some diplomatic intervention.

"Don't get me started on you, Ford. You might be a dream wielder"—I suck in a breath; I didn't realize they knew—"but that doesn't mean you are automatically awarded my trust."

"We should really be getting home," Azalee says without looking at Roz, stepping past them, but Roz isn't done yet.

"Azalee, stop this. I'm not going to ask you again."

Azalee presses her lips together, nodding.

I doubt any of us in this room are buying that answer.

CHAPTER 37

AZALEE

Gabriel follows me back to my house in his car. I slam my fist into the steering wheel as I drive. I get Roz is the head of the coven and they need to protect them—I really do. But why the hell can't they see that's exactly what I'm trying to do too? I'm just a little more *hands on*. We're getting so close to uncovering what's really going on and being able to prove that dream wielders are being framed. I can't stop now, not this close. I might not know how to save Iniko or the Nightmares yet, but I can save Meera.

"The number might be a good lead," I say as I exit the car. Moonlight dances across puddles in the bumpy driveway. It must have rained while we were at Roz's.

"I can get a trustworthy contact to look into it. I might be able to trace the origins." Gabriel's hands are shoved into the pockets of his cloak, his face hidden in shadows.

"It's probably a burner."

"Probably."

My soul aches to reach for him. Press my body against his and let his fingers take me to another place for a few hours. But my head hurts, too full of questions that never seem fully answered.

"How do you think Meera works into this? Is she just collateral damage for association with me?" I ask to keep thoughts of his naked body at bay. "All of these other dream wielders were drugged, and the victims were lone wolves paid to show up. That pattern doesn't fit with Meera. She and Grant were together of their own free will."

He runs a hand through his hair. "What did Meera say when you saw her today?"

My eyes narrow. "How did you know that?"

"The Captain informs my grandfather if you or your mother visit. I heard them talking," he says, lips turning downward. I want to kiss away the worry lines etching his devastatingly handsome face.

"Of course he did." I kick a rock as we walk to the front door. "Meera said everything was blurry—just like when Iniko tried to see it."

"Maybe she *was* entranced?" Gabriel holds the door for me as we go inside.

"But I don't know why she was targeted in the first place—hating my family doesn't feel like a good enough reason to break the pattern." I flop onto the sofa, Gabriel sitting beside me. "If the High Witch just wanted dream wielders implicated to spread fear, the Jane and John Does made sense. Meera feels personal somehow, but also it's stupid risky. Which doesn't feel like a move the High Witch would make in a plan like this."

He puts his arm over the back of the sofa, playing with a strand of my hair, before resting his hand on my neck. "If something doesn't fit the pattern, there must be more to it."

Heat rises in my chest as his aquamarine eyes roam over me. "What?"

"I'm sorry," he whispers, thumb rubbing circles beneath my ear.

My brow furrows, panic running through me. "For what?"

"For not taking you up on the offer to come here after my accident." There he goes admitting he's wrong again. I could get used to this Gabriel.

"It's okay. You aren't the first dream wielder to turn me down." Slowly, I run my hand over his bicep, feeling the muscles under his cloak.

"I always knew deep down dream wielders weren't dangerous. That you weren't." His fingers trace lines on my upper thigh. "But I hated myself for becoming a thing my grandfather and brother would despise. They were all I had."

"I get it now, Gabriel." I place my hand over his heart, feeling the steady beat. "I should have understood instead of being an ass about it when you ignored me."

He leans in, kissing my lips with a ghostly touch. "I was scared of what would happen if I let you teach me. If I opened up myself to this world. It was nice for once not to dream."

I swallow hard. "I know what you mean. I never dreamed about my father's death; it was a blissful escape."

"Will you teach me after this is over?"

"To dream wield?" He nods, a cautious smile appearing on his face, and butterflies fill my stomach. "Why me? There are a lot of other witches with more experience and patience."

He hovers over my mouth, teasing me by getting almost there and stopping before I'm satisfied. "Because of what I might dream about."

"Oh? What would you dream?" My eyes drift closed as my body arches into him.

"About you."

"Totally understandable." I smirk. He leans forward to kiss me, but I stop him. "If we solve this, save the day, and you get to be all heroic, what will you do after? If the High Witch . . ." I trail off.

"If he's guilty?"

I nod. "What would you do if you could do anything? Go be a spaceman?"

Flopping back onto the couch, he plays with a throw pillow. "I tried not to think about what else I could do. Never seems productive. I was always going to work for the High Witch."

Staying silent, I let him find his way. It's one of the things I learned when dream wielding for therapy. I can guide someone to an answer, but it works best if they make the last discovery themselves.

His Adam's apple bobs while his analytical brain formulates a solution. "When this is over, dream wielders won't suddenly be accepted. That's going to take education and policy changes. I'd like to be a part of that."

An unfamiliar warmth spreads across my chest. I'm used to him making me hot, but not like this. He sounds like he really cares about us—dream wielders. "I want to provide therapy sessions at The Retreat," I say. "Not just for dream wielders to cope with their trauma, but for anyone. Witches, non-witches, dream wielders . . . Nightmares. I think we could do some real good."

He links our fingers. "I think you could too."

"Maybe we could do it together?" I hedge with a shrug, hoping he doesn't see how much that would mean to me. I'm not used to letting people glimpse that side. I always have to be the strong one.

"I'd like that."

"Yeah, I bet you would." I wiggle my eyebrows.

"What am I going to do with you, Azalee Saunders?"

"I have a few ideas." Grabbing his shirt, I tug him closer, his mouth finally connecting with mine. I pull at his cloak, removing each layer of clothing that keeps us apart.

Heat blazes across my skin as he takes his time kissing down my neck, along the soft curves of my breasts, over my navel, stopping to look back up at me. "Azalee," he whispers into the sensitive skin of my hip bone.

I run my hands through his silky hair, lifting his chin so our eyes can meet. I trace the lines of his lips, and he responds by kissing my fingertips. The heat growing inside me aches to have him closer, to fill me up until I erupt, but something else tugs on me—a force running parallel to the life debt string I've become familiar with.

"What?" he whispers, moving back up until he's sitting beside me again.

I shake my head, swallowing. "Nothing." Pushing him to lie flat on the couch, I straddle him, undoing the buttons of his jeans to get rid of the last pieces of fabric keeping us apart.

He stops me, wrapping his fingers around mine. "Do you feel it?"

I raise an eyebrow. "Oh, Gabriel, I definitely feel it."

His laugh is low, a deep rumble that sends shivers down my spine in the best way. "I would think you would feel that, but not what I was referring to." He places my hand on his heart and then puts his over mine. "The golden thread, it feels different."

Pressing my lips together, I nod.

"Do you think—"

I crash my lips into his, not letting him finish the sentence. Because I know what he was going to say. I've never felt a soulmate bond, but the sparkling white light that dances across my senses as I sink into him and let him carry me away sure as hell feels like something special.

My phone alarm wakes us the next morning. I untangle myself from him on the couch. "Gabriel . . ." *Fuck.* I did not mean to turn this into a sleepover. But apparently my body didn't get that memo.

"Mhhh," his hum vibrates against my neck.

"Time to face reality." I kiss him on the cheek before getting up.

He grabs my leg to keep me from moving. "Come back to bed."

I lean over, his hand sliding up my thigh and to the under curve of my ass. "Sorry, Lover Boy, I've got places to be. And so do you." I rip the blanket off him.

"You're not the cuddle-in-the-morning type of girl, are you?"

Throwing his clothes at him, I say, "Please, you already knew that."

Reluctantly, we get dressed, and I walk him out. "I'll check back later and let you know if I found out anything about the number," he says, lingering at the doorway. "I feel like we should talk about some stuff . . ." He trails off.

"Nope." I pull him in, kissing him as he smiles against my lips. "I'll see you later." Last night, asleep in Gabriel's arms, was the first night in days the nightmares hadn't come. I should be grateful; maybe it wasn't anything other than stress, but I don't feel relieved.

Because nightmares don't always start as scary, sometimes they trick you into thinking you've entered a dream.

Gabriel didn't say what time he'd come by tonight, so after my shift at The Retreat, I stopped by the hospital to visit Mom before heading home around seven. I busy myself by cooking lasagna and researching a location spell to find where the High Witch has hidden the Nightmares. Making dinner from scratch was what I needed to occupy my mind and hands. The doorbell rings at half past, and I take a quick look in the mirror before answering the door.

But Gabriel isn't standing on my threshold. *"Meera?"* I nearly choke on the word. "What are you . . . did you break out?" I scan behind her to see if she's been followed.

Her bright smile lights up her face. "I love that you think I'd be so calm if I busted out of jail. Can I come in?"

"Yes, yes, of course. But Meera, what happened?" A million questions bombard my brain.

"They let me go." She grins, heading to the kitchen. "Is that your world-famous lasagna?" She peeks into the oven.

"They let you go? Why?" Numbness stretches through my limbs as I think how this could be another trick from the High Witch.

"The evidence wasn't strong enough to hold me. I guess that lawyer was pretty good. They said something like, *We'll be keeping tabs on you.*" She mimics a grouchy officer. "And that was that. I'm a free lady."

I'm ecstatic she's not locked away, obviously, but why let her go? Even if we all know she didn't do it, surely the High Witch would convict her as an example, no matter her innocence.

What's the play here? Is this a trick set up by the cops to catch us?

Wait—what am I doing? This is the first lucky break I've gotten and I'm trying to logic it away. After all the other shit I'm still dealing with, I should just thank the Gods and not fuck up this gift.

Take the win, Azalee, you might not get many more.

"You should have called. I would've come and got you."

She waves me off. "No big deal."

I run over, drawing her into a bone-crushing hug—a weight lifting from my shoulders. "I'm glad you're out, Meera. You have no idea . . ." I pause, swallowing to stop the tears burning my eyes. "It was tough without you."

"And your mom in the hospital," she adds, grabbing water from the fridge.

"Yeah, having both of you gone, it felt so lonely . . . Wait, who told you about Mom?" My brows knit together. I don't remember telling her, but I've been preoccupied the last few days.

"I heard one of the officers talking about it." She frowns for the first time.

"Did they say anything about more dream wielders being attacked? Is there a trend?"

Gabriel and Mom would say it isn't my job to protect all the dream wielders, but I feel like it is. If I sit around waiting for someone else to do it, more people could get hurt.

"Can we not talk about jail right now? Please?" She gives me puppy dog eyes. "I just want to eat your lasagna and binge-watch a horrible cheesy reality show."

"That sounds perfect." There's plenty we need to find out, but right now, I have my friend back and want to enjoy that for a night. We can deal with the oddity behind her release in the morning. Everyone keeps telling me I need to take a breather, maybe I should finally listen.

We're halfway into our third episode of the most over-the-top reality show I could find and our second helping of lasagna when the doorbell rings. "Expecting company?" Meera asks.

"Keep watching. I'll be right back." I grab a mint before I open the door to the face I was expecting earlier. "Hi. There's still some lasagna if you're hungry." I beam. He's feeling increasingly like a real person and less like the High Witch's grandson.

The muscles in Gabriel's jaw pop as he ushers me inside. "I found something . . ." He stops short when he sees Meera sitting on the sofa. "Meera, I thought—what are you doing here?" His expression is unreadable.

"Jailbreak!" She throws her hands in the air, shaking her head wildly.

"They released her." I grin. "There wasn't enough evidence. I told you something was weird about it."

Gabriel keeps his voice quiet. "Can I speak to you privately?"

"I know you want to keep things secret, lest they get back to the High Witch, but with Meera here, we've got an extra pair of hands to help uncover the truth."

"I'd prefer to talk to just you." Deep wrinkles crease his forehead.

I study him, sweat building on my palms. "Meera, we'll be upstairs." She nods, not taking her eyes off the TV.

I lead him to my bedroom. "What's up? Did you find anything from that number?"

Shutting the door, he runs a hand through his hair and over his face, letting out a sharp breath. "I don't know how to say this . . ."

I cross my arms, fisting my shirt to steady my hands. "You're making me nervous." Is he about to tell me he regrets helping me? Or maybe this has all been a setup since the beginning. I thought it was odd that Gabriel suddenly decided to help me. I should have questioned that more.

"Azalee, you were right about the number; it was a burner. It'd already been disconnected when I called it." He fiddles with a set of crystals hanging from my vanity.

"Okay. We figured that might happen." If this was his bad news, he's being a little dramatic.

He shoves his hands into his pockets. "I decided to look into my grandfather's files. I figured if he were involved, there would be records of the phone calls or the money. He is obsessive about keeping records."

I shift my weight from one foot to the other. "Is there a point coming?"

"Remember how we thought Meera's murder was different?" At my silence he keeps talking. "Meera wasn't supposed to be there. She was supposed to facilitate getting Grant to his house and another dream wielder was supposed to show up and be blamed. Apparently, Grant had been vocally opposing some research into dream wielders the High Witch requested and he needed to be silenced."

I shake my head, blinking rapidly. "I don't understand. What do you mean Meera was supposed to *facilitate* getting Grant home?" My dry mouth makes it hard to speak.

He steps closer, resting his hands on my shoulders. "The escort from last night, the smaller one, was Meera. She's been working for my grandfather all along."

The world spins as the light above flickers in and out of my vision. "No." I stumble away. "No, Meera isn't involved with the High Witch. You're wrong."

His face pinches. "I looked at dozens of files. I tried to find another explanation, but it was there in black and white. Meera's been finding the dream wielders because she knows what to look for. He recruited her because she was in the best position for access to the coven because of her friendship with you."

"No." I can't breathe. The air in my lungs is a lead balloon. It's poison, and if I keep breathing, it will kill me. "Meera is my best friend. She has always protected dream wielders." *Oh Gods, the pressure is overwhelming.*

"Azalee—"

"Stop!" The scream rips through my throat. My blood boils. Gabriel takes a deep breath—calm—he's always so *damn* calm. My vision turns red as he opens his mouth to speak. I can't listen to him anymore. "Get out." The words are a growl.

"I understand—"

"Get out." I push hard against his chest, my hand slipping between the gap in his shirt, touching his skin. The world is ripped from us as I drag him into a nightmare.

CHAPTER 38

Azalee

Freezing salt water lashes at my skin as the wind howls like a wolf. White-capped waves batter the tiny fishing boat Gabriel and I cling to for our lives. The thundering storm has us in its clutches, and with no land in sight, escape is futile. My wet hair and clothes hang from my body, chills shaking my frame. Gabriel has an oar in each hand, trying fruitlessly to move us.

A wailing echoes in the distance, but Gabriel pays it no mind.

Is it in my head?

I try to remember how we got here—to remember anything at all. But concentrating is useless with the hammering in my skull, followed by shooting pain in quick bursts.

I press my hand along cracks in the bottom to stop water from seeping in.

Too many.

Too many.

Too many.

Shaking my head, I silence the spiraling thoughts. Frozen water covers our feet and ankles—we're going down.

Suddenly, we're standing in the middle of a crowded town square. The inhabitants have pitchforks and torches with eyes of gleaming red.

Gabriel is no longer beside me. Instead, he's chained to a mammoth log at the front of the crowd. Bloody, angry welts cover his face. His clothes ripped to shreds.

The screams are deafening, but this time, it's not coming from inside my head. The strangers around me yell incoherent words, saliva dripping from their chins as they spit at Gabriel. I press my hands to my ears to drown them out. I attempt to shove my way out of the crowd, but the more I move, the harder they push back. Their hands claw at my clothes, my face, their nails drawing blood.

I throw my hands over my head and yell, "Leave me alone!" Even though I feel the words scraping my throat, no sound leaves my lips. I curl into a ball, squeezing my eyes shut, waiting for them to consume me. But they don't, and the hands recede. The voices stop, and the world is silent.

Too silent.

Silence is the sign of more to come, something lurking in the shadows. Silence is a warning.

Breaths don't come easily as I open my dry eyes, glancing around at the grass dancing in the wind.

Something's wrong.

The grass is blood red. Running my hand across the blades, I jerk back as a sting shoots up my arm, several cuts forming on my fingers. My blood drips and intertwines with the landscape. A drumming starts beneath my skin, the beat pumping in my veins, consuming all thoughts but it.

There is nowhere to hide. A sharp cliff descends into thick fog. When I glance behind me, Gabriel is still chained to the pole. His mouth moves, but I can't hear him.

I tilt my head, watching. The grass grows, twisting around my legs, locking me in place. A hooded figure appears behind him—something is familiar about their attire, but I can't remember.

How did we get here?

The man pulls the hood down and reveals himself as the High Witch. My body jerks, but I'm held in place. The High Witch clicks his fingers, and a lit torch appears in his hand.

Gabriel's eyes widen as we both notice the bed of logs at his feet. The muscles in his neck bulge, the veins protruding as he opens his mouth and fails to scream his plea.

The weeds grow more constricting, like a boa strangling its prey. There's something I should remember. I drop my chin to my chest, clamping my eyes shut.

Why am I here?

Why am I here?

Where is here?

A nightmare.

My head snaps up as the High Witch places his torch on the woodpile at Gabriel's feet. The smoke rises in twisting curls. Resisting is making this worse. I become very still, slowing my breath and calming my mind.

This isn't real.

This is a nightmare.

Wake up.

Wake up.

Wake up.

"*Wake up!*" I'm screaming as my eyes crack open to Meera standing in the doorway to my bedroom, face stricken, Gabriel pale as a ghost and still beside me.

I rip my hand from Gabriel's chest like it's on fire.

"I heard yelling," Meera gasps, fingers covering her mouth, wide eyes taking in the scene. "I ran up . . . I didn't . . . What happened?"

Shaking, I scoot away from Gabriel. Nausea overpowers my senses and I vomit on the carpet. "We need to . . ." My voice is raspy, broken pieces. Neither of us moves. My hands turn white, veins popping as I clasp them. I don't want to touch him.

"Is he?" Meera gapes at Gabriel's unconscious body. His chest rises and falls with ragged breaths—but at least he's breathing.

"The emergency kit in the dungeon," I say, my voice stronger this time. "Get it. Now." I unclench my fists, flexing my fingers before wiping the sick off my lips.

I am not a Nightmare. I am not a Nightmare.

I scoot away from Gabriel. "Meera, the kit." She gives me another wide-eyed stare before disappearing.

I'm careful not to touch his bare skin as I drag the quilt from off my bed and place it over him. Exposure to Nightmares can cause shock. I need to keep him warm. I let my years of training guide my movements.

I stare at him, not blinking, biting my lip so hard I taste blood.

"Here." Meera's voice startles me as she thrusts the kit into my hands.

Meera, my friend. Meera, who is always there to lend a helping hand.

Meera, who is working with the High Witch?

Gabriel's words echo through my mind.

I kneel next to him, pulling out various potions. "Can you light the blackthorn and cleanse the room?" I ask, glancing up at her, trying not to let the panic show in my voice.

I don't know what I'm expecting to see—she looks like Meera. I try to read her aura, but my head is too groggy to get a clear picture. I hold in a sob as I turn back to Gabriel.

"Shouldn't we take him to Roz?" she asks, cleansing the room with the purifying smoke.

"The kit has everything we need to offer aid." *After an encounter with a Nightmare,* I don't say out loud. "Besides, Roz is the last person I should bring my problems to at the moment."

Opening Gabriel's mouth, I pour in a potion of dream wielder making. A mixture of echinacea, ginkgo, ginger, and lavender. "Come on, Gabriel," I whisper. My hand reaches for his tearstained cheek, but I stop short.

What did I do?

I let him go. The nightmare didn't have total control over me. That's a good sign.

Meera finishes with the blackthorn, leaving the smoking sticks in a copper bowl by the bedside. If she was a traitor working for the High Witch, wouldn't she jump at the chance to get me locked away with the other Nightmares?

"What's going on?" Her voice is cautious.

I stand once I see Gabriel's breaths are coming in deep, even strides. "I need to see Iniko." I grab her arm, pulling her into the hall and downstairs.

"Az, I don't think that's a good idea, considering what just happened. You need to rest." She tries to detach my fingers, but I don't let go, even as her bare skin grazes mine. "Can we talk about what you did? I'm your best friend."

"I'll explain later."

"What good will talking to Iniko do? He can't hear you." Her voice is sharp.

"Actually, he can." The crystal necklace Gabriel and I made is still around Iniko's neck. I need to see if he can clarify a few things.

Like if my friend really did betray me.

I take the steps down to the dungeon two at a time. "Meera, come on," my voice echoes as I call from the bottom of the stairs.

"I should wait up here in case Gabriel wakes up."

I walk up a few steps to see her better. "I can't do this without you. Please? It will only take a few minutes." I hope, because my head is pounding and I might throw up again. What happened to Gabriel, what *I* did to Gabriel, is eating away at me.

Meera shifts on each foot before giving in and coming down. "What is it I need to do?" Meera was never a fan of being with the Nightmares, but she was never downright frightened of them like she is now.

I explain the spell to her as I unlock Iniko's door. "You won't have to do anything except stand there and channel your energy to mine."

Stepping into Iniko's room, Meera is so close behind I might as well be giving her a piggyback ride. "Hey, Ink," I say quietly. I squeeze my crystal before grasping Meera's hand. "Let's dream."

Once again, we're back in his childhood bedroom. It was easier this time; nothing resisted me, almost like the nightmare had welcomed me. Iniko sits on the floor at the foot of his bed, throwing a baseball against the wall and catching it when it returns. The thud of the ball reverberating through the dream makes my skin hum.

"Iniko?" I sit beside him. I don't know if he'll remember the last time. If the nightmare burns out the good things, or if he thought it was part of a twisted game to make him think for a moment he was free.

"You came back." Each word causes a visible cringe on his features.

"I told you I'd never leave you alone." I squeeze his hand, the baseball rolling under the bed.

"It's good you came. Time is fleeting—not much of it left." When he peers at me, there's no light in his eyes. His clothes hang limply off his bony frame, his skin ashen and dull.

I pinch my leg to keep from falling apart, from telling him about my nightmares. He doesn't need the burden. "Time will take us all one day, but I promise your time is far from now."

"You always loved to make promises you had no control in keeping." He shakes his head, like he's clearing a fog, and folds his legs, shifting to face me. "Why did you come back?"

I copy his position. This is how we used to sit when sharing our deepest secrets. "I . . . I need you to search the future. I need to know about Meera."

He raises an eyebrow. "What about her?"

I spill my guts, telling him what Gabriel said and how it can't be true.

He stands, pulling me with him. "Let's take a look."

The world spins, a pastel-colored rainbow blending around us. Images come and go, but nothing sticks. Then we land in a candlelit room.

The High Witch sits behind a large desk. "It's done?" he asks.

I turn, the world swirling like ripples in a lake, to see the person behind us he's speaking to.

"I located the dream wielder. It'll be taken care of." Meera's head is bowed, hands held tight behind her back.

"Iniko?" I croak. He puts a finger to his mouth to silence me.

Shrouded mist darkens the room. Only Meera and the High Witch are lit. "This is the third time you've screwed up. This dream wielder should have been in jail days ago." The High Witch glares, face beet red.

Meera's throat bobs. "I'm sorry, sir. It'll be handled this time."

"Good. We have to move on with . . ." His words fade as we slip back into Iniko's room.

"Why did we leave? He was about to reveal his plan."

He rubs a hand over his face. "Seeing is hard enough, but stuck in here . . . it's like I'm Seeing through another layer of fog. Things don't stick."

"Could you be Seeing it wrong?"

"Everything I See is a *version* of the future. Nothing is set in stone. But Az, you heard what he said. Even if this is a possible version, he mentioned events that have already come to pass." Iniko's volume goes in and out like a broken radio.

I slump onto the bed, shoulders rounding forward as I stare at the ground. "Meera betrayed me—*us*. She's been working for the High Witch the whole time." Tears slip from my eyes. Gabriel was right, and as a thank-you, I brought him a nightmare.

"Why don't you ask her?" He runs a hand over my head, his fingers sending icy chills down my spine.

"I don't—" But the words are cut off as a sharp pain shoots through my head. Before, I could feel Meera's energy giving me power, but now there's an empty void.

Iniko's mouth opens, and moths fly out. I trip backward, shoving myself off the bed and catching my leg on the frame. His face disappears into a cloud of ash. The thumping of the baseball against the wall begins, but the baseball is still under the bed.

I scramble for the door, but the handle disappears. The blood in my veins runs cold. I claw at the wood to force a way out. "Iniko, we need another—" But Iniko is gone. The room melts into shades of gray. I pound on the door with my fists, feet, every part of my body that might make it move. I have to get out of here. The nightmare is gaining back control.

I'm not sure if it's Iniko's nightmare or mine.

The pain of a thousand faceless voices fills my ears.

Breathe. Breathe. I hear my mom's voice, training me. *You will never be stuck in a dream of your creation. You're in control. Breathe, hold, and exhale.*

I made this dream in Iniko's head—I can get out. Breathe, hold, and exhale. I blink up at the ceiling in Iniko's cell. He's on his bed, staring at the wall, and Meera is nowhere in sight.

CHAPTER 39

Gabriel

Abomination.

Filth.

Monster.

Dream wielder.

Whispering voices nip at my ears, cutting them a thousand times as warm blood drips down my face. My arms are tied behind my back around a log atop a hissing pyre.

I squint through the flickering flames, the smoke stinging my eyes and blurring my vision. Ever-increasing waves of pain intensify with each breath. When will my body finally shut down and save me from this torture?

Salvation never comes.

I burn on the pyre, skin bubbling off and sizzling when it hits the flames.

"It's what you deserve, Gabriel." The High Witch's damnation cuts through the angry whispering of an unseen crowd.

Azalee's face appears in the sliver of space between the fire's orange tendrils. Then she's gone from one blink to the next.

"You shall suffer for all that your kind has done." The flames accelerate at his words.

Logs explode beneath me, and I collapse, knees banging into hard stone. They crack and break, the skin soft and moldable from the heat.

Suffer.

I will, for now, until eternity.

CHAPTER 40

Azalee

I grip the back of my head; a sharp pain radiates from where I hit it on the cement. I must've fallen off the bed when Meera let go of my hand. Pressing myself onto my elbow, I roll over so I can get up, but my stomach lurches, and I throw up. Ignoring the burning in my throat and lungs, I heave myself off the frigid, moist ground. Iniko doesn't stir as I stumble out of the room. In the hall, Meera is walking toward the stairwell.

"Why did you break the connection?" I blink, vision tunneling as I press my hand into the rough stone to keep upright. The dregs of the dreamscape cling to me. Tangy bile saturates my tongue, but I manage to keep from hurling again.

"I thought I heard someone." She points upstairs, avoiding eye contact.

I stare at her, tears forming. "Tell me it isn't true."

She scrunches her forehead. "That what isn't true?" Her voice wavers.

"Meera." The words crack.

Her lips press into a tight line; her throat bobs like she's having to swallow down sick. "You don't understand. I didn't have a choice."

A hole rips open in my chest. "How could you? The High Witch?" This isn't real. My hand is still glued to Gabriel's chest—the nightmares playing with me.

Please let this be a nightmare. *Please.*

She fists the sides of her cloak, the fabric a shimmering distraction to her betrayal. "Exactly, Az, the *High Witch.* He is the most powerful person around."

I scrape my nails into the stone, welcoming the pain. "You lied to me!" I scream, the echoes of my hurt reverberating through the dungeon. "I'm your best friend, and you've lied to me this whole time." The light above us flickers, the room swaying in front of me. Now that I really think about it, I don't actually know that she had an alibi for the other murders. Sure she was with me around those times, but never during the actual event. I overlooked that detail because I couldn't even fathom that Meera would be involved.

"That's rich. You want to tell me what the hell happened up there with Gabriel?" Her teeth are bared. It's as if a stranger has possessed my friend's body. "Got something you've been hiding too?" She laughs bitterly.

"That's not at all the same, and you know it." But the heat rises in my cheeks at the accusation. I wasn't lying to her. I just didn't want to burden her with my problems when she was accused of murder. But maybe none of that was true.

Her eyes are wide, face colored with . . . is that *fear*? "You almost killed Gabriel. That's Nightmare shit. It's only a matter of time before the darkness takes full control. If I hadn't been there to stop you—"

I press a hand to my ear to drown her out. "Meera, the High Witch *is* killing people and putting innocent dream wielders in jail. That is the real problem here, not me."

"They're nobodies. They don't have families that will miss them."

I feel like she punched me in the gut. I don't know the person standing in front of me.

"We made a pact to help. After everything with Iniko . . ." My breath comes in short bursts. I can barely see her through the glaze of tears. "How can you say that about those people?"

"Because I do have a family!" she bellows, finally losing her tenuous hold on this situation. "And if I don't help the High Witch, they'll die."

"What do you mean?" For a second, the world stops hurling me into oblivion. Finally, some clarity. An explanation for why Meera betrayed me.

Her tongue flicks over her teeth, eyes swimming. "He took them, Az. My parents didn't just decide to go on vacation to visit my brother." She's begging me to understand now. "The High Witch took them and will kill them unless I help him." Tears roll down her face. She wipes them away with the back of her hand.

The anger in me seeps away. "Meera, you should have come to me. I could have helped. Mom could have—" I reach for her hand, but she jerks away.

"No, I already tried to tell you once, and it landed me in jail as a warning." That's why Meera's arrest didn't match the other cases, why she was freed. "He said if I attempted to tell you again, he *would* kill them—no more second chances. This is the price I have to pay to get them back, and I'm willing to pay it." The tears have dried, and the face of absolution has replaced it.

"You're going to pay with other people's lives? Do you think that's what your parents would want?"

She laughs, cold and shrill. "Don't you play high and mighty with me. If the situation was reversed and it was your mom he took, you would stoop this low in a heartbeat."

I open my mouth to tell her she's wrong, that I wouldn't sacrifice innocent people to save her. But I can't get the words out because deep down, I know I would do anything to save my mom.

"Okay, what's done is done, but you don't need to do it anymore. I can help you. Gabriel can help you. We have enough evidence to stop the High Witch. You can be the final piece of the puzzle we were missing."

She shakes her head, jaw tight. "If anything happens to the High Witch, my parents die. He won't make it swift either. They will suffer unimaginable terrors before the end comes. I'm not risking them for a long shot."

"You're going to let him kill more people—imprison more dream wielders and turn the world against us." My heartbeat thumps in my ears, growing louder with each breath.

"I don't care!" The scream rips through the hall, stirring the Nightmares in the rooms around us. "I don't care," she says quieter, but that's almost worse. "I would let him kill half the world to get them back."

I step away in horror. "What about me? It's only a matter of time before he comes after me too."

She pauses, the first sign of regret flashing across her features. "You have always been my best friend, and I'm sorry that your nightmares have gone this far. But I can offer you one last promise: Once you're no longer able to, I'll make sure nothing happens to your mom."

"Too late," I mutter, thinking of Mom lying in a hospital bed.

"I'm sorry," Meera says, frowning as she heads for the door.

"Wait." I grab for her, but she shoves me back. "We can work through this. Please. There has to be another solution." But she's always been quicker than me and reaches the exit first.

"I'm sorry." Then she slams the door as the runes she carved into it glow bright, the magic locking me in.

She trapped me with the Nightmares.

CHAPTER 41

Azalee

"Damn it!" I pound against the door until I bleed. But even my blood can't break the locking spell.

A whisper in my ear sends a tingle along my neck, my hair standing on end. *Your fight is done; come sleep.*

Shadows pass over the corner of my vision. My head snaps around, but I'm alone. The hall is empty, the doors locked.

I cover my mouth with my hand to hold in my sobs. Hot breath fills my lungs as I slide down the rough door, landing on the ground with my knees bent. I rest my head against them, exhaustion bombarding me.

One step forward, two steps back.

When Meera showed up tonight, I was elated for the first time in a week. I thought something was finally going right. With her at my side, we could break this case open and show the world what the High Witch has been up to.

I understand why she did it. I *do*. If the roles were reversed, I would've taken the High Witch up on his offer too, but it would've been to dismantle him from the inside. Meera doesn't have any interest in that. She wants her family back and doesn't care if others die in the process.

This adds another layer of trouble: When I confront the High Witch, I need to make sure Meera's family is safe. But first, I need to figure out where the hell they are. Gabriel might be able to. Except he's lying unconscious right now, and I'm stuck in a dungeon where no one will hear me scream. Just like when I scream in my nightmare.

Okay, I need Gabriel to know where I am. Since he's unconscious, the only way I can talk to him is if I dream wield. Which again, I can't because I'm stuck here.

I could astral project.

I need to make sure whatever runes Meera used won't keep me from projecting my consciousness out of here. I run my hands along the crudely carved marks. I don't think she was planning on locking me in. She improvised when she realized I wasn't giving up.

My hand tightens into a fist. It would be so much easier to give up. But I can't turn my back on the dream wielders when I'm this close. I have to save Meera too. She's not locked in a cell anymore, but she's still a prisoner. I know she betrayed me, all of us, but the Fates didn't give her many options.

Taking a deep breath, I let it all go, pushing myself off the ground. My body is weak from the nightmares, but I don't need my body for this. The flow of energy feels the calmest in the center of the room—as calm as a dungeon full of Nightmares can be—so I set up there. Astral projection requires me to open my mind and free myself from the burden of my body. I'm kinda looking forward to shaking off the physical for a bit.

I reach into my trusty bag, grateful I brought it with me. First rule of dream wielding: Always be prepared. I pull out a large honeycomb crystal in its raw shape, but the polishing makes it look like I'm holding actual honey. A small blue calcite goes into my other hand.

The hard cement amplifies my pains when I lie on it, but I ignore it, settling myself into stilled silence. I need to close my eyes, but instead, I stare at the cracked ceiling. What if I close my eyes and the nightmare comes back? I bite hard on my lip, gripping the crystals.

I can do this.

There is no other way. Steadying myself, I shut my eyes, focusing on the in and out of my breath, not sleeping but entering a deep trance state.

Next, I must connect with the vibrations of the dreamscape, of the world beyond the physical. I imagine my body lying on the floor, my spirit being pulled from it into the astral plane.

Is Meera out there right now, finding another dream wielder to frame? Another person to kill?

I squeeze my eyes tighter. I try again, bringing my focus back to my breath, the feel of the energies of the universe around me. Slowly, pressure builds in my bones, my head, pressing outward against my skin, colors exploding. When it subsides, I float into the astral plane.

The dreamscape is different from when I connect directly with another person. When I enter someone else's mind, it's of their creation, but here is the creation of the universe, the heart of it all. The energies of everything caress me like being held in a warm embrace.

Nothing hurts. Nothing weighs me down; there's just peaceful assurance. I could stay here forever.

I need to find Gabriel, but I don't know where to start with the whole universe before me, the energies of billions.

I play a film of Gabriel in my mind: the way he moves, speaks, the taste of him—no, it's not his body I need to find, it's his soul. I think of his kindness, his shining aura, the way I feel when he holds me, and his smile. Because the smile isn't just of the body, it's a peek at the soul underneath.

Then I pull on the greatest tool I have. I grab hold of that golden thread, finding a white one alongside it, a bond of the souls—in its early stages, this rare bond is delicate, growing stronger as time passes and the connected souls become one. The light bursts through me. I follow the string until I sense him. I reach out with my mind, gently pressing until I crash through into his dream.

The feeling of the universe is gone. It's only Gabriel and me. I'm in Salem City Cemetery. Gabriel sits on a short stone wall near the back.

His hands press into his thighs as he stares with a vacant expression across the sea of graves. Threatening clouds douse us with a cool mist.

When Meera, Iniko, and I were in middle school, we came here at night to scare ourselves. A heaviness weighs on me when I think I might have lost them both. On cue, my feet sink into the grass with my change in mood. I can't get distracted in a dream; it will take the reins, and I have a mission to complete. I wrench myself up from the rich mud.

Gabriel hasn't looked up or made any indication he knows I'm here. "Gabriel." I crouch, gazing up at his face. His hair is soaked, skin nearly translucent. Blood drips from his lips where he's bitten them through.

"The spirits dream of many things, screams and nightmares, but peaceful things, like rivers and streams," he rambles incoherently.

"Gabriel, I'm so sorry I did this to you." His hands are ice cold as I grip them tight. "I know you must be in pain, but I need your help. I'm locked with the Nightmares. I need you to come let me out."

His dead eyes stare at the cracked and broken graves. He doesn't move. Maybe he can't. "She doesn't see, not with eyes of green, she doesn't feel with hands of cream, she doesn't dream . . ."

"It's okay," I tell him. "I'm here. You're safe." My reassurance goes unheard.

I usually don't like to force dreams, but I'm running out of time. I push myself to my knees, the mud squishing under me. I gently take his face, moving it until he's looking at me. "Gabriel, listen to me. I'm stuck, and I need your help. Hear me, please hear me." I stare into his unfocused eyes. "Gabriel, I don't have anyone else." A tear slips down my cheek.

His finger catches the tear, eyes shifting to it. "Water of salt flows out the sea. A drop in the ocean once gone is seen."

Time for plan B. I pull him into a kiss. His body doesn't stiffen in response, instead, his hands wrap around my waist, dragging me up to him. The kiss deepens, his hunger for it palpable, searching for the warmth he desperately needs. My hands slip through his hair, guiding him back to me.

"Find me, Gabriel," I breathe into his ear as he kisses down my neck. This time, he stiffens, his breath ragged against my skin.

He pulls back, cupping my face—his eyes bright and alert. "Azalee." His fingers run over my lips. "Azalee."

"This is a dream."

He traces my face, his eyes returning to mine, understanding in them. "A dream."

"I'm locked in with the Nightmares. You need to come get me out." The stones rattle around us.

One beam of light breaks through the clouds. "The Nightmares dream of horrible things, like screams and pain and a life unseen."

He's slipping away. "You need to wake up."

His thumb rests on my bottom lip.

"Do you understand?"

Eyes closed, he nods slowly. When he opens them again, he looks right at me. "I'll find you."

The dreamscape of the universe tugs on me, my spirit drifting back to my physical body. "Wake up, Gabriel. Wake up." I scream it over and over until the dungeon comes back into view, and it's only the Nightmares and me.

CHAPTER 42

Gabriel

My eyes fly open, a cough sputtering out of me. Shaking takes over my whole body as I turn on my side and vomit onto the floor.

"Where . . ." I try to speak, but another coughing fit takes over. I spit to clear my mouth. Blinking, I take in the unfamiliar bedroom and the warm quilt wrapped around me. My head is fuzzy with images of fire and smoke. With nightmares.

Azalee.

I scramble to my feet, wobbling on weakened legs as I race out of the bedroom.

"Azalee." My desperation echoes through the dungeon's stone walls as I trip down the stairs. I slam my shoulder but barely feel it.

I hear rustling behind the wooden door. "It worked." The relief in her voice is palpable. "Are you okay?"

"I had the weirdest dream," I say. "Not sure if I'm out of it, to be honest."

I can only see her eyes through the cutout, and they're filled with worry. "This isn't a dream. Do you think you can get me out?"

I examine the door; rudimentary marks are slashed into it. "These are interesting runes." Pressing my fingers into the indentions, I feel the haphazard magic, chaotic and troubled.

"I have them over here too."

"I've seen them before. My grandfather uses them on occasion to lock doors." My eyes flick back to hers. "Why are the High Witch's runes down here?"

"Meera." She licks her lips, eyes swimming with barely contained tears. "Did he tell you how to bypass them?"

"No. But I learned on my own." I grin. "Hold tight. I have what I need in the car. I won't be long."

This potion is of my own making. I gather agrimony, bergamot, chili, salt, and comfrey, tossing it into a copper bowl I find in Azalee's kitchen. Muttering my spell, I add three drops of moon-infused water and royal honey. Then I light it on fire. I usually like to brew it a little longer, but we don't have time. Besides, the runes aren't very strong, so it should be enough to break the spell.

"Stand back," I say, returning fifteen minutes later with a bubbling potion.

"Is that going to burn the door down?"

The singed herbs tickle my nose. "It's going to break any spells binding the door shut."

Azalee wraps her hand around the window between us, getting on her toes to see me better. "Wait, would that include the spell tied to my blood?"

I frown; I didn't think about that. "Yeah, it's pretty potent."

She looks over her shoulder at the locked cell doors. These won't be affected, but if the Nightmares pass those defenses, there'd be nothing stopping them from walking out of the house. She must think it's worth the risk because she says, "Do it."

"Stand back." I pour the potion on the door while chanting the second part of the spell. A burning scent fills the air as the runes on my side glow bright orange. There's a clicking, and the door opens. "Pretty handy, huh?"

"You or the spell?" She scrambles to my side and quickly closes what's left of the door.

"What happened?" I ask, following her upstairs to her living quarters.

"I was an idiot," she says when we return to the living room, sitting on the couch. "You were right. Meera is working with the High Witch." She tells me what Meera confessed and why she locked Azalee in the dungeon.

"How could I not have seen it?" Azalee's face is pale, lips trembling. "I missed the signs with Iniko and now with Meera. Am I just a shitty fr—" She grabs the back of her head as the painful scream rips through her. "Argh!"

"Azalee, you need to lie down." I know what she did to me. She pulled me into a nightmare. I have to tread carefully—that's a symptom of the late stages of Nightmare progression. Maybe I can still bring her back, but push too hard, and it might lead her straight over the edge. I need to reduce her stress, but knowing Azalee, that won't be easy.

"No." She closes her eyes, taking long breaths. "You were right about Meera. Which means we're out of time."

I rub her back in slow circles. "I know what Meera means to you. I don't blame you for thinking I was lying."

For what you did to me.

She opens her eyes. "But I shouldn't have reacted like that . . . I'm so sorry." She doesn't confirm what we both know happened. "The last few days, you've been nothing but trustworthy. You've had my back. I wanted the truth, and when you presented it, I freaked the fuck out."

I shift, words measured. "About that . . . Azalee, you should tell someone." I know Roz isn't my biggest fan, but they might be able to help.

Leaning forward, she covers her face. "Can we not talk about that right now?"

There's a long pause. "It's been an eventful night. We can discuss it in the morning."

She looks at the clock like she just realized it's nearly midnight. "No. We need to find where the High Witch is hiding these people."

"Right now?" I frown. My palms sweat at the idea of confronting my grandfather.

"We need to make a finding spell—a powerful one."

"Do you know how to make a spell strong enough to break through the protection charms the High Witch no doubt has surrounding that place?" I ask. "My grandfather is a masterful ward caster. And while potions are my specialty, he's had decades longer to hone his skills." I don't know if I'm good enough.

"I know *of* a spell. I just don't have the ingredients. But I know who does." She leaps up, grabbing her cloak off the hook.

I follow her to the door because there isn't much point in arguing with her. She's going to do this with or without me. And I'd much prefer the former.

"You remember when we saw that medium?"

"Yeah?" My head is still fuzzy from the nightmare, and it takes intense concentration to keep up.

"When we were there, I noticed a golden rutilated quartz—a big one. Ones that large are extremely rare and exactly what we need to boost a finding spell."

My lips press into a thin line. I picked that medium initially because she had no ties to my grandfather, but I don't like bringing more people into our plans than we need. "You think she'll just give it to us?"

"It doesn't hurt to ask."

"I'm sorry, it's not for sale," Opal tells us when she finally answers the door. The shop was closed, but when you bang on a door long enough, people answer or call the cops. Thank the Gods, it was the first one.

"Please, this is important," Azalee begs, keeping her foot in the door, preventing Opal from closing it in our faces.

"Everything is to those who seek something." Her hand runs along the chain at her neck.

"More people are going to die if we don't do this," I say.

She studies me with graying eyes. I keep my gaze strong. She shifts to Azalee's pleading face and, after a minute, nods, opening the door for us to enter.

"How much for the golden rutilated quartz?" I withdraw my wallet.

"As I said, it's not for sale." She pulls her red shawl tight, long hair hanging down her back.

"Then why did you let us in?" Azalee rests her hands on the wooden display table, fingers gripping a stone covered in runes that lies upon it.

Opal lights candles around the cramped room. The flickering casts a moody glow about the darkened space, stirring the scent of anise and cloves toward us. "I will help you find what you seek, but you must do it here. The golden rutilated quartz can be dangerous in the wrong hands. I cannot let it leave this building."

I open my mouth to offer more money, but Azalee interrupts. "Okay, we'll do it here."

We tell her enough but not too much so that she can figure out what we're doing. She doesn't seem interested in knowing. That or whatever spirits are floating around here already informed her of our plans.

Walking around, I find breathing hard in certain areas, like an invisible presence clogs the air. Spirits are everywhere, but they must travel here in hordes, hoping Opal will connect them to who they have lost.

"They won't bother you," Opal tells me. "They're only observing."

"Do you ever want a break from all of it?"

She smiles softly, fingers running along the fabric adorning her reading table. "If I were lost and trying to find my way home, I wouldn't want someone to turn their back on me."

I watch her face, deep with worry lines, but how much of those are from the sorrows of others. "Doesn't sound like an answer."

"Answer enough, I think." She glides over to the spot we've set up to perform the spell. She places the golden rutilated quartz down next to the spell bowl. "I will leave you to finish the incantation. You are welcome to stay until the spell is complete."

"How long will it take?" Azalee asks me, watching Opal disappear behind the curtains in the back.

Once Azalee showed me the spell, I took the lead since my magic is stronger on this front. We're sat on the wood floor, the spell cloth laid between us. "Depends how strong the spells are protecting the place we seek, and since it's the High Witch—I imagine it will take a while."

"Why do you think she let us in?"

The shop was always small, but with Opal gone, it feels like it's closing in on us. She kept the spirits at bay, but now they have free rein.

"I don't know, maybe some spirit told her we were the good guys." I pour in the last of the ingredients, muttering the incantation as I stir, the contents turning a bright white. I hand Azalee a copy of the spell. "We need to read this together and think about finding what the High Witch has hidden. When it becomes translucent, we'll uncover what we seek."

"What is hidden must come to light. Guide us to this unseen place; we seek it for a noble deed." The liquid glows but doesn't change. It's going to be a long night.

CHAPTER 43

Azalee

I wake up to the smell of coffee and someone gently shaking me. I blink, expecting to see sunlight, but it's still dark. "The spell?" I mumble, still acutely aware of the nightmare that chased me through my sleep, calling me, whispering to stop fighting.

"It's done." Gabriel hands me a cup of coffee, green eyes searching my face, but thankfully leaving the conversation there.

I take the mug without any intention of drinking it. "What time is it?"

"Three a.m."

Moving from the cushioned window seat, I kneel before the bowl. The glowing has subsided, leaving a clear potion. "Did you look?"

He shakes his head. "I waited for you."

I take a deep breath, grabbing the silver goblet Opal picked for us. I dip the cup in, filling it with the potion. "Bottoms up." I lift the chalice to my lips, but Gabriel grabs my wrist.

"If we complete the ritual, my grandfather will know we're seeking what he's hidden." Firelight dances across his features that I want to memorize completely.

A powerful caster can be warned by a finding spell. It was one of the only hesitations about performing it. But it would take too long to find the place without magic, and Meera might have already tipped him off that we're onto him. "We have to risk it."

"If he knows we're coming, it might be a trap."

I'm coming to appreciate Gabriel's more methodical approach, which is helping to balance the scales against my action-first mantra, but tonight isn't the time for slow and steady. What did Mom say? *A single ripple could cause a tidal wave.* Well, it's coming and we need to get fucking moving before our boat is sunk.

"We'll leave right away. It's the middle of the night; he might not act until morning." I bring the cup back to my lips, taking a long sip. It's cool and refreshing, like an untouched spring on the mountainside. I hand the chalice to Gabriel.

He drinks the remainder of the potion. "We should see the place we're seeking in our minds. I don't know how—" The words are torn from his mouth as images fly into our minds' eyes, almost like memories.

There are trees everywhere, a forest. A manor painted the deepest plum, but it's wasting away, unkempt, abandoned—or meant to look that way. I see the path like I've been there a hundred times. A stone garden full of crying statues.

I open my eyes moments before Gabriel. "A manor in Salem Woods, deep inside."

"It's not far away from where the last attack was with Amina," he adds, running a hand across his lips. "If we'd gone in the opposite direction, we would've found it." Gabriel helps me to my feet.

"You don't have to do this." I gaze up at him, relishing the warmth of his body pressed into mine. "He is your grandfather."

"Why do you keep trying to push me away?" Hurt flashes in his eyes.

"I'm not. I just know you don't have a lot of family. I don't want you to feel like you've lost everything."

"I haven't lost everything." He tilts my chin, kissing me softly. The ravenous passion from the other night is still tugging at us. But this kiss is a port in the storm we've dived headfirst into.

"The High Witch," he continues, "is facilitating the murders of innocent people for his vendetta. I've tried for years to understand, to search for the good I thought must be hidden there. But I'm afraid my hunt was futile. Doing what is right isn't always easy, but it doesn't mean it shouldn't be done."

For so long, I hated him because of his grandfather, thinking they were one and the same. But I was wrong. Just because he stayed with his grandfather didn't mean he was the same person.

We thank Opal before we leave. "The spirits," she says as we walk out the door. "The ones shadowed in darkness, will you free them?"

"We'll do our best." Maybe that's why she helped us. Her interests didn't lie with the living but in ensuring the dead reached their final resting place.

I know this plan is stupid. But what choice do we have? No one is publicly campaigning to help dream wielders—so I will have to do it in the cover of darkness.

I turn back for a last glance at Opal as we get into Gabriel's car, but she's already inside. The alcove to the door is dark, all the lights out, but crouched in the corners scratching to get inside are creatures hidden in darkness. I look away, but I'm not fast enough; they turn, smiling—teeth dripping with blood.

I close my eyes, count to three, and open them again. The creatures are gone, and the street is silent. "Azalee?" Gabriel follows my gaze to the shop. "Did we forget something?"

I press my lips together, shaking my head. I'm afraid if I spoke, the only thing that would come out is a scream.

Gabriel parks his car on the edge of the woods, and with our phone lights guiding us, we take the rest on foot. Waiting until sunrise would've been easier, but night will keep us hidden, and time is of the essence.

Now that we've tipped our hand, we must act before the High Witch can move the prisoners.

Also, I don't know how much longer I can keep going. I'm seeing nightmares in real life now—the creatures at the door haunted me the whole way here. This is the final stage before I become a Nightmare. But I can hold them off a little longer. Then Mom and Roz can figure something out.

I can fight it.

Just keep looking forward. Ignore the shadows creeping at the sides of my vision. They aren't real.

Gabriel is real.

Grabbing his hand, I squeeze so hard I can feel his pulse against my palm. "Are you okay?" he whispers.

"Fine."

The manor comes into view after thirty minutes of deep-woods trekking. If we hadn't been looking for it, I would've passed right by. The once grand manor looks like it's about to collapse any minute. Half the shingles are missing, likely from years of storms. Fallen branches have cracked windows in the upper stories, giving the impression no one has called it home for decades. What a perfectly creepy place to conduct your villainous deeds.

There's no movement or lights, but he must have security guards or wards, even if we can't spot them. Since going through the front door isn't the wisest plan, we walk to the gardens on the side of the building. Damp leaves and dirt scents tickle my nose, making me sneeze. We pass the weeping statues I saw in the vision, white-tinged marble angels crying into their hands—wings cast down, shoulders slumped in pain.

I want to keep going, but Gabriel stops, fingers running along the stone, coming back covered in dirt. "Can you feel them?" he whispers.

I frown. The world only responds to me with emptiness. The hum of magic surrounding us is lost to me—another symptom of a Nightmare.

"Feel what?" I move closer, struggling to keep the shaking from my voice.

"The spirits. I can sense them, but it's dark and cold." He touches the weeping statue nearest us.

I put my hand on it too, but I can't detect anything—just the cold seeping into my skin. "We'll come back for them, but we have to get the others first." He nods and follows me, but I find him glancing back as we walk away.

We wander around the house's perimeter until we see a whitewashed door leading into a basement—perfect place to lock up your Nightmares. The heavy padlock doesn't budge as I yank against it. We have a vial of Gabriel's unlocking potion left, but only enough for one use.

There is a window near the door, too small for me or Gabriel to get through, but Meera might fit. Too bad she isn't here to help us. My head snaps to the woods, a crunching noise drawing my attention.

"What is it?" Gabriel scans the woods. "Do you see something?"

"I thought I heard . . ." I close my eyes, lungs struggling to harness my ragged breaths. *Stop it, Azalee. It's not real.* "I . . ."

"It's probably an animal. All the same, let's hurry."

I know he didn't hear it because there's nothing to hear. But that doesn't stop the crawling sensation on my skin.

I crouch, using my shirtsleeve to wipe away the grime on the window. I shine my flashlight through the glass. Bile chokes me when the conditions inside are revealed. There are dozens, if not more, of people with their arms above their heads, hands, and feet locked in shackles and fastened to bolts on the wall. It's hard to tell, but it looks like these are the Nightmares. I fruitlessly try to record the scene with my phone, but the wards make the images useless. I press my eyes shut as tears sting them. Gabriel touches my shoulder, but his warmth feels so far away.

"We have to get them out," I choke as rain patters against the roof.

"We will, but we need to scout the rest of the place first."

"I can't leave. Look at them." My voice gets louder than it should.

"We can't just let them free. If they wander off, they could hurt themselves or someone else. We'll come back and make sure we can get them somewhere safe."

He's right; I know he is, but a piece of my heart chips off as I walk away. I keep picturing Iniko stuck down there. This is the vision he saw, why he had to warn me. If we don't stop the High Witch, this might be the fate that awaits all Nightmares—*awaits me.*

We find a back door, and after checking the grungy windows, we can't see anyone inside. This is a large manor with plenty of places to hide. We can't let our guards down just because everything's been smooth sailing so far.

The door is locked, but not with magic. "We have to break the window," Gabriel whispers. "Then you can climb through and open the door."

Breaking windows sounds more like my thing. "That'll make too much noise."

"There are at least four visible locks on that door, and possibly more I can't see. Taking the time to pick each one eats away at our already limited time."

"Okay, fine, break the window."

He searches the ground until he finds a rock big enough. "If we hear any movement inside, we run for those trees." He throws the rock through the window near the door. Smashing glass echoes around the quiet woods, but when the sound dies, there is silence again.

I take off my cloak and lay it over the edge of jagged glass. Gabriel helps lift me, and I climb inside. I hiss when I catch my arm on some wayward glass. I slip my cloak back on, examining the entryway I've landed in. It looks like the staff entrance.

I open the door for Gabriel—he was right, there were two hidden locks. "Should we split up?" he asks.

I raise an eyebrow. "You need to watch more horror movies because that is never a good idea. We stay together, checking room by room."

"This could take a while." His eyes drift up the dusty stairs.

"Then let's not stand around."

Thick dust coats everything on the first floor, and none of it looks like it's been disturbed for years. We also come up empty after searching the second floor. If it weren't for the Nightmares in the basement, I'd think we had the wrong house.

Stepping onto the third floor, I'm second-guessing myself. "Shouldn't there be guards? Where are the other hostages? There's not the slightest hint there has ever been anyone in these upper rooms. Maybe we fucked up the finding spell? Or the High Witch could have multiple stash houses. Maybe he already killed Meera's parents or—"

"Maybe this is a trap," Gabriel finishes my thought.

"Starting to feel that way." It took us almost an hour to get here. That might have been enough time for him to set an ambush.

I stop when I reach a door with freshly carved runes. This is the first sign of new magic we've seen. Everything else was dusty books and herbs from years gone by. "Gabriel." I point to the symbols matching the ones Meera used. "We need to use your potion."

Gabriel performs the unlocking spell, the runes glowing brightly as the lock clicks. We exchange a glance before I slowly twist the handle. We shine our lights in to see three people asleep on beds. They don't shift as we move toward the first bed.

"Tali!" I run to Meera's mom, who is lying unmoving on the white sheet. I put two fingers to her neck, checking her pulse. "She's alive. They must be under a sleeping draught."

"Same with these two," Gabriel calls from the other side of the room.

My hands shake as I search in my bag for the wake-up potion. If I can get Meera's family out of here, Meera won't have to stay with the High Witch. I force Tali's eyes open and dispense a few drops into each.

"Tali, it's me, Azalee. Open your eyes, please." I stare at her frozen body. "Damn it. We need to get them to Roz." I pull Tali to sit, propping her up on the wall.

"Azalee." Gabriel places a hand on my shoulder. "How do we get all three of them out of here and to the car? It's almost two miles."

"We carry them." I grunt, lugging Tali to a standing position, but she can't stay upright without my help.

"And the Nightmares? What do we do with them?"

The blood pumping in my ears is so loud I can barely hear him. "We have to save them." I lose my grip on Tali, and she slumps onto the bed.

"We will." Gabriel wipes a tear from my cheek. I don't remember crying. "But we need help. We can't take them all ourselves. The car isn't big enough and is too far away."

"The other dream wielders!" I say. "If we find them, they can help carry everyone out." We should have thought this plan through, but I didn't expect there to be this many Nightmares, and I didn't expect Meera's family to be unable to walk.

Time was running out. I *had* to act. I had to.

"They're probably going to be enchanted like Amina," Gabriel says. I know he is trying to help, but it's infuriating.

"If they're like Amina, they'll be easily manipulated. We can tell them what to do." If they're also asleep—I can't think about that right now. I have to see this through, which means we need an exit plan. Cell service is nonexistent, so calling for reinforcements is a bust.

"We've been through the whole house. Where could the dream wielders be?"

I stare at Meera's sleeping family. My thoughts keep getting lost in the foggy abyss of my mind.

Think, think, think.

Where would the High Witch keep dream wielders? "The basement." I jump up and nearly knock him over as I race from the room.

"With the Nightmares?"

"Of course. He thinks we're all the same. He would keep them together." It's hard to hear how loud I'm being with the thundering in my head. I should slow down, make my steps light, but I have to get to the basement.

The stairs threaten to crack beneath me, but I reach the ground floor in one piece. The lonesome hoots of the owls outside are the only noise. I rip open the wood door we guessed leads to the basement and start down the rickety stairs, the wood sagging and groaning beneath my feet.

Gabriel grabs my arm when he catches up with me. "Azalee, we need to be careful."

"I know they're here," I whisper, voice strained.

"Okay, but someone else might be too."

I blink, eyes stinging from the stirred-up dust. I take the rest of the stairs gingerly, Gabriel close behind.

No locks or runes hold the door at the bottom of the stairs closed. The knob twists open with little effort. The room is dark like all the rest, but the small window near the rafters brings in enough light to see the people chained to the walls. They're standing on a dirt floor with nowhere to sit or lie.

From outside, they all looked like Nightmares, but down here, I can see the difference. Chained among the frail Nightmares are the dream wielders.

I shake the shoulders of the nearest dream wielder, careful not to touch his skin. While I'm pretty sure he's not a Nightmare, better safe than sorry. His eyes flutter but don't open. I shake him again. "Wake up. You need to wake up." His eyelids move rapidly, opening this time before closing once more.

"Gabriel, we have to . . ." The words die in my throat when I turn around and see a hooded figure behind Gabriel. The stranger puts his hand to his mouth, unfolding his palm and blowing blue powder into the air.

The world fades into darkness.

CHAPTER 44

Gabriel

The baby-blue powder misses hitting my skin by millimeters as I dodge to the left. But Azalee isn't so lucky. It hits her full in the face, her eyes widening before she collapses to the ground.

Ignoring the urge to run to her, I duck to avoid the assailant's grasp. A satisfying crunch follows when I kick him in the knee. Not taking the time to celebrate, I spin around, elbowing him in the nose. Blood flows onto his black shirt while he fumbles in his pocket. Before he can open the new hex vial, I grab his wrist, twisting his arm and dislocating his shoulder. He screams, writhing in pain as I land a final blow to his face, letting him thud to the ground.

I move to Azalee, drawing her into my arms; I avoid the powder as I check her pulse. It's slow but steady. Lifting her into my arms, I head for the stairs but backtrack when I hear clambering footsteps. I gently lay her against the wall, then conceal myself in the shadows. Adrenaline still pumps through my veins, making me jittery for the next scuffle.

Three men burst through the door. I jump on the closest guy, punching him in all the right places, but I'm outnumbered. A searing fire erupts along my spine as wetness seeps into my hair, my legs becoming jiggly as the potion works its magic. The other two pull me off the third and secure my hands behind my back. But not before they each take turns slamming their fists into my stomach.

"The High Witch would like a word with you," the guy I whaled on says, spitting blood onto the floor.

I wrench my arms, trying to wiggle out of the cuffs, but all I accomplish is getting another punch to the gut. I look down at Azalee as they haul me up the stairs. My stomach drops as I lose visual of her.

I'm dragged through the living room and taken to what we missed: a bookcase with a hidden room behind it. Inside are my grandfather and brother. I'm tossed into a chair and secured with a rope.

Logan's dark eyebrows furrow into a deep frown, his ordinarily jovial face devoid of mirth. His gaze is locked on the wall behind me, avoiding eye contact. Grandfather looks like a king lording over his castle, unbothered as he leans against the fireplace, swirling a scotch.

"Gabriel, I didn't want it to come to this," he says, shaking his head, stare finally landing on me. "I had such hope for you. Your parents had such high hopes. I thought you'd be my pick for the next High Witch now that I know my end is near. But instead you betrayed your brother and me." He motions to Logan, whose hands tremble in white-knuckled fists.

"Logan, I don't know what he told you, but he's lying."

The High Witch scoffs. "My truth is easily proven. Do it," he says to one of the henchmen behind me.

He advances, ripping the buttons on my shirt open to reveal my bare chest. I stiffen as Grandfather hands him a glass jar with a deep-black liquid swirling with purple. "Nightlock," I whisper. "I thought your crop was destroyed?"

Grandfather smiles. "I had other gardens. As I taught you, Gabriel, always have a plan B."

The henchman untwists the lid.

"I will show Logan what you are."

My eyes widen.

They throw the potion on my chest, the one that will reveal what I truly am. At first, I only feel the cool liquid, but slowly, a buzzing starts on my skin, and then it's like a thousand wasps are burrowing their stingers into my chest.

I clamp my jaw tight, grinding my teeth to keep my pain inside. I don't want to give him the satisfaction. I squeeze my eyes shut until the fire subsides. I blink past the tears to look at the High Witch.

He's frowning. "This proves nothing."

I glance at my chest, where the black potion is dripping down my skin. If I had dream magic residue on me, it should have traced the lines of my veins up my neck and to my head. But it didn't—because I've never dream wielded on my own.

Logan finally looks me in the eyes, face clouded in confusion. "Maybe Gabriel isn't a . . . dream wielder." He chokes on the last words.

Without proof, the High Witch only has speculation. I could keep on lying to hide who I am. There might be strategic benefits to keeping my secret just a little longer. Logan won't hate me—a huge incentive—and Grandfather, while he surely won't trust me now that I was caught breaking in here with Azalee, might still be convinced to do the right thing as long as he believes I'm not doing it just to save myself.

But I was never doing it just to save myself, and I don't want to lie to my brother, not anymore.

"Logan, I'm so sorry I lied to you. I just didn't know how to tell you. The way we were raised, I knew how you would react because it's how I did. I hated what I became after that night, hated myself. I didn't want you to hate me too. You're the only family I had."

"So, you're admitting it then?" Grandfather pushes. He wants to hear me say it. And it's long past time I did.

I sit up as straight as I can, holding my head high to muster a bit of dignity. "I am a dream wielder." My voice is steady, even as my heart rattles in my chest.

Logan's eyes widen as I watch him connect the dots of the events that led to me becoming a dream wielder. "That night? When she saved you . . ." Guilt etches his face. "This is my fault."

"No, *no*, it's not," I insist. "You are not responsible for what happened to me. The Fates are."

"But . . ." Logan's eyes slide to Grandfather. Neither of us ever talks about Logan's indiscretions. "You were only there because of me. If I—"

My stomach sinks, but I cut him off. I need the High Witch's focus to stay on me. I'll direct his fury into my path and away from Logan like I've done our whole lives. "Grandfather, the dream wielders are not the monsters you've made them out to be. And the Nightmares . . . it's not their fault. There has to be a compromise that doesn't condemn our fellow witches."

He glances at Logan, but thankfully returns to me. "Why would I listen to you? You've been lying to your family for two years. I only recently became aware of your affliction thanks to Meera's insider reports. I was appalled that this abomination had been allowed to live in our home."

This is what I feared most. That when they found out who I was, they'd hate me. But it doesn't hurt like I thought it would. At least not with Grandfather, not after everything he's done. But the betrayal I inflicted on Logan is another story. And now he's also saddled with the guilt of thinking this is somehow his fault. I never blamed him, not once.

"I wanted to tell you, but I knew you wouldn't understand." I try to reach my brother.

"After everything that happened to your grandmother and I, not to mention your parents." Grandfather shakes his head.

Logan frowns. "Our parents died in a car accident."

"That's what I told you because I wanted to save you the pain and embarrassment. There was a car accident, and your dear mother was killed in the initial crash, but your father was not. We brought him to a private hospital. Thank the Gods, his injuries were minor, and he was going to make a full recovery." Grandfather dabs at his eyes with a handkerchief. "But he was devastated by the death of your mother. The trauma was too much for him. It was mere days before we noticed the signs of dream wielding."

My body shakes. "Dad survived? What happened to him after that?" My rough voice fills with anger.

"We all know that there's no cure once a dream wielder is created. That it is only a matter of time before they become a Nightmare."

"That's not true!" I fight against my bindings, but they only grow tighter. "Logan, he's lying to you. Dream wielders are not dangerous monsters."

"Silence. I will not have an abomination spout lies to my grandson. Your father became a monster, and I did what I had to do to protect you and this family."

"You killed him."

"A sacrifice your father would have understood had he been in his right mind. He witnessed firsthand what happened to his mother and would not have wished the same fate on himself."

Logan's face pales as he glances between the two of us. He looks like he's going to throw up. I want to push my point further, but my words won't come as my vision tunnels.

I open my mouth, slurring, "What . . . you . . . did me?"

Grandfather eyes me like a hawk narrowing in on its prey. "You will still be useful yet, Gabriel."

CHAPTER 45

Azalee

My thoughts are sand, cascading down a slippery slope, the hazy memories from my last moments coming back to me in snippets. I flutter my eyelids, but they feel like someone glued them shut. Gritting my teeth, I pry them open with sheer force of will. Regretting it immediately when sunlight blinds me before I slam them shut again.

Take two.

I squint just enough to get a peek at my surroundings. I'm in an unfamiliar part of the manor's ground floor. Thick rope cuts into my skin, where my arms are tied behind my back on a rickety chair that wobbles unsteadily at the slightest movement. Weak rays of early-morning sun filter through the dirty windows.

How long have I been asleep?

Gabriel. I have to get to him. A strong, thick hand pushes me back down as I attempt to get free. It's the same bulky figure from the basement who knocked me out with a potion.

"You can't hold me here," I say, mustering more courage than I feel. I hope he can't hear my heart rumbling like a stampede in my chest. The man stays silent. We're the only ones here—well, us and the things lurking in the corner with pointed teeth and bloody mouths. The minutes tick away as I formulate my escape plan.

"Good, you're awake," the smooth voice of the High Witch says, as he comes in through a hidden bookcase door.

"Where's Gabriel?" I thrash against my bindings. The hooded guard doesn't even bother to stop me this time. Probably just happy to let me waste my energy.

"Not here." The High Witch gives no further explanation as Meera and Logan follow him inside, shutting the door behind them. I bite hard, tasting blood. I want to hate her—I *should* hate her. She betrayed not only me but all the dream wielders and Nightmares. But I can't, she's my best friend. I've always known she'd do anything to protect those she loved.

"Meera, don't do whatever this is," I beg, looking at her and not the High Witch's humorless smile. "I found your family. We can save them. You don't need to hurt any more people."

She frowns. "Why didn't you leave it alone, Azalee? I told you I'd never hurt you. But now . . ."

The High Witch's too-white teeth gleam in the morning sun. "Now you've made it so much worse. For you, obviously, not for me. This worked out great for me."

"Gabriel was right; this was a trap." The creatures in the corner move closer.

The High Witch laughs, and it's so charismatic I want to throw up. "Of course it was a trap. You don't think I know when someone uses a finding spell on me?" His face sobers. "I didn't lure you here, Azalee. You trespassed of your own accord. Anything that happens now is your own doing."

"I wasn't going to sit by and let you continue to kill people." The darkness pumps through me, the hate and anger burning away the light.

He chooses his words carefully. "Something had to be done."

"I know all about your plans," I say. "You'll be caught soon. I hope you like prison. I'm sure you'll do great there."

"I'm not going to prison." He nods to the guard. "And neither will you, but first, we have some formalities to cover."

The guard pulls my jacket and shirt back to expose my shoulder and clavicle.

"What are you doing?" I curl inward to protect myself, but I can only move a millimeter. "Stop!" I yell as he pulls a familiar jar from his pocket—the nightlock potion.

"You should learn to be more thorough," the High Witch says as the guard throws the potion onto me.

"Gods," I hiss as a thousand tiny needles dig into my skin. *"Fuck."* The searing travels across my chest, up my neck, and over my face. Nausea rolls through me as the pain becomes unbearable.

"No need to confess like your mother," he says. "The proof is written all over your skin."

I press my lips together to hold in a sob as I see the black potion has traced the lines of my veins across my chest, and based on the pain, I'm guessing it goes across my neck and face.

The creature slithering around on the floor bares its teeth, green saliva dripping from its yellowed mouth.

"It doesn't matter. Others know I'm here." I attempt to buy myself some time. "You're not going to get away with this."

"No one knows you're here." He indicates his head to Meera. "This secret is between you and Gabriel. Meera told me everything."

My throat burns. Meera has been doing his bidding to protect her family, and while I don't agree, I understand, but she didn't have to tell him all that. She could have kept that information to herself. She sold me out. *Again.*

The darkness widens its hold on my mind. The creatures' heads twist at odd angles, their claws scraping across the floor as they move closer. They're the only clear things. The rest of the world is becoming fuzzy. "Why are you doing this to dream wielders?" It takes more strength than usual to get the words to move out of my mouth, my tongue heavy inside it.

"I don't need to explain myself. I am simply doing what I must to protect Salem and all of humanity." He stares out the window covered in grime.

"I know you're dying and you think this needs to be your final act." I try to reason with him. "And I understand our powers can be scary from an outside perspective—that you've suffered from wrongdoings with it yourself. But they aren't inherently bad. In fact, we can help people through so many things. If you just—"

Dust swirls around him as he walks. "What I can do is make sure there are no more dream wielders poisoning this earth. That whatever dark magic you possess withers and dies."

"You think by locking us up—killing us—you can stop more dream wielders from being created? Dream wielding isn't inherited, it appears when it wants. Fate decides, not us." He's trying to wipe us out with a tactic that will never succeed. Which means the killing will never end.

"The ability to infiltrate dreams, to create nightmares, is a plague on all of us, and like my forefathers in Salem, I will eradicate it."

"Magic can't be destroyed by mortals. You must know that." I shudder as the ropes cut into my arms as I strain to release myself.

"Watch me."

My guard unties me but keeps the ropes around my hands as he drags me to the door.

I struggle against him, but he's got a good foot on me.

"I want to show you I have zero tolerance for dream wielders. No matter who they are." We follow behind the High Witch and Meera, the creatures running past me and into the woods. In the front yard, a pyre is assembled, and in the middle of the logs, tied to a vast pole staring straight at me, is Gabriel.

CHAPTER 46

Azalee

"Azalee," Gabriel roars, struggling against the ropes binding him. "Run!"

I need to free Gabriel before they do something I can't reverse. "He's your grandson," I scream against the roaring in my ears. My shoulder pops as my captor fights against my attempt to escape.

The sunlight dances across the High Witch's unworried face. "He is nothing. My grandson died two years ago." He opens his palm to reveal a lighter.

"Grandfather, can we talk about this?" Logan's eyes are wide.

"Logan, you know I have no other choice."

"No. This isn't Gabriel's fault." Things run through the forest around us, cracking branches, leaves flying—no one else notices the blinking of red eyes behind the trees. The life debt he owes me burns between us. That gold thread pulled tighter than it's ever been. The wisp of white string is too weak to do more than shiver in the breeze. The bond is newly formed, it hasn't had time to strengthen, and now it's going to sever before it ever gets the chance.

"Azalee . . ." Gabriel knows what his death means for me. "Let her do it," he offers as a last-ditch effort to save me. Because if I ignite the flame that takes his life, I'll survive.

I should want that. Weeks ago, I might not have cared that Gabriel would die. But I do care now. *Gods, I care.*

The High Witch flicks the lighter open. "Having your hand be the killing blow is a rather tempting offer. It'll fit nicely into our little narrative. You were so keen on figuring out what I was up to; now you can play the part of the dream wielder imprisoned for murder. Release one of her hands," he says to my guard.

Untying the rope, he slips my left arm free. I shove against him, and he barely moves.

"Meera, make yourself useful and keep hold of her."

Meera tentatively takes my arm. All the nerves on my skin are on fire. The slight touch feels like an iron clamp. "Meera, *please*?" My voice cracks as tears trail down my cheeks.

"Azalee . . ."

"Enough." The High Witch's fingers encircle my arm as he places the lighter into my palm, narrowly avoiding touching my skin. If he had, perhaps I could have shown him what a Nightmare can do. He leans down and whispers in a hot breath, "Do it, or I'll make sure he suffers an even more painful death."

My stomach rolls, bile climbing up my throat. I look up at Gabriel, and he nods. *It's okay,* he mouths.

None of this is okay. I can't save anyone.

"Do. It. Now." The High Witch's voice is miles away.

Meera shakes beside me.

"I'm sorry," I say, flicking the lighter and throwing it on the pyre. The smell of burning wood fills the air, the fire igniting quickly. There must be an accelerant on the wood. The High Witch didn't want to wait around for a natural burn.

Gabriel's face, which was decisive moments ago, breaks into fear. "Logan, I'm sorry . . ." But his words fade as the crackling fire sings its anthem. There is nothing left for him to say. He twists at his bindings, trying to get higher up the pole, but it's useless. The flame licks his skin, melting it from his bones.

No, no, no.

Mom flashes through my brain. She's sitting in a hospital room right now, thinking I'm safe at home, where I told her I'd be.

Screaming roars overpower the raging fire as the world spins. I need to cover my ears, but the ropes won't let me. Pain radiates through my arms as I wrench them to escape. I let out a sharp breath, closing my eyes, and counting to three before I open them again. I can't see Gabriel anymore; the fire and smoke are too thick.

My fault. It's my fault he's here.

"I'm sorry, Azalee. You might not believe it, but I never meant for any of this."

Meera.

I think?

The screaming is deafening. The world is the wrong color—things creep out of the forest.

We have to run.

They will find us.

They will tear us apart.

Words are caught in my throat—choking me. I'd claw to get them out, but I can't move my hands.

"Az, are you okay?" Meera's face is stretching, the skin melting off her bones. "What are you doing to her?" she screams at the High Witch. "You're hurting her." Meera shoves the man off me, hands shaking as she loosens my ropes.

"We had a deal. Your family's safety for helping me. You do this, and it violates that agreement."

Meera ignores him, freeing my hands. I sway as the ground beneath me rumbles. Does no one else see the creatures creeping toward us? I look back to Gabriel, but there is nothing left but roaring flames. I try to speak, but bony hands pull my mouth shut, the words trapped inside.

Meera extends her hand, but I push her away; the creatures are at her back—horrible gray things with teeth for eyes and mouths for hands. The hooded man reaches for me, and I grab at his face, clawing at the bare skin. The world explodes into bright white. He staggers back, and I do the only thing that makes sense—I run.

Wind thrashes at my skin, cutting me. I need to outrun them. I stumble through the weeping statues, their invisible hands tearing at my clothes. I rip my cloak off, letting them have it.

The creatures are close, their breath sticky on my neck. My legs wobble as I stagger through the woods. The trees become thicker, the branches catching on my shirt, the roots making me trip.

I hit the ground hard, teeth rattling inside my skull. The last light of the misty morning fades away as the darkness closes in. The creatures howl their approval.

Then, for one brief moment, everything is frozen. But the darkness remains—will remain. The scream now is my own. Hot tears stream down my face. The creatures stare at me, eyes blank voids.

The darkness is a smooth hand against my cheek. *"Sleep now,"* it whispers, one voice and many. *"Sleep. Your fight is done."*

I want to fight it, have been fighting it for weeks. I've been resisting, but I know now ignoring it has only made it stronger, brought me closer to the never-ending dark.

"Sleep." My eyes grow heavy but don't close. The world is fading away, even with open eyes. *"Darkness is all you will know. All you deserve."*

I failed all of them—Mom, Gabriel, Meera, Iniko, the dream wielders, and the Nightmares.

"Dreams are not your sanctuary. They will bring you no resolution."

I don't deserve a sanctuary.

The creatures move again, mouths opening wide, jaws unhinged, their teeth rotten and yellow. The woods fade as darkness reigns.

I close my eyes.

My heartbeat, the blood pumping through my veins, slows. It might have stopped altogether; I can't feel it anymore.

I surrender. I'm exhausted, and the darkness beckons me in with the sweet relief. Part of me knows something is wrong, telling me this isn't the way. But it fades just as the sunlight did. Clarity comes as I realize what I've given myself over to, but it's too late; I can't pull myself back out of the darkness.

I am a Nightmare.

CHAPTER 47

Gabriel

As the fire licks my skin, raging higher until it consumes my view of everything else, I realize that today might not actually be the day I meet the Gods. The fire is scorching, eating away at the logs beneath my feet, but I feel none of it. It's simply a warm caress against my skin, like a loving embrace. Arms still tied behind my back, I survey my skin to see if the heat has melted it off, but it hasn't. Nor has it touched my clothes.

I'm not burning.

It's an illusion. Grandfather wants to make Azalee think I'm dying. But what is the larger motive at play? The hatred I saw on his face earlier made me believe in his conviction. He wanted to kill me. So maybe it's not *his* illusion.

Logan . . . it has to be him. He's skilled enough to brew a potion capable of stopping fire. Gods, let it be him. Let my brother still care about me. Or at least not hate me enough to want me dead.

Now that I'm not being burned alive, I can focus on undoing the ropes and getting Azalee and me the hell out of here. I assess my current predicament. I'm well secured, but there aren't any runes on this pole that I saw. Until now, all I could hear was the raging fire, but a deafening scream cuts through the crackling.

Azalee.

Wrenching my arm forward, I'm treated to a pop and burst of pain as my right shoulder dislocates. It hurts like a bitch, but it gives me enough leverage to slip my arms out of the ropes. Fighting through the wave of dizziness, I take a deep breath, regretting it when I choke on smoke. Just because the fire isn't killing me doesn't mean that smoke inhalation won't.

My right arm hangs limply at my side, out of commission. Slowly, I wiggle my left hand through the orange flames, testing the limitations of the spell protecting me. Just like the rest of me, I don't feel anything but a soft warmth from the fire.

Steeling my nerves, I grit my teeth and jump through the flames. Without seeing where I'm throwing myself out to, I land hard on wet leaves, my already dislocated shoulder catching the brunt of my fall. Pain ripples through my body, and I almost black out. Forcing fresh air in and out of my lungs, I manage to keep awake and stumble to my feet.

I expect to be greeted by another ambush of guards, but the group is in chaos.

"Find her, you worthless idiots. She can't have gotten that far." Grandfather points to somewhere in the forest. My eyes quickly scan the scene. Azalee's gone. On the ground, huddled in the fetal position, is the guy who was holding her.

Just as I'm staggering away, Logan spots me. He tosses a handful of seeds in the air, and the garden explodes with color as each one bursts into a full-bloomed flower before releasing their own seeds that repeat the process as they fly on the wind like confetti.

Hidden from the others, he runs to my side while the rest are preoccupied. "You need to get out of here, Gabriel." He helps me stay standing, eyes full of panic.

"You saved me?" My throat burns from ash.

"I wasn't going to let you die—even after everything. Just go so my good deed isn't for nothing." He shoves me away.

Numbness creeps down my arm, which is only slightly better than the blinding pain. "Logan, I don't think I can make it." My body feels like I'm wearing cement shoes.

"We'll go together." Meera slings my good arm over her shoulder, which, given our height difference and the many pounds I have on her, isn't much help.

"Logan, come with us. You don't need to stay with him." I don't want to leave my brother with this monster.

"I can't" is all he says before disappearing into the lessening cloud of flowers. As much as I want to chase after him, I'm in no shape to do so.

"You betrayed Azalee." I fight against Meera as she drags me into the woods and away from the fire that's masking our escape. "Why are you helping me?"

She easily keeps going since I'm too weak to stop her. "It wasn't supposed to go like this. I never . . ." Her body shakes against me.

"Where's Azalee? Did he hurt her?"

Meera grunts as I lay more weight onto her, my legs still wobbling from whatever potion they gave me earlier. "She ran into the woods."

"Then we have to find her."

Her eyes scan the trees as we clamber through the forest, not as fast as we should be going since it won't be long before they come for us. "Gabriel, something happened to her . . ."

"All the more reason to find her. Azalee!" I attempt to step away from Meera, hoping I can grit my way through. But I stumble and fall to my knees.

In the dense forest, only a minimal amount of light comes through.

"You're in bad shape," Meera says, grunting as she helps me stand.

I mumble, unable to say much more. Reaching inward, I search for that golden rope linking us together. I always know when Azalee is near, but all I feel is cold. Even the budding bond neither of us wants to mention is absent. Where is she? Could she have gotten farther away than I thought?

I keep my left hand on my right elbow, pressing my arm into my side to stabilize it. But I grind my teeth against the pain. "She thinks I'm dead, doesn't she?"

"You were supposed to be."

We've only been searching for a few minutes when we hear footsteps in the distance. "The High Witch's men will catch up. They're ex-military, we don't stand a chance."

I'm so cold. My fingers are barely able to move. "We can't just leave her."

"She may have made it back to The Retreat. If so, we'll meet her there."

Meera's right. That might be why I don't sense Azalee's pull.

Footsteps crunch nearer. It makes me physically ill to know that if Azalee is still in the forest, we're leaving her to the wolves. But I'm growing weaker by the minute, my vision tunneling. "Okay, my car's nearby."

I must pass out on the drive back because I wake to Meera shaking me. "Help!" she yells, opening my car door, but I'm too far gone for her to carry me alone.

Roz and Genevieve race out of the house and help Meera get me inside.

"Is she here?" I manage to say as they lay me on the couch. A vision of Azalee and me making love only a few nights ago makes my eyes sting.

Roz comes to my side and begins administering healing.

"Where is my daughter, Meera?" Genevieve asks.

"We . . . we lost her in the forest."

"It was a trap," I croak as Roz makes me swallow a bitter, grainy potion.

Roz's eagle eyes watch Meera, but they remain quiet. I don't know if they're aware of Meera's collaboration with the High Witch. Azalee and I didn't have time to tell anyone.

Genevieve spreads a cloth onto the coffee table, lining tarot cards in the center. "Let's see if any spirits know where she is." Genevieve's eyes move rapidly beneath her lids as she summons ghosts to help her. After a few minutes, she opens her eyes, face pale. She swallows hard. "The High Witch has her. But worse than that, Azalee has become a Nightmare."

CHAPTER 48

Azalee

Curling my shoulders in, I rub my hands up and down my bare arms, fighting against a never-ending chill. Snow falls in heavy, wet flakes as the wind thrashes it into me like a million tiny razor blades. Blizzard conditions mean I can't see more than a few inches in front of my face. Where my feet should be are blue Popsicles doing an impression of feet. I don't know what happened to my boots.

Did I lose them in the foot of snow somewhere back? I've been walking for . . .

Gods, it feels like an eternity.

But I'll be there soon—wherever it was I was going. My body shutters, teeth chattering in an attempt to warm itself. Hypothermia is bound to kick in anytime. A deep chasm widens in my stomach, hopelessness settling into my bones. It's no use; I'll never make it.

Exhaustion pounds at the door in my head. *Sleep, sleep, lie down, and sleep,* it whispers.

Won't it kill me? I ask.

What if you're already dead? the voice responds.

A strangled sob catches in my throat. I can stay awake a little longer. I busy myself searching my pockets once again for anything that might give me some relief.

My fingers catch on a smooth metallic object. A lighter. I withdraw it, not remembering how it got there. I flick it open and ignite the flame. It dances in the wind for a second before extinguishing.

Flames. Fire. Pyre.

Whispers of a memory race along the synapses of my brain, but the ice and snow cover up the course, just like my surroundings.

Squinting, I spot a sign with an arrow. But it's in a language I don't understand.

Where am I?

Teeth chattering harder, I feel them shatter in my mouth—broken shards, cutting into my lips and gums. I spit them out, covering the snow in speckles of blood.

A screeching to my left draws my attention. I look just in time to see a blue car slam into a tree. The branches shake, causing them to release a honey-colored sap onto the car and trapping the person inside. Racing over, I slip and fall to my knees, jarring and rattling my whole body like an earthquake from deep in my gut. Unsteady, I get to my frozen feet.

Sticky sap covers me when I yank at the door handle. "I'll get you out!" I call to the person inside, wiping the window so I can see them. Their face is distorted, jaw unhinged as their eyes stare blankly at me. They're dead.

I can't help them.

I can't help anyone.

You can't even help yourself, whispers the wind.

Stumbling, I stagger away from the vehicle and the smell of decaying bodies. I just keep running. I don't know where to go, and I don't seem to be getting very far, but maybe if I just keep pushing . . .

"Hello?" I yell into the wind. "Is there anyone here?" Snow usually muffles sound, but I hear my echo as if it's cascading into a giant empty cavern.

I collapse to the ground, strength finally giving out. Ice cracks beneath me, a frozen lake splintering into a thousand pieces. Letting the tears come, I press my body into my knees and cover my head.

I'm useless. I deserve this. I ruined everything I touched.

"Azalee!" Someone calls my name from a distance, but I don't move.

Let me die.

"Azalee, do you hear me?" The voice is closer now, right in my ear.

I blink up at the shining halo around the man's head. "Who are you?"

"I felt you were here. I came as fast as I could." As he speaks, his face becomes clearer.

"Iniko?" Frozen tears make my face stiff.

"There is no warmth to give here." He places his cold hand on my cheek, causing my shivers to increase. "I'm so sorry." He pulls away. "Can you walk?"

Looking at my feet, I shake my head. "I can't feel them."

"Just try." Putting an arm under mine, he heaves me up with great effort.

"What's happening? Where am I?" It's painful, but I manage to stand.

Iniko leads us toward a gray door, standing alone in the trees. "I wish I could've warned you, but I didn't See it clear enough."

"See what?" Every word causes another sore to open in my mouth as it fills with a metallic tang.

Darkness greets us when he opens the door. "That you and the nightmare had become so acquainted."

We step through, and we're in the bell tower at The Retreat. "Are we in your nightmare?"

The crevasses under his eyes are so pronounced they look like black holes. "Not exactly. It's no longer just my nightmare. It's yours too."

"I don't understand?"

Something is wrong. Run. Run. Run.

Gabriel? Is that his voice? I left him. I burned him.

"Oh Gods. No. No." I grab hold of my head, slamming my palms into my skull to force the memories away.

Iniko rips my hands back, fingers so tight on my wrists he leaves red marks. "Azalee, you're a Nightmare."

"How?"

"You know how. The same way all Nightmares are created."

"I thought I was fighting it."

His smile is sad. "We all think we can handle it."

I look around, expecting to see the usual sights of Salem from up here, but they aren't there. Instead, it's the nightmarescape. Each way I turn, I see a new horror. Some I'm familiar with: grasslands filled with snakes, a stormy sea, and an overgrown jungle with flickering torches. Others are new: monsters with sharp fangs crashing through abandoned buildings, a volcano oozing red-hot lava. And so many more beyond my vision; only the screams tell me they're out there.

"Am I making you up? Are you here to haunt me for what I let happen to you?"

A creature flies across the dark sky behind Iniko's head. "I could ask you the same thing."

"How do we know what's real? Or is none of it real?" I press my hand into my chest and feel no beating heart in return.

"You're the dream wielder—you tell me. How real are dreams?"

I lick my lips, coating them in blood. "As real as nightmares."

CHAPTER 49

Gabriel

"Knock, knock," Genevieve says, leaning against the doorframe to the spare bedroom. "How are you feeling?" The weight of her earlier discovery casts a shadow across her features.

I run a hand through my shower-wet hair. The residue of Fire Retardant Logan used was hell to scrub off. My skin is going to be pink for hours. "Roz's potions pack quite the punch." They'd given me something for pain while they set my shoulder and then topped me off with a system cleanse herbal mix of Roz's creation. My bones are still vibrating. "But, all things considered, I'm good to go."

"If you need more time to rest, don't rush on our account."

I shake my head, buttoning my shirt and slipping on my shoes. "I need to find Azalee."

"While you were in the shower, we did a finding spell with no luck. The High Witch knows that we'll be seeking him. He's guarded himself accordingly." Genevieve's words tremble, and my heart sinks.

I run my tongue along my teeth, the citrusy aftertaste of Roz's spell still coating my mouth. After the adrenaline wore off, I couldn't stop shaking. Almost being on fire will do that. Roz prescribed a strong calming draught, but I only took half. I didn't want to dull my senses when there was work to be done.

"Mrs. Saunders, I want to apologize. I didn't mean for this to happen to Azalee."

She raises her hands to silence me. "Call me Genevieve. I don't blame you, Gabriel. I know my daughter, and nothing would've stopped her from going there." She plays with the ring accompanying her crystal necklace. "If it's anyone's fault, it's mine. I should have seen the signs that Azalee was unwell. But like a fool, I thought there would be nothing my strong-willed daughter couldn't overcome."

If we only had to save Azalee from the High Witch, that would be difficult enough, but getting her back is just the first step. No one has ever been saved from the fate of becoming a Nightmare. What if we've already lost?

Stiffness creeps along my neck, and I rub deep to reach the muscles. Azalee and I spent so long fighting each other that I never thought I'd miss her like this. The thread connecting us was a pain in my ass, but now I'd give anything to feel it again.

Genevieve's eyes clear as she looks up from her hands. "You're welcome to stay as long as you need. Dream wielders always have a home here."

"That's what I am now, isn't it?" Do I look any different now that my confession was made? Are the words I used to consider sins written across my skin? I search for something within that indicates a life-altering event. But I just feel empty. I need a strategy, a focus.

"It's what you've always been. Dream wielding magic might appear after a trauma, but it's always inside us. The power just manifests when we need it." She walks over, placing a hand on my shoulder. "I hate to ask this, but I have to. Will you be all right?"

My body stiffens because I know she's not just asking in a general sense. She wants to know if I'm going to transform into a Nightmare.

I've spent so long denying my magic that, despite everything, I actually feel better. Which is a fucked-up thing to say knowing Azalee could be being tortured right now. So, yeah, I'm out of my godsdamn head worrying about her, but no Nightmare urges.

"I appreciate your concern, but you don't need to worry about me. I'm good."

Her eyes, so much like Azalee's, make my chest hurt. "I do believe you are. Would you like to come downstairs? The coven is meeting in a smaller capacity, but I think it's about time you made an appearance."

"I'd like that."

"When you're ready." Genevieve leaves me alone once more.

Gathering my thoughts, I exit onto the landing.

"You look like shit, but I guess we all do." Meera stands from a chair near the window.

Instinctually, I step back, my body tingling as it assumes a fighting stance. Meera helped in the end. Which is all well and good, but I read what she was up to, and I'm not sure I can fully trust her.

"I was just wondering if you were going to tell the others what I did?"

I cross my arms, shoulder only twinging a little. "I should. You're part of the reason we're in this mess and why Azalee succumbed to the nightmares."

Her face crumbles, eyes darting to the stairs like she's ready to bolt.

"*But* I don't think Azalee would want me to do that. And if you're really here to help, we could use it. You have inside knowledge of what the High Witch has been up to." Stepping past her, I head downstairs, stopping briefly to add, "But if I think for one second you're still working for him, I'll take justice into my own hands."

"I didn't tell the High Witch about the life debt you owe Azalee."

I frown, glancing over my shoulder. "Is that supposed to make up for what you did divulge?"

She stays silent, pursing her lips.

"Didn't think so."

Downstairs, a group of ten witches has gathered, along with Genevieve and Roz. The latter's keen eyes track Meera and me as we slide into the last two seats.

"What we've feared for decades has finally come to pass." Roz gets right to business. "The High Witch has never been our number one fan, but he's finally taken an action that puts all of us in immediate peril. With the head of magic against us, the tide has shifted far beyond our favor." Roz doesn't mention Azalee's abduction.

Despite the grave news they delivered, most of the witches seem more preoccupied with me. "What's the Ford boy doing here?" An ancient man with dark, wrinkled skin points a finger at me. "Are we using him as a bargaining chip?"

"Gabriel is one of us. Which means he has a place at this table, just as any of you do," Genevieve says.

"What if he's a spy?" A witch glares at me through purple spectacles. I can't blame her. It's what I would think if the roles were reversed.

"I'm not a spy. I want justice to prevail just like the rest of you." I keep my tone even—the voice I've used with many politicians.

"Don't pretend you know anything about us," she spits.

"Seraphine," Genevieve starts.

"It's okay," I say. "She wants an explanation, and I'm happy to provide. You're right. I haven't been a part of this community before, but that doesn't mean I don't know what it feels like to hide who you are. To be scared shitless that I was going to mess up and reveal who I was to the wrong person. I've seen firsthand what the High Witch is capable of, and I don't want that fate to befall anyone else."

The witches exchange looks around the table, but no one speaks against me. I don't think they'll be inviting me to their Halloween celebrations, but it's a start.

"Gabriel, do you have any insight that might help us?" Roz keeps the meeting on track.

I wish I had more to offer. "We know the High Witch is using Nightmares to carry out the murders that he's been framing the dream wielders for. He's been holding both of them in a manor in the forest, under heavy spells. But now that he knows we're onto him, he could change tactics. However, knowing him, I don't think he will. He'll just be more careful about it. He won't expect any dream wielders to confront him directly because if we did, he'd twist it into us covering for each other."

This is the first time I referred to dream wielders as *us* and *we*.

"If we could connect with Azalee, she might be able to help," I add.

A young Latina woman perks up at Azalee's name. "Where is she, by the way?"

Genevieve's lips purse. "I'm afraid while trying to save our kind, Azalee was taken captive."

Worried expressions fill the table. "I'm sorry." The man who called me out takes her hand.

"So, how did you plan on talking to Azalee?" The witch traces a blue vein under her nearly translucent skin down her arm, reading them like others would read tarot.

Before I can answer, another pipes in. "What if Genevieve dream wields through the astral plane?"

Azalee did that with me, but the problem with that plan now is that the Nightmares can't be reached that way.

"The High Witch has warded against that, I'm afraid," Genevieve says. I don't know if that's true, but it silences the witch. The discussion drifts into what they need to do to protect the dream wielders at The Retreat and in Salem at large.

I get it; the coven's priority is the group as a whole. But my main concern is Azalee—who knows what the High Witch might do to her out of spite. When the meeting adjourns, we're no closer to rescuing her.

"I need to talk to Logan," I tell Meera.

"Are you insane?" Her eyes widen. "You're just going to wander into the belly of the beast?"

"He's not going to hurt me."

Meera shakes her head. "The High Witch has eyes everywhere."

"You do what you want, but I can't sit around and let Azalee die a slow death in a prison somewhere."

I thought finding Logan at school would be a long shot, but as I hide in the shadows of the alcove, it's the only plan I have. Meera was right; it's stupid of me to seek him out, but after everything, I need to see my brother. I dip my chin, pulling my black baseball cap lower as a group of kids walk by. Logan's first class should be letting out any minute.

The muffin Genevieve forced me to eat swirls in my gut. If Logan isn't here, the next options are the High Witch's office or home. Both of which will be swarming with guards and, I'm sure, orders to arrest me on sight.

In a matter of hours, I lost my whole family. It didn't happen in the way I thought it would, but the outcome I was worried about for years still came to pass. You can't outrun the Fates.

As students file out, I scan the crowd. Near the back, I spot him. He's alone. The usual social butterfly looks like he's had his wings clipped. Careful not to make a scene, I follow a few paces behind him, hidden in the masses, until he takes a left, and I see my moment.

"Logan," I whisper as I grab his elbow.

Logan's eyes narrow. "Gabriel? What the fuck are you doing here?"

"I needed to talk to you," I say, leading us into a doorway hidden from the main road.

Yanking away from me, he shoves his hands into his pockets. "The old man's looking for you. You shouldn't have come."

I've been practicing what I was going to say, but with him in front of me now, it doesn't feel like enough. "Logan, I'm sorry."

"You said that."

"I just—I wanted to tell you. I did," I add when he rolls his eyes. "I didn't tell you because . . . I didn't want you to hate me."

He frowns, looking offended. "Gabriel, I don't hate you because you're a dream wielder. I hate that you lied to me. It was me and you against the world, and you couldn't even trust me with your biggest secret."

"If I could go back, I'd change things."

"No one can change the past." He looks around. "Is that all you wanted to say? Because I have to be somewhere."

"No. Do you know where Grandfather took the prisoners he had at the manor?"

He scrubs a hand over his face. "I don't. We left before them. The old man just told his goons to move everyone."

"What about Meera's family? Are they still alive?" She risked the loss of her family to help Azalee and me. Maybe I should be giving her a bit more credit.

"I don't know. It's not like the High Witch is giving me priority access to his plans."

I level him with a serious stare. "Do you think he could?"

"I don't want any part of this, Gabriel."

"Grandfather is a bad guy. I need someone to help take him down from the inside." For the first time when I look at him, I don't just see my little brother. I see the man he's grown into and the burden he's carried all his life hidden beneath the surface of his mask.

"You were the one who told me the old man was always looking out for our best interest. That we should trust his plans. Now you're telling me that was all bullshit?"

For a split second, it's my six-year-old brother standing before me, the one who needed me to defend him on the playground. It was my job to protect him. I kept us close to Grandfather because that was the only safety net I knew. I was too young to see the scope of things beyond our tiny bubble. I wish I didn't have to ask him to do this, but I don't have a choice. "I was wrong."

"You never admit to being wrong."

"That's how you know I'm serious." My smile turns into a grimace.

A muscle pops in his jaw. "I'm not as good a person as you are, Gabriel. I use the Ford name to get away with things and get even more. I'm not the type to stick my neck out for people I don't even know."

It kills me to hear him talk about himself like this. "You are a good person. Don't sell yourself short. I know you'd never just sit by and let people die if you could stop it."

"I don't want to die," he yells, eyes wide. "Don't you get that? You saw what the old man did to you. And you're his favorite. What do you think he'll do to me? He runs this town, this country. There's nowhere we'll be able to go as long as he's in charge. I betray him, and I'm next on the pyre."

"Not if you help me take him down. I won't let anything happen to you, Logan. Can you please look into where he's hiding those people? Then I can save them and get Grandfather implicated in the process."

He shakes his head. "I'm sorry. I got to go." Flipping up his hood, he walks away.

CHAPTER 50

Azalee

The ground rattles as the bell tower shakes violently. "What's happening?" I white-knuckle grip the railing.

Iniko doesn't respond, staring blankly out into the darkness as the railing breaks away and clatters to the abyss below.

"Run." I grab Iniko's hand, yanking him down the stairs.

"Where are we going?" He blinks like he just remembered I was here.

As if on cue, a thunderous roar erupts outside, and the stairwell seems to be growing faster than we can get down. "Do you think you can jump out the window?" I stop abruptly, and Iniko rams into my back.

"Yes. But I don't want to."

"No choice." I snatch a brick from the ground and throw it into the glass. It shatters, blood dripping from the cracks. "When in Rome," I say as I vault out of the broken death trap. I'm flying through the air, farther than my ability should take me. I land on something squishy in the middle of a jungle.

"Son of—" My scream gargles in my throat as the worms wiggle across my skin from a giant puddle of them I'm lying in. "Gross, gross, gross." I scramble to my feet, Iniko falling into me from his catapult.

"We can't stop." He barely notices the worms burrowing into his legs.

I brush furiously at my arms as I race to keep up before he disappears into the thick foliage. I push a large palm leaf out of the way as it smacks me in the face. Swallowing the burning taste of bile, I realize I've been in this place before—the jungle and the woman with the pointed teeth.

While I can still see the residue of the nightmares in Iniko's eyes, it's less so. Or maybe we're just seeing through the same lenses now.

"Iniko, how did you find me?" Last time I went into his mind, it felt like the nightmare was actively pushing me out. Maybe it's like when an animal can smell a human, it'll stay away. Before, I smelled wrong, but now I smell like it.

Not a comforting thought.

"Honestly, I don't know." Vines curl around us as we trudge deeper into the moonlit jungle. "I was just there." He motions toward the nightmarescape in the distance. "And then I saw you in a vision. You were freezing to death, and at first I thought I was Seeing the future in the real world, but then I realized that it was here."

Humid heat radiates in the air. I pull my hair off my neck, fanning myself. "Do you often meet with other people? Because, as far as I could tell, the nightmarescape was pretty lonely. Unless, of course, the people are part of the horrors."

Torches flicker in the distance. Peeking between the trees, I spot what looks like a circus tent. A creeping sensation makes me raise my shoulders to my ears. The distant sounds of music trickle on the dewdrops. I know she's there before I see her. A woman in a sparkling flapper dress waves at me to join her. She smiles, her mouth full of razor-sharp teeth. I shudder, forcing my gaze away.

"I see people more often than you might think. But most times, I assumed they were phantoms come to haunt me. I kept my interaction to a minimum."

I clasp my throat, the thick air making it difficult to take deep breaths. Then it hits me. "The necklace."

"Necklace?" Iniko pauses his stomping, looking around like he's worried what might pop out.

"When I came to visit you, Gabriel and I performed a spell, and the most important component consisted of two necklaces, one for each of us. It's what allowed our connection to be strong enough to break through the nightmare. We were both still wearing it. Maybe that's letting us stay bonded even now."

Iniko nods, insects flying around his head. "That makes sense. The few times I tried to talk to anyone, it never worked. It was like we were speaking different languages." He looks at me with aching familiarity, almost like he's been waiting his whole life for this exact moment. He's a Seer, so maybe he has. "But it's like I always told you, you're special. Maybe it just had to be you."

Iniko starts walking again, jumping at the slithering on the forest floor.

"Are we lost?" I ask.

"It's a nightmare, we're always lost."

Comforting.

"I thought of Nightmares as solitary figures, but they're not," I say. "Like when I astral projected to find Gabriel and I could see all of the dreamscapes, the nightmarescape must be one place too. But it's only penetrable if you're a Nightmare. That's why I've been here before."

Iniko doesn't speak for several minutes. Maybe the nightmare never gave him time to think about things other than horrible tragedies and running for his life.

I keep going, ignoring the increasing movement and sounds of people in the jungle. "Maybe we could find other trapped people in the nightmare and work together?"

"It's possible. I've noticed my ability to hold off the darkness is stronger with you here. By no means a fortress, but it's easier."

Maybe I've been thinking about this the wrong way. It's not a matter of saving each individual nightmare but working together to save them all at once. "Do you think there's a way to knock out the entire nightmare realm?"

Haunting violin music whistles through the wind. "I don't think nightmares can be destroyed. Just like the sun and the moon, nightmares have their place in the grand scheme of the universe."

"Okay, maybe not *destroyed*, but weakened? Enough to get the trapped people out?"

"How exactly would you—" But Iniko's words are cut off as his face distorts in pain.

"Iniko, stay with me." I feel the nightmare dragging us apart.

"Someone's coming." A black hole sucks Iniko away. I tell myself this isn't real, but that's the thing, it is. I'm a Nightmare now.

"Oh, darling, you truly are the prettiest thing," a soft voice says behind me. I turn to see the woman with the sharp teeth. "We missed you. But it looks like you're here to stay now."

One minute, we're standing among the trees, bugs nipping at my skin, and in the next, we're inside a black-and-white-striped circus tent. I'm once again spread eagle, arms and legs strapped down with leather ties to a roulette-style wheel.

"I haven't done this much. But practice makes perfect." The woman in the flapper dress is twisting a knife in her fingers. "I'd say don't move, but you don't really have a choice."

The wheel begins spinning, picking up speed. Nausea rolls through me, and I vomit, the force of the twirling causing it to fly back into my face.

Through the blurring world, I watch the woman throw the knife. It hits the side of the wheel, bouncing off. "Rats. Good thing I have more chances." She waves her hand, and a whole case of knives appears beside her.

Rotating faster, I'm unable to move as she throws an endless supply of weapons. Some split the wood between my legs, and others penetrate my skin. Pain seizes my entire body as I dry heave.

I don't know how long she keeps hurling the knives, but it feels like an eternity. I can't close my eyes no matter how hard I try. I'm forced to watch and feel every single moment. Most of the world is a blur of striped tents and sneering knife throwers, but then I see someone in the seats.

It's the other woman from my nightmare, wrapped in the same tattered shawl, her hair twisted into a loose bun. The knife thrower is enjoying herself, pointed teeth dripping with blood as she squeals in delight. But the other woman's face is drawn into a pinched grimace. Her pain looks as torturous as mine.

She's not part of the nightmare; she *is* a Nightmare, like me.

Words are ripped from me before I can even form a sentence. Forcing my breaths to slow, I remind myself I'm a dream wielder. I know how to control dream magic. This might be a nightmare, but they're only different sides of the same coin. I also have the advantage of being new to this place. The longer you're submerged in the darkness, the harder it is to fight it.

I swirl my tongue around my mouth to cure the dryness. "Help me," I croak.

Tears stream down the woman's face as she remains trapped in that chair. "I couldn't help you before. I can't help anyone. They just keep dying."

"No, they don't." I grit through each word like it's ripping bits of my flesh away to speak them. "This isn't real. We're stuck in a nightmare. We can fight it together."

She still looks dubious.

"Stand. I know you can do it. I believe in you. I believe that you can save anyone."

You're going to save the world. The words Iniko spoke to me all those years ago come roaring back. I don't know if they're true, but I let them fill me up like casting a spell.

Hope and belief in yourself are the first things the darkness rips away. If I can give some of that back, maybe she can wrest control.

The pain melts away from her face. "I can save you?"

"You can save me. And I can save you."

She leaps from the chair, knocking it down as she grabs a knife and stabs it through the other woman's hand. Screaming, our captor disappears.

The wheel slows as the other woman rushes toward me and helps get me off.

I collapse into her, legs weak. "Thank you."

"I've never been able to do that." Her eyes are alight. "Who are you?"

"I'm like you. But I know a way out." The heavy weight crushing my shoulders lightens ever so slightly. It was nice to work as a team—even if it took a little longer to coordinate us both to the same goal. I wouldn't have been able to escape this without her, nor she without me. Nightmares feed on isolation and loneliness—togetherness might just be the nightmarescape's weakness.

CHAPTER 51

Gabriel

Driving up to the gates of The Retreat, I'm greeted by a wave from the attendant as he lets me in. Not long ago, I stood here with the police captain, waiting to interrogate suspected dream wielders. Now I'm one of them.

I debated not returning. Everywhere I go, I'm putting those people at risk, but there's something I can only achieve here.

Just as the cathedral comes into view, the music pumping through my speakers is interrupted by a news bulletin. "This just in: A double homicide is being reported near Gather's Bridge. We're just getting information, but as many fear, this looks like another dream wielder attack. We will bring you all the latest as we—" I jab the button, silencing the lies.

So much for Grandfather lying low.

When I pull up to Azalee's house, Meera is waiting outside. She motions for me to lower my window. "Genevieve thinks it's safer for us to stay in the back of the property. Open the door, and I'll show you where to go."

I get out of the car but leave it running. "You go. I'll meet you there after I do something." I head toward the door, but her next question stops me.

"Did you find anything out about my parents?" She's been putting on a good facade since our escape, but I hear the crack in her shell.

"Logan didn't have any info about the prisoners."

Her eyes are glassy as she nods, getting into my SUV and tearing away.

Genevieve answers the door, looking behind me. "Meera was supposed to take you somewhere safer."

"I get it. And I'll happily oblige, but I need to see Iniko first."

Ushering me inside, she says, "Why is that?"

"I saw my brother, but he doesn't know anything about where the High Witch moved Azalee and the others." And I'm not sure he's even going to help. "Until we figure out how to gather more intel about that, we have to work with the resources we do have."

I know my way to the dungeon and stride ahead, not waiting for Genevieve's permission.

"How exactly is Iniko going to help?" Genevieve follows me down the stairs and past the door I destroyed getting Azalee out barely twenty-four hours ago.

Even though she won't like it, I owe her the truth. "Azalee and I performed a spell that allowed us to dream wield and interact with him in his nightmare." I withdraw a necklace identical to Iniko's from my pocket. I made a quick pit stop on the way here to pick it up. "He's wearing the same one."

"That sounds like dangerous magic. Give me the necklace." Genevieve holds her hand out.

"We didn't have a choice." If I'd known Azalee was already suffering from symptoms of a nightmare, I wouldn't have let her do it. But that's a moot point now.

She's still waiting for me to hand her the necklace. "I'll perform the dream wield and see if I can talk to him."

"I need to be the one to do it. I performed the original spell. It's going to require my magic." I'm not sure if that's true, but I need to do this. If I'm going to embrace who I am, I have to do the dream wield sooner rather than later.

"Gabriel, if you want me to put my life and the covens' in your hands, you're going to have to do better than that." Her eyes bore into me. "Why have you risked everything for a people you were actively trying to destroy only a month ago?"

"I might not have embraced my magics before, but I was still pursuing justice from within the High Witch's office the best way I knew how. So I was never trying to destroy you. But once I saw all the evidence for myself and spent more time with . . ." I trail off.

She doesn't budge.

I dip my head, sucking in a breath of stale air. "It was Azalee. She was the final stepping stone that made me realize I couldn't straddle both sides if I wanted a change." I meet her eyes again. "Azalee and I—Gods, it's more than complicated, but I won't—I *can't* stop until I know she's safe." My voice breaks.

Studying me a moment longer, she nods, continuing, "What do you think Iniko will be able to tell you? He's been down here for almost a year."

"He can still See. He showed Azalee where the High Witch held the prisoners before. Let's hope he can do it again."

"I appreciate you wanting to do this, Gabriel, but do you know how to dream wield?" Genevieve stops short of opening Iniko's door.

"I know the steps, despite not having used the magic personally. I've done a lot of studying, and I'm a quick learner." I use the voice taught to me my whole life, which doesn't allow for negotiation.

"Spoken like a true Ford." It doesn't sound like a compliment. Despite offering me sanctuary, I don't think she cares for me. Probably blames me for what happened to Azalee.

That'd make two of us. But she must believe that my feelings for Azalee are true and that we both want to save her and the others trapped with her.

She lets me inside as I explain her part in the spell. "Just keep hold of my hand." She takes it, and we approach Iniko's bed.

"Hey, man. Ready to talk?" Squeezing the necklace, I focus my energies. *I'm a dream wielder. This magic is mine to control.*

I take his hand and let him pull me into his nightmare.

Everything is shrouded in gray smoke—the blue door in front of me swings on a hinge, creaking echoes from it. I walk through the steps of reminding myself I'm in charge. This spell is my doing; I'm only visiting the nightmare. I place my hand on the handle and push it open.

I'm dropped into a minefield, an explosion bursting to my right tosses me ten feet in the air before gravity slams me into the ground. I cover my ears as another bomb explodes. Scrambling to my feet, I zigzag to avoid getting hit with debris.

"Iniko!" I scream.

I spot him chained to a Humvee near the road. He squints, using his arm to brush the dust off his face from the aftermath of the bombs. "Gabriel?" he yells.

My clothes soak in what I hope is water as I jump over a busted pipe and skid to a stop next to him. "Sorry to drop in so suddenly."

"It's been . . ."

"Too long. It's good to see you—even if it's not the best location for a reunion." Another bomb explodes overhead.

"I'm getting used to that. I missed you, man." His smile is cracked and broken, but I see my friend peeking out of it.

I give him a brief hug before getting back to business. I examine the chains to see if I can undo them, then remember I can manipulate this dream. Closing my eyes, I picture the chains snapping. When I open them, nothing has changed.

Hello. Something tickles the back of my neck, and I spin to see empty air. But I feel the presence pressing itself against me.

"It's not real. It's just the darkness sniffing you out."

I shiver despite the heat. "Let me try again." Instead of closing my eyes, I stare at the chains like I have X-ray vision until they bust apart.

Iniko rubs his wrists. He looks better than the real him sitting on the bed, but his face is still too sunken to be healthy. "Thank you."

"Iniko, I'm afraid I need your help."

"I bet you do. Come on, I told her someone was coming." He turns and, without waiting for me, walks down the road.

"Told who?" With my added height, it doesn't take me long to catch up. "Iniko, look, I have to tell you something."

He waves me off. "I already know."

"Did you See it?" My chest seizes.

"In a manner of speaking." In the middle of the road, Iniko stops at a rusty pay phone box.

He opens the door and steps through. I don't have a choice but to follow him. When I step out, I recognize Azalee's living room.

I sense her before I see her. That life debt glowing brightly as it tugs in my gut, followed by the flickering soulmate bond.

"Gabriel?"

My heart jumps into my chest when I turn and see her standing next to the fire. Before I have time to think about the implications of what's happening, I draw her into my arms. This can't be real. I'm in Iniko's nightmares, but she feels so close. She's not as solid as she could be, but it's better than nothing, even if it's just an illusion.

I look at Iniko over her shoulder. "Do your nightmares often tease you with things you can't have?"

"Yes, but this isn't a tease. That's Azalee."

She pulls away, smiling sadly as she traces the lines of my face with a featherlight touch. "The joke's on me, right?" The despair in her voice breaks me. "The nightmare is showing me a ghost."

I want to kiss her, taste the sweet nectar of her lips, and feel every inch of her skin against mine. But I can't. "Iniko, Azalee isn't here. She's stuck in her own nightmare." Saying it out loud makes it hurt even worse.

"Iniko?" Azalee's brow dips into a deep V. "Care to explain what's happening right now?"

"Gabriel isn't dead. He used your necklace spell to find us here," Iniko says. "And Azalee is a Nightmare, but she's not in her *own* nightmare. Turns out things are more connected than we realized."

Skepticism still colors Azalee's face as she studies me. "You didn't die in the fire?"

"Logan used Fire Retardant to protect me." I move my hands over her face, her lips, touching her like she's made of glass. "You're really here?"

She nods, hope blooming in her eyes. "I think this might be how we win."

"Where are you?" I ask. "The High Witch took you."

She frowns, that shadow of darkness I saw in Iniko's eyes lurking in hers. "Right. I hadn't really contemplated where my physical body was. But okay, good to know."

"So, you're in here with the other Nightmares?"

She nods. "We think this nightmare realm is one giant place where all the Nightmares go. And the longer you've been here, the harder it is to remember what you're trying to get back to. Eventually, you become part of the landscape and forget that other people are around. But I saw someone, and we worked together to stop the nightmare's torture. We can do that with others."

"Together, Azalee and I are stronger than I've ever been," Iniko adds.

I can't take my hands off her, worried if I do, she'll disappear. She doesn't seem to mind. "Okay, but waking the Nightmares up isn't going to save them from the prison the High Witch locked them in."

"Gabriel, you have to find that."

"Is there any way you can see beyond the nightmare to your physical location?"

Azalee raises an eyebrow at Iniko. "Have you ever been able to see your cell?"

He squeezes his eyes, closed lids moving rapidly in memory. "Maybe? Things all blend together."

Azalee taps her finger against my chest. "If we can start breaking down the walls of the nightmare, robbing it of its strength, then maybe we can pierce through the veil and see where we are."

A sharp force tugs in my head, Genevieve reeling me back to the real world. "You work on that, and I'll come back as soon as I can."

The pressure in my head increases, but I pull Azalee into a kiss. It's so close to being the real thing but has a bitter aftertaste of nightmare. Before I hear her goodbye, I'm ripped back into the real world.

"Gabriel, take the tunnel on the side of the house and follow it as far as it'll go," Genevieve says, tearing out of the room.

"What's going on?"

"There's a raid on The Retreat."

CHAPTER 52

Azalee

When Gabriel disappears, that warm glow of our connection does too, leaving me colder than I was before. A voice whispers in the far reaches of my mind that I'll never get warm again. I shake my head. Letting despair have even the slightest traction while stuck in a nightmare could be catastrophic to any progress we've made.

"Okay, so now we have a plan." I rein us both in, not liking the way Iniko's eyes have begun to glaze over. "I need to figure out where I am in the real world so we can get that information to Gabriel."

Iniko scratches a little too intently at his face. "Sure, simple."

"I saved a lady today, Ink. She and I worked together to overcome the nightmare's hold. When it happened, I felt a lessening of the darkness. This is going to work. We just need to find more people. So, any idea where we can do that?"

"Why don't we see what's behind door number one." I follow him out the front door and enter into a warehouse. The loud percussion of a thousand drums bombards my ears, the vibrating making my teeth chatter. Lights flash in every color from all angles like we're at the world's worst disco.

Squinting, I scream, “How the hell are we supposed to find anyone here?” I can barely tell what I said. The nightmare isn’t going to make this easy for us.

But easy has never been my cup of tea.

Iniko presses his hands against his ears, motioning with his elbow to a man seated at a drum set. His hands drip blood down the sticks and onto the drums he’s banging. Blood splatters his brown face, eyes wide and bloodshot like he’s been sitting there for days on end.

I approach from behind and gently touch his shoulder. “Hello?”

He doesn’t slow his playing. I scan the floor, looking for a way to unplug his kit, but thousands of cables are running everywhere like snakes.

I pull Iniko’s arm away from his ear, cupping my hand over it and screaming, “Find how to turn this off!”

Getting low to the ground, I follow every cable, but it fruitlessly leads to more lines. In dreams, we can learn lessons, heal, or live out a fantasy. Is there an aspect of that in nightmares too?

Before I can contemplate the dynamics of the nightmarescape, I return to the present. If I can’t find where these unplug, I’ll just have to make a new stopping point. Light blooms in my vision as I call upon my magic, the nightmare fighting me, but I manage to summon a pair of scissors. Grabbing the nearest cord, I start hacking at one after another until the music cuts.

I hold up the frayed cords in one hand and scissors in the other.

“You were always good with creative solutions.” Iniko grins and warmth fills my chest at being back in league with my favorite wingman.

The man at the drums hasn’t noticed the music’s stopped. He continues to bang away, the offbeat cacophony almost worse than the deafening music. I cup his cheek, turning his head toward me. “You don’t have to play anymore.”

He blinks. “I have to. He always makes me keep playing.”

"Whoever that is, they aren't here. You don't have to do anything you don't want to." My body hums with the power of that statement. The nightmare doesn't like that. But it can kiss my ass. "What's your name?"

"Orion." He looks around like he's seeing this place for the first time. "Where am I?"

I debate lying to him, but the truth is what will set us free. To have the power we need, we have to know what's going on. "You're in a nightmare. But don't worry, we'll get out of here."

I need all of us to make that reality.

The three of us head through the next door. This time, we exit into a hospital hallway. But unlike the welcoming, bright cleanliness of Salem Medical, this is dingy, dark, and smells like rotting meat and sewage. The chipped walls are a nicotine yellow, with suspicious stains scattered along the bottom. Above us hangs a sign: MAXIMUM SECURITY ASYLUM.

Great.

As creepy as this place is, we couldn't have wished for a better door, because this is apparently where lots of people get stuck—at least based on the amount of screams I hear. An asylum makes sense as a theme lots of people would fear.

"Watch out," Orion yells, shoving me to the side as a large man dressed in white scrubs comes at me with a syringe. Iniko jumps on his back, scratching at his eyes, while Orion uses one of his drumsticks to stab the guy in the stomach. Iniko leaps off before the orderly falls to the ground.

"Thank you." I press a hand to my rib cage. "Find an unlocked door. We need to save whoever we can to weaken the nightmare." We each take a side, yanking at door handles down the hallway.

"I got one," Iniko says as a door flies open.

"Me too," Orion yells.

"Go. I'll take this one." The next handle I grab singes my skin, but I grit my teeth, shoving it open.

Leaving the others to their rescues, I enter a room with electrical equipment and a woman strapped to a chair. As I get closer, I realize it's Inez. She's the first I've seen from the dungeons, other than Iniko, but they must be here somewhere. Tears sting my eyes when I remember I told Inez's mother she'd be safe, but I'm still far from fulfilling that promise. The contraption around her head looks like something they used in old-school lobotomies, her body writhing against the electrical current.

Instead of looking for a plug this time, I grab a stool and chuck it at the machine. It explodes in a burst of sparks, and I cover my head against the searing light before the hospital is drenched in darkness.

A few emergency lights click on, giving the space an eerie red glow. Inez lies limp in the chair. I press two fingers to her neck; no pulse beats there. I recall her mother wanting so desperately to save her daughter, and use that love to strengthen my resolve.

I need a defibrillator. But from the little I can see, this room has only instruments of torture. Knowing time isn't on our side, I begin CPR. I took a class because I was in charge of lifeguarding at The Retreat last year. My compressions are messy, and my arms tire much faster than usual.

I clamp my jaw, tasting blood as I clip my tongue. My arms are ready to give out on me when she opens her eyes, gasping for air. My shoulders sag in relief. Sweat stings my eyes. "Welcome back to the land of the living, Inez."

Or the Nightmares—but semantics.

"Azalee," Iniko calls from the door, a kid no older than ten by his side. "We got to go. There's more burly orderlies on their way."

Inez grips my arm, her ice-cold fingers digging into my skin. "Are you an angel?"

"Most certainly not. But I can help bring you out of this hell."

She looks at Iniko and me like we're ghosts, and maybe that's what we are. But she takes the scalpel I hand her all the same.

Carrying my weapon, a saw that looks like it could hack through bone, we head into the hall. Because of the explosion in the electrical room, it's dark except for a few emergency lights. Orion and the man with him are already fighting off an orderly nearly seven feet tall. Not caring what damage I do, I head for the other bad guy, slicing and stabbing anything that gives.

Blood splatters the hall, and if this weren't a nightmare, I'd throw up from the metallic smell, but it's not real. And the more people we gather for our cause, the more that sentiment gains power. "This way." I motion as voices trail from farther down the hall.

As we start running, I test a theory. I imagine a wall growing up between us and our pursuers. The more numbers we collect, the weaker the nightmare's hold becomes. My dream wielder magic is growing in strength. A wall does appear, but it's only half height and already crumbles at the edges, but it's something.

We stumble into an exam room full of horrors. There are five beds; each contains someone getting tortured in an archaic fashion. "Pick a bed and start saving," I tell the others. "Show them they can beat whatever hell the nightmare conjures."

As we each help a lost soul, the room becomes increasingly brighter, as if we're flipping switches and illuminating the world. I don't know if the others can feel it, but the debilitating hopelessness in my gut is disappearing.

Once we've saved everyone in the room, I seek out Iniko. "I didn't let myself think it was truly possible," he says, eyes full of tears as he takes in the group. Each one is still looking worse for wear but strong.

"None of us knew this was the solution. I spent the better part of a year trying to save you on the outside and got nowhere." I squeeze his hand. "But now we know how to save Nightmares. How to save you."

"I knew. I told you, you'd save the world one day."

I frown, voice rough when I ask, "Did you See this?"

A familiar faraway look eclipses his features. "Bits and pieces. I saw the trails of fate and its possible outcomes."

"Did you know you'd become a Nightmare? Is that why you had us try to activate your dream wielder magic?" My ears ring, years of memories clicking into place.

He offers a guilty smile. "I couldn't tell you. You would've done anything to prevent it. But while the path wasn't ideal, I knew in my bones, down to my deepest cells of magic, that if I let this course of fate play out, you'd save the Nightmares, that you'd save me."

"Well." I swallow the lump of emotions this revelation has dug up. "That was kinda fucked up, not going to lie, but then I'd probably have done the exact same thing, so guess I can't yell at you." Then I add, "Until we're out of here, anyway."

"Your mom would be proud, you know," he says.

Tears clog my throat, and I clear it with a cough. Thinking about Mom is only going to make me sad. "I'm going to try to see where the High Witch is holding me. Take my hand?"

But he doesn't respond. His eyes are glazed over, staring unseeing through a frosted window. I grab his hand, and he draws me into a vision.

It's cloudy, but as Iniko's hand clenches into a fist, the smoke clears, and Gabriel appears.

My heart leaps, and I want to run to him, but then I see his arms are shackled behind his back. "What's happening?"

Iniko's face pales. "Retribution."

CHAPTER 53

Gabriel

"You have to hurry, Gabriel." Genevieve stops at the bottom of the stairs in front of a blank wall. She moves her hands in a practiced pattern, revealing runes carved into the stones. "Take this tunnel to the end." She steps away, and the stone slides backward, revealing a hidden passageway. "I have to go."

"Come with me. You don't know what they'll do." There's banging at the door, followed by muffled shouting.

"I know exactly what they'll do and am not afraid. You need to find Azalee. Go, Gabriel." She shoves me into the tunnel and runs upstairs.

My instinct is to go after her and fight whatever stands in our way. I'm not afraid of what the High Witch will do to me, but I am scared of what they'll stop me from doing: finding Azalee.

Going against everything inside, I turn my back on the fight, closing the stone wall and encasing myself in darkness. I trail my fingers along the rough interior, slowly getting a feel for where I am. My feet slip on wet floors, and scurrying behind me makes me jumpy. But there're no sounds of doors being blown open or officers pursuing me.

Once I've got my bearing, I break into a run—stale, cold air whips across my face. I trip on something, my shoulder slamming into the wall. I've been going for about five minutes when a soft glow develops at the end of the tunnel. Slowing, I walk the rest of the way, ears keen for anything indicating danger.

Frantic voices cease as I approach.

"Gabriel." Meera sighs when I emerge into the light of a bunker. "Where's Genevieve?"

Despite the chill, I'm drenched in sweat. I swallow to get moisture in my mouth. "She stayed behind."

A few other witches are dotted around the room. Just like in the tunnel, we appear to be underground with no visibility to the outside. Safe, but strategically limiting.

"What's that?" I stride toward a set of television screens on the wall.

"It's CCTV cameras of the different parts around The Retreat," the witch says from a seat in front of a computer.

I point to one of the views. "Can you make that bigger?" They click on the video, and it fills the entire screen. "Is there sound?" On screen, Genevieve is being hauled outside, and an overwhelming mass of officers circle her. They force her to her knees as the sound kicks in.

"Witnesses placed Gabriel Ford at the scene of the double homicide last night. They saw him fleeing in this direction. We have reason to believe that you're harboring him." This voice belongs to Captain Mendoza. It feels like someone surprised me with a kick to the abdomen. This accusation shouldn't shock me. But after decades spent trying to be the perfect Ford, knowing my grandfather's vendetta always came first still knocks the wind out of my sails.

"I do not know where Gabriel Ford is." Genevieve remains the picture of calm. Azalee's nerves of steel mimicked in her mother.

"You're impeding an investigation. If you do not provide Gabriel Ford to us, we will arrest you instead and make you an example for all those who defy the High Witch's protection of this city. We'll also take those Nightmares we found hiding in your dungeon."

There's a collective intake of breath from the dream wielders around me. Numbness creeps into my limbs, and a buzzing in my ears makes it hard to hear the rest.

"Do as you must," Genevieve says.

Without waiting to hear more, I head for the door.

"What are you doing?" Meera grabs my arm and yanks me to a stop.

"I'm going to turn myself in." It's the only thing I can do. I can't let somebody else go to jail for me. Because I know what they will do to Genevieve, and Azalee would never forgive me for letting that happen. I'd never forgive myself.

"They'll kill you. The High Witch is not going to let you get away a second time."

"Let him do it," someone snarls. "It's his fault we're in this mess."

"They're right." I stare down Meera, challenging her to argue otherwise.

"But," she whispers. "I did—"

"I'm buying you time," I cut her off. "Find the others." I don't let her argue further, bounding up the metal stairs and outside to my SUV.

The officers turn their weapons on me the moment I roll up to the gravel driveway.

"Turn off the car and step out of the vehicle," a voice booms from a megaphone.

I put my hands up as I exit the car. "I don't want any problems. Neither Genevieve nor anyone else at The Retreat knew I was here."

Three officers are on me in a matter of seconds, cuffing my arms behind my back.

"Get him back to the station," Captain says. I'm hauled into a police car, head down, so I can't see what they do to Genevieve.

Eyes follow me through every step of booking at the police station, not bothering to hide their curiosity.

These people, who looked at me with admiration only weeks ago, now glare at me like I'm a monster. Because, according to them, I committed a double homicide. But more than that, I'm a dream wielder. I don't know if I should plead my innocence or reveal what the High Witch has done. I doubt the sycophants on the payroll would believe me. But I need to buy time. If I die at the hands of another, so does Azalee. Still, I know she'd say it was worth it to save her mom.

"Captain," I say after I'm processed and confined in a cell. "You've known me for years, do you really think I'm capable of murder?"

"The High Witch informed us of your dream wielder magic." He barely looks me in the eye before averting his gaze.

"I am a dream wielder, but neither I or the others did this." I lick my lips, the words resisting only momentarily before I speak, knowing full well what waves my frothing accusation will create. "The High Witch is doing this."

Mendoza scoffs.

"You have witnessed firsthand how hard he's riding the police to cast the blame on dream wielders. These murders have been orchestrated by him all to help further that unlawful bill. I can give you the evidence to stop him, so you can be the real hero of Salem." I try to play a bit to his ego. "But I won't be any help locked up. Keep me in cuffs if you need to, but just let me out of here and I can show you." Can I? Not exactly, but I'll do my damnedest. Azalee's recklessness is rubbing off on me.

His jaw tightens, face pinched. I know what it means to stand against the High Witch, so I shouldn't be surprised when he says, "Save it, Gabriel. Only prayers to the Gods can help you now." He shakes his head as the door slams behind him, the hollowness echoing like a tomb.

A few hours later, another group is let in. When Iniko enters last, I know it's the Nightmares from The Retreat. I did this. If I hadn't been there, they wouldn't have taken them.

My new cellmates look so scared and fragile as they're shoved into a single cell by officers in full protective gear. They've removed the bed, forcing them to stand or lie on the floor. I want to reach out and comfort Iniko, but it's too risky. They took away my necklace and crystals, so without that, the nightmare's likely to gain control.

"I'm sorry, Iniko." I get as close to the bars as possible without being in his reach. He still wears his necklace, so at least I can take some comfort that he and Azalee might be together.

When dinnertime arrives, I expect an officer to bring me some gruel or rat stew, but it's Logan with a sandwich. "Gods, Gabriel, what did I tell you?" He slides the tray between the bars. "You should be halfway to the Caribbean by now."

"You know I couldn't do that."

"I can't get you out of this." He glances at the Nightmares, visibly shrinking back. "Or them."

My stomach growls out of habit with the smell of food, but the thought of eating sickens me. "I know. I'll figure it out. Have you found Azalee?"

"Gabriel." He frowns. "You're going to be executed tomorrow. Do you understand that? You have to start worrying about yourself." His voice cracks.

"I owe Azalee a life debt." Logan balks at another of my secrets revealed. "If I die before that's repaid, she dies too. So I *am* thinking about myself, but I can't not think about her too." An invisible fist squeezes my chest, the pain nearly bringing me to my knees. I will not be the death of her.

"All this for a girl, huh?" His eyes wear the cunning look he gets when he's learned new gossip. "You must really like her."

I glance to my heart, looking for the white thread, but like the life debt, its absence is a gaping hole. "It took me by surprise too."

"Do you love her?" His brow furrows.

"I . . ." I've never been in love before, so I don't have anything to compare it to. I haven't had a chance to breathe with the speed that things have changed all around me, but I can't see the path I'm on leading anywhere else. But what I do know for certain is this: "I can't live without her."

Logan rubs the back of his neck. "I still haven't found them."

"But you were looking?"

"Yeah, I was. I got some feelers out to some guy who owes me a few favors. But then I heard they brought you and some others in. I had to see for myself."

"I thought you hated me?" I can't even pretend it doesn't pain me to say it.

"I never hated you. You're my big brother."

Fuck. I didn't know how badly I needed to hear that. My circumstances are less than ideal, but this is a boost to set my wheels spinning again.

"They're framing me for a homicide."

Logan's eyes fill with tears. "I don't want to lose you, man, but I'm just one guy. He's the High fucking Witch."

I take his hand through the bars. "You won't have to do it alone. Find Azalee; she can help you." But I have no idea how the hell I can save the rest of us.

CHAPTER 54

Azalee

As I watch Gabriel being hauled away in cuffs, disappearing into the smoke of Iniko's vision, pressure erupts in my brain like a vise grip squeezing it. I stumble away from Iniko, clawing at my face to alleviate the unseen force.

"Azalee." Iniko's intrusion into my spiral is a million miles away. "What's happening?"

Gods, leave me be. I squeeze my eyes shut, counting to ten, and then there's silence.

Prying them open slowly, I settle into my new surroundings. The smoke has evaporated, and I'm in my room, but not the room at The Retreat. This is my childhood bedroom in our old house. I'm wearing a soft-pink nightgown and cuddling a sleeping black cat.

A thud.

A bang.

A crash.

Jumping out of bed, I race through the hallway, stumbling down the stairs to where my father is crumpled on the ground. The masked men turn and look at me before bolting out the door.

"No, no, no." I sway as dizziness overtakes me. I've never dreamed about this night—it wasn't possible since it made me a dream wielder.

Skidding on my dad's blood, I run out the door to catch the murderers I never could. Dirt and rocks shred my feet as the mysterious men disappear into the endless night.

I never even saw their faces.

I'm alone.

Wails erupt from deep inside, scratching their way through my lungs and out my throat.

I close my eyes, plummeting to the ground. Cold earth doesn't greet me. I'm back in the twin bed, clutching my cat.

The stage reset.

Not waiting to hear the sounds of death, I'm out of bed and heading downstairs. But just as I reach the last riser, the assailants give their death blow to my father's head. Blood splatters everywhere; Dad's eyes widen for just a second before he collapses.

"No!" I scream, the only thing I can manage. *I'm useless.*

I chase the men outside, but they disappear once more. I turn to go back inside and trip, hitting my forehead on a rock and blacking out.

When I wake, I'm in that *fucking* bed again. Trapped in a loop, I continue trying to save my father, but I can't, and I can never catch the men responsible. Where before my heart was banging against my rib cage, now I feel only numbness. The black hole of despair opening wider with each round.

The next time I get downstairs and see him crumpled on the wood floor, I don't chase the murderers. I drag my dad's corpse into my arms, hugging his body as my salty tears mix with his blood.

"Why didn't you save me?"

Brushing hair from my face, I look up to see the ghostly figure of my father standing above us.

"If only you'd been faster, you could've stopped them." Hate fills his translucent features.

My whole body aches. "I was a child," I sob. "I tried to find the men who did this to you. But they were too quick, and my legs were too small."

"If you'd never been born, I wouldn't be dead." He spits at me in disgust. "I would've been with your mother on her business trip. But I had to stay home with you. You killed me. It's your fault."

My body shakes with tears I thought long dried up. "I can't save anyone."

"No, you can't." His truth slithers through me like a flesh-eating disease. "You couldn't save me, you can't save Iniko, or your mother, or Meera, or Gabriel. Everyone is going to die because of you."

He's right. I never deserved them.

Banging rattles the front door, and I slide away from it, my pink nightgown coated in blood.

The door bursts open, pouring light into the room as Iniko walks inside. "Azalee." Rushing over, he yanks me up.

I fall into his arms, sobbing against his shoulder. "I can't save anyone."

"That's not true." He brushes hair out of my eyes so I can see him. "Your father was unsavable. If you'd gotten to him sooner, they probably would've killed you too. This moment that made you a dream wielder changed your life and made you who you are." He spins so the ghost of my father is out of sight. "That thing is not your father. It's a figment of the nightmare. You know your real father doesn't blame you for what happened."

"I just wanted to save someone."

"What do you think you've been doing? You've saved people in this realm. You saved me every day."

As Iniko holds me, I squeeze my eyes shut. I let the truth of his words sink in. I was just a kid. As much as I wish I could've changed that situation, there's no way. I realize that's what I've been doing ever since then. If I was fast enough, if I didn't slow down, stop to think, I could outrun whatever danger was coming. But that didn't work—wouldn't have worked in my dad's case. Only once I took a moment to breathe, to let others help me, did I finally see the results I'd always been craving.

I couldn't outrun the bad things. The only way was to let others help me carry the burden as we made our way through to the other side.

I turn back and look at my father. "I love you, Dad, and I miss you every day. I couldn't save you, and I really am sorry for that, even if it wasn't my fault. But now, I'm going to save myself."

He disappears, and as he does, I close my eyes and breathe fresh air. That's when I see—not this world, but the other.

A room full of stones with names carved into it. Dirt covers the ground and walls, vines growing out of the ceiling. There's a stained glass window, but no light penetrates it. Behind the prisoners shackled around me are glass boxes with objects inside them: dolls and flowers.

A crypt.

"Iniko, that's it. I know how to get out of here. I had to face the original trauma. The thing that made me a dream wielder. I can see where I am in real life. If I push against the membrane, I think I can get through."

Iniko's smile is sad. "Good. Go, save the others imprisoned with you and Gabriel."

I take his hand, gripping it so tight it stings. "I will, but I'm not leaving this nightmare without you."

His body shakes as fear cascades across his features because he knows that if you have to face your original trauma, he has to go back to his brother's murder.

"It's okay. I'll be with you the whole time."

CHAPTER 55

Gabriel

The sun has barely risen when they drag us from the cells to our damnation at Proctor's Ledge. I'm shackled in the front of the transport van while the Nightmares are in the back. From the side mirror, I can see Iniko's sunken frame. Does he know where he is? Or understand what's about to happen? If this is how we meet our end, perhaps it is better he doesn't. He'd just be leaving one nightmare for another. At least in the other place, Azalee is with him.

Dark clouds loom threateningly on the horizon. Perhaps the Gods have come to watch us petty humans take out our fear on one another.

Three hanging ropes stand ready to take the lives of witches accused of magical crimes on the gallows platform. Punishments of old to match crimes committed with magic. I've never been to a public hanging before. They rarely happen now because people know better than to use magic in a crime. The sentencing is always harsher and swift.

I thought when my time came to an end, I'd feel more than numbness. Where's my heart raging to fight against the dying of the light? I wonder if I'll see my parents again. Wherever they are, I hope they'll understand I did what I had to.

As numb as I feel about myself, the same can't be said for my thoughts on Azalee. The second my neck snaps under the weight of my own body, Azalee will die too. I can't let that happen.

But with my hands chained, the metal etched with runes, and dosed with potions to keep me from breaking out, my options for escape are near impossible. Logan is searching for the others and proof of the High Witch's guilt, but he's had only a handful of hours to do it.

As we're shuffled out of the van, a few Nightmares snag my attention. Most of the time, their faces are vacant or etched with fear, but two are glancing around, very clearly aware of their surroundings.

"Can you hear me?" I say to one of them.

A guard hits me in the ribs, knocking the air out of me. "Prisoners aren't allowed to talk."

We aren't allowed a trial, jury, or judge either.

Ignoring him, I continue, "Do you know where you are?" I'm greeted with another sharp whack to the back of my head; warmth pools in its wake.

But it was worth it because the Nightmares look at me and nod. Nightmares do not interact with us, not ones as far gone as this group. That means something has changed. Iniko, however, remains the same, dashing a little bit of my hopes.

We're brought to wait in an old stone house from Salem long ago. I hear the crowd growing just outside the walls. Tears prickle my eyes, and I pinch them closed. I will not show fear. My head hangs low as I sit on an overturned log, arms still strapped behind my back. A dozen guards surround us in full protective gear. Ready, should the Nightmares decide to lash out. Maybe they should? It would offer a good distraction.

"Gabriel?" A familiar voice cracks through the silence.

Lifting my head, I see Iniko staring at me. I jump to my feet, but a guard quickly shoves me down.

"What happened? Is Azalee okay?" My words are fast. The guard hits me in the jaw with the butt of his rifle in response.

He points the gun at Iniko. "Next person to talk gets a face full of holes. The High Witch will understand. I'll tell them you were trying to escape."

I lock eyes with Iniko. He offers the slightest of nods. He looks worse for wear, but that determination has returned to his eyes. If he's awake, maybe Azalee is too.

Fifteen minutes later, we're pulled onto the hanging platform. The crowd is enormous. All walks of life have come to see the spectacle: employees from the High Witch's office, other political figures, and sycophants I'm surprised aren't selling merch with dream wielder hate written on it. I spot dream wielders too, Roz among them, their face devastated as they look over us. And in the very back, heads down, are Meera and Genevieve.

As the commotion settles, the High Witch gets onstage. This is the first time I've seen him since my escape, and I don't miss the utter disdain in his eyes. He doesn't speak to me; he just shakes his head and turns to the waiting crowd.

"My fellow citizens. We are here under grave circumstances. Our town has been riddled with murders the last month, and I know we are all scared. But as you can see, I have captured some of those responsible." He waves an arm to us. "These dream wielders have set upon our town and used it as their hunting ground. It is my duty to make sure all magical powers are used safely by all citizens. That is why swift and decisive action is needed. These criminals will be punished as the old ways demand. I will rid this town, this country, of those who seek to use magic for ill deeds."

The High Witch glances sideways at me, then back at the crowd. "I must deeply apologize, for my own grandson turned out to be one of those monsters who was taking innocent lives. As I have always stated, I let nothing stand in the way of justice—even my own flesh and blood. In a few short weeks, you will go to the polls and vote on a bill I have proposed that will further allow us to seek out these criminals before they can act. I encourage you to vote *yes* so tragedies such as this will not happen in the future."

Justice, what a load of bullshit. He instilled in me that he was on this crusade because a dream wielder ruined his family. But he's done far more to destroy the Fords than any other witch. He killed my father and I'm next. I always knew the High Witch didn't give love easily, but now I don't believe he's even capable of giving it at all. The only love he ever had was for his power. That soulmate bound he claimed to have with my grandmother was probably bullshit too.

The High Witch nods to the executioners. Iniko, another Nightmare, and I are led to the waiting ropes, the nooses slipped around our necks.

How do I stop this from happening? *Words.* It's the only power I have left.

"He's lying," I yell to the audience. "The High Witch is not who you think he is. Not who *I* thought he was. Listen to your conscience. You must see that this isn't right. He is using these dream wielders and Nightmares as puppets to orchestrate his own storyline. We did not commit these crimes. The High Witch did. He is the murderer. He made you fear what our magic could do, but the only witch controlling you is him."

My words ring through the shell-shocked crowd.

A low hum thrums in the air as whispers start, but I don't think it sets in. Of course they suspect I'd say anything to save myself. Why should they believe me?

Once my words have started, I can't stop. "Don't let him manipulate you into creating the world he wants, by believing his lies as divine prophecy. I know we don't want a Salem, a world, where we fear our neighbors, our friends. Our home is a community filled with so many vibrant people—don't let him taint that with his prejudice."

There's rustling in the back of the crowd as a group pushes to the front. "My brother is right," Logan shouts, emerging from the masses. "And I've brought the proof you need to believe him."

Standing by his side is Azalee.

CHAPTER 56

Azalee

My breath seizes as I stare at Gabriel with a rope around his neck, perched on the gallows. Bruises pepper his handsome face, and his usually neat hair is disheveled—but his eyes are full of resolve when they meet mine. Next to him is Iniko, and while I'm thrilled to see him alive and alert, my happiness is short-lived at the stark reminder of the executioners waiting behind them.

Forcing the quivering out of my voice, I stand tall, picking up where Gabriel stopped. "The High Witch has abducted and imprisoned dozens of harmless dream wielders and Nightmares—framing them for the murders of those innocent victims. All this is a mirage to dupe the citizens of Salem into doing what he wants. As Gabriel said, do not let him manipulate you into becoming a monster like him," I say, moving toward the gallows, Logan acting as escort. I lock eyes with as many onlookers as possible before staring down the High Witch. "He claims dream wielder magic is used for control, but I only see one puppet master on this stage."

"Puppet master? The people of Salem elected me for guidance. I have and will always do that in the way I best see fit." If looks could kill, his glare would light us on fire. "Clearly, this is another dream wielder scheme to save themselves. They have nothing but spoken falsehoods to back their claims. No actual proof."

Logan uses his prestige as a Ford to try to sway the crowd. "That's bullshit. I found the place where he was holding them hostage. I can take the police there right now."

"Hostage? Is that what we call imprisoning dangerous criminals? I was simply housing them in a facility far enough away from the town to minimize the risk of them hurting anyone. I'm helping people, as I have always done for the last forty years. If you did have evidence otherwise, I would happily explain myself for any misunderstandings."

We don't have proof beyond our words. When Logan told me that the hanging was happening now, we didn't have time to find more evidence. We've left a few dream wielders at the prison to keep searching or find a way to disable the wards so they can take photos, but nobody has contacted us yet to say they found anything.

"If you had the spirits of the murder victims, perhaps they could tell the truth to the mediums among us," the High Witch suggests. "But I am told magic is being used to hide the spirits away. No doubt by the killers to protect themselves."

Spirits. Opal wanted us to release the spirits, but I've been a little too distracted to follow through. She said the spell locking them out was powerful.

The sun peeks from behind the clouds, catching on the High Witch's large, rare red-beryl crystal necklace. That would certainly be strong enough to make a holding spell.

Blood pounds in my ears as I move toward the High Witch on the platform. My gaze quickly darts to the stairs on the side. If the spell is linked to that necklace, breaking it should free the spirits to spill their beans.

"Dream wielders have walked among you for centuries." I lay out my story, taking one stair at a time. I don't want to tip my hand. The security that should be on me hesitates as Logan stays close by. Uncertainty flickers in their gazes as they watch the youngest Ford acting as my bodyguard.

"When in history have we ever lashed out and killed people? Dream wielders have been feared forever. But other than a few bad apples—which no witch or human could say they don't have either—what have we ever done as a whole to provoke that? Just the idea of us is enough for you to condemn an entire group." I'm on the platform with him now, but two guards flank him on either side. If I lunge for him, they'll come fast—I have to be faster.

"The High Witch has used that fear to whip you all into a frenzy. He manipulated the narrative by staging these attacks to play out in a fashion that would make dream wielders the monsters. You've been used—don't let him use you anymore."

Before my words settle, I leap forward, wrenching the necklace off him and slamming the crystal to the ground. It explodes in a burst of light, and shards of yellow fly everywhere.

"Seize her." The High Witch's command is drowned out by high-pitched screaming.

For a second, I think I'm back in the nightmare, but this wailing is coming from the crowd.

Several people in attendance—including Opal—clutch their heads, eyes racing and rolling back in their skulls as the spirits that I just unleashed bombard them. The deceased are now able to tell the truth about how they were murdered to the witches who can listen.

The medium standing nearest Captain Mendoza stares at the High Witch with haunted eyes. "The girl speaks the truth. The spirits have told us how they ended up in the clutches of the Nightmares sent by the High Witch. The ghosts were gagged from speaking their truth."

The other mediums in the audience nod their agreement. Confusion colors the features of the rest of those in attendance.

The High Witch snarls at me. "You meddling bitch. You and your rotten family have upended decades of work. So what if I had to grease a few wheels to get things moving? The lives of the many outweigh the need of the few. Sacrifices had to be made to ensure the safety of the whole." Withdrawing a vial coated in gold, he yanks off the cork, and I know immediately when I see the orange smoke emitting from it how dangerous it is, as do the people closest to us, who gasp right before he throws it at me.

"Azalee!" I didn't see Meera bound up the stairs until she shoves me back, the full force of the hex hitting her.

Simultaneously, a loud bang cuts through the chaos, a burst of fire erupting in my chest. I grip it like I've been shot. But I'm not bleeding. The High Witch's face goes slack before he falls forward with a thud. Standing behind him, holding a gun, is Gabriel.

CHAPTER 57

Gabriel

"Dream wielders have walked among you for centuries," Azalee says, slowly approaching the High Witch like she's eyeing down a lion. "When in history . . ."

"Roz?" I hiss, keeping my attention locked on Azalee, but quickly glancing at Roz, crouched behind me. Luckily, all eyes are on the plea Azalee is professing to the audience.

They twist open a jar, painting symbols on the cuffs. "Hush now, boy. I'm trying to get you free." My arms grow warm as Roz's counterspell works its magic and unlocks my shackles.

I cast the rope off my neck, and my breath comes easier already. As if in slow motion, I watch my grandfather pull a golden vial from his pocket, casting the lid aside, the potion emitting an orange smoke.

"No." My heart rages and vision narrows on Azalee. Only one potion is housed in gold and produces a smoke that color with such a dense cloud. Stone Cold hex.

A bewildered guard stands with his back to me, his two sidearms ripe for the taking. I shove him to the side, ripping the gun off his belt. Barreling toward the High Witch, I pull the trigger as he tosses the vial.

I had a split second to decide which gun to grab—the one with the bullet or the one with the subduing potion. It would be so simple to take the High Witch out with a single blow. I've been trained to shoot to kill—I won't miss. But is that the justice I want? Killing the High Witch would end his reign of terror, free Logan and me from under his boot, but is that the right course?

He pulled out a killing potion, easily recognizable by everyone in attendance. After the chaos dies down, calmer heads will prevail and understand I didn't have a choice but to stop him. He'd be gone. He killed my father, tried to kill me—twice. Whatever life I could have had, he stole from me and Logan. Stole the lives of those murder victims, the dream wielders, the Nightmares. How many other tragedies have happened because the High Witch willed it?

Change doesn't happen right away, but without the High Witch around to fan the flames of fear, we could see real progress toward acceptance and understanding of dream wielder magic.

A split second isn't a long time to make a life-altering decision, but that is often where they happen. The High Witch *needs* to pay for what he's done. The people need to see that a leader, even one with as much power as my grandfather, can be held accountable for his crimes. He deserves to sit in a courtroom and have the full extent of his monstrosities presented in front of him for the world to see. Death is too swift a punishment. He wanted his legacy to be genocide; instead he should have to live out his dying days in prison knowing that he failed.

That is the fate he deserves. Which is why the Fates and I both guided my hand to the gun with the subduing potion.

My future was always set in stone, but with the explosion of the liquid, I shattered it into a million pieces.

Logan said the High Witch's reach was too far for us ever to be free. *Well, brother, I freed us. I won't let him mold you into the next version of him he tried to make me.* Salem has lived under the rule of a Ford for so long; let's see what happens when it gets the opportunity to spread its wings.

Let's see what happens to all of us.

Everything occurs in the space of the second it takes to exhale. From one breath to the next, I've changed the course of fate. The liquid coats the old man's face, his body stiffening before he collapses.

As if the potion has penetrated my own skin, I clutch my chest, bright gold filling my vision. I lock eyes with Azalee and we know in that moment that my life debt to her has been fulfilled. But despite the gold thread between us evaporating, the white thread tying me to her is stronger than ever. I know in my deepest cells, I will nourish and tend this bond, protecting my soulmate until my dying breath, until we are reunited once more in the afterlife.

But Azalee's gaze doesn't linger on me as she drops to Meera's fallen body.

CHAPTER 58

Azalee

I'm frozen. My breath comes in short bursts. "Meera." I drop to my knees, bile rising in my throat as I take in the wide, vacant dead eyes of my best friend.

Meera's skin is a deep blue from the hex, frame rigid like a block of cement. The Stone Cold hex. Death would have been instant. She didn't suffer. That should bring me comfort—but the grief only grows. I concentrate on finding an aura, but the colorful spirit no longer resides in this body.

Not Meera. Tears stream down my cheeks, pooling on her skin like she's nothing more than a fallen statue. Not caring if the hex is still potent on her, I try to pull her into me, but two sets of arms drag me off her.

I kick and struggle against them, but my body is still weak from the days stuck in the nightmare.

Gabriel's familiar scent surrounds me as he holds me tight against his chest. "Shhh. I got you." He peppers kisses into my hair, hand cradling my head. "Gods, Azalee. I'm sorry I wasn't quick enough."

I'm immune to whatever chaos is happening around us—the rest of the world is only shades of gray. My sobs are ugly, soaking his shirt, but he doesn't pull away. "I never got to tell her I forgave her. She died thinking I hated her." Pain rips open my chest, a raw nerve forced to face the world with no armor.

"No, she didn't." Gabriel's tone is strong and assured. "She knew how much you loved her, and she loved you too. That's why she saved you."

Pressing my hand into his sturdy chest, I look into his eyes. "You saved me." I acknowledge, for the first time, the unconscious High Witch lying feet away from me, his face stained in a deep purple from a potion. Gabriel stopped his grandfather from attacking anyone else. "That's why the life debt isn't there anymore. That golden rope connecting us is gone." I move my fingers to his heart, and the delicate white string curls around my hand like a loving embrace.

He wipes tears from my cheeks. "I don't need a life debt to be connected to you. You have me forever." Our souls will forever be two parts of one whole.

Grief still colors the world. I know from experience that isn't a shade you can ever completely get rid of. Still, when I focus on Gabriel's glowing aura, the soft yellow-indigo of the dream wielder, and the purple hue of the inner ring, I know he means it unconditionally.

"Is he dead?"

"Did you see the hex?"

"Get an ambulance!"

"He tried to kill her!"

The voices of confused citizens rise up around us. Gabriel pulls me in tighter as Iniko drops down on my other side, taking my hand and squeezing it. None of us moves as we watch the healers take the High Witch away on a stretcher. Captain Mendoza spares Gabriel a curt nod and mutters something I don't catch before ordering his officers to take statements from the crowd and to put a detail on the High Witch.

"To protect him?" one of them asks.

Mendoza's voice is solemn. "To arrest him for attempted murder—but it appears that won't be the last crime we charge him with."

Epilogue

Azalee

Months later

In the end, Meera did save her family, but at the cost of her own life. After we buried her in the cemetery at The Retreat—a beautiful ceremony with dozens of pink peonies—her family moved to Florida. It was too hard to be here after everything.

I curl my hands around my cup of coffee, soft flakes of snow falling onto the lake's thin ice as smooth as glass. I had a gazebo put in nearby and dedicated to Meera.

"You're going to freeze out here." Gabriel comes up behind me, putting a cloak over my shoulders. It smells like him.

"No, that's why you're here." I nuzzle into him, resting my head on his chest like I have every night since we both almost died. We lose ourselves in each other's bodies, and for those long hours, everything is precisely as it should be. I can't believe we fought it for so long, probably because my soulmate and I are too stubborn for our own good.

There was a brief moment after the High Witch's arrest when the authorities were trying to piece all his crimes together that I thought I might lose Gabriel again. He attacked the High Witch. No matter how shitty the man was, he was still a powerful entity. But when the dust settled, and the dozens of eyewitnesses—including the police captain—verified the High Witch was attempting to hex me, Gabriel wasn't charged with anything.

We're still a long way out from the High Witch going to trial, but his lawyers are already building a case for his innocence. Which means we're working with the state to make sure that doesn't happen. But despite the evidence against him, there is still the fear that he'll get away with it. He might be behind bars, but the High Witch still has a lot of allies in Salem and across the country.

My fear pales in comparison to what Gabriel and Logan are feeling. The High Witch was a monster, but I still see the anguish in Gabriel's features now and then when he doesn't think I'm watching. He's mourning the grandfather he thought he knew and starting over again with a new family structure. Logan and Gabriel's relationship isn't quite what it used to be, but I know they're finding their way back to a new normal.

We all are.

I take another sip of coffee. "I was just getting some fresh air before your lesson."

Kissing my forehead, he says, "Are you sure you're up for this?"

I slide my hand up his chest and over his lightly scruffy face. He's adopted a more casual state since leaving the High Witch's office and joining me at The Retreat. "You ask me that every day."

"I guess"—he kisses my fingertips—"I'm just hoping you'll go back to bed with me instead." His green eyes burn with desire, lighting my own internal flame, and I almost say yes.

I look over my shoulder at our small house built into the trees. After everything that happened, we both wanted somewhere quiet to be alone. Luckily, The Retreat has lots of places like that.

"Later, I promise." Heading to the house, I turn when I hear a car approaching. Even months later, when things have started to settle in Salem, and we're making strides to stop the prejudice against dream wielders, I still have the moment where panic grips my chest and I brace for disaster.

But so far, it hasn't come.

There's an election coming soon where the citizens will vote for a new High Witch. With so many decades stuck under one man's thumb, the race on who will take the seat has been heated. I floated the idea that Mom or Roz should run, but they both nixed it quicker than zit-removing potion. They're happy to keep working at The Retreat, offering expanded dream services not just to dream wielders but to anyone who wants them.

"Morning," Iniko calls, waving as he exits the car. "I brought pastries." He holds up a bag from his favorite shop. I think it's his favorite because of the flirtmance he's having with the guy who runs it.

He stops when he reaches us, smirking. "Unless I'm interrupting something?" He nods to Gabriel's hand low on my back.

"Oh, you most certainly are, but I've made it a sport by now," Logan says, coming out the front door. "So you're welcome to join my team."

Logan doesn't live with us, but some weeks it feels like he does. He's over so much, Gabriel set up a makeshift bedroom for him in the loft. Though neither will say it, I think the two brothers like to keep eyes on each other—perhaps worried their grandfather's allies might seek them out in the dark.

Gabriel was terrified he'd lose his family when the truth of who he was came to light, but having Logan steps away is a reminder that his nightmare didn't come to pass.

As Logan quickens his pace to get by us, Gabriel grabs his backpack and yanks him to a stop. "What's that?" Taking Logan's chin, he moves it so Logan's right eye is cast in early-morning light. Half of the skin is normal color, but the other half is black and blue.

Logan cringes as Gabriel pokes it with his finger. I'm assuming just to be a dick since it looks wicked painful. "Ouch." He attempts to step back, but Gabriel's grip is strong. "It's nothing."

Gabriel is my family now, which means Logan is by extension. So, if Gabriel is worried, I am too. "It looks like a poorly applied concealing cream to cover a black eye."

He manages to escape Gabriel's grip. "I'll have to sign up for a cosmetology class next semester." The quip is quick as lightning, like his always are.

"Did you go to the fighting rings?" Gabriel's voice drops, eyes roaming the rest of his brother for unseen marks.

"After your experience there? Fuck no." Logan is no stranger to unwise decisions, so it was a fair question.

"Then what happened?" I can feel Gabriel's worry radiating off him. I slip my hand into his to let him know I've got his back. Iniko stands still, eyes bouncing back and forth like he's watching a tennis match.

Logan scratches the back of his neck, searching the trees like he's a bird-watcher. "It was just some guy in my English class who had one too many things to say about *current events*." He doesn't like mentioning the High Witch's arrest. I see the shame he tries to hide that he didn't catch on sooner. "Short story shorter—he had a lot of feelings and took it out on my face."

"Logan, why didn't you tell me?"

He shrugs and waves off the concern. "Nothing to tell. I handled it. He's not the first person to lecture me about being a Ford and I'm sure it won't be the last."

"We're both Fords. We're in this together."

Logan glances at me, then nods. "I gotta get to school. If someone calls me a bad name on the playground, I'll run right home." He offers a dimpled grin before heading toward his SUV.

"That was interesting," Iniko finally says.

"Logan will be fine," I add.

"Someone punched him and he didn't even tell me. I should call the school."

I can't help but laugh at my ever-lawful soulmate. "I don't know how much that will help. He's not your ten-year-old brother anymore. You have to let him handle his own shit sometimes or he'll never learn."

Gabriel's jaw is tight and I kiss him to make it go away before grabbing the bag of goodies from Iniko. "Let's go in; it's time for your lesson."

Iniko and Gabriel have been training their dream wielder powers together. It's been therapeutic helping them. Which is what we plan on doing once they're ready to dream wield unassisted.

I'm going to open a clinic in the spring here at The Retreat to help with trauma. We will welcome anyone, but specialize in dream wielders and those showing symptoms of Nightmare progression. Now that we know how to fight the nightmares, I'm hoping eventually we can stop anyone from being lost to them.

But that's a long road.

I spent so long going full speed ahead without ever stopping to breathe. I've learned a lot in these past few months, including that it's okay to slow down and live in the moment. I almost lost everyone I love—did lose one of my best friends. I don't want to take this time with the ones I have left for granted ever again. So, now things move a little slower, but I don't mind anymore.

Gabriel has been partnering with the secretary of education to implement school programs to teach about dream wielders. We'll start small here in Salem, but the hope is it will become a nationwide thing.

I lean against the doorframe, watching Gabriel and Iniko settle in, and my heart has never been so full. I've been controlling dreams for so long, but never in my wildest ones did I picture this. Two people I love working together to make a better world for all of us.

All we need is the power of dreams to make it happen.

Acknowledgments

As someone who has experienced vivid dreams their whole life, I've been constantly fascinated by what they mean and how they work. When I combined that interest with my love of all things Salem (which started with *Sabrina the Teenage Witch* in the '90s and continued when I discovered I had ancestors in Salem during the witch trials), *The Nightmare Keeper* was born.

I have so many people to thank for helping bring this book into reality. My mom for being my first and biggest fan and listening to me endlessly chat through plot points and daydreams. My dad for your support and excitement. Anna, Hannah, Elizabeth, and Scarlett for helping and encouraging me through early drafts. Your talents are even greater than your kindness (which is unending).

To my wonderful agent, Jem. From the second you read this book, you have been so enthusiastic and worked your own brand of magic to get us here. I couldn't ask for a better partner. To Lauren Plude and Lindsey Faber, my editors. Your championship of this story was such a joy to experience and work alongside. Your creative input and love for the characters really made this the best experience.

To everyone at Montlake who worked on this story and showed it all the love.

About the Author

Vienna James has been a storyteller since a young age, when she would spend hours coming up with intricate lives for her dolls. When she is not lost in her world of stories, she can be found drawing digital art, thrifting, and binge-watching her favorite TV shows for the hundredth time. She also writes YA contemporary romances under the pen name Cara Stout. She lives in Salt Lake City, Utah. For more information, visit www.viennajamesbooks.com.